# *Wolf Eyes*

## *By*
## *S.L. Kotar and J. E. Gessler*

Ahead of the Press
St, Louis, MO

Library of Congress Cataloguing-in-Publication Data

Wolf Eyes
/ S.L. Kotar and J.E. Gessler
ISBN      KINDLE       978-1-950392-30-8
ISBN      PAPERBACK  978-1-945594-99-1

Manufactured in the United States of America

**Ahead of The Press Publishing**
**St. Louis, Missouri**

TABLE OF CONTENTS

# "WOLF EYES"

## DEDICATION

This book is dedicated to Timothy Dalton and Zelah Clarke. And to Amanda and Erin who are, of course, Meg and Storm.

SLK

And JEG, always

# CHAPTER 1

In the vernacular, it was raining cats and dogs. To the tall, spare man standing at the window, nose pressed to the cold glass, "cats" meant mousers in the field, while "dogs" referred to a shepherd's best friend. At the moment, and for many moments past, the man had no use for any type of four-legged creature.

That time was irrevocably gone.

The wetness from the sudden storm swept across the Scottish moors, covering the whole earth, as far as the piercing grey-green eyes could see, with mist. Had the man been outside instead of in, he could not have seen his hand in front of his face.

Which is exactly what the bank manager had said to him, less than two weeks gone by.

"The times have changed, Mr. MacDhui. Yuh have not changed wid them. Yuh canna see yer hand in front o' yer face."

The man, so addressed, had not replied to the bank manager. There was nothing to say which had not already been said.

"Ah'm sorry fer ya, but there's nothin' Ah kin do. Not a thing. Yuh're behind on yuh're loan payments to the Bank, an' that's all there is to it. Yuh understan' it's not my doin', don't yuh?"

Ian MacDhui did not understand. He had not understood anything clearly since his beloved Megan had died three years ago. This made survival in the three-dimensional world difficult, if not impossible.

"Yuh're to pack yuhr belongin's an' be off the property in two weeks. That's the best Ah kin do fer yuh, Mr. MacDhui." When Ian failed to reply, the bank manager had wrung his hands in a gesture of hopelessness he did not feel. It was not his land which was being repossessed. He was, after all, only doing his job. "We've a'ready sold off yer dog an' yuhr sheep to the Conglomerate, so there's no use yuh frettin' aboot them."

And then he had added, out of politeness, "It's all fer the better. All you small sheep men will have to give in to the Conglomerate sooner or later. They have the money an' the New Technology on their side."

It was always pronounced New-Technology and spelled with a capital "N" and a capital "T."

When a bank manager or a Conglomerate officer spoke the words, their voices were filled with respect. When a sheeper pronounced them, the words dripped with bitterness.

"Yuh men of the old ways. Yuh fought the introduction o' new methods to sheer sheep, an' yuh canna afford the special feed which makes the wool rich an' thick."

The bank manager spoke with a regional dialect, although he had gone away to University and attempted to obfuscate his roots by speaking as a City Man. The fact he had not succeeded placed him in contempt by both Insiders and Outsiders.

"No' better."

Those were the first two words Ian MacDhui had spoken. The sound of the man's voice so startled the bank manager he took a step back, as though fearful for his life. Or afraid to further contaminate himself by association with a man who had fallen by the wayside of Progress.

"Two weeks," the bank manager firmly repeated. He wished to be certain the former sheepman understood. He did not want a scene when the constable came to place a shiny new padlock on the front door of the simple, one story stone home with the thatched roof. The shareholders of the Conglomerate had specifically warned: Not Again.

It was bad publicity. Emotional outbursts riled the remaining families, brought recriminations down on the heads of those who put profit ahead of tradition.

It was not so long ago when the banner in one of the small, weekly newspapers had proclaimed: "The Godless Have Come Amongst Us." Shares in the Conglomerate had fallen three points before the ruckus faded away.

Before the dead and dying had given up the ghost and gone quietly to their rest.

The problem, as the bank manager saw it, was the sheepers – the men and women and their scrawny, dirty children – who did not know their time had expired. It was a new age, the dawn of technology and science, where sheep were mated by syringes filled with foreign semen, rather than in the natural way. It was, they said, "to ensure consistency of quality," as though a ewe were not a living, sentient creature, entitled to a moment of passion before she reproduced her species for the benefit of Mankind.

Gone were the days when a sheep dog was the most important asset a man possessed. Vanishing forever were the family-owned farms, the small flocks and the men who walked the lonely moors in unconscious imitation of their Savior.

The harvesting of wool had become Big Business. Money could only be made when expenses were sheered to the bone, when inexpensive, unfeeling machines replaced man and dog; when privately owned, unproductive "units," were merged into huge, impersonal, government-sanctioned conglomerates.

The world was changing. In light of synthetics, foreign competition and a move away from scratchy, itchy, old-fashioned wool, tradition was expendable.

In fact, it was on life support.

Almost as dead as Ian MacDhui's heart.

Moisture from the humidity formed on the glass and dripped down the pane, making imitation tear tracks on Ian MacDhui's reflection. Yet, when he sniffled, it was from cold, not the tumultuous emotions racking his soul.

He had not cried in three years; not since Megan died. He would not cry now. He told himself he had forgotten how.

It was not the first lie Ian ever told himself, but it was one of the more destructive ones.

And as enduring as flint.

Megan Clarke MacDhui would understand his inability to cry, he told himself. Looking down from heaven upon his ramrod frame and hollow, red-rimmed eyes, she would comprehend the reasons his heart was hard. She had been, after all, the one great love in his life, his reason for existence. Without her, any semblance of happiness was vanished like dew in the hot, midday sun.

Without her, Ian MacDhui was a stone.

There were only two slight problems with this self-evaluation, this denial of love and life. Those very tangible "problems" stood behind him, hidden from sight by a long, floor-length curtain. Both were the spitting image of their father; tall, lean, dark-haired, with an other-worldly air about them which set them apart from the rest of humanity.

Their mother, Megan, nicknamed Meggie, had exclaimed, when handed the second of her offspring immediately after birth, "We've another copy of you, Ian, an' Ah'm not sure that's a good thing or a bad thing."

The proud father had stooped to kiss both mother and daughter, declaring, with tears of joy streaming down his handsome face, "'Tis a good thing, an' no denyin'." To which the infant had lustily agreed, howling her approval.

From that moment forth, Gail MacDhui had been called "Storm," not so much, as it turned out, a play on words with her given name, as from her temper and self-righteous avowal of always being on the side of right.

The new baby made a perfect complement to her sister, two years her senior. Margaret, called Meg, had already established herself as the "spittin' image" of her father, in form as well as temperament. It did not take long for her to initiate her sister into the ways and mysteries of "Clan MacDhui." From the time of Storm's birth, the children were constant companions, more twins than siblings separated by two full years.

Everything Meg had learned she taught Storm, saving the younger from making the same mistakes. The children were not duplicates, exactly, for Meg was the stolid one, gravely quiet, while inwardly smoldering. Storm, as befit her name, was the wild side of her parent, the darkly intense, fiercely combative offspring of Megan and Ian. Where Meg was reasonable, Storm dismissed counter explanations with a wave of her hand and a flash of her grey-green eyes.

"Storm is too much like yuhr father fer me to reason with," Meggie had explained to her elder daughter shortly before her own death. "It is therefore up to yuh to be the patient one in this clan. Listen to what's said and dinna make up yuhr mind until yuh've heard all the facts. Use reason instead o' emotion, an' guide yer father an' sister, for they're both hotheads, the lot of 'em."

"Ah shall leave that to yuh," Meg had defiantly replied, starting into her mother's blue orbs with a look which might have pierced steel, or parted the waters of the Red Sea.

"But when Ah am no' here, bairn, it is to yuh they will look. Stand thy ground ag'in them, for they are not ones to reason, but to feel. Tis a world where a body must have both emotion an' logic. Be their calm side."

To which Meg had replied a second time, "Ah shall leave that to yuh."

"An' when Ah'm gone?" came the sad rejoinder.

"Ah dinna know what yuh mean," the worldly nine-year-old had replied with as much hurt as denial. When her mother had not answered, she continued, lower lip protruding in classic MacDhui fashion, "Yuh canna go, fer Ian MacDhui needs yuh. He canna stand alone. He is not a tree but a man, an' being naught but a man, he needs yuh. As does Storm," she added, including herself as an unspoken component of her sister.

When the mother's silence persisted, the child stomped her slender foot on the hard, bare floorboards of their home and raised a clenched fist upward in the traditional direction of heaven.

"Ah am puttin' Yuh on notice," she declared to the Almighty. "Ah dinna have to tell yuh that Ian MacDhui –" for he was never called "father," or "dad," but always by his first name, or more commonly by both first and surname, "canna survive without Megan MacDhui. They were created fer one another, an' that's all there is to it. Separate one frum the other, an yuh have ha'f a man, ha'f a woman. Ah know Ah dinna have no business tellin Yuh yer job, an' Ah'm not. Just puttin' Yuh on yer guard no' to make a mistake."

It was a unique relationship Meg MacDhui had with God, childlike and complex, informal and blunt. If it were God's business to see to the proper running of His earth, then He had better get it right the first time. Meg had little patience for mistakes. If He were perfect, as her mother had taught, then He did not need to be told. But just in case He was wavering, she would set the record straight.

Calmly.

That was, after all, her place in life. Meggie MacDhui had told her so.

When Meg MacDhui discovered God's will was not her will, nor did it coincide with Storm or Ian MacDhui's will, she had abandoned her belief. It was little they asked from life, and little they received. If God could not – or would not – spare one indispensable life; if He would not or could not restore to health one True Believer in the form of Megan MacDhui, she saw no point in further communication.

When God saw fit to take back the mother of Meg and Storm and the wife of Ian to His own bosom, the nine-year old child realized she would have to take matters into her own hands. A god who would separate Ian from his soul mate was not a loving god and of no more use to her.

"He's brooding," Meg whispered, staring at the back of their father.

"He's no' brooding," Storm declared in rare disagreement with her sister. "He's plannin' a counter-attack ag'in the bank."

"It's too late fer counter-attacks," Meg replied slowly and with perfect calm. As much as she would have denied it, her mother's words had marked her destiny. She had become, in fact, the calm MacDhui, the logical, reasonable MacDhui. Which did not mean she was a quitter. Nothing on earth – or from any higher region – would sway her from any course she believed in.

"We are to be off the property in two days an' two nights. An' we shall be. We are goin' away," she added without enthusiasm. "On a journey of Grrreat Consequence," she added, rolling her R's in the familiar dialect of her Scottish ancestors. "Yuh heard Ian MacDhui. We've new worlds to conquer."

"How kin we conquer new worlds when we hav'na conquered the old?" came the sour interrogative, punctuated by a flash of shadowed eyes.

"We're doin' what Megan MacDhui wanted us to. We're goin' to the New World. Yuh know that," Meg defensively whispered, least the idea and its implementation be brought down upon her shoulders.

"Ah dinna know inny such thing," Storm spat, then immediately hushed as Ian's broad shoulders flinched and his leg jerked. "Quiet," she warned, more to herself than her sister. "Dinna disturb him."

When Ian's ghostly shape resumed its solitary vigil at the window, Storm continued her argument with Meg.

"Ah dinna remember what Meggie dreamed."

"Then ask Ian MacDhui to tell yuh."

"Yuh tell me," came the demand. Meg's shoulders sagged in uncharacteristic defeat.

"It's better if Ian does. He remembers better than Ah."

"Yuh dinna remember, either," Storm accused.

It was an old argument.

"I *do* remember. It's jest that... Ian puts it better, is all. He kin conjure up the spirits," she tried in a pitiful tone. "He's got the gift."

"Aye," Storm agreed, her voice, like her hope, trailing off into moor mist. She hesitated, then tugged gently on Meg's sleeve. "Ah want him to tell me now. Ah want him to make Meggie MacDhui cume alive fer me."

"He canna do that," Meg replied with a harshness of tone meant to quell any further objections. "She's dead an' buried in the ground these many years. Leave her there."

It was a statement meant to cut, but the blade turned both ways, causing Meg to quiver under the sharp, cold, stinging pain. The passage of three long years had taught her it was hard to be twelve years old and head of a family. Hard to be without a mother's loving care, a mother's gentle hand to guide her.

Hard to always be the adult, to have all the answers, to be the windbreak in the storm. Hard to give solace when there were none to return her own need for succor. None but a father, rendered half a man by God.

Before either child could recover, they were shocked out of their hurt by Ian's sudden movement. He turned, squinting his wolf eyes toward the curtain they hid behind, piercing through the cloth to look beyond.

"Meg. Storm," came the summons. His daughters shriveled from the not-to-be-disobeyed tone.

"The bastard's got eyes in the back o' his head," Storm complained.

"An dinna be callin me a 'bastard,'" came the stern rebuke. "Me parents married right an' proper, up in yonder church. The self-same church Megan Clarke married Ian MacDhui," he continued, referring to himself in the third person. "The self-same church yuh two will be married in."

"An' he's got a predator's ears," Storm remarked before stepping boldly into the small outer chamber, lower lip protruding in anger at having been detected. "An' Ah dinna see how we kin be married in that 'self-same' church of yuh'rn, Master MacDhui, seein' as how we're aboot to undertake a journey o' three thousand miles. We'd have to flap our arms like birds ta git back here fer inny marrin' up. So what do yuh say to that, Wolf Eyes?"

Her question was meant to hurt, but by softening it with the inclusion of their pet name for Ian, she eased the thrust from fatal to painful.

"Ah'm goin' out," he chose to reply, ignoring both her pout and her words. "Cover fer me."

"Out?" Meg demanded, small fists placed safely on either hip. "Yuh canna go out. They're havin' a party back there fer yuh," she reminded him, indicating the muffled noises coming from an inner room. "It's supposed to be a goin' away party, if Ah remember correctly. Wid yuh the guest o' honor. It's a poor party, them celebratin' alone."

"Make some excuse," her father replied, waving his hand in a futile attempt to brush away her objection.

"What would that be, now?"

"Ah dinna care. Yuh're the one with the glib tongue. Think up sumethin'."

Storm made a deprecating noise deep in her throat, then rolled her eyes.

"That's easy. We'll tell them there's more ale cumin' an' they won't notice if rain drops turn to pound notes."

"Aye," Ian agreed, then added quickly, "That's mean."

"Fancy that," she nodded. "It was meant to be. What they're really celebratin' is that it's yuh what's goin' and them what's stayin'. Fer now."

Ian digested her words, then drew his lips into a tight line.

"Tell them... what yuh will."

Ian sighed, wrung his long, nearly bloodless fingers together in a gesture of hopelessness, then crossed silently to the outside door. Had he been no more than a wisp of wind; had he been a wolf on the prowl, he could not have moved more silently.

Almost before they knew it, their father slipped away, into the moist, dank night. With a little imagination, mixed with a dose of dread, the girls might have convinced themselves he had never existed at all.

Storm turned to Meg, tugging urgently on her sister's sleeve, appealing to her with wide, shiny eyes.

"We've instructions," Meg protested, but her words held no conviction.

"It's Meggie MacDhui's orders Ah'm obeyin'," Storm reminded her. "Yuh told me them yuhrse'f. Never leave him alone in the moors. He'll git lost," she added, less assured.

"She dinna mean lost, as in lost his way. Ian's a moor man an' he could find his way out o' inny fog or mist or rain. He's a wolf, yuh know. He roams wid his instincts, not jest his eyes an' his nose. Cume what may, he'll return."

"What 'lost,' then?" Storm demanded.

"She meant... lost in his mind, not his body. Lost... in thought. Lost," she choked, "in his memories."

"An' iffn he's lost that way, he'll git lost in his body, an' then where will we be? It'll be 'takin' into care' at the children's home fer us, an' as to that, Ah'd rather be dead!"

"Hush yer mouth," Meg warned, shuddering. "There'll be no talk o' that. Besides, yuh heard what he said. We're to make excuses fer him."

"Yuh make them, then. Ah'm goin' after him."

"He's too far ahead. Yuh'll never find him in the fog. An' before the hour's out, it'll be a full-blown storm. Yuh canna track a man in a storm."

"Aye, yuh kin," Storm protested, putting a hand to her head. Meg understood the implication.

"Jest wait here. Ah'll go in an' see how the party's goin'. Dinna leave without me," she reiterated.

"No. Ah won't."

More than a promise, Storm's words were a vow. She and Meg were tied to one another by blood, linked by intertwining souls, attached by common desire, made one by love. Had the roof blown off in a terrible wind; had the floor upheaved from the horrific might of an earth tremor, Storm would have remained, rooted to the spot, waiting for her sister.

That was the way it was between them.

They were, after all, the daughters of Ian MacDhui, and Ian MacDhui was half man, half wolf. No less could be expected from his cubs.

# CHAPTER 2

Mist and fog covered the earth, effectively shrouding it into varying shades of greys and blacks. The moors were devoid of color. Were a man to slit his own throat, he would have bled black under the low, heavy clouds.

The moon was full, with a faerie ring around it. What light it might have brought the night-blanketed land was lost in layer upon layer of cumeulonimbus and stratocumeulus clouds. There was an uneasy stillness to the setting, a tension, a sense of potential energy, held at bay. The sounds which penetrated the moors were muffled, stifled, ominous. The eerie fluff of a bird, waken from sleep; the tiny, ineffectual squeal of a field mouse as the talons of an unseen enemy curled into its flesh; the lonely moan of wind across barren rock, whispering of times long gone, of civilizations long dead.

The moors were slumbering peacelessly, in expectation of some interloper, the appearance of an intruder, the transformation of shadow into substance. Seemingly unwilling to witness the explosion of kinetic power, the moon winked out, dropping a curtain over both the living and the unlived.

A moment, a minute, then the unnatural rustling of swirling fog, the bending of a wild weed suddenly crushed by powers beyond its control. Then suddenly, by imperial command, the wave of a hand, the curt dismissal of one born to rule, the clouds were whisked away from the full moon. Shadows were immediately set to life, dancing among the ancient Celtic stones, while ghosts of the drowned and the murdered, hidden for eons deep within the marshy bogs, were temporarily unshackled from the fingers of mud and slime, to wail their lamentations.

It was the bewitching hour, when the Powers of Mystery ruled the world. Shakespeare's three witches stirred the contents of their bubbling pot, while black-winged creatures soared the sky and slimy, slithering snakes hissed and spat and struck with the venom of the unredeemed.

Into this stew of past and future, timelessness and imagination, the howling of a wolf shattered the illusions of rhyme and reason. Once, twice, three times the solitary wolf howled, and each time the moon appeared to glow brighter, seemingly at the beck and call of the wild wanderer.

A pause, then the chirp of a cricket, the rasp of a grasshopper, before the howling began anew. It was an unearthly, desperately solitary howl, a plaintive cry of urgency, without comprehension. Up and down the scale, deep-throated, notes tailing off as one song ended and another began.

There was in the howling that of the wild and the savage, the godless and the redeemed; the shriek of love lost, responsibility onerous, future pressing too close to present. Less than a prayer yet more than a wish, the howls echoed over the hills, sunk to the level of the swamps then bounced upward, striking the clouds a glancing blow before twisting their way heavenward and disappearing.

"Ahwooooool," the beast articulated, first loud then soft, then loud again. "Ahwooooooolllllll...!" It was the ear-shattering sob of early Man crawling out of the slime, the heart-rending misery of the acknowledgement at Calgary.

What once was, could never be again; no safety in a retreat to the swelling oceans of the past. What will be was written in the hard-hearted hearts of *homo sapiens,* in a language undecipherable to the human race.

"Ahwooool!" And then "Awoool!" but not from the lone wolf. These were two new voices, responding to the first. "Awoooooooool!"

Neither the same pitch, nor the equal in experience, these howlers from the pack were the untried, untested young ones, eager to explore, to fight and bite and establish their own order to the world.

"Awhoool!"

And "Ahooooo," the leader signaled in wordless communication. "Come to me and we shall bay at the moon together."

More swirling through the ground fog, little waves and eddies of angry grey mist, disturbed by the passage of sleek, eager wolf cubs. Noses wet from fog, ears pricked with excitement, they joined the older creature at the rim of a cliff, skittered at the edge, sending bits of stone and myriad pebbles to their death a league below.

"Awool!" and "Ahoool" and "Aaaahhhwhoooo," chimed the voices in a chorus of blended spirits. And then silence, punctuated by the panting and the heavy breathing of excitement held at bay.

They waited and waited and waited a bit longer while the echoes grew as cold as last night's slaughtered lamb. Only when the silence had reclaimed the land and the moon had misted over, did the tails tuck and the claws receded, making merely humans out of noble canines.

"Ah tolt yuh to stay behind an' cover fer me. Yuh had yer instructions." There was no accusation in the tone, but more of resignation.

"They're singin' and dancin' to the music on the radio an' they dinna feel no pain. They won't be lookin' fer yuh until the signal fades at one o'clock."

"Aye," he said as his thoughts trailed off. Then, more forcefully, "Ah wanted to be alone."

Storm brushed back her long, dark hair from her child's eyes and shook her head.

"Ah remember what yuh said."

"And what was that?" he inquired in a huff.

"The day of the lone wolf is past."

"Ah never said that," he denied, moving away and shaking his shoulders. "Ah never said that," he repeated into the moors and the grey-black heather.

"Yuh did." Not accusation, but fact. A patient reminder.

"It t'was on a night like this," Meg took up, her eyes slanted in remembrance.

There was a crack of thunder, then a flash of lightning, temporarily illuminating the landscape. It improved the vision of the past miraculously.

Meggie MacDhui cuddled her two-year old daughter inside her warm, woolen cloak, effectively sealing in her mother's warmth, while denying access to the cold, prying fingers of a harsh March wind. Storm made a small movement of protest, brushing back the tip of the cloth so she could watch her father.

Ian stood five feet away, tending a skittish fire. His long, dark brown hair appeared black against the backdrop of the night, falling in elf locks across his brow. The moon, flirting with rain clouds, occasionally sent slivers of bright, silver light, magically illuminating the crevices of his face, highlighting at irregular intervals his long, straight nose, a corner of ear, the deep cleft of chin.

"Ah've brought more marsh moss," Meg announced, appearing out of nowhere from behind the dominating presence of the crag. She paused to readjust her precious bundle, resting against the lee side of the ancient stone formation, then dropped to one knee and cautiously added fuel to the fire.

"Once we've a good flame, Ah'll add some sticks," Ian observed. She nodded, then cupped her hand and blew on the hesitant orange heat.

With skill, born of many winter nights spent on the moors, a bit of luck and the shifting of the howling wind, the fire suddenly leapt to life. The addition of sticks, then several larger branches, brought a modicum of comfort to the clan.

Rubbing his reddened, chapped hands over the fire, Ian ran his tongue across his lips, cleared his throat and began.

"It t'was a story Ah believe yuh requested," he said, addressing the statement to Meg. The four-year old nodded solemnly.

"Aye. It was a story Ah requested."

"Have yuh a preference?" her father inquired, knowing full well what his child would ask.

"Ah want to know aboot the wolves."

"Have Ah not told yuh that story befer?" he demanded. "What aboot a different story? Perhaps Ah should tell the one aboot –"

"Wolves!" Storm shouted. Then, with a kick of her foot to emphasize her request, "Wolves."

"Yuh had better tell them aboot the wolves," Meggie suggested, a kind, knowing smile radiating over her face. "An' me, too. Ah believe Ah have forgotten parts o' the story meself. What was it aboot the alpha wolf, now?"

"Oh, that," Ian agreed, thoughtfully scratching his chin and staring gravely out into the un-seeable moors beyond. "Aye. The alpha wolf. Well," he continued, settling down, cross-legged in front of the fire. "There's many people what believe the wolf is a solit'ry beast, but that's a misconception."

Meggie whispered the meaning of the word into Storm's ear, just loud enough for Meg to catch her words, as her elder daughter positioned herself, in imitation of her parent, by the fire.

"Wolves are no' lone animals, a'tall. They hunt in packs. They have a strict social order."

Moving with the deliberate care of a tall man aware of his grace, Ian stretched a hand out, engulfing Meg's tiny one. This was the signal for her to reach out her other hand and take that of her mother's. This link complete, Meggie slipped her fingers over Storm's right hand while Ian took the tiny fingers up in his other, effectively completing the circle.

"The pack is dominated by what's called the alpha male, which, to yuh, is known as a 'tupp,'" he continued, leaning close and raising an eyebrow to accent the word. "His mate is called the alpha female."

"That's yuh," Meg whispered to her mother. Meggie nodded in solemn acknowledgement.

"These two beasties are the dominant breeding pair. All the other wolves in the pack help raise their young."

"Who is in our pack to help raise us?" Meg asked.

"Well, now, that's the peculiar thing aboot the MacDhui clan. We're a group onto ourselves. We've no others, just us four. Yer mother an' me take care of yuh, an' yuh take care o' one other. That's the circle within the circle."

"There's another circle, Ian," Meg persisted, shifting positions so she could see both parents. "Storm an me take care of yuh two."

"True," he nodded. "But on the whole, Ah'd say it was me an' yer Mum who do the lookin' after."

"No!" Storm burst demandingly into the conversation. All eyes turned to her.

"No, child?"

"No."

"It's yuh who'll be lookin' after us, then?"

"Yuh need lookin' after."

"Too wise," Ian lipped soundlessly to his wife, who blinked the tears away. Then, louder, "We were speakin' o' wolves. Now, let meh see.... Wolf pups cume in inny color – there's pure white, pure black, grey, brown, or inny coloration in between. As they grow, their colors may change. Color plays no part in the worth o' an animal to the pack; a lesson worth applyin' to human bein's."

He released Meg's hand, stirred the fire with a stick, paused to watch his poker flame, then blew it out and reattached himself.

"Why do wolves howl at the moon?"

Ian considered, then shrugged.

"Ah dunno. Ah'm not fer certain inny one does know. There's a mystery aboot the moon – call it a yearning. By bayin', a wolf – or a man – is barin' his soul. He's puttin' the Lord on guard he's not content wid his lot in life; he's suspectin' there's more to the Universe than meets the eye, an' he'd like a taste o' it."

"But when a wolf howls, it sounds like a lone wolf."

"Aye, it does. But isn't it often that when yuh hear one wolf howl, pretty soon there's other wolves howlin', until there's a whole passel of em' cryin' their hearts out?"

"Aye."

"That's the rest o' the pack lettin' that lone wolf know he – or she – is no' alone. An' that's a good thing to know, for bein' solitary leaves a horrible empty hole in a creature."

Meggie squeezed Storm close to her bosom, eliciting a tiny grunt, before turning her attention to Ian.

"Yer father an' Ah never want yuh two bairns to be alone. Yuh must protect one another. Haven't we a'ways said yuh must run as a pair?"

"That's right," he agreed. "Yuh, Meg, must watch out fer Storm, fer she's two years younger than yuh. An' you, wee one," he continued, staring into the minuscule eyes of Storm. "Haven't Ah a'ways said yuh'd catch up to yer sister? Two years makes a big difference now, but in a bit yuh'll notice that difference gits smaller an' smaller."

"Twins," Megan agreed, kissing the top of Storm's woolly head. "We'll send yuh to school together, an' see yuh're a'ways in the same grade. That way, even though yuh may find yuhrselves in a strange place, yuh'll never be alone."

"We'll never be alone because we have yuh," Meg protested. "We're a pack. Remember?"

"Ah remember. But the pack grows, changes members –"

"No!" Storm cried, struggling to free herself from the confines of the cloak, as though baring her body would protect her naked soul. "Our pack remains the same. Yuh an' me an' Meg and Ian MacDhui. That's four," she added proudly. "Four."

"As it was in the beginin'," Meg agreed.

"Not so, child," Meggie reminded her. "In the beginin' there was only one MacDhui, an' that was yer father. Ah was a Clarke befer Ah met him."

"Yuh were a'ways a MacDhui," Storm persisted angrily, clenching her fists in rage. "Yuh were a'ways married to Ian."

"No. That's an untruth, an' yuh know it."

"Ah dinna know it! Ah tell you, Ah know what Ah know, an' Ah know yuh was a'ways a MacDhui."

"It's a'right, Storm," Meg comforted her. "We're a pack now."

"It's not a'right, an' dinna yuh be tellin' me. Meggie MacDhui, Storm MacDhui, Meg MacDhui an' Ian MacDhui. That's the way it is. That's the way it'll a'ways be!"

"Go on with yer story, Ian," Meggie ordered. But it was not the night to be issuing orders.

"Ah've said enuf. Ah've sheep to tend." Breaking the circle, he stood on cramped legs, stamped his feet, then shook himself. "Tis a cold night. Yuh three shouldna have cume out onto the moors wid me. Ah'll be takin' yuh home in the mornin'."

He was not ten steps into the distance before he was lost to sight behind the crag and the murk. There was no safety for Ian MacDhui, however. With the biting wind to his face, he heard the howls of three wolves at his back.

"Ah've got to protect the sheep," he muttered. But it was not from wolves the danger would come. And he knew it. The danger was more insidious, less understandable than beasts on the prowl for their nightly repast.

A pack of hungry grey and white and black and brown wolves; ten thousand hungry grey and white and black and brown wolves were preferable to the evils lurking in the dark of the Scottish landscape.

A shepherd might scare away an animal but he could not defend what was his against the Unknown. That evil stalked the MacDhui clan and neither a sheep dog nor a man's love could keep it at bay.

Ian MacDhui stuffed his hands in his pockets and stared away from the two quiet forms at his side. He snuffled, coughed, then cleared his throat to cover his raw emotions.

"Yer gettin' a cold," Storm innocently observed.

"Aye. Ah might be," he agreed, removing a hand and brushing his arm over his face.

"Might turn to pneumonia," Meg diagnosed.

"Or leprosy," Storm added.

"Never mind that," Ian protested. "Yuh heard what that damn doctor said. There hasna been a case o' leprosy in the British Isles fer years."

"Aye. Three or four, at least," came the child's reply. Meg was trying to make him smile.

"We need to go back," Storm interrupted, abruptly changing topics.

"Ah dinna want to go back! Ah tolt yuh – go back an' cover fer me. Why dinna yuh do what Ah ask?"

Storm lashed out with her foot, kicking a stone. The projectile went hurtling down the slope, making soft thuds as it hit and bounced, almost in the rhythm of a beating heart.

"Yuh tell us aboot there not bein' inny more lone wolves, an' then you think o' yerself as a lone wolf," Meg pointed out. She reached a hand to his arm, wrapping her fingers around his sinewy muscle. When he tried to shake free, she tightened her grip.

"Ah'm the alpha wolf and Ah've lost me mate!" Ian cried, turning away. "Leave me alone."

"We'll not leave yuh alone, so there's no sense yuh askin'," Storm protested, her own ire rising. Her sister had a more direct approach.

"Then git another mate."

"What?" Ian gasped, trembling. "What are yuh sayin?"

"Yuh heard me."

"No. Never. Ah've had the one great love in me life that no man befer or since will ever have. The one... perfect love." Steeling his muscles, Ian hardened his soul as his words turned bitter. "God saw fit to take yuhr mother frum me – frum us. He's made me a lone wolf. He's made His statement: Yuh're a lone wolf, now, Ian MacDhui. Ah heard Him."

"That wasn't God," Meg spat. "That was yuh talkin' to yuhrse'f."

He started to shake his head, then sighed and surrendered.

"What makes yuh wise beyond yer years?"

It was Storm who chose to answer.

"We were born that way."

"Aye, yuh must'a been, fer as sure as the blood's the life, yuh dinna git it frum me."

"Yuh kin say that ag'in'!"

He registered her words, then finally smiled. That smile spread until the contagion mutated into a laugh. As soon as the children registered that he was not laughing at, but with them, they joined in, the sounds of their love clinging to the hills, like the faded echoes of a pack at bay.

# CHAPTER 3

The rain had not slackened by the time Ian, Meg and Storm retreated into the small entrance chamber of their home. All three were wet to the skin, dripping huge, spreading pools of water onto the floor.

As they removed their soggy outerwear, Ian made a low noise in his throat over the mess.

"Dinna fear," Meg quipped. "If God had no' meant fer puddles to form, He wouldna have created rain."

"There's a thought," Ian agreed, running his hand through his stringy, shaggy mane, then casting the bangs back over his head in a gesture of casual indifference. He was a handsome man, but his appearance had ceased to interest him after the passing of his cherished wife. Good looking or ugly, prince or frog, he was a widower with two small children to raise. He could not conceive of a reason to care about his looks.

The girls would tolerate him, whether he turned heads or cracked mirrors.

"Go take a peek," he urged his daughters, "an' see if the party's still goin' on."

"Yuh can hear that it is," Storm complained, but went as directed. She was back in a moment.

"Jest the right time to make an entrance wid a keg o' ale in yuhr arms."

He started to smile, then correctly interpreted her expression and shrugged.

"That will be the last, then."

"What are we savin' it fer? Christmas?"

His shoulder muscles quivered from the well-directed blow.

"An' where did yuh git that sharp tongue, lass?"

"At the auction last year in Old Edinburgh. Did yuh not see me bid on it? Why, there Ah was, wavin' me hand an' jumpin' up and down –"

"No. Ah dinna see you bid on inny such a thing."

"Yuh missed it, then. Go on."

Ian disappeared into the small closet, wrapped his arms around a keg of ale, then sucked air through his nose, hoisting the heavy barrel as though it weighed no more than a lamb.

"Stand clear," he ordered.

"Dinna drop it," Meg directed as he passed, knees slightly bent under the weight of his burden. Her words were not meant as a warning about the keg, but rather as an admonition not to abandon his demeanor as host and refreshment-supplier. It was a party, after all; the type of going-away celebration meant to hide, rather than reveal, emotions.

"If Ah crack a bung hole in this keg an' no one drinks this good ale," he announced ahead of his arrival, "then it'll be a waste. An' as inny good Scot knows, it's a sin to waste a drop o' innythin' intoxicatin'."

To the ears of the partygoers, already as well saturated as if they, too, had been out on the moors, his words rang cheerful and inviting. To his daughters, who knew better, the warning was shrill and empty.

"He'll be a'right," Meg whispered. When Storm did not reply, she shifted her gaze from the closed entranceway to her sister and repeated the statement.

"Aye," the younger hesitantly agreed. "He has to be. Doesn't he?"

To which the elder made no reply.

When the men and women assembled in the parlor saw Ian's gift, they raised their glasses in toast.

"The perfect host!" they chanted, eager for the relief contained inside the keg. While it would not ward off the cold of failure, it held the promise of temporary forgetfulness from the outside temperature and the changing clime of a world they could no longer control.

"We wondered where yuh were! Did yuh go all the way to Aberdeen, now, to buy us drink?"

"Awk, no," Ian grinned, easily falling into the safety of slurred speech and swimming brain. "Ah brrrrewed it out back, so it's fresh as mornin' milk."

"Aye, but a lot more damagin'!" approved a man pushing his way toward the front. "Poot a spigot in that thing an' let's get at it."

"No sooner said than done."

With a deft, well-practiced motion, Ian placed the keg between the wooden arms of a home manufactured frame, inserted a spigot, tested it by spilling some of the amber liquid onto the floor in a false exhibition of wealth, then stepped back. After two men helped themselves, they positioned their bodies next to him, both slapping him on the back. Their levity was as rehearsed as their drinking.

"Well, Ian, it's no more sheep dip yuh'll be wallowin' in, cume summer," Thomas articulated between burps.

"Aye, think of it, man," his brother, Louis, agreed. "We'll be knee-deep in lambin' an' yuh'll be a fine, fancy gentl'man, paradin' down the streets o' New York City!"

Thomas Campbell wiped his lips on his worn shirt sleeve, drank again, then nodded in well-intentioned support. "Think o' it, Louis. We'll be receivin' a postie card frum the Statue o' Liberty, an' standin' underneath it will be our old pal, Ian MacDhui."

It was a game they were playing, but in the telling, there was always the hope the story would come true.

"Smilin' as big as yuh please, without a care in the world."

Ian grabbed for Thomas' mug, drank deeply from it, then handed it back. Under the harsh light of three burning lamps, his natural pallor made his face appear waxen. The skin of his face, drawn taut by a smile, revealed more skull than joviality.

"Yuh paint a pretty picture, boys. Ah hope it cumes trrrue."

"Of course it will," a middle-aged woman agreed, joining them with the familiarity of one long used to the company of men. Hers was a hard face, character lines crisscrossing her features until they might have done good service to a mapmaker. "Look how we've decorated yer home, Ian – with paper streamers an' balloons. Even Willum Bennes brung two lamps to make cheer."

"Tis very beautiful," Ian thanked her, pausing to stare around the room. A half dozen stools had been set up in a semi-circle around the fireplace, while bits of colored confetti littered the floor. "Right nice. A fine party it is. Ah only wish..."

But what he wished was not any part of reality that decorations, lamps or neighbors could influence.

"What he wishes," Louis continued, taking up the slack with a toothy grin, "is that we all write him letters, tellin' him how miserable we are."

"Ah dinna wish innythin' o' the sort –"

"We'll be writin' him letters," Mae joined, "An' they'll say, 'Dear Mister MacDhui, we heard tell yuh struck it rich in America. We're cumin' fer a visit an' a loan. Yers truly, Mae an' Louis an' Thomas."

They all pretended to laugh at her joke, attempting, by loudness, to ignore the undertone of fear it brought to the surface.

Before their forced merriment had died down, a deep rumbling voice startled them back to time and place.

"An' how will you be strikin' it rich, Mister MacDhui?"

All four turned shifty, accusing eyes toward the newcomer, challenging him to explain why he burst the bubble they were riding on.

The speaker, an elder statesman in the county, squinted his eyes at them, knowing the intent of their states, but made no attempt to mitigate his question. Rather, he withdrew a hand-carved briar from the oversized pocket of his patch-pocket tweed jacket, then dipped it into a sheepskin pouch. After adjusting the groves in the stem, honed by worn teeth, into his mouth so it fit comfortably, he directed the unlit pipe toward Ian.

With a shaking hand less drunk than sober, the host struck a match. Holding the flame over the charred bowl, he withstood Angus Meager's puffs of smoke into his face. When the old man was satisfied, he blew out the match, now burned to Ian's fingertips, readjusted the briar and continued his one-sided conversation.

"Ah asked yuh what yuh intend to do in this New World yuh're goin' to, Mister MacDhui. That which will bring yuh fame an' fortune."

"Ah never said Ah was goin' to git fame and fortune," the younger man replied with a confused sniff and a hurt tone.

"Aye. True. It were these others what were sayn' it. He'll rob a bank, Ah suppose?" he asked, directing his cruelty to Louis Gwynn.

"Awk, no. Ian's a bright boy. He'll latch onto sumethin'."

"We were all 'bright boys,' onst, an' what has happened to us?" None of the four vouchsafed an answer. "Ah'll tell yuh what's happened to us. We're too dumb, the lot o' sheepers an' sheeper's wives, to see the handwritin' on the wall. We shoulda sold out when them 'conglomerates' cume to buy our land."

"But Angus," Thomas protested, tugging nervously on a stray thatch of thinning blonde hair. "They was offerin' pennies on the head. They were no' makin' us a fair offer."

"Fair offer? Fair offer, yuh say? Now, mebbe it were fair, considerin' how cheap we'll be sellin' when our own loans cumes up. Cheap," he emphasized, puffing on his pipe, "as in *free*. The same kind o' free as what Ian done. Foreclosure, they call that kind o' free."

"You canna believe that!"

"Ah do, an' Ah'm sayin' so. We're all as good as cooked an' in the stew. An' there's plenty more 'mutton' and 'lamb' to go in it befer there's none o' the old-timers left."

"But the gov'ment – what they've been sayin'. How they mean to help –"

"They mean to help them what's makin' money, so's they kin bring in more money. Do you suppose them in the capital gives a tinker's dam aboot those who are fallin' by the wayside?"

"But... what does them conglomerate men know aboot sheep?" a young man, new to the group asked. He was Brian Campbell, Thomas' boy, old enough to drink by privilege of having been a shepherd since he was out of nappies. "Do they know how to stare a sheep in the face an' know if it's poorly? Kin they pre-dict the day the lambin's agoin' to start? Do they know how to run a sheep dog, Angus?"

Angus shook his head, reached into the opposite pocket and brought out a large box of kitchen matches. He lit his own pipe this time, shaking his head as though the conversation were actually of little import to him.

"Ah dunno. Ah doubt it. But it dinna matter. What matters is them conglomerate-types got all the money in the world behind 'em. They're the ones what kin afford to undersell wool to poot the likes of us outta business. An' they will. Won't they, Ian?" he demanded, turning his back on the life of the party.

All eyes save Angus' turned to Ian. He hesitated, opened his mouth for a quick rejoinder, then shut it, clamping his teeth down on a pipe he did not possess.

"Speak, man," Angus demanded.

"Ah dinna know. All Ah know is the bank called me loan an' Ah couldna pay."

"Dirty, rotten bastards. We shoulda burned that bank down an' hung that Outsider by his balls to the nearest tree," Brian cried. The desperation was apparent and the men moved away from him, fearful least they find themselves in the Bank Manager's position.

Had Ian the fire in his belly he once had, he would have had a different reply. But Megan Clarke MacDhui's passing had poured water over his passion, reducing heart, and thereby courage, to fading embers.

"It was legal; it was his right. Ah pledged the wool an' the price o' wool fell. They called me loan an' Ah lost me farm."

"But that's what Ah'm sayin', man," Brian protested. "They dinna have to call it. He coulda give yuh another year. Like what they done in the past."

"The past is dead," Angus replied for him, determined to play devil's advocate.

Ian's hands clenched but his voice reflected only an impotent rage.

"What's the point o' arguing it? Ah was a land owner an' now Ah'm not."

"An' now yuh think the grass is greener in this New World o' yern?"

This time, Ian's face flushed with true emotion. With an angry gesture, he grabbed Angus Meager's pipe from between his lips, held it a moment with a thought to crush it, then hurled it across the room. The briar struck the wall and broke. A hush descended over the room faster than if an air raid siren had shattered the calm of a Sunday morn.

"Yuh've no right. New York was Meggie's dream an' yuh know it. It was all she ever talked aboot. She saw us there in New York, she said so." Jamming his finger in the old man's face, Ian pushed him back, the grey of his eyes turning black with betrayal. "Yuh talk of none o' us seein' what was cumin' – of us holdin' out when them Big Boys furst cume. Well, Meggie saw the future. She dinna want her bairns brought up in a land what's no longer ours. She started savin' an' weavin' that dream o' hers right then an' there. 'Take daughters an go,' she said, an' that's what Ah'm doin'. She had the money poot aside frum her own mother."

His hands clasped together in dire need to explain the point.

"'Dinna spend this on land, Ian, me darlin',' she said. "It's to take yuh an' Meg an' Storm to New York. 'Apply fer yer passport,' she said an' so Ah did. Ah've the papers, all right an' proper. Papers wid me name stamped on 'em. An' Meg's and Storm's. We're to go an' Ah'll no be robbin' banks to make me livin'. Ah'll git a 'respectable job,' jest as Meggie said Ah would. Yuh mark me, an' go to hell."

When the words were drained from him, Ian comprehended the terrible breech of etiquette he had committed. Still trembling, he backed away, looked wildly around himself, then stumbled toward the newly opened keg of ale. He opened the spout, then realizing he had no glass, grabbed one from a man standing near him, filled it to the brim and guzzled it.

There was a long moment of silence. Then, to cover their own shame, the men began to clap in rhythm to his swallows. When Ian finished the mug without pausing for breath, a rent of triumph split the air.

"Aye, that's showin' them!" Brian cheered. It was not so much the feat as the need for victory which spurred the youth on. As others took up the cry, Brian raced to the mantle and grabbed a large silver trophy cup from its place of honor.

"Remember this, Ian? Use this, if yuh dare. Fill it wid ale an' drink it down."

The tall, stoop-shouldered man with the lope of a wolf and the eyes of a child grabbed the cup, kissed it reverently, then hugged it to his breast.

"Remember it?" he cried, turning in a circle to dare any man to deny him his memory. "Remember it, yuh ask? Aye, Ah remember it. Look here, on the engravin'. Ah kin read it well. It says, 'First Prize, Edinburgh Fair. Ian MacDhui, wrestlin' champion, 1960."

"They said a moor man coulda beat their champ, but yuh did, Ian," a voice from the back yelled over the din of other men's memories.

"Fair an' square," Ian boasted. "He was as big a bruiser as inny man alive, yet Ah whooped 'im. An' they give me this here trophy, an' a cash prize fer doin' it."

The men began to clap again in the traditional rhythm of heart beats and swallows. Ian opened the spigot, filled the trophy nearly to the top, then brought the cup to his lips. Staring out over the silver-plated rim of his treasure, he understood the need, the craving for him to succeed.

"Bottom's up!" he cried and began to drink.

As his Adam's apple bobbed to the tempo, Ian drank the harsh, dark ale. More than a man's portion, it was a giant's drink he undertook. There was no thought of failure. Better die trying than disappoint. Life was too bitter, too filled with dregs for this moor man to fail. No longer a sheeper, stripped of his land by the interlopers, he was a champion, wrestling a moment of triumph for his onlookers.

The clapping grew louder with every swallow until the whole room swelled with noise. No one else brought glass to lips; no one dared breathe for fear of breaking the spell. Fifty pair of eyes trained on the solitary drinker, begging the fates, praying to the gods to give them back a hope, to reclaim the evening from the hardened heart of Angus Meager.

Rivulets of ale dripped from the cup but no one noticed. They had eyes only for Ian's face.

"Drink, man, drink," Brian, the boy, whispered.

"Yuh kin do it," Thomas, the shepherd prayed.

"Ghost o' Meggie MacDhui, watch over yer man," Mae, the wizened old matron summoned with reverence.

"Drink!"

"Drink!"

"Drink!"

Drink for those who had gone and for those who remained. Drink for the quick and the dead. Drink for the past to put off the future.

Drink for the deeds not done, for the bank manager who yet lived. Drink for the death of the Conglomerates and the new ways. Drink for the children and the unborn, so they would know pride, however fleeting.

Drink for the moor men and the moor women and the moor children who cannot help you.

Drink for yourself, for in the ale is the sleep of death. Drink for the liquid running from your mouth which waters the cold sod covering your love.

Drink, drink, drink until the trophy cup is dry.

Clap, clap, clap away the sands of time going pit-pat, pit-pat, pit-pat in the hour glass.

One swallow, another, longer in coming, then a third and a fourth and then, with a yell of agonized, tortured, bursting lungs and a stomach near to rupturing, Ian MacDhui finished the ale, staggered, looked around himself with bleary, blood shot eyes and dropped to his knees.

The cheers which rent the air were of Celtic ancestors tearing down Hadrian's Wall. A wall which had stood for 1,800 and some odd years and would stand for as many more.

"He's done it! He's drunk it all!"

"God bless yuh, Ian MacDhui!"

"The moor man has triumphed over evil-doers!"

They crowded around him, those who clung to their land and their sheep and their dying ways, arms and legs tangling in frenzied fury to be the first to touch the champion. Then, with drunken eagerness, they pulled and tugged and yanked until he was hoisted into the air, their standard, risen to top mast.

"He's done it!"

"God as my witness, Ah never thought it could be done."

"It's a miracle!"

With Ian on their shoulders, the men and women paraded him around the room in a dizzying pace, laughing and crying and singing, the words as slurred and indistinct as the whirl of emotions.

"No matter!" Thomas cried, tears streaming from his time-etched face. "No matter what, the Old has won a victory over the New!"

"The old! The old" another screamed, and that became the rallying cry. God for Harry, Scotland and Saint George, it was all one now, the old against the new, the Celts and the Romans, the Welsh and the Irish, the sheep and the shepherds.

"Ian!"

"Ian!"

"Ian!"

Without the memory that Ian was now of the new, the old turned back. Within a day and a day he was away to the New World, and they were left behind.

But it was not a time for deep thinking, and the party was not a *bon voyage* but a reaffirmation of man over beast, of a Christian defeating the hungry, devouring lion; the eradication of Conglomerates and the bending of the knee to old testaments and unwritten promises.

When they finally tired and lowered him to his feet, Ian tottered backward, caught himself, then plunged forward, finally steadying himself against the wall with an unsteady hand.

It was not much of a bow, but much was not required.

"Ah've never turned down a challenge in me life," he declared, eyes rolling upward in his head. "An' Ah never will. Whatever it takes, Ah'm the man fer it."

"Ian, you kin do innythin'!" Louis declared, pausing to blow his nose in a red and white checkered handkerchief before slapping the celebrant on the back. By way of acknowledgement, Ian burped loudly.

Taking this as a signal of approval, the men and some of the older women gathered round to slap him. Each subsequent burp brought more cheers, bowing and scraping.

"Yuh've done a great thing, Ian MacDhui," Angus Meager remarked in low, choked tones after the crowd had moved off. Ian stared at the withered representative of Tradition, pride shining through his ale-soaked face.

Words failed him. Rather than stutter through the acceptance of such a great compliment, he wrapped his arms around the old man's ancient shoulders and wept like a baby.

"Aye," Meg MacDhui agreed, watching her father from the protection of the foyer. "Yuh've done a great thing. Yuh've been the sacrificial lamb."

"Amen to that," Storm replied, fists clenched at her side. Then added so gently her sister turned to stare at her, "Ah wonder what else will have to die befer inny other 'great things' are accomplished."

It was not a question but a statement. Meg's reply, if she were going to make one, was lost to the loud, strident, retching sound of a man vomiting.

# CHAPTER 4

The clouds obscured the moon and the faerie ring around it, casting the small front yard into pale, depressing shadows, nearly indistinguishable from the more substantial shapes of human beings.

"Go' night," Ian waved from the open door. His voice was hoarse, barely audible over the sound of a poorly tuned automobile engine kicking over. When it gasped, shuddered, then died, Ian repeated his farewell, but this time, without the wave. It was all he could do to stand, leaning against the frame.

The motor started on the next try and the last of the partygoers left, disappearing into the murk, leaving behind only the lingering stench of ill-combusted fuel and the tracks of bald tires.

Without remembering why he was standing at the door, Ian hiccupped, spat a mouthful of bile-tinged saliva, then lifted his eyes, but not his head upward, toward the direction of the moon.

"Where are yuh?" he piteously demanded. When no answer was forthcoming, he hiccupped again, made a low, gagging noise, then staggered back inside the house. The door was left ajar.

There was no need asking why. On most nights, the door to the MacDhui home was left open an inch or two.

For the elves and the faeries to come and go as they pleased.

"It would be a sad day, indeed," Meggie had once observed, "if one o' the wee people cume callin' an' we dinna hear their knock on accounta their voices bein' too low fer us to make out."

Thereafter, the door was always left open and no MacDhui was ever heard to complain "aboot the bugs an' the critters gittin' in." It was a small price to pay for making an elf feel welcome.

Ian was drunk. He had consumed more ale this night than on the accumulated nights of thirty years past. While his world had often been out of control, seldom it was that the living room couch, the four chairs and the fireplace swam with alarming disarray.

His legs buckled, nearly toppling him. As he stumbled, one stray foot landed on a red balloon, bursting it. With a moan of surprise, he tipped an imaginary hat and back-stepped as quickly as he could.

"Ah beg yer pardon, ma'am," he apologized. "Ah dinna see yuh."

He cocked his ear, heard an acknowledgement to his words, smiled crookedly, then continued his journey toward the hearth, where his champion cup had been left in the melee. Surprisingly, there were two trophies. It took him several jabs into thin air before he retrieved the real one.

Holding it up toward his face, he saw, not his own reflection, but that of Megan's. Reassured by her bright, all-knowing eyes and her beautiful, youthful face, he sniffed and kissed her.

"They said Ah couldna win this, Meggie, me darlin'. They said the boys frum Edinburgh a'ways win. I remember what *yuh* said, Meggie – yuh said Ah was more brains than brawn, so Ah had better not fight, because iffn Ah lost inny more up here," he indicated, tapping his forehead, "yuh'd have to be the head o' the family.

"Do yuh remember that, Meggie? Oh, how we laughed. Laughed, because Ah a'ready knew yuh was the head o' the family. Yuh was the realist, the one wid her feet on the ground, while Ah was the dreamer, wid his head in the clouds.

"What kinda combination was that to make a marriage on, Ah ask yuh?" he demanded, turning the cup until he found a face better suiting his mood. "What was they sayin', Meggie, when the too tall, ugly moor boy asked the great lady to marry him? They said she could do better. They said she was the most beautiful lady in the whole o' Scotland, that's what they said. An' they was right, too. Right as rain. Ah had no business courtin' yuh, Megan Clarke, but Ah did. An do yuh know why?

"Why, because Ah was head an' heels in love, that's why. An' Ah told yuh so, dinna Ah? Ah told yuh, yuh was meh dream, an' yuh said there were lots o' dreams in this wild world – lots an' lots o' dreams – an' yuh could be only one of 'em. No, Ah said. That's untrue. Yuh're the only dream Ah need. Ah'll dream o' yuh, an' yuh do the dreamin' fer me. Ah'm a sheep dip man an' yer a watercress an' chive lady."

He laughed at their shared joke, then sobbed and kissed the cup once more. But his breath had fogged the metal so he could no longer find her image. With a desperation bordering on panic, Ian turned and turned the cup until the effort dizzied him. Hiccupping and sobbing, he rubbed his hand over the tarnished silver until a pair of eyes reappeared. Satisfied, he continued his soliloquy to the dead wife, whose eyes watched the live husband through the orbs of two small children standing immediately behind him.

"Yuh married me an' we was the happiest man an' woman on the face o' the earth. Wasn't we, Meggie? An' yuh said all sorts o' silly things to yer sheep-boy, did ya not? All sorts o' things Ah couldna unnerstan'. Yuh told me yuh was married to the most handsome man yuh had ever laid yer eyes on, an' took me to a mirror. An' what did Ah see – Ah saw me own face, starin' back at me. What a shock!"

He laughed, shook his head, then steadied himself as the room betrayed him again by spinning on its old foundation.

"Yuh're talkin' in circles, Ah said. Ah cume to see who yuh was really talkin' aboot an' Ah see meself. An yuh said, that's right, Ian. That's what Ah been tellin' yuh. Wid a face like that, yuh could stop a trrrain in its trrracks."

He rolled his R's, took delight in the sound and repeated the sentence.

"Wid a face like that, yuh could stop a trrrain in its trrracks. Oh, Megan, yuh a'ways could see a silver linin' behind the darkest rain cloud. That's why Ah fought them burlies at the Fair; why Ah rolled up me sleeves an' went at them like a wild thing. Ah wanted to win sumethin' fer yuh – to show yuh Ah was worth sumethin' – not just a boy frum the moors, a man who dinna know inny more aboot the world than sheep an' lambs an' dogs.

"Yuh were me first an' only love, Meggie Clarke MacDhui. Ah never had looked at one single gal until Ah laid eyes on yuh, and what did yuh do? Yuh turned me world upside down! That's what yuh did. Upside down."

With a lopsided grin, Ian grasped the trophy with two hands, spread his legs, then made a good-hearted attempt to turn the world upside down. As he did, however, he lost sight of her reflection.

"No!" he cried in fear. "No! Ah canna lose yuh ag'in. Cume back, yuh hear?"

But the face and the memories were all gone. Ian tripped over his twisted legs, tumbling to the floor, dropping the cup as he fell. The rim of the trophy pinged against the hardwood, then bounced dully on its side, creating a irregularly shaped dent.

"Oh, meh God," he cried, repossessing the prize and rubbing at the mark. "Ah've hurt ya! Ah've hurt ya, ag'in!"

The reply, when it came, originated from a source far closer to earth than heaven.

"Yuh never hurt her an' it's time yuh went to bed."

"Ah did!" he cried. "Ah hurt her because she died –"

"Yuh know better than that, an' we'll no be arguin' that old argument wid you this night," Meg explain, resting a hand on her father's hot face. "It's past time yuh've gone to bed."

"Bed?" he reiterated uncomprehendingly. "Bed? What's bed to me? What's bed to a man what's lost his wife? An' dinna know no more aboot bed. Ah dinna care. Ah'll never go back to bed ag'in."

"Aye, yuh can an' yuh will. Now git up, fer yer too heavy fer us to carry. Git up on yer two legs, or crawl like a beastie if yuh canna, but git to bed!"

"Where is she?" he screamed, blind hand searching for the form he knew so well. "Where is she?"

"She's waitin' fer ya in bed. Now, dinna keep her waitin'."

Meg shuddered under the weight of her lie, but held her ground against Ian's frenzied stare and Storm's angry accusation.

"Dinna tell him that. It's untrue."

"Ah know it's untrue!" an injured Meg replied. Then, with stoicism born of dire need, she turned and faced her sister. "Dinna be remindin' me o' what we all lost!"

"It's a sin to lie."

"Aye. An' it's a greater sin to let him sleep on the floor this night. Or are you gonna pick him up an' carry him to bed?"

"Ah kin try," the child pouted. When Meg remained quiet, Storm reached down in an effort to raise her father.

"Yuh canna make a bird wid a broken wing fly, no matter how many times yuh throw it up in the air."

"Who's talkin' aboot flyin'? Ah'm gonna git him on his feet. Besides," she continued, refusing to admit defeat, "he's no' a bird. He's a wolf. A wolf will chew its own paw off to git outta a trap."

"True," Meg agreed. "But then it crawls under a bush to die, for a wolf canna hunt wid three legs. Think o' that, Storm MacDhui."

"Ah'd rather have 'im die under a bush than in a trap."

"He's not in a trap."

"A lie is a trap."

"A lie is a lie he'll no be rememberin' in the mornin'. A lie is a thing a man kin live wid, because he kin outlive a lie. Or mebbe turn a lie into a dream an' make it a truth. He canna outlive a trap."

"Ah dinna understand yuh."

But Meg did not understand herself, and made no more argument.

"Cume to bed, Ian. It's long past yer bedtime an' yuh need yer sleep. There's plenty o' dreams to be dreamed an' they're all waitin' fer yuh."

"Aye," he sleepily agreed. "Ah'll go."

When their father was carefully placed in bed and tucked in with all the deft four pair of loving hands could manage, Meg bent over to kiss his fervid brow. As she did, Storm slipped quietly away. It was more than ten minutes before she returned. Meg eyed her suspiciously.

"Where did you go?"

"Just around," came the evasive answer.

"Answer me, for we had better no' have secrets between us."

Storm hesitated, then stared defiantly at her sister.

"Ah cleaned the trophy."

"And?"

"Ah packed it."

"Packed it – where?"

"Wid me things. Ah packed it away – an' yuh know the reason."

Storm narrowed her eyes in challenge, but got none.

"Aye," Meg sighed. "Ah know the reason." She started down at the sleeping form, shaking her head sadly.

"We mustna let him pawn it."

"No," Storm agreed. Then in a more hushed voice, added, "Nor his weddin' ring, neither."

"Awk," Meg cried, jutting out a hand to stop Storm from removing Ian's ring. "Yuh canna do that. He would never...." But the thought died a bitter death on her lips and she averted her head as Storm worked the ring from their father's finger. Once done, however, the younger child shook with a sense of betrayal.

"Yuh shouldna ha' done that," Meg pursued, knowing full well the deed was not a crime but a measure to prevent one.

"It's as much ours as his."

"No... it's not. It's a bond, a promise between a man an' a woman. It had nuthin' to do wid us."

"We're the product of that bond," Storm insisted, eyes dry, yet emotions running. "She was our mother. That's sacred, too, isna' it?"

"Sacred? Aye."

"Yuh've seen that look in his eyes befer – seen him whirl the ring around on his finger; Ah dinna have to tell yuh what he was thinkin'." But she did have to tell, if not for Meg's sake, than for her own. "'It's money in the bank,' he'd be thinkin'. Money fer food, or shelter or whatnot."

"There's a lot o' 'whatnots' in the world," Meg confessed. "But, he'll miss it. They're be a terrible row over it when he wakes up."

Storm shook her head, on steadier ground.

"He'll no be lookin' fer innythin' when he wakes up. His head'll be hurtin too bad. An' after that, we'll be movin' out; gone. Gone," she repeated, letting the word harden her heart.

"What are yuh goin' to do wid it?"

That answer was ready. Storm produced a thin cord of latigo from her pocket. In a moment, she slipped the simple band through it, knotted the ends of the leather, then placed the enclosed circle within a circle around her neck. Both children stared at the ring, suspended on the cord a moment, before Storm slipped it under her shirt.

"Safe," she declared.

"That's a terrible burden yuh'll be wearin'."

"No more'n what yuh a'ready have. Ah want meh share."

There was a long moment of silence before Meg tried one final time to dissuade.

"He'll think he lost it." There was accusation in her voice, but it was not directed at Storm, but rather at the dead mother and the tortured father. "What iffn he asks me if Ah've seen it?"

"Yuh've seen it an' yuh hav'na seen it," Storm shrugged. Then added gently, with the faith of a child,"Iffn he really wants it back, Ah'll give it to him. To poot back on his finger. An' he'll have to swear on Meggie MacDhui's grave never to pawn it. That's my condition. Are we agreed?"

"We are agreed."

"Swear it."

"Ah swear it... On my love for him who sleeps to wake, an' she who sleeps not to wake."

"Ah swear it on me beloved moors. Them what's part o' me fer now an' forever. Megan MacDhui had a dream an' that was her dream but it wasna mine. Ah swear Ah'll cume back here," Storm vowed with all the intensity of her being.

Meg hesitated, then the nearly ten-year old and the twelve-year old shook hands. The pact was sealed.

To bind it in affection, they both bowed and kissed the brow of he who slept the short sleep. Not the sleep of the just, but the repose of the betrayed.

Betrayed not by his beloved daughters but by a Fate and a Will more powerful than earthly bonds.

"Come," Meg declared, brushing away the cobwebs of the past. "We have work to do this night."

Work of a nature, less holy in a religious sense, than sacred in an ethereal way.

The fire crackled with intensity, the orange-red-blue-tipped flames eagerly consuming the dried moss and twigs. A different fire, a time well beyond that of other fires which had ever burned on the moors. It was not to loosen the tongue for story-telling, nor to warm the hands of a shepherd's children over on a cold, rainy night.

This crag, the lee side of which protected the worshipers from the rain and the wind, was a private place, a chapel carved by centuries of unrelenting weather. Small enough to protect the forms of two children, it had stood one thousand years and would stand another thousand, as wild and untamed as the weed-grasses and the natural selection of beasts, both two- and four-legged which called it home.

Standing between Meg and Storm was a ewe. The sheep was quiet, placid, disturbed from sleep yet not alarmed. These were shepherd's children come to fetch her with dog and staff. Hers was not to question.

The hour was late and the moon near setting, yet it was as distinct in the heavens as though painted on canvas, forever a reminder of eternal light over God's brown and green and purple-flowered moor.

"There's a ring around the moon."

"Ian says that means it's a faerie moon. Good luck."

She did not have to repeat their father's teaching. It was part of the ritual.

"Ah hope that's true."

That was not part of the ritual; doubt in the face of gospel. Yet as moons set and suns rose, it was as predestined as life and death.

Placing a hand of the wool of the ewe, Meg took in a deep breath, then began the words, speaking in a low, sing-song chant.

"By the light o' this faerie moon, an' in the presence o' this sheep, made sacred by Jesus, the Shepherd who oversees all, we make this sacrifice."

Removing a small pocketknife from her jacket, Meg handed it to Storm, who sterilized and made pure the blade by suspending the fire-forged steel over the heat. When it was running red, she gave it back to Meg. Clenching it tightly, Meg held it up toward the moon for a blessing, then deftly severed a small tuft of wool from the animal's neck.

With the wool in one hand, Meg took the point of the knife and made an incision in the long finger of her own left hand. When a significant droplet of blood formed, she absorbed it with the sheep's outer protection. This act done, Meg gave both knife and wool to Storm.

Using her left hand, for she was left-handed, Storm repeated the ritual, drawing blood from the long finger of her right hand. She, too, wiped the smear onto the wool, then closed the knife with a snap and buried in inside a pocket.

"The blood is the life," she swore. Then holding the newly consecrated sacrifice over the fire, she dropped it onto the eager flames. In an instant the host was consumed. "Fire is purifying," she recited.

Meg nodded solemnly, never taking her eyes from the flames.

"We, Meg MacDhui an' Storm MacDhui, offspring o' Ian and Megan MacDhui, do hereby make this vow."

"An' take this oath," Storm continued. "We swear to be loyal to one another; to be proud an' honorable –"

"To keep the faith –"

"To love an' protect Ian MacDhui; to watch over him, an' see no harm cumes to him."

"We swear before this faerie moon, while standin' on these moors o' our ancestors, an' by this blood sacrifice, to let no person, nor no thing cume between us. To fight to the death for what is right and fair."

A second passed, then another, two heartbeats long. When the wool was vanished and the flames lowered, they whispered an "Amen."

"Go now, ewe," Meg told the animal. "Back to where yuh belong. Back to the moors an' the grasses an' the wind an' the rain. Back to what yuh know; we're off to what we dinna know. Think kindly o' us, fer we love yuh an' all yer kind."

"Dream a dream fer us, for we're dreamin' the dream o' another," Storm continued. "An' we'll be far away when yer time cumes to lamb. Dream... of the MacDhuis... an' what they were."

"Dream of the MacDhuis – an' what they are to becume," Meg firmly amended.

The ewe hesitated, then wagged its tail and slowly moved off. In a moment the animal was lost from sight around the crag and down the path to join the others of its kind. From the herd came the faint sound of bleating, then all became silence once more.

"This is our land," Storm protested, digging her fists deep into her loose-fitting trouser pockets. "An' Ah'm cumin' back. Ah belong here."

"Yuh were born here an' a part of yuh will always be here. But yuh canna say yuh belong here."

"Ah kin say what Ah please." Her lower lip trembled, then tears welled in her child's eyes. "Ah hope the aeroplane crashes!"

Before Meg could respond, she ran away, face pressed into the suddenly sleeting rain. Meg hesitated before following, wiping her own eyes with a hand she would not let her father see tremble for the world.

"It's never easy to dream another's dream. The trick is, to find some goodness in it an' make it yer own."

Storm did not hear her, but the admonition was not meant for the ears of a nine-year old. And, perhaps, neither were they meant for the ears of a twelve-year old.

# CHAPTER 5

The rain tapered off at dawn, bringing with it a dubious sunrise. The air hung heavy, damp to breathe, while clothing clung to the body like a toad skin, ill-disguising the bones and muscles beneath.

"Good morning," Ian called, his voice in contrast to the ashen-grey complexion and bloodshot eyes he peered at the world through.

His daughters, hanging a bed sheet over the last naked piece of living room furniture, jumped at the unexpected sound.

"Good morning," Meg responded, matching his optimism with forced gaiety. When Storm did not speak, he addressed her, winking by way of private signal.

"What's the matter wid yuh? Cat got yer tongue?"

There was a pause before she found the courage to answer.

"Ah dinna own a cat. An' if Ah did, Ah'd never give it meh tongue." Then, when his face fell, she pried open a corner of her heart. "Can yuh not see? Ah'm hung over, so please keep yer voice to a low roar."

Her attempt at humor brought a smile as wide as the Atlantic Ocean to Ian's face.

"So. Yer hung over, are yuh? An' what do yuh know aboot bein' hung over?"

Meg poked Storm with her elbow and the answer, if there were one, was consigned to the upper regions of silent thought.

"How aboot some breakfast?"

"Breakfast?" Ian questioned, regretfully rubbing his queasy stomach. But it was not a morning to refuse. "Great. What have we?"

"Porridge is on the stove. An' yuh'll be wantin' bacon?"

"Ah suppose we ought to eat whatever's in the ice box. What we leave Ah told Angus Meager to cume an' take." When the statement fell on sad faces, he clapped his hands to catch their attention. "No sense startin' out on a Great Journey with our bellies rumblin'. But Ah thought to finish the packin' an' here Ah see yuh two are up befer me an' the work's a'most done."

Storm's eyes flickered quickly to the pale indentation on Ian's ring finger, then jumped to his face, which she searched with innocent earnestness.

"Will they have porridge in the New York?"

"O' course they will. What do yuh think, those people eat? Day-lilies an' mustard fer breakfast? They're jest like us, yuh know."

"Then they're all in a heap o' trouble."

"Why is that?"

"They're as poor as church mice."

"Awk, off wid yuh now an' no be lookin' at things with a gloomy face. Ah thought yuh were an adventurer – a kindred spirit to the wanderin' Celts who conquered jest aboot every square inch o' every piece o' land worth havin'."

"Ah'm a shepherd."

"Well... that's the same thing. Now git. Ah smell the porridge burnin'."

The porridge was not burned. The three MacDhui's finished their meal, then sat around the table, wiping their lips on well-worn linen napkins. These napkins, acknowledgement of better times and table manners of "fancy folk," had originally been placed around each plate by Megan, who believed in maintaining decorum at the dinner table. While she ruled the house, and consequently the dining table, the family ate with forks properly fitted into the left hand. The knife was placed by the side of the plate, used only to cut, never to spear. Spoons were reserved in the silverware drawer, only seeing the light of day to assist in the consumption of soup or dessert.

Meggie, Ian frequently remarked, was a sheep of a different color. No one else of their acquaintance used napkins, and a knife was considered a necessary component of bringing sustenance to the mouth.

It was as well for the MacDhui clan that neighbors seldom partook of food at their table, or the "peculiar ways o' Mrs. MacDhui" would have made her a legend in her own lifetime.

Their offspring were required to wash up before eating, even when victuals were prepared over a camp fire, and never, ever, were any of them seen in town without well-pressed clothes. Ian, not a swearing man by nature, was never heard to raise his voice to Meggie, while Meg and Storm, both outspoken and hot tempered, were banished to their room if they so much as spoke one word in anger in the vicinity of their mother.

Megan MacDhui, *nee* Clarke, was a shepherd's wife in heart and soul, never failing to make the required appearance at lambing time to bless the ewes, or to roll up her sleeves and aid in the delivery of hard births. She never complained of boots traipsing muck across clean floors, never chided moor men for two weeks growth of beard during their long intervals away from home, and was known to whip up a pot of stew good enough to win a ribbon at the local fair.

On the other hand, she was seen more than a few times reading a book to Ian while he lay, head on her lap, the two of them settled under the spreading leaves of an ancient shade tree.

Megan Clarke was raised on the moors, but she was not a moor woman by blood. Her parents died in a motor accident while she was yet a babe, and the child was raised with her cousins by a distantly related aunt and uncle. The inheritance she received from her dead parents was placed in an account, bearing her name. This vast sum of ten thousand pounds was never touched by her step-parents, despite the legitimate claim they had on it.

When curious neighbors complained that Megan's money might be put to use helping the large family survive hard times, instead of "rottin'" in an Edinburgh bank, her guardians had shrugged away the question, failing to provide a satisfactory answer to well-intentioned inquiries.

"Fair was fair," the neighboring sheep families muttered to themselves, scratching their heads in wonder. Ten thousand pounds would pay the taxes, buy a new roof for the family dwelling and add a comfortable treasure to the few pennies stashed under the mattress for a rainy day.

"It's no' ours," was all either Charlotte or her husband David Wayne would say. "It wasna left fer us."

Not even when David fell off a crag and broke his leg, putting him in hospital for a fortnight was that legacy touched. Nor, truth be told, did Megan offer it. She was, people said, an "odd one," a foreigner.

Falling in the middle of the Wayne children, age-wise, Meggie performed both the duties of sister and servant. She was never heard to complain about the arduous life of a moor girl, though many supposed she would take her money and run at the first opportunity.

Megan Clarke was not tall by moor standards, but she had strength equal to any child her age, and was not above putting her shoulder to the wheel to get a wagon out of the mire, or to hoist a half-grown sheep and carry it out of a steep valley. She was soft spoken and polite, religious and book-learned, yet when fire sparked out of her deep blue eyes, no one dared cross her.

She understood right from wrong, yet her idea of right and wrong did not always coincide with that of others. When confronted with a problem where she fell on one side and the family on the other, it was they who ultimately altered their opinions.

Meggie had the power to bewitch, the moor folk whispered behind her back. During the black of a moon she might be seen wandering the lonely sheep trails without a light, or picking her way amongst invisible stepping stones through the swamps, never wanting for any other companion than the whispering night breezes or the low-flying night birds.

Neither a witch or a gypsy, exactly, Meggie was known to consort with the wee people and once appeared at church wearing a small flower in her hat, the like of which had not grown on the moors for two hundred years.

A gift from the faeries, she had said. No one doubted it.

When acquiring full woman's status by attaining the ripe old age of sixteen, the moor people expected her to pack her bags and return to the mysteries haunts of her birth parents, from whence she came. When Megan gave no indication of imminent departure, they speculated she was only biding her time, waiting, perhaps, for the fulfillment of some prophesy, whispered into her ear by the elves.

It was not her legacy of ten thousand pounds which brought the boys from as far away as Glasgow to court her, but the wild, untamed beauty of face and limb which attracted them. She was one of a kind; a lass with a laugh as clear as the tinkle of a silver bell and a scowl as dark as the storm clouds of October.

"She's no' a Wayne an' she's no' cut out fer the harsh ways o' a shepherd's life," they said, the folk of the moors and the heathered meadows. "She's a Clarke an' she'll no stay here. Let one o' them city boys make her a respectable offer an' we'll never see hide ner hair o' her ag'in."

"Respectable," was a word often on the lips of Meggie Clarke.

Come to pass, it was not "one o' them city boys" with flashy smiles, motor cars which raced like the wind, or scholars with parchment University degrees who gained the fancy of Megan Clarke, but the tall, glum, dark haired boy from "up beyond" which caught her eyes and netted her love.

Ian MacDhui was the seventh son of a shepherd and his wife, born into the world in the month of March. He came, Ian's mother said, "wid the lambs." Dirt poor and educated enough to sign his name on a piece of paper when payday rolled around, he was taciturn by nature, half man, half wolf, with no better destiny awaiting him than hard work and bitter frustration.

Having left home at fourteen when his family could no longer afford to feed him, Ian first hired himself out as a shepherd, keeping lonely vigil with the beasts and the crags.

"Dumb, he is," they said, meaning lacking in intelligence, rather than the kinder "mute." He took his pay with nary a word and disappeared into the hills, shunning the campfires of other men. He had, it seemed, no taste for the tall tales and boasts of those who had no dreams.

The only time Ian ever smiled was at lambing time. In this joy, he was not alone, for it was the season when even the harsh hills and glens relented, adding a bit of purple and green to the barren landscape.

"Tall as a mountain an' a companion fer no one but sheep," the moor people said, paying him his wages, then shying away, for like a wolf, he could turn at a moment's notice, teeth bared, a growl in his throat.

No one ever knew how they met or when. The first inkling anyone had of Ian and Meggie as a couple was when they appeared, hand-in-hand, at a dance one wet, windy spring night. Their appearance was the cause of considerable speculation. Gossip rang over the little Scottish town like church bells, first tentative and low, then rapid and deep.

"What does she see in him an' how kin he hope to hold onto her?" they muttered behind cupped hands. "He's naught but a brute wid his feet in the muck an' his brains in his pockets," they agreed, for they could not see the gentleness for the gruffness, the beauty beneath the grime, or comprehend the hopes and dreams behind the darting, challenging grey-green eyes.

Because she was not daughter but niece to the Waynes, no one in the sheeping community expected Ian to present himself at their hearth, asking for her hand. "He'll knock her on the head an' drag her away," they said, and waited for the day when Ian and Meggie disappeared forever off the face of the earth.

"She's destined for better'n the likes o' him," Angus Meager predicted. "She's sowing her wild oats an' will leave that poor beast wid a broken heart. He'll howl at the moon till his spirit cracks, then he'll fall off a rock an' be dead till Doomsday."

"He's turned her head wid his animal charm," Thomas, brother of Louis, remarked. "She's niver seed innythin' like him, an' he'll eat her up befer he's through."

Contrary to expectations, Ian had showered and shaved and presented himself at the Wayne's door late one night, and, hat in hand, requested permission to wed her.

"Yuh've heard, Ah expect," David Wayne, master and guardian replied, "that she has a legacy to bring to the union. Tell me true if that's why yer courtin' her." To which Ian had blushed, stammered an incomprehensible reply and departed, without either permission or blessing.

The MacDhui married the Clarke in the tiny church on the hill. No one from the village was invited, including the Waynes. The minister's old handy man served as witness. As far as anyone ever knew, not one penny from the dowry was ever touched.

The couple set up housekeeping in a small, rough-hewn home, purchased with the wages Ian had saved over the years. They were, as the expression went, as poor as church mice, yet never was one word of complaint heard from either.

Just as Ian went about raising sheep, Megan went about raising Ian. Books in hand, she followed where he went, reading to him, teaching him to cipher, making the dusty dates and obscure names of history come alive to his open, eager mind.

"She's made a new man outta him," they all agreed. But what they could not come to a consensus over was if this were a good thing or a bad thing.

There was never any doubt in Ian's mind, for under her loving hand, he transformed from a boy to a man, from a beast to a gentle human. Many were the chuckles behind his back he earned, for drawing out a chair so his lady might sit, or rising to his feet when *she* entered a room.

His acquaintance with soap and razor raised eyebrows, while his carefully washed and ironed shirt and trousers made him a marked man at church and grange gatherings. A tip of his hat to the village girls caused great consternation among the women and not a few shakes of older and wiser heads.

"She's put a spell on him a'right," they agreed. "His consort is a changeling, faerie born yet human bred."

"Beware," they said, "She'll fill his head wid clouds."

To which Ian MacDhui replied not one word. For him, joy was of the kind mere mortals could hardly comprehend.

When their first child was born, a wee slip of a daughter, men feared the worst, for it was their experience that a man like Ian "would be raging hell" for a boy and have no use for girls. But at the christening, when the proud father presented his offspring to the minister, there were tears of happiness streaming down his cheeks. The naysayers were hard pressed to explain.

"Wait," they predicted. "In a year's time there'll be another, an' this time, it had better be a boy."

It was more than two times a twelve month before the next MacDhui made an appearance, in the form of another daughter.

"Now cumes the fury," they said, in expectation of cataclysm from the sire. They were rewarded with a fury fairly received, but in the guise of a "Storm," for Ian was as happy as a lark carrying his two female children on his broad shoulders over the land called MacDhui.

When asked one night past quitting time at the King's Arms pub he had tarried in on his long journey home, Ian had laughed at the question of when there would be an heir for his small family.

"Ah've two heirs a'ready an' Ah couldna be a happier man," he declared, eyes bubbly with ale. "Ah'm the happiest creature on the face o' the earth."

"An' how kin that be?"

"Ah've three to love where befer Ah had none," came the simple, honest reply.

"So who's to work yer land wid ya?" they inquired, dumb astonished.

"There's me an' Meg an' Storm and Meggie MacDhui," he replied, wiping his mouth on a threadbare handkerchief and waving his good-byes. "When a man has love, all things is possible."

Which, forever after, labeled him as touched in the head by elf dust, or bewitched by the charms of an Otherworlder.

"Ah guess we had better pack these, too," Ian sighed, staring with forlorn fondness at the napkin. The napkins came from the rag collection, carefully cut into squares and sewn around the edges, so the ends would not unravel.

"Napkins," Meg replied dryly, "is one thing we'll never be widout. Ah dinna think there will be inny worry aboot making new when we git to New York. Yuh might say, we have a replenished supply jest waiting to be converted frum overalls an' drawers."

"Dinna let yer mother hear yuh talk like that," Ian warned, then caught himself and turned away.

"Never mind," Storm quickly volunteered. "When yuh git a respectable job in New York, we'll have money enuf to buy linen napkins."

"Aye," Ian agreed, turning back with wet eyes. "What am Ah thinkin'? Yer right, o' course. When Ah git a respectable job in New York, all things is possible."

"Respectable job" was Megan's expression and consequently, the MacDhui's mantra. It was an insuperable part of the Quest.

The expression hung, like low-lying fog in the valley, before Ian spoke again.

"Cume, now. It's high time we said our good-byes. It's out back, first, to the graveyard, Ah think, then when the trunk is packed an' we're ready to go, it's off to see the Angel." His plan was met with long faces. He tried smiling, an effort not lost on the children. "Am Ah right, or am Ah wrong?"

"Yuh're right," Meg reluctantly agreed.

"Ah'm a'ways right," he cheerfully replied. "Am Ah not?" The silence evaporated the children's answers. Clearing his throat, Ian agreed for them. "Ah'm right! So it's off we go."

Pushing his chair back, a leg scraped against the bare floorboards, making a distraught, grating sound. He winced, looked down, then scuffed the mark, giving Meg and Storm the opportunity of getting up and departing before him.

If sorrow made a kirk yard, then the wandering spirits would find a ready home amongst the abandoned furniture and threadbare napkins of the newly departed MacDhuis.

# CHAPTER 6

It was called a scratch garden for obvious reasons. A small patch of earth, hewn out of rocks and wind-swept dirt, was encased by a small twine-and-stick fence, more for show than purpose. Several plants, half weed, half cultivated, stuck their green leaves upward and their roots downward, neither movement particularly inspired. That they lived at all was testimony to the perseverance of nature and the stubbornness of life to survive against all odds.

Beyond the patch was a small cemetery. A number of peculiar grave markers lifted their own lifeless forms upward toward the sky and hopeful redemption. From the appearance of the dismal, haphazardly placed remembrances, a positive outlook was less than certain.

It might have been the final resting place of well-beloved MacDhui pets which had perished over the years, but was not. Rather, the burial yard represented, if the names were to be taken literally, the interment of kitchen utensils.

Squatting down beside a large, stained handle protruding from the dirt to a height of a foot and a half, Ian rested his hand casually on top, then wound his finger through the once shiny silver-colored hanging loop.

"Good-bye, friend pots an' pans. We'll a'ways remember yuh."

"Good-bye, fryer," Meg acknowledged, directing her attention toward where the curved lip of metal shone through the ground. "Yuh made good doughnuts in yer day."

"Good-bye, electric oven," Storm declared, louder though less assured than her sister and father. "Yuh taught us a lesson we'll no soon fergit."

Without stooping, she restlessly placed the toe of her shoe against a tangled pile of twisted metal. On one of the larger "bones" was painted the word, "Electric."

"Perhaps," Meg sniffed bravely, "We'll have a new oven in New York."

"If we do," her father declared, plucking a wild flower from beneath the shadow of death and placing it on the grave, where it immediately wilted from the hot sun, "we're no gonna use it. Ah doubt we'll be able to afford to pay fer the damages."

He laughed, looking from one girl to the next. As they caught his eye, they laughed with him.

"Aye," Meg agreed. "We'd have to live like a Conglomerate president to keep buying new electric ovens at the rate we could explode them."

"An' iffn we took out the wall of a flat, there'd be all sorts o' explainin' to do. Ah imagine landlords dinna take kindly to tenants destroyin' their property."

"But Ah thought yuh said we'd have a house of our own," Storm suddenly protested. The two pair of older and wiser eyes turned to her with troubled pity.

"We will," Ian promised. "In time."

"When Ian gits a respectable job," Meg supplemented.

"Sure. Sure." The encouragement was loud and positive, perhaps to instill belief in the speaker more than the recipient. "But we hav'ta save our money at first. No one goes to New York City an' buys a house right off."

"Yuh said we would," Storm stubbornly protested. "Yuh said we'd have a house wid green grass in the front an' trees in the back. Ah canna live widout trees, Ian MacDhui. Where are the birds to land iffn we dinna have no trees? An' what am Ah gonna climb when Ah want to stare off into the distance? Answer me that," she demanded, fists clenched under her chin in obvious anguish.

"There'll be stairs to climb," he chided, eager to end the argument before his own courage tumbled to earth. "An iffn yuh want to look into the distance, we'll go to the Statue o' Liberty. Ah hear yuh kin take a ride near to the top. Would that be high enuf fer yuh, then?"

"Only if Ah kin look east an' see Scotland." When he made no reply, Storm kicked viciously at the remnants of "Electric," bending the already unrecognizable and decayed corpse into a new, though no less redemptive shape. "Will Ah be able to see that far?"

He started to answer in the negative, then stood and turned his back on her.

"Yuh know the answer to that as well as Ah do. Yuh've Meggie MacDhui's atlas in yer bookcase an' we've poured over its pages time an' time ag'in."

"If Ah canna see Scotland, then Ah dinna want to go."

"Yuh had better poot –"

But he was restrained from elucidating where Storm had better put her complaint by a gentle hand on his darkly tanned, muscular, working man's arm.

"She knows, Ian MacDhui."

"Then why is she askin' ag'in?"

"She's jest askin', that's all. Jest fer the sake o' speakin'."

"Aye. Well, sumetimes it's better no' to speak."

"Ah'm a free Man, an' Ah'll speak me mind whenever Ah please," Storm informed him, moving into a fighter's stance. "Tell me Ah canna, an' we'll have it out, right here."

Ian flinched, then ran his hand nervously through his long locks.

"Ah dinna want to fight. Ah'm done fightin'. Fightin'," He added bitterly, "is fer losers."

"Yuh may not want to fight, but Ah was born kickin' an' screamin' into this world, an' that's the way Ah am. Am Ah not called 'Storm'? What do yuh think Ah'm called 'Storm' fer, if not because Ah'm a fighter?" Taking a deep breath, her temper roused, she clenched her fists and continued.

"There's no life worth havin' iffn someone hands it to yuh on a platter. Ah've heard yuh say that a time or two, Mister MacDhui. Have yuh fergot so soon, or is all this dreamin' aboot New York gone to yer head? Not even yer own dream," she finished, challenging him by protruding her lower lip. "It's Megan MacDhui's dream what's kept yuh alive an' kickin'. Mebbe it's time yuh got a dream o' yer own."

"Yuh had better put that lip back in your head," he warned, taking a step closer.

"Or else what?"

It was an act of defiance of the most primitive kind. His shoulders jerked spontaneously before he reined in his temper. Knotting his fingers behind his back, Ian kicked at a clump of dirt, then retreated.

"Ah've give up that kind o' fightin' fer yer mother's sake, an' even if Ah hadna, Ah wouldna raise a hand to yuh. Ah've never touched yuh in anger, an' Ah never will. Mark my words, Gail MacDhui an' dinna stand befer me wid yer fists clenched."

"Or else what?"

"There must be an echo around here," Meg loudly declared. "Ah believe Ah jest heard that question asked no' a moment gone by."

Her intervention gave Ian the moment he needed to calm his jangled nerves. With a misshapen grin, he squared his broad shoulders and pointed to the house.

"If yuh've finished yer packin' then go an' load the truck. We've one more place to go befer we're to be at the Aeroport an' Ah dinna want to feel rushed."

Storm quivered, a wilted leaf under an interminable sun, then backed down. With a surly shake of her own dark locks, she turned her back on her family and walked, stiff-legged toward the house which was no longer a home.

"Go wid her," Ian pleaded with his elder daughter. "She's young an she dinna understand."

Exactly what Storm did not understand was left unsaid.

It was Meg's turn to comply with the request. She made a motion, then paused, looking over her shoulder as she spoke.

"Do yuh?"

It was unfair, but she was only twelve years old.

Truth be told, had she been thirty, she would have asked the same question. The difference was, she would not have expected an answer.

"Ah unnerstan' that God helps them what helps themselves."

It was a trite answer, an answer out of the pages of a book written by author or authors unknown. There was much to be said for anonymity.

"Ah understand that, too, Ian MacDhui. But not in the same way yuh do."

Her tone was not meant to be ominous, but the words spoke for themselves.

"Off wid yuh," he shooed. "Harsh words is no way to start a Great Adventure."

"We canna start what we hav'na finished."

"Go! Go! It's finished, Ah tell yuh! Done an' buried."

"If that's the case, we have nowhere else to go an' it's off to the aeroport."

As tears came into her father's eyes, Meg regretted her pointed thrust, yet it was too late to retract the sentiment. Confused and guilty, she stared upward into the muted expanse of sky, then hissed through the gap in her front teeth and walked away. Ian watched her for a moment, then glanced downward at the graves of the unlived.

The wilted pedals of the yellow wild flower met his gaze, holding his eyes transfixed.

"Don't yuh start," he warned, wagging a finger at it. "What's dead will be reborn. Remember that."

*Ah will, if you will,* it waved at him as he wavered.

It was all the hope he was going to get.

"Enuf, then," Ian pronounced.

It would have to serve as an "Amen," which was a far cry from a hallelujah.

Though the trip to the kirk yard was short in distance, it seemed to take forever in time. With Ian driving and the two children squashed in the front seat alongside him, there was little opportunity for conversation. It was enough to hold one's bones together as the ancient pickup sought out and dove mercilessly into each and every pothole.

"If Scotland ever offers a job to inny one fer the detection and proper identification o' holes in the road, Ah'll nominate this ol' horseless carriage," Ian said, making a gallant attempt to break the silence.

"That would be nice," Meg agreed, staring with desultory eyes through the windscreen. "If they put a bounty on every hole, we'll be wealthy fer sure."

"We will not," Storm growled. "Fer after today we'll no be here an' this ol' horseless carriage, as yuh call it, will belong to Thomas and Lewis. So if yer thinkin' they'll be a bounty, we had better stay."

For her trouble, she received a sharp blow on the ankle bone, delivered with expert and deadly accuracy by the heel of her sister's shoe.

The cemetery had nothing to distinguish it. As burial places went, it was of recent dedication, being no more than one hundred and fifty years of age. There were no royal bodies resting within its consecrated soil, no notable Names. It was said some famous battle had been fought near its south gate over one thousand years ago, but even the local historian was hard put to name it.

The grave markers were flat, weather-worn and inexpensive. Most of the letters, carved into the limestone, were faded beyond legibility. Those still bearing the names of the dearly departed, boasted accomplishments no greater than "Father," or "Shepherd." The few with "Mother," or "Wife," were distinguished by birth and death dates depressingly close together.

Because its blanket of patchy green weeds and sun-dried grasses covered the poor and the destitute, it more closely resembled a potter's field than an honorable estate for temporary repose. No one standing at the rusting, wrought-iron fence looking inward could swear with any certainty that Gabriel's trumpet would wake any of its slumberers.

"Look," Storm pointed. "There's a new one, just dug. Ah wonder who it's fer?"

Meg did not look and Ian did not hear.

The truck, like a faithful dog, could have found its way through the twisting and turning road, which was, in actuality, no more than a two-sided track, without help from its driver. The ruts were enough to keep the wheels in line, and the oft-traveled route had long ago been memorized, even by so mechanical a servant.

Left, left, right, left, stop at the corroded pump to fill a cup of water, then turn left again and down the incline, too modest to be called a slope.

Half way down this portion of the drive, the engine wheezed, coughed, shuddered then figuratively gave up the ghost. Out of habit, Ian jerked the key in the ignition to give himself the semblance of having turned the machine off.

"We're here," he announced. Like the coughing and wheezing of the engine, his patter never altered.

Faded with time and dulled by repetition, yet never changed, the sentence represented two constants in the parade to eternity.

"We'll get out, shall we?"

The question was rhetorical. Ian reached out, opening his side by sticking his hand through the open window and disengaging the latch. Storm, closest to the door on the left, merely put her shoulder to the naked metal and pushed. The hinges moaned as the door slowly opened.

"Tis a fine day."

Had thunder and lightning cracked across the low-hanging heavens, he would have declared it a "fine day."

Rituals died a slower death than mortal bodies.

They let him go alone, lingering behind on the excuse their legs were shorter than his. When Ian was fifty meters ahead, Meg and Storm stopped altogether, squatting in the tall, unkempt weeds to pick wild flowers.

By the time Ian arrived at Megan MacDhui's earthy tarrying place, he was as solitary a being as ever walked the earth.

Falling to his knees, he carefully trickled the contents of the tin cup over the violets he had planted lifetimes ago, then bowed his head and pressed his hands together.

As the tears rolled down his cheeks, he addressed she who no longer had ears to hear.

"Meggie... Meggie, me Meggie. Ah've cume to say farewell. Ah've the children wid me, Meggie. We're all packed an' ready to go."

From the distance, a bird began a short series of sharp trills. He waited in respectful silence for its mate to reply. When no further song was sung, he lowered himself onto the grave, pressing his face to the tiny, unmarked stone, tracing the uncarved letters, m-y-l-o-v-e, where the name should have been.

"Meggie, God forgive me, but Ah wish it were me lying in this cold grave an' not yuh. Why did yuh have to die an' leave me here, alone? Why dinna yuh take me wid yuh, Megan? Yuh know what yuh swore; yuh remember, do yuh not? Till death do us part. But it was never supposed to be yuh who died. Till death do us part, Meggie, but why did it have to be so soon?"

The bird called again, this time singing a more plaintive song.

"How am Ah to do this great thing, Megan? How am Ah to take yer daughters to a new country widout yuh?"

He paused again, but this time he was not waiting for the distant bird, but for a well familiar, cherished voice. A voice from the past calling to him as he addressed a future more frightening than everlasting sleep in an unmarked hole.

"Yuh were the one who talked o' goin' to New York, Meggie an' we're goin'. Just like yuh a'ways said we would. Off to a new country an' a new start. There's no goin' back, now, meh love. But how am Ah goin' to leave yuh here, a'by yerself? Will you not be lonely? Will yuh not think Ah've abandoned yuh?"

He heard another sound, neither of a bird nor of a wife. He did not turn around to meet the gaze of daughters, too much like the living embodiment of their mother.

"Megan Clarke MacDhui, Ah've cume to ask yer blessin'. Can yuh no say a word to ease me heart?"

Meg's hand reached out, but this time it was the younger child who stopped the older. With a non-verbal denial, Storm restrained her. Better not to make a move; better not to make a sound which might be interpreted for a heartbeat, as an answer from the grave.

"Megan, fer better or fer worse, in sickness an' in health, Ah loved yuh. Ah love yuh, still. Ah crave yuh, ache fer yuh. Widout yuh, Ah've no' the body of a man nor the soul of a lover. Ah'm jest a shadow, Meggie, an alpha male widout his alpha female. Who said it was supposed to be like this? Who set the trap yuh fell into? What evil spirit brought down upon me head this emptiness?

"Where is that loving God yuh believed in, Megan Clarke MacDhui? Where was He when Ah begged fer mercy? Where was He when yer wee bairns cried in their cradle fer the comfort o' their mother? Where are yuh when Ah need yuh most?"

If poets held sway over the pitiful destinies of Mankind, then surely Megan Clarke MacDhui's stone would have wept, for the words were wrung with poignancy. But poets held no power, nor did the dead rise to bless or wish Godspeed.

No miracles here.

"It's time to go, father. Time to go."

Words as old as the dawn of death.

"Go? Go? How am Ah to go an' leave me Megan behind?"

"Yuh're not leavin' her behind," came the faithful pronouncement. "She's cumin' wid us."

"How be that, then? Am Ah to dig her up?"

There was a touch of madness in the wail.

"She's cumin' in spirit."

Ian pressed his palms flat against the earth and raised himself a quarter inch.

"In spirit, aye, yuh say. But how do Ah know? How kin Ah be sure?"

"We're sure."

"We prayed on it, Ian. We prayed under the full moon. The howlin' moon."

"Aye?"

"Iffn yuh pray fer sumethin' under the full moon, then it has to cume true. That's what the faeries say. That's why they put a ring around it."

"A ring, aye, that's what Ah've heard a'right."

His right hand went to his left, but before flesh touched flesh, Meg stopped him, turning his head away from his unborn loss.

"We made sacrifice. Blood sacrifice, wid a ewe."

"The blood is the life, Ian MacDhui."

"Yuh    made    sacrifice?    An'    what    was    the    answer?"

"The answer was, we have a great aeroplane to catch. It'll fly us up into the clouds. Remember? Up near heaven. Like Meggie MacDhui a'ways said. Remember the dream."

Had she been alone, she would have cried for the lie, but no power on earth could have made her shed tears before her father. Weakness was for others, not for the daughters of a shepherd and a shepherd's wife. Not for the cubs of an alpha male and an alpha female wolf.

"Ah remember."

"Ah thought yuh would," Storm remarked with caustic familiarity. "Yuh're no' touched in the head an' yer no' deaf. Fancy, now. Take a handful o' earth. I've a bag to poot it in."

She removed a small, well creased brown paper sack from her jacket pocket and handed it to him. He smiled bravely while his lips trembled.

"Ah never thought o' that."

"That's why yuh have us: to do yer thinkin' fer you."

"An' Ah thought it was the other way around."

They made no further speech. Ian wiped his eyes, then lovingly scooped up a small handful of dirt and grass from the grave, carefully depositing it into the receptacle. They waited until he had folded the top down three times, then reached out their hands, each helping him to his feet.

"We're off'n a great adventure, Meggie," he said, addressing not the grave but the bag. "An' yuh're to cume wid us."

It was a small comfort, but they were, after all, only wee people.

# CHAPTER 7

The wind was the same wind. The moors were the same moors. The night sky reflected back upon the earth the same dark images it had done for two million years.

For all practical appearances, nothing had changed.

To a creature standing on the moon and staring at the Earth, be it human or otherwise, the only manmade structure visible to the naked eye was the Great Wall of China. Nothing, with or without the aid of telescopes, could see the very slight alteration which had occurred on the Scottish highland several hours since.

A large, bright, shiny-new padlock had been placed on the door of Ian and Megan MacDhui's former home. A pre-printed sign, of the type for sale in small shops all across the United Kingdom, had been hammered into place above the lock. It was slightly off center, but it was doubtful anyone would notice.

The sign read: No Trespassing. Private Property.

And then, in the thin, scratchy scrawl of a bank manager or a magistrate's clerk, the words "This property currently in repossession," had been added in ink. The pen had skipped in several places, due, certainly, to the glossy sheen of the paper or the slant of the cursive penmanship.

A careless examination might have revealed, "Tis properly rent in possession."

Whatever the words, whatever the meaning, real or imagined, there was no one there to read them. The family which had so lately called the "property" a proper home, had moved on.

No one, it should not be questioned, standing on the moon and looking toward Earth, would care to read it, even if they could.

No one from England or Ireland or Wales; no one in Scotland; no one in the county and no one driving by would tarry long enough to make out the sentiment.

That left only one being with the power, if not the interest, to decipher it. And He, it might be imagined, was busy elsewhere.

The Great Aeroplane which whisked the remaining members of Clan MacDhui westward was itself curiously impersonal. Made of metal, fastened with sundry nuts and bolts, soldered and molded into the familiar shape of a transcontinental "flying iron horse," it rose and fell with the precision of an automatic pilot.

The air was breathable, the temperature chill but not uncomfortable, the food tasteless if not sustaining, the drink adequate and utterly comfortless. Those who worked for the airline themselves were faceless nonentities, bit actors whose sole mission in life was to transport goods and commuters from Point A to Point B. Their smiles were perfunctory, their uniforms pressed, the name tags generic.

Smith, Jones, Zacorowitz, Delgado; pilot, engineer, flight attendant, navigator. Had they been mass murderers or traffic accident victims, their names and faces might have been the same.

The aeroplane, the staff, the terminals of arriving and departing passengers, the hustle and bustle, the noise, the silence, all similar, all sterile.

These items were not part of the dream, merely windmills to be passed by or through on the long and winding road toward the Quest.

Time continued, neither faster nor slower than on any other day. Second hands swept around watch faces, big hands moved faster than little hands. Over the course of one Atlantic crossing, lives were engendered, souls departed, lovers enriched one another, school children repeated lessons by rote; commuters arose and retired, fortunes were made, stocks dipped in queer sounding places like Nasdaq and rose on common pseudonyms such as Big Boards.

Men died for the preservation of invisible boundaries, women perished in childbirth; boys slit one another's throats in gang wars, while girls were tortured under the guise of religion.

The world, created in the short span of six days, as the oral historians would have the faithful believe, went about its activities, unaware of larger issues. Diseases were spread, second-generation antibiotics were administered, mountains erupted, spewing lava over an eight mile radius and wiping out all life for a generation.

Endangered species slipped off the charts of evolution, cockroaches thrived.

Such was the nature of the beast.

The planet, as an irregular green and blue jewel in the heavens, had a lot of explaining to do, yet there was no time to listen for excuses.

Time, like bank managers and Conglomerates, waited neither for Man nor beast, and prayers, directed up into starry, unpopulated galaxies, went unanswered.

The MacDhuis, pushed, shoved, bone weary and made deaf, not by the constantly changing altitudes of the mechanical bird which had brought them to the new world, but rather by the buzzing of ten thousand voices, the honking of a million car horns, the blare of seven-hundred and thirty-three unintelligible loud speakers and the commingling of twenty thousand radios, moved away from Customs not their own, into the glare and glitz of the Big Apple, known, some three thousand odd miles away, as The Dream.

There were thirty people standing at the bus stop, all lost in their own thoughts, neither seeing nor noticing the drama unfolding before them. They were New Yorkers, after all, and had learned from birth to ignore what they could not alter.

"Why is it so noisy?" Storm demanded in a childlike, whiny voice. Placing her hands to her head, she closed her eyes and moaned.

"Cume now," her father encouraged, his own spirits jaded to the point of breaking. "They call this rrrrush hour."

He trilled his "R's" in a familiar manner, hoping, by association, to ease his own tensions.

"This is New York," Meg tried, her ears so plugged she could barely hear herself speak. "It's a'ways noisy. We'll git used to it. We read aboot it in a book. Remember?"

But Storm was only nine years old going on ten and the reading of a book, now lost from memory, was a nonexistent comfort.

"Ah dinna want to live in a place Ah canna hear the wind on the moors! Ah wanna go home!"

"But yuh are home, darling," Ian began, failing to convince himself. The height of the buildings was dizzying and the unfamiliar, low hanging sky, not of weather but of smog, depressed his put-on optimism.

"Yuh'll feel better when we git to a place of our own," the elder daughter said, in her best Megan MacDhui tone. "Everythin's frightening when it's new."

"I'm not frightened!" Storm cried, pulling away from the fingers wrapped round her arm. "Ah'm out o' place. Ah dinna belong here. Ah'm a sheeper an Ah canna raise me sheep in this dirty city."

Before her sister or her father could think of stopping her, she bolted away, sprinting with legs of rubber out into the continual stream of traffic. Oblivious to oncoming motor vehicles, she wove her way, first left, then right then straight ahead, seeing nothing but her overpowering urge to escape.

Crying out in frightful dread, Ian dropped the luggage he was clutching, trembled a moment, then plunged after his child.

"Stay here!" he screamed back at Meg. "Watch the bags an' wait fer the bus. Hold us a seat!"

He might as well have demanded she stop the earth from rotating on its axis, but he was a newcomer and did not know he could not alter what others ignored.

"Storm! Storm! Cume back!"

She was ahead of him fifty yards, then one hundred, dashing pell-mell through the busses and automobiles, ignoring the flashing lights, the cursing, the obscene gestures. These were unknown factors, and therefore meant to be ignored. They stood between her and freedom and that must not be.

"Storm! Storm MacDhui!"

Words lost in space. For the good they did, never uttered.

Storm became the frightened lamb and he the shepherd, loping after his charge with the grace of his namesake, the wolf. Not hunting, but protecting, he twisted one way, then another, hand instinctively to his head to hold on the working-man's cap, once a badge of identity, now a distinction of oddness.

"Storm! Ah'm cumin'! Wait fer me!"

Like time, or a being out of time, she waited for no man, neither shepherd nor wolf. She was an alien, a green card, a tourist, a lost prodigal. Running on the energy of the condemned, she made it safely to the opposite side of the intersection, then started down another street, labeled by numbers higher than the pounds in her mother's legacy.

"Storm! Storm!"

The storm was coming and she was only Gail.

No one stepped aside, no one made the slightest attempt to catch the runaway child. Ian darted past faceless men, women, executives and tourists, tireless, on the hunt for what he had lost. Had the asphalt opened up underneath his feet, he would have crawled out of the hole and continued. Such was his nature, his destiny, his calling.

"Storm! Storm!"

Through another intersection then across a barrier of permanently parked cars on the thoroughfare, before his grasping hands caught her and his all-powerful arms wrapped themselves around the frail, struggling body.

"Storm! Caught yuh!"

She struggled, scratched, bit and clawed, then kicked and screamed before giving in to the horror and falling limp against his warm father's body.

"Ah'm dyin'," she gasped, sobbing into his chest. "Ah canna breathe."

"Yuh kin," he gasped, sucking in air through distended nostrils. "Yuh kin. Jest take it slow."

"Ah canna breathe!" but polluted air forced its way into her child's lungs and she lived, despite her agony.

"There, there," he soothed, running the flat of his hand against her fly-away hair of deep, rich brown. "It's a'right. It's a'right."

"How kin it be a'right? We dinna belong here."

"Aye, but we do. We will," he corrected, piteously.

"But how?"

"We'll find a way."

"The noise."

"The noise will die away. It's rush hour; yuh heard me say so. It'll fade away."

She sobbed, rubbing her eyes with balled-up fists, then bent her head back to look up to him.

"Fade away? Yuh promise?"

"Aye," he lied unknowingly. "Ah promise. Have Ah ever told yuh an untruth?"

She was only nine years old and could be excused for believing him.

He was only thirty-three years old and could be excused for having a dream.

"We'll go back, now."

"Back?" she whispered, meaning one thing while he meant another.

"Aye. Back." Back to the bus stop. "Befer we miss our place."

When her knees gave out, the father wrapped his arms around her and carried the precious burden back, the way they had come, slower, more reserved, without the power of terror to drive them.

Meg was standing where they left her. The only difference between then and now, was that she stood alone. All of the other passengers had mysteriously disappeared. As he approached, Ian smiled bravely. It was a meaningless gesture.

"Ah found her," he announced. Since Meg had already ascertained that fact for herself, she made no reply. He tried again. "It was good, in a way. For Storm to go runnin' off like that. Gave me a chance to stretch me long legs after all that inactivity."

"A man stole yer haversack," Meg said, her face impassive, her words almost so.

Ian stared blankly at her.

"What?"

"The haversack yuh threw at me. Befer yuh run off. To stretch yer long legs."

"Are yuh sure?" he inquired, looking around as though the bag had merely been mislaid.

"Ah couldna hold everythin'. He grabbed it as he boarded the bus."

Ian considered long before replying. When he spoke, he had assumed the helplessness Meg felt.

"Mebbe he thought it was his."

"Ah tried to get it back – but he jest pushed me aside an' pushed his way to the back o' the bus."

"Dinna the driver try to he'p yuh?"

"He paid no mind. When Ah shouted at him, he shut the door in me face an' drove off."

"Ah guess he dinna unnerstan'."

"He understood," she pronounced with meticulous clarity.

"Well.... we'll have less to carry."

Storm squirmed in his arms and he dropped her gently to the asphalt.

"That bein' the case," she whined, "yuh shoulda given him the rest, too."

"Never mind," Ian warned, his weariness breaking through. Seeing Meg was about to cry, he pasted a brave smile on his face, then stooped to kiss her on the forehead. "Yuh done fine. Had Ah been standin' here all alone, he woulda taken it frum me, too."

"No," she responded, lifting her chin in defiance. "Not frum yuh. Yuh're a champion. Yuh have the winner's cup to prove it."

"Aye, that's right. But these city fellas... they're tough. Like rats. They know how to do things so's a body canna stop them. Ah bet if yuh saw a constable an' notified him, that rat woulda had a card or a name tag stuck on our baggage. Then it'd be our word ag'in his. And who do yuh think would win?"

She wavered, wanting to believe. Her pride had been hurt and defeat was a bitter pill.

"Yuh think?"

"Ah not only think, Ah know. So there we have it. Yuh did what yuh could, an' Ah'm proud o' yuh. So let's put it behind us an' get on wid what we have to do." He made a show of searching his pockets, patting them with exaggerated clumsiness before looking back at her. "Do yuh have the book? The one what explains this crazy system o' money?"

Meg retrieved the book, a corner of which was conspicuously sticking out from her pocket and opened it.

"What do yuh want to know?" she inquired, needing to feel useful. "Whatever it is, Ah suppose will be in this Very Useful Book."

It was a familiar joke and he grinned broadly.

"Ask friend book how many pennies makes up a United States pound note."

"They're not called 'pound notes' in America," Storm piped up, eager to show off her knowledge.

"What are they called, then?" her father inquired, pushing aside his cap and scratching his head.

"Dollars," came the prompt response.

"Aye, that's right."

"And they dinna have an engravin' o' the Queen on them, either."

He appeared startled, his brows knitting in the center.

"Oh? Are yuh sure aboot that? Ah canna imagine any paper bein' worth innythin' widout ol' Queen Bess' picture on it. Whose picture do they have, then?"

"Oh, lots of people," Storm continued. "Presidents."

"Presidents? Oh, that's right; Ah forgot. They dinna have a queen here. They elect their prime minister an' call him a president. Queer ducks, these Colonists. And who are we to blame fer that?" he challenged Meg.

"King George III."

"An' frum what House?"

"The House of Hanover."

"Aye. Won't have innyone sayin' we're uneducated peasants."

"Ah bet there isn't innyone in New York who knows that," Storm bragged.

"Well, there might be a few," Ian conceded. "There's lots o' Universities here. But no one yer ages, Ah'm sure," he added, restoring the smiles to their dampened eyes. "Now: read what that book says aboot how we're to git around in this jungle."

Meg flipped through the pages of the dog-eared "Facts and Conversion Tables for Tourists."

"It says," she ad-libbed, "that we wait another half an hour fer a bus to take us around. An' that we pay befer sittin' down or the driver'll shake us up."

"Ah'd like to see him try," Storm added, swaying a moment from weariness, then leaning against Ian's leg. "But Ian, we're no' tourists. So how can that book do us inny good?"

"Well, aye, in a way we are," he began, then bit off his words. "Inny way, we're as dumb as tourists, so Ah dinna expect the book will mind."

"Dumber," Meg tried, grinning through a veil of sudden exhaustion.

Ian matched her grin, then wrapped an arm around her, drawing both children close.

"So – we wait. That's nuthin' new to Clan MacDhui. An' yuh know what they say: All things cumes to those who wait."

"Then let's wait fer that stranger to cume back wid our haversack," Storm responded, turning her face to Ian's body so that her words were obscured by the close proximity.

"That's not waitin'," he teased, smoothing her hair. "That's expectin' a miracle. Why dinna we find a bench to sit at?"

"Ah wouldna," Meg advised. "Ah saw a lady try that one over there, an' she stood up right away, cursin' a blue streak."

"Why was that?"

"Pigeons."

"She sat on a pigeon? Then Ah'd'a thought it'd a been the poor wee bird what'a done the squawkin'."

"Pigeon *shit.*"

"Oh. What was that sign we saw – the one we saw on the man's case – the one on the plane?"

"Shit Happens," Meg supplied.

It was as much of a welcome as they were apt to get.

# CHAPTER 8

"Why is it called the Sea Breeze Apartments?" Meg inquired, staring forlornly at the seventeen story building which was to become their new home.

"What's an apartment?" Storm asked, nearly on top of her sister's question.

Of the two, it was not difficult to decide which to answer.

"In America, they call a flat an apartment," Ian explained.

"Why?"

"I've forgotten now, but yer mother told me once. I think it's because either 'flat,' or 'apartment' was originally a French word an' they either did or dinna want it."

"Thank you," Meg replied for both. "That clears it up wonderfully."

Ian cheered considerably, failing to note the sarcasm.

"Ah thought it might."

Standing on tiptoe, Storm sniffed the air.

"It smells more like offal to me. If that's what their sea breezes smell like, I dinna want inny part o' their ocean."

"We're a bit away frum the water. Ah bet it smells more like what we're used to when yuh kin see it."

"Ah bet it doesn't."

"Let's go up, shall we?"

"Let's go home."

"This is home," Ian replied, allowing a trace of tired discouragement to seep into his voice. "Contracted through the agent in Scotland. So let's make the best of it, shall we?"

Together they climbed the steps to the front door. Ian rang the bell. No one answered.

"Mebbe no one's home," Meg hesitantly suggested.

"Mebbe they've all died of smell poisoning," her smaller half volunteered.

"I'll jest ring it ag'in. Perhaps nobody heard." After the third try, he fashioned a weak smile over his lips and glanced toward one of the overhead window sills. "Let's count the pigeons while we're waiting."

"Why?"

"Because it's sumethin' to do. Because we ought to know how many there are."

"Aye. There's a respectable job; pigeon counter. Excuse me, Mister Pigeon. I'm takin' a survey o' the number o' pigeons in New York City. Besides yuh and Mrs. Pigeon, how many in yer nest?"

He laughed mirthlessly.

"Ah kin think o' worse jobs. Besides, Ah like pigeons. They're very intelligent creatures. An' beautiful. Look at the coloration o' that one."

He pointed out a bird with striking fluorescent green and purple feathers. Neither Meg nor Storm followed his direction.

"Ah like pigeons, too, but we better not git too fond o' them, as we're likely to be eatin' them fer supper."

"Never mind," he warned, turning away from the birds and back to the door. A resounding pounding on the paint-peeling frame finally elicited a response.

"What-you-want?" a man with a beer belly, acutely accentuated with a not-overly white undershirt inquired.

"We're the MacDhuis. Frum Scotland. Yuh had a letter we were cumin'."

"And a deposit," Meg reminded the landlord.

"The MacDhuis? From Scotland? Yeah. I thought you were due earlier."

"We missed the bus."

The landlord stepped aside a quarter of an inch, forcing Ian and the children to squeeze past him. As she went by, Storm took in a deep sniff, then rolled her eyes.

"It's obvious they didn't name this place after him!" she whispered to Meg.

"He's got 'breezes,' a'right," she agreed, hiding a smirk behind her hand, "but Ah dinna think they have innythin' to do wid the sea."

"You – wait here," the man ordered to the children. "You," to Ian, "follow me. You gotta sign the lease agreement. Then I'll give you your key."

"A key?" the Scotsman inquired as he followed the man into a first floor apartment.

"That's right. A key. It's for locking and unlocking your door. Maybe you don't need locks and keys where you come from, but you need one here. Anything what's stolen from your apartment ain't my fault. The management's not responsible for lost or stolen items."

"If our belongin's are stole, Ah'll know where to look fer 'em," Storm dryly remarked. Fortunately, the man was either deaf or uninterested in her opinion, for he made no comment.

While they waited for their parent to return, she flipped through the paperback tourist book.

"There's nuthin' in here aboot 'locks,' an' 'keys.' Ah wonder why."

"Yuh dinna wonder why, an' dinna be smart. When Ian gits a respectable job, we'll be outta here in two shakes o' a lamb's tail."

Storm returned the book to Meg's pocket and shuddered.

"It's fair creepy here."

"We won't be here long."

After a moment's hesitation, Storm placed a hand on her sister. Her voice was low and frightened.

"Promise?"

"Ah promise," the diminutive adult vowed. "Megan MacDhui would niver have wished this upon us. A week at the most. Mebbe two," she added, for fear her sister would hold her to the statement.

Stamping in place as though to warm herself, Storm peered around Meg at the landlord's door.

"What if he's muggin' Ian?"

"Why would he do that?"

"It's New York City, isn't it? They do a lot o' that here."

"Yuh're makin' that up."

"Ah am not. Shamus McClory told me all aboot it. He said New York City is a terrible fierce place to be."

"Shamus McClory's niver been beyond the borders o' Scotland. How would he know?"

"He said a fella frum the Glasgow told him. An' that fella knew because he'd been in the army an' roomed wid a fella what's spent time here. He said –"

"Oh, hush! Too much 'he said.' Ah thought yuh had more sense than that."

"Ah do. But he said so."

"No one's gonna mug Ian MacDhui. He's the strongest fella in the world. Iff'n that man gets tough, Ian'll pop him one in the nose. He's not the sort what's gonna take back-talk or threats. He's no' scared o' nuthin' in the world."

"Aye," she agreed, reassured. "But then, where is he?"

As though hearing her question, Ian emerged from the apartment, dangling a key from his fingers.

"Here it is," he proudly displayed. "A key. To our very own apartment. Shall we go on up an' take a look? The stairs is over there," he indicated.

"What aboot the lift?"

"It's rightly called an el-e-vator, an' it's out o' order. It's the stairs fer us, but we're used to walkin', are we not?"

"That answers one question," Meg grunted, hoisting up the baggage set on the floor by her feet. "They call it an 'apartment' building becuz it sure as hell ain't a flat building."

Ian chuckled while loading the rest of the luggage into his arms.

"Now you're soundin' like the Margaret MacDhui Ah know an' love."

As he opened the warped, splintered door marked "Stairs," a feral cat spurted through, hissing angrily as it passed.

"Welcome to New York City," the known and loved elder daughter remarked.

"Watch yer step," he urged as the family began their upward trek. "Where's there's cats, there's –"

"Mice," Storm finished quickly.

The stairwell was narrow, erratically lit and cluttered with trash. Sidestepping both the cat and rat droppings, they climbed seven flights to the eighth story. The door here was propped open by a brick, despite a sign warning "Fire Escape. Door to remain closed at all times."

While Ian searched for number 721, Meg removed the brick and let the squeaky-hinged door ease shut.

"Why are yuh doin' that?" her sister demanded.

"We're following the rules. The sign says the door should remain closed."

"Ah kin see we're going to be popular here," Ian agreed. "No one kin say we're back-moorsmen, what don't unnerstan' a proper sign. Here we are."

Without thinking, he tried the knob, only to discover it locked. With an embarrassed noise, he dropped the baggage then inserted the key into the hole. When it did not turn, he applied more pressure. Nothing.

Placing his shoulder to the door, Ian gave it a solid shove. With a protest of old wood, the door opened.

"Nuthin' like followin' the rules."

"Home, sweet home," he declared over the last.

Flipping on the light switch, clan MacDhui stared in dumb stupefaction at their apartment. The flat consisted of three rooms, one large kitchen-living room and two bedrooms, the doors of which stood ajar. A faded tweed-colored carpet with a nap one hundredth of an inch high ran the length of the living room, then ended in an inglorious death at the doors to the bedrooms.

A couch, three cushions long, was placed in dead center of the main room. One end table, utterly devoid of paint or lacquer, and a wooden card table, doing duty as a dining area, with four folding chairs placed around it, completed the furnishings. In the kitchen, a small, four-burner stove, refrigerator, sink and oven made up the amenities. A well-traveled ant trail led from one end of the room to the next.

"At least we'll no be wantin' fer company," Meg declared. "A little short on conversation, mebbe, but what they lack in chattin' they'll more than make up fer by numbers."

"We'll see what we kin do aboot them onest we're settled. Let's look at the bedrooms."

Stepping around the ant trail, Ian crossed the bare room, sticking his head inside the nearest sleeping chamber. What met his eyes was no more cheerful than that which he had just left. His children followed his gaze.

"Ah'll bet when the bank comes to repossess this place, they'll decide to give it back," Meg remarked.

Inside the "furnished bedroom" was one twin-sized bed, its naked mattress sagging depressingly in the middle. A dresser, which might have done service for the denizens of a World War I flop house, was placed to one side. There were no chairs. An un-curtained side window was open. Storm poked Meg with her elbow.

"Ah bet the glass's busted. That's why it's open."

"It's open to let in some fresh air," her father reproved, without having the nerve to test his theory. "It'll look better when we put up some curtains. Let's check the other bedroom."

The next room was a carbon copy of the first, except that the bed was queen-sized. The lower drawer of the dresser was missing.

"Yuh two kin have this room," Ian bravely determined. "We'll switch dressers so yuh kin have the better one. When I find some wood, Ah kin repair this. It won't look so bad when we're moved in. Will it?" he completed, turning to face his daughters.

Neither had the heart to disagree. That would have been crossing the line between disappointment and despair.

"Ah think," Meg tried, "that what we need is some tea. Things a'ways look better wid a kettle boilin' an' a pot o' hot tea steepin'."

"That sounds fine! Shall Ah go out an' fetch us sume milk?"

"No!" came the reply, spoken simultaneously by both children. Then, "We dinna want yuh to go out now. We're all tired. In the mornin' we'll see about the amenities."

His appreciation was apparent.

"Tea it is, then widout milk. But jest fer tonight. Tomorrow is the start o' a new day. Cume, Storm. Yuh bring one o' those dinin' room chairs in an' sit on it whilst Ah do sume unpackin' and get the beds made. That way, we kin drop off into sleep in no time. Ah dinna know aboot yuh, two, but Ah'm aboot as tired as Ah've ever been in me life."

While Ian went about making the bed, Meg retired to the kitchen, where she turned on the tap, watching with curiosity as the old pipes hissed out stale air before issuing forth a trickle of water. Before trusting her beloved kettle to the suspicious smelling liquid, she stuck a hand under the water, then brought the cupped fingers to her face. Sipping it did little to appease her doubts as to its drinkability.

Being practical, however, she abandoned her mistrust and filled the kettle. Once placed on the front of four equally-sized burners, she experimented with the stove, eying it critically for a flame to jump out at her. When none did, she held a hand over the coil. It was warm, growing hotter.

"This canna be good," she mused, remembering their first and only experience with an electric stove. "Ah was hopin' to avoid this sorta creature."

While keeping a wary eye on the kettle, she carefully removed cups, saucers and napkins from her bag. When the warped, stained condition of the dining room table drew the corners of her mouth down, she changed her mind and removed the items, spreading a thin, red and white checked cloth over the top, then dotting her handiwork with three matching napkins. The sight of Megan's much treasured table cloth did much to restore her waning spirits.

"Tea in a minute," she called.

When she did not get a reply, she walked gingerly to the bedroom. Storm was seated in the chair, head drooping onto her chest, while Ian was stretched out on the bed, fast asleep.

"Aye, well, rest while yuh kin," she whispered. "Ah'll have tea ready befer Ah call yuh."

Retracing her steps, Meg wearily unwrapped the blue willow tea pot, setting it beside the matching cups. Next, a tin of English breakfast tea and a tea ball was retrieved. As their first meal in a new land, it had little to recommend it but familiarity.

Given the circumstances, however, it was more than she had hoped for.

When the cheery whistle of boiling water summoned her to the stove, Meg reverently poured hot water into the pot, swished it around, then dumped it into the sink. The sink did not drain.

Taking the stainless steel tea ball, she filled it two-thirds full with loose tea then draped the chain over the lip. Filling the pot to the brim with water, the room soon assumed a more pleasant odor.

Giving the tea adequate time to brew, Meg set a small sugar cube into each cup, then poured the hot beverage into each. Only when everything was to her satisfaction did she go to her father and sister.

"Ian MacDhui, Storm MacDhui, tea's ready."

She had not expected either to wake. Fearing least they be disappointed not to be roused, she first went to her father, shaking him gently on the shoulder.

"Ian. Wake up. Jest time fer some tea befer yuh sleep."

He stirred, cried under his breath, then fought her summons by sinking deeper into the land of escape.

"Aye, Ian MacDhui," Meg whispered. "Sleep. Yuh've worked hard enuf fer it. Who am Ah to wake you, now?"

Turning away from her father, Meg paused briefly to brush a strand of hair from Storm's lightly furrowed brow, then padded out of the room on the balls of her feet. Such an attitude was second nature to her, for she was, after all, the offspring of an alpha male and an alpha female.

From habit, she crossed to the table and dipped the end of her finger into the liquid. The familiar gesture finally brought a smile to her soft, youthful features.

"Yuh're right, Megan MacDhui. Tis not the accepted method o' testing the temperature o' the tea. But as Ian would say, iffn there's no one aboot to witness the deed, then it's as a crime undone. And as Meg MacDhui would say, there's been enuf crime committed on the MacDhui clan. It's aboot time their luck changed."

She took her own cup and sipped carefully, drawing the liquid up through nearly compressed lips, then swallowing. After wiping her lips on the napkin, Meg repeated the ritual until she had drunk from all three cups and used all three napkins.

"Tis not much o' a toast Ah'll be makin' alone, but Ah believe the occasion requires some sort o' puttin' God on notice."

Clutching the third tea cup in her hands, Meg held it out and then up, after the fashion of an ancient sacrifice.

"Ah'm no' much fer praying' an' that Yuh know," she began, lowering her voice so as not to be overheard from a waking sleeper. "Ah've had precious little to thank Yuh fer an' Ah'll no be tellin' Yuh inny news there, either. But Yuh brought Ian an' Storm an' me safely to this New Land, an fer that we're all grateful. Ah think it would have served Yer plans better iffn Yuh had spared Megan MacDhui. She was the heart an' the soul of this family. It's her dream we've been livin' and it's becuz o' her that we've made this journey."

Stiffening her resolve, she took in a deep breath and resumed her "toast" which was woefully short of bread. And milk.

"Ah dinna remember her much, but she lives fer Storm an' meself through Ian MacDhui's eyes, an' through his eyes, she canna do no wrong. It would be a cryin' shame if things were to turn bad an' he be forced to give up her dream. It would hurt his love an' that would cume close to destroyin' him. Ah'm asking Yuh to take that into consideration befer Yuh throw us plague and famines, as Yuh did the Israelites, long ago.

"Ah'm thinkin' there's only so much inny man, woman or child can bear befer they lose what faith they have. Ian MacDhui has a good heart. When the books close on him, Ah'm thinkin' the judgment will be kind an' gentle. Yuh might spread some o' that unnerstandin' around now widout doin' too much harm.

"And as fer Storm MacDhui, Yuh understan' she's young an' she's had to live widout a mother's care. She's a temper, right enuf, but she's proud and fair. She has the birthright to walk wid her head held high an' her eyes bright. Give her time to grow an' she'll never disappoint Yuh.

"As fer meself, all Ah kin say is that there's a lot Ah dinna comprehend aboot this great wide world o' Yuhrs. If Ah had me choice, we'd no be here, an' that's no secret. But we are here an' Ah'll try an' do me best. Ah'm not askin' fer a handout an' Ah'm not askin' fer what Yuh might call a miracle, because Ah know there's many more in need then us. Jest look favorable an' mebbe stay Yer hand here an' there until we're on our feet.

"Iffn that's too much to ask, then Ah'll unnerstan' we're on our own, an' Ah'll not be botherin' Yuh ag'in."

She hesitated, then added, "Amen."

Her last act of her first day in the New World was to walk a still-sleeping Storm into Ian's bed. After drawing a blanket over them, Meg crawled in the other side and dropped off before the echoes of her prayer had faded.

# CHAPTER 9

"What are yuh doin'?" Ian inquired, rubbing his knuckles into half-open eyes. Storm turned away from the window from which she was hanging out, her own eyes slanted, but for a different reason.

"Ah'm listening to the noise," she declared.

"Ah dinna think you'd hav'ta open the window to do that," came the droll response.

"It started aboot half an hour ago, an it's been gettin' worse since. It's frightful."

"It's the sounds o' a big city wakin' up."

"City, hell. It's all them automobiles an' busses an' planes goin' overhead. We might as well have rooted ourselves at the aeroplane terminus."

"Never mind that cussin', Storm MacDhui. We've agreed to leave our cussin' behind, in the Old World."

"Ah never agreed to that. Besides," she pursued, pulling back into the apartment and slamming the window closed, "iffn we give up cussin' and swearin', we'll niver fit in like natives. Yuh ought to hear what Ah was jest listenin' to down below."

Against his better judgment, Ian looked down as his daughter rattled on.

"The man doin' it was all dressed fer a funeral or sumethin'. He had on a suit o' clothes what probably cost fifty pounds." She whistled appreciatively. "Yuh wouldna believed it. An the brogans he was wearin' on his feet – Ah swear, yuh coulda used 'em fer a mirror to shave in."

"Ah doubt he was goin' to a funeral," Ian thoughtfully replied. "No' at this hour. Ah niver heard tell of buryin' innybody at this time o' the morning. He musta been goin' to work."

Storm gave this careful consideration, then her eyes opened to the size of saucers.

"Yuh may be correct in what yuh say, Ian; but iffn that's the case, yuh're in a wee bit o' trouble, 'cause yuh dinna have nuthin' like that to wear. An iffn yuh did, Ah canna imagine yuh dressin' like that every day. Yuhr body would sure leap outta yuhr clothes."

"I canna say Ah look forward to it. But then, Ah suppose there's lots o' respectable jobs out there what don't require a man to look like a preacher."

"Or a conglomerate president," Storm darkly added.

"That, either," he nodded enthusiastically. "Where's yer sister?"

"Ah dunno."

"Yuh dunno?"

"She was gone when Ah got up."

"Gone where?"

"Now, iffn Ah knew that, Ah'd a tolt yuh in the first place, wouldn't Ah?"

"We got to find her. She mighta been carried off in the night."

"Aye; by the gypsies," Storm agreed.

"Not by the gypsies. By bandits. Yuh see them all the time on the tellyvision. They're fearful common around here, Ah expect."

"She might be held fer ransom."

"What are yuh sayin'?"

Storm drifted away from the window, wandering aimlessly into the kitchen, where she filled the kettle with water as she spoke.

"Ah suppose we'll have to buy her back. It'll be pricey, Ian, no doubt. Ah suppose whoever took her figured we was rich tourists."

"Yuh dinna say!"

"Aye, Ah do. No doubt there's lots o' tourists stolen from the Sea Breeze Apartments. A kidnapping ring. Ah've heard tell o' such things."

"My God, why dinna yuh say sumthin' befer this?" he demanded, rushing to her. Ian placed his hands on her shoulders and swung the child around so she faced him. "We've got to call the po-lice right away. How am Ah gonna do that?"

"Yuh could try hollerin' out the window. There might be a uniformed bobby hangin' around. Or we could look in the Tourist Book. Ah bet there's a whole chapter on how to call the po-lice."

Having read the Book cover-to-cover and knowing there was no such chapter, Ian's wolf-grey eyes finally lit with a hint of belief that he was being put on.

"Ah see," he remarked. "Poor Margaret, in the hands o' robbers an' murders. Yuh're not scared o' being kidnapped yerself, Ah take it?"

"Me? Dinna be daft. Ah have a secret weapon to protect me."

"What's that, then?"

"Ah brung a bag o' sheep dip to carry around. Iffn sumeone gits too close, Ah'll hit 'im over the head wid it. See how one o' these fancy-pants New Yorkers likes a taste o' that."

"Yuh brought no such thing, an' Ah kin see you're pullin' me leg. Where-is-yuhr-sister?"

"She ought to be cumin' through the door aboot now," Storm predicted.

As Ian turned away from his youngster, the door flew open, revealing his elder daughter, grocery bag in hand. His jaw dropped the proverbial length to the floor.

"Good mornin'," Meg greeted. "Ah see yer up, Ian MacDhui. Ah was beginin' to wonder if yuh'd becume a big city man a'ready an' was gonna sleep till noon."

"Right as rain Ah'm a big city man, young lady, an' where, in the name o' the Conglomerate, have yuh been?"

She grinned at his expression, which had become *the* derisive expression adapted by the moors-men to express contempt.

"Shoppin'."

"Ah kin see that," he pursued. "But where? How did yuh know where to go?"

"Ah asked directions."

"Of whom?"

"There was a drunk on the corner. His name is Albert MacPhearson, an' we had a chat."

"Yuh had a chat wid a drunk on the corner named Albert MacPhearson?"

"There must be an echo around here," Storm observed.

Meg nodded agreeably.

"Aye. An' he said Ah'm the furst person he's ever admitted his name to, since he fell off the wagon. That means –"

"Ah know what it means!" came her exasperated father's retort.

"Aye. Well, around here he's knowd as 'Drunk Al,' an' he lives on handouts an' sleeps in a 'flop house.' Ah asked him if it were better'n the Sea Breeze an' he laughed. Said it was the furst laugh he'd had since the Big One."

"World War Two?"

"Nay. The Fourth o' July last year. He said there were so many drunks rollin' around in the streets, he had a very successful night o' it."

"Drinkin'?"

"Rollin' other drunks."

"Oh, me God."

"His 'capital gains' has lasted him near till now. An' yuh know what else he said?"

"Ah canna wait to hear it."

"He said his great-great grandfather cume from Scotland."

"An' Ah bet his name was MacPhearson," Ian tried.

"No. It was Scott, of all things!" Meg laughed. "He had niver spoken to a real, honest-to-Christ-living-Scot befer. In fact, he tolt me, he doubted there really was a place called Scotland. Then Ah tolt him there damn sure was, an' explained all aboot it. We struck it off, right quick."

"Ah kin hear that yuh did."

"Aye, Ah did. An' he knows everythin' they is to know aboot New York. They dinna call it New York *City,* by-the-by. The natives drop the word 'City.'

Apparently, when yuh live here, they dinna acknowledge no place else as 'New York.'"

"What aboot the state o' New York?"

"Ah guess that's only used for postal addresses. Innyway, he told me where to go, so Ah went."

"An' he dinna steer yuh wrong?"

"One Scotsman to another? He did not."

"They call that honor among thieves," Storm inserted. Ian shot her a warning glance.

"Well, yuh've had yer first great adventure in the city o' New York."

"Aye, Ah have. An' iffn yuh two want breakfast, yuh had better wash up, 'cause Ah'm near to starvin'."

"No argument there," Ian agreed. "What have yuh in that bag o' magic tricks?"

"Ah've what they call 'oatmeal,' an' a pound o' bacon, an' coffee an' cream. An' a dozen eggs and a loaf o' pre-sliced bread."

"Ah'm droolin'," Ian professed, which was not far from the truth. "Cume on, Storm. Let's be washin' our hands an' then helpin' yer sister wid the victuals."

While they washed, Meg set the prize possessions out on the table. In less time that it took to shake a leg, they were clustered around the treasure, eyes wide with delight.

"Ah think, Ian declared, "we'll eat it all, on accounta it's our furst meal."

"Aye. Yuh mighta had yer first meal last night, but the two o' yuh dropped off to sleep like new-born lambs."

"That's past history," Ian laughed, his deep rumblings of delight bringing smiles to his daughters. "Right now, Ah could eat two-thirds o' a bank president."

"Ah could eat the Conglomerate!" Storm announced.

"Eatin' hog is one thing, but consumin' pisin' is another. We'll have to settle fer real, honest-to-goodness food!"

The ceramic pot was readied and soon the room was filled with the fragrance of steeping tea. Without ceremony, Ian deposited the entire pound of bacon into the pan, then licked his lips, letting his tongue linger over his sharp canines.

Meg made the oatmeal while Storm toasted bread by holding the slices over the hot burner. They worked in silence until Ian grunted in surprise.

"This bacon is flakin' off," he dubiously observed. "Is it supposed to do that?"

Meg inspected the pan, where the sizzling slices of fat had begun to separate.

"Sliced," she diagnosed.

"Aye, Ah know what 'sliced' is, but why are the pieces so thin?" Holding one up with his fingers, he stared through the nearly translucent meat. "Ah kin see through it. This musta gone through the packagin' wrong. Who wants to eat a slice o' bacon yuh kin see through? How is it yuh know what yer eatin'? What's to get yer teeth into?"

For once, Storm had the practical answer.

"Ah want to eat it, an' iffn my teeth dinna know what it is, my mouth will tell them."

"Well said," Meg championed. "It's near ready. Sit down befer it gits cold an' Ah hav'ta listen to another sermon."

"Ah've done preachin'," Ian announced, immediately plopping himself down in the dining room chair. With the food spread out before him and the girls seated, he interlaced his fingers and bowed his head.

"Almighty God, Ah thank Yuh fer providin' us this repast." He paused for the children to add their thanks.

"Almighty Lord," Meg continued, "Ah hope there's a lot more like it cumin' 'round the bend."

"Almighty Lord," Storm concluded, "Ah dinna know if it were Yuh, or rightly Ian an' Meg MacDhui who produced this breakfast. Ah would hate to give me thanks where thanks wasna due."

"Canna yuh not think o' sumthin' a wee bit more respectful to say?" Ian demanded.

"Aye," she agreed. "When it's Yer turn, could yuh kindly provide us wid real porridge instead o' this mush? Ah'd be thankin' Yuh respectfully then, an' while Yer at it –"

"Amen," he interrupted and waited for the duet of "Amens" to follow. When they did, he supposed God would accept the offering and dug in.

Between the three of them, Clan MacDhui consumed the pound of bacon, the dozen eggs, half a loaf of something labeled "bread," and six servings of "mush," smothered in cream.

"Wid tea to wash it all down," Ian decided, rubbing his stomach, "Ah declare meself full."

"Not bad for a heathen repast," Meg agreed.

"It goes a long way toward explain' why that man was cussin' so loud this mornin'," Storm added. "Eatin' this city food will do terrible things to a man's bowels. Ah bet he had cramps like to kill a horse."

Ian guffawed, spewing forth bits of bread crumbs lingering in his oral cavity. Meg and Storm made a deliberate point of counting the cracks in the ceiling while he picked them up with the wet end of his finger.

"That point o' etiquette bein' over," he muttered, completing the task, "what do yuh say we make like tourists today an' have a looksee at our surroundin's?"

"Ah suppose we had better."

"Aye. An' we'll look fer a bobby while we're out, in case Meg gits taken ag'in."

"Ah was the one what was 'taken,' Storm MacDhui, an' Ah'm hoping yuh two will put on some cheerful faces."

"Oh, Christ! Ah think we fergot to pack them!"

Which made Ian laugh again, proving he had remembered his happy face. It was good to hear him laugh and the two children exchanged knowing glances.

"Iffn we're goin' out, yuh had better put on yer Undertaker's suit."

"Never mind. Ah'll dress cumfertable like, an' yuh do the same. We're tourists fer the day, Ah said, an' we might as well look like it."

"That won't be hard."

"Oh, yer both right sassy this mornin'. It cumes frum being full in the stomach an' light in the head. What was it that beetle said aboot little Oliver Twist? Too much meat in yer bellies."

"Ian, iffn yuh call that bacon 'meat,' then Ah'm expectin' yuh to bring home a herd o' cattle fer dinner."

"Up an' at 'em." Pushing himself away from the table, he stretched, burped then scratched under his armpits. "No fleas, here," he added.

"Give them time. The woman next door has cats an' Ah saw them scratchin' as Ah went out this mornin'."

"Cats? She keeps cats in a flat? The poor wee beasts. They must feel cramped. Where do they run? And what do they hunt fer their meals?"

"Ah saw her feedin' 'em outta a can."

"A can?"

"Aye."

"Strange."

"Sure is. Wid all the rats around here, yuh'd think they could earn their keep," Storm supplied. "But Ah guess like everythin' else in this City, they're lazy."

"Ah never heard tell o' a lazy cat. Them's workers by nature. Like me. An like yuh. Iffn a cat's not huntin' then its sick."

"A city kin make a beast sick. It changes nature," Meg softly announced.

"Well, Ah'll no be changin' me nature. Ah'm a proud man an' Ah'll be earnin' a respectable wage soon. No city will ever change me. Or not you, neither. Cume on. Let's go out an' see the sights."

"What aboot the dishes?"

"We'll clean up when we git back. Right now, Ah'm as restless as a free-born barn cat, there's no denyin'."

"There aren't inny barns in New York," Storm sadly demurred, but Ian was not listening. The time for words was past. It was the dawn of a new day. There was adventure in the air.

"Adventure," Storm might have added, "what smells like garbage."

# CHAPTER 10

It was a day to play tourist for the new immigrants. A day to familiarize themselves with the new world they had decided to cast in their lot with. A day meant to dispel the devils of the past and make peace with the spirits of the present.

It was not until they arrived at the United Nations building that they truly began to comprehend the enormity of where they were.

Taking off his cap, Ian stared at the great place with awe. Breathing through his nose, mouth half agape, he was humbled as a seedling before a mighty oak.

"Yer mother would have loved to cume here," he reverently whispered. "The home o' world peace. The one spot on earth where representatives frum all nations kin talk widout guns. If ever there was a woman who believed in communication, it were she. God rest her soul, an' may she be granted the power to travel, in spirit form, to these hallowed halls. Ah canna imagine but that there are many in Heaven who cume here to see this place."

Returning his cap to his head, Ian stared around himself, nostrils to the wind, as though he were seeking the scent of those souls who paused to do penitence before the earthy shrine of the hope for freedom.

"It dinna do much fer Northern Ireland," Storm observed. If Megan MacDhui were to visit earth in spirit form, she could think of other places she would rather have her go.

"Awk, shut yer mouth. Peace in Northern Ireland will be achieved by talkin', an nuthin' else. In the end, it will no' be the threat o' guns which solves the problem, but by men an' women sittin' down and facin' one another, eyeball to eyeball. Violence is never the answer; the bully canna win."

"Then why did the Bank win?" Storm pursued.

Meg shot her a sidelong look but the warning went wide.

"The bank dinna win," Ian continued, turning away, his brief, unexpected moment of communication with Meggie MacDhui shattered. "We was a'ways plannin' on cumin' to New York an' here we are. It's true enuf it hurried us on our way, but yuh hafta look on the bright side."

"Which is?"

"We're pioneers: explorers, set on a journey o' great adventure. We're treadin' new ground, seein' new sights. How, in the name o' God, could Ah expect to expose me daughters to all this?" he asked, spreading his arms wide, "iffn we had never left our wee nest in Scotland? The world was meant to conquer; not wid arms, Ah mean, but wid sights an' sounds an' smells. What chance did either o' yuh two have back where we cume frum? Nary a one. Yuh'd o' growed up in the same rut Ah growd up in, penny poor and pound scarce.

"Here, where life is spinnin' around yuh, yuh're exposed to new ways, different challenges. Yuh dinna have to be jest a sheeper's daughter, marryin' another sheeper an' raising yuhr children wid no hope fer tomorrow. Here yuh kin grow up to be a scientist or an educator."

"Or a bank manager."

Ian grabbed Storm by the shoulders and shook her, face flushed.

"A'right, a bank manager, then. It does not hav'ta be a dirty word, yuh know. Ah'm sure there's bank managers what have helped people achieve their dreams. Have yuh never thought o' that?"

"Never."

"Well, yuh had better reconsider yer hard heart, Storm MacDhui. No good ever came to him what has a closed mind."

The earnestness of his emotion, the tortured sparks flashing from his grey eyes mesmerized, then slowly eased Storm away from her bitterness. His warning that she had gone too far, pushed not her, but him to the edge of endurance, sank in.

"Aye," she respectfully deferred. "Yuh have a point. Ah shall try an' keep it in mind."

He held her, breathing heavily, a moment longer, then, finally realizing she had backed down, released his hands, then clasped them together, left over right.

"Let us move on."

"Aye," Meg added, her own hands clenched behind her back and out of sight. "Let us move on."

"Where shall we go?" Ian inquired, making a valiant attempt to restore his former good mood.

"Ah would like to see the ocean," Storm volunteered. His head perked up, eyes instinctively shifting toward where he knew the water to be.

"Aye. Then we can kill two birds with one stone. Ah want to see Ellis Island. There's a place yuhr mother spoke of wid such depth o' feelin'. It's the first stop on American soil an immigrant makes when cumin' to the U-nited States. There's talk o' them pootin' up the names, yuh know, o' them what's cume befer us."

"Will our names be there?"

"No, darlin'. It's the names o' them what cume a long time ago."

"The pioneers," Meg volunteered.

"That's it! Right as rain. Ah want to see the new beginnin's fer so many what have paved the trail."

"Ah want to breathe the air," Storm admitted.

"Well, Ah shall look, an' yuh shall breathe."

"Ah hope yuh breathe, too," the youngest tried, her smile tentative.

"An' Ah hope yuh look! Onward an' upward, me hearties."

Interlocking hands, the three set off for Ellis Island.

"The wait's an hour before your boat is ready," the ticket seller explained to the three pair of shining eyes. "You can sit over here," he indicated, pointing to a series of benches so crowded with people it might have passed for a mass transit vehicle, "or you can wander around. But you had better just stand in line. You can stop off at the Statue of Liberty and then take another boat on to Ellis Island or you can stay on the boat an' go right through. Boats come by there every fifteen minutes."

"Thank yuh kindly," Ian acknowledged, taking the three tickets. "It's very exciting. Yuh must be proud to work in such a place."

The youth hesitated, then shrugged.

"They pay minimum wage and my feet hurt. I can say my patter in my sleep."

Not understanding the word "patter," Ian smiled brightly.

"Then yuh must have fine dreams. Cume, children. We have an hour to wait. We shall look around befer we go stand in line."

"It's like a circus," Meg remarked, staring in open astonishment at the various troupes and individuals performing along the grounds. "Like the fair," she added. "Remember when we went to the fair, Ian?"

"Aye, Ah do. Look at that man jugglin'."

They pushed their way through the curious onlookers to stare at a man keeping a set of balls high flying. After nearly five minutes, he tired of the game, deftly catching the balls and dropping them into a pocket. When his hat went round, Ian dropped a coin into it. It made a dull thud against the few dollar bills. For his concern, he received an angry look from the juggler.

"Thanks a lot, Dad," he grumbled. "That and another like it will buy me a cup of coffee."

Storm made a move toward the man but Meg stopped her.

"Ian an' Ah saw a man juggle fourteen balls at one time at the Edinburgh Fair," she announced. "Ah guess yuh'll jest have to try harder befer yuh earn a dollar frum us."

Caught off guard, the juggler paused, considered, then leaned closer.

"Fourteen? Really?"

"Aye. An' a grand sight it twas."

"At the Edinburgh Fair? Where's that? In Yonkers?"

"Ah dinna know where 'Yonkers' is. Edinburgh is in Scotland."

"Oh. I thought you talked funny."

He passed on without further comment. Ian turned to Meg.

"Yuh're brave to speak up like that. An' Ah had pure forgotten that juggler we saw at the Fair. Fourteen, was it, now?"

"Something like that," she admitted, staring after the man with contempt. "It mighta been fifteen or sixteen. Mebbe twenty. An' Ah dinna talk funny. He ought to listen to hisself sumetime. Ah could barely unnerstan' him."

"Aye, he *was* hard to make out. Well, let's move on, shall we?"

"Ian, where is Yonkers?" Storm asked, tugging on his sleeve as they walked away.

"Ah dinna know, honey."

"Why dinna yuh know? Yuh know everythin'."

"Ah wish Ah did, but yuh know that's an untruth."

"When we were at home, yuh knew everythin'," she persisted.

"No one knows everythin' but God."

"No! Yuh know everythin'. Ah want to know where Yonkers is!"

"It's by the capital. That's Albany, New York. We read that in the book."

Placated, Storm began looking around with new enthusiasm. It was Meg who remained troubled, lagging behind so she could stare at her father without being detected.

While not exactly certain where Yonkers was, her well-studied geography of the Empire State did not place the city anywhere near Albany. She did not believe Ian thought it there, either. Therefore, he had lied, merely to satisfy Storm's demand. Meg had never known him to issue a falsehood before. His doing so now disturbed her greatly.

She would have to watch him more carefully.

"This Battery Park is a fine place, is it not?" Ian was chattering for the sake of hearing himself talk. "So many people, an' Ah would imagine they are all tourists, here to see where their ancestors furst cume ashore. It's very exciting to see how they have prospered. It bodes well fer us."

"What is that statue, Ian?" Meg asked. Her own enthusiasm had faded into near nothingness, but to remain silent would only serve to arouse his suspicions.

"Let us git closer," he suggested. "Oh," Ian continued, reading the words, "Tis a statue dedicated to the Merchant Marine."

"Tis a right fine statue," Storm remarked, eyes wide. "But why is the seaman reachin' into the water like that? Is he fishin'?"

Ian scrutinized the figure a moment, then shook his head. Before he professed ignorance, however, he remembered his last failure and looked around.

"Excuse me, madam," he said to an elderly, salt and pepper-haired woman standing nearby. Taking his cap from his forehead, he grinned and indicated the work of art. "We're new here an' me daughter jest asked me why the seaman is reachin' into the water. Could you kindly enlighten us as to the significance?"

"Certainly," she beamed, pleased to have been asked. "You can't tell now, but as the tide goes out, you can see the hand of a sailor coming out of the water, reaching for help. The effect is rather startling. It is a dedication to the aid and the courage of the sailors in the Merchant Marine."

"Tis a fine thing," Ian remarked, throat constricting at the love so beautifully expressed.

"Yes. I have come here several times and always been moved by it."

"Did yuh have a loved one in the service, then, mum?"

She smiled sadly. "My husband was a sailor in World War II. A red-haired boy with bright blue eyes. You're from Scotland, aren't you?"

"Aye," Ian replied, matching her smile with a wide one of his own. "How did yuh know?"

"Your accent. *My* parents came over on a boat from Ireland many years ago, when they were young. I'm hoping one day they'll inscribe the names of the newly arrived immigrants on a wall plaque at Ellis Island. If they do, my sisters and I will gladly pay to have them listed. I think about it a lot. Don't you think it would be a very inspiring tribute? If the letters are raised, I'd like to think you could put a piece of paper over their names and rub the back of it, so that when you remove the paper, you'd have a duplicate of what's inscribed there."

"Ah have never heard of innythin' like that, have yuh, Meg?" he asked, turning to her. She slowly shook her head.

"No. Ah have not. But Ah like the idea o' it."

"Are you going over to the Island?"

"Aye."

"You will be very moved by all the exhibits. They have suitcases from some of the immigrants and photographs of their faces. If I knew the name of the boat my parents came over on, I could get the entire history of it. But I don't know it," she regretfully added, leaving her listeners with a small hole in their hearts. "They never spoke of it to us. Just 'a very crowded boat.'"

"We cume over on an aeroplane," Storm informed her. "An' we dinna stop at Ellis Island, a'though we're immigrants, too."

"They don't stop here anymore. But you're as much a part of the history of this country as my parents were. I wish you well."

"Thank yuh. Ah appreciate that," Ian replied for his clan. "An' the great Statue o' Liberty – have yuh been there, too?"

"Oh, yes, certainly. When you take the boat over, you can stop at the Statue and walk up it, if you like. I've taken my own daughters up in it. Once you've done that, you can take another boat to the Island. I think they stop every fifteen minutes, but mind the time; the boat rides close early. Three o'clock, I think."

"That's a good thing to know. Ah appreciate yuhr kindness."

"It's my pleasure," she replied with sincerity.

As Ian and Storm moved on, Meg shyly approached the beautiful woman.

"Would it be too much iffn Ah were to ask yuh a question. If yuh dinna know, yuh dinna have to answer."

"Please do."

"Kin yuh tell me where 'Yonkers' is?"

To which her informant swelled with quiet joy.

"Of course I can tell you where Yonkers is. In fact, I grew up there and my oldest child was born in Yonkers. It's very near here, in fact."

"Ah see. Not near Albany?"

"No, no. In the city, here. Albany is upstate. I live close to Albany, mow. It's one hundred and sixty-two miles away by throughway."

"Ah see. Thank yuh."

"You're welcome."

Meg sauntered away, head hung low with too much knowledge. It would take more than Ellis Island and the Statue of Liberty to make her forget what she would rather not have known. Yet, it was her duty in life to observe Ian MacDhui. She had never imagined such a task to be an easy one.

Being the keeper of the flame never was.

After touring the Statue and Ellis Island, Clan MacDhui was tired and hungry. Rather than pay the exorbitant prices charged along the waterfront, they opted for a bus ride to Central Park, where Storm could "see sume trees."

"What do yuh say we hop into this restaurant an' buy our food an' take it to a park bench?" Ian suggested. When neither child voiced a contrary opinion, he slipped through the doors and merged into a waiting line.

"What'll it be?" demanded a boy behind the cashier's counter.

"Ah'd like three ham-burgers, three sets o' French fries an' three drinks."

"What size fries, what kind of drinks?" came the bored response.

"Pardon me. It's the first time Ah've ever been in a place like this. It's very large; so much to choose frum. A man could git quite lost. How aboot large French fries an' small drinks?"

"What kind of drinks?"

Flustered, Ian attempted to make sense of the flavors while two men behind him gave him an intentional shove.

As befit a man of breeding, Ian turned and smiled.

"Ah'm new here," he apologized.

When the men made no further comment, Ian turned back as the cashier spoke.

"Nine dollars and fifty-three cents."

"So much?"

Removing his farmer's purse from his pocket, Ian attempted to count out the unfamiliar money as the two behind him snickered.

"Hey, look at this guy. He's got a little purse. Where'd you get that from – your Barbie doll collection?"

Ian turned back once more, surprised to be ridiculed over so common an item.

"This? It's me pocketbook." He tried a smile, demonstrating how the item fit into his pocket. "See? Ah keep it in me pocket."

"It's 'is 'pookitbouk,'" the heckler imitated. "What planet are you from, where a man carries a pocketbook?"

"Ah'm frum Scotland."

"And he's right off the boat, I bet," teased another. "I didn't think they let fags into the country."

"Fags?" Ian frowned.

"Isn't Scotland where they make shortbread?" laughed another, pushing closer to have a look at the peculiar creature with a funny dialect and a woman's purse.

"Aye, they made shortbread in Scotland, but –"

"Must be hard on you fags, havin' crumbs in your bed all the time."

"Nine dollars and fifty three cents," repeated the clerk with a total lack of concern.

Swallowing his confusion, Ian handed the man a twenty dollar bill and received change which he did not count. This new incident added to the onlookers' amusement.

"I hope you're rich, man, the way you tip like that."

"Oh, they're all rich in Scotland. Isn't that where they raise kangaroos?"

Confused and hurt, Ian allowed himself to be shoved into another line where a different employee pressed a greasy bag into his hands.

"Move along," came the order, which he obeyed with alacrity.

Emerging from the restaurant, Ian looked wildly for his daughters, nearly panicking before spotting them at the corner. Hurrying toward them, he pasted a grin on his haggard face, while indicating the park.

"Ah'm ready to sit down."

Crossing at the traffic light proved a new experience for the aliens. Upon realizing no one followed directions, they waited through three turns of "Walk" before scurrying behind a short man with a poodle as he navigated the harrowing trip across the street.

Before the MacDhuis could find an unoccupied bench, a jogger approached. Rather than run to their side, the man brushed past them, nearly knocking Meg off her feet.

"Hey!" Ian called, face flushing with anger. "Yuh cume back here an' say yuh're sorry. There was no call to do that!"

"You were in my way," the runner in a two-hundred dollar outfit called over his shoulder.

As Ian made a move to go after him, Meg caught him by the arm and shook him off.

"Ah'm hungry, Ian. Let's eat befer the food gits cold."

He hesitated, clearly torn, then let his shoulders sag.

"A'right," he agreed. "But where shall we sit so as to be out o' the way o' these New Yorkers?"

"Under a tree," Meg suggested and they traipsed slowly toward an unoccupied spot. Sinking down onto the ground, Ian opened the bag. Inside were two hamburgers, one fries and a soda, half spilled because the top have been placed incorrectly.

"Is this what yuh ordered?" Storm demanded. His smile this time was not meant to fool.

"Ah'll look in the bag next time. An' count me change."

Distributing the food to Meg and Storm, he placed a French fry between his lips, then heaved a sigh and tossed it away.

"Ah've lost me appetite."

Storm took a bit of her burger, chewed it a moment, then spit it out.

"Bein' pioneers is hell!"

To which neither Ian nor Meg had the strength to disagree.

# CHAPTER 11

The window was open and a slight breeze moved the new curtain, reincarnated from a flowered pillowcase. A pigeon landed on the sill and stared in with avian fascination at the occupants of the strange menagerie.

Ian, Meg and Storm were sitting around the kitchen table, reading various sections of the newspaper.

"Did yuh see this?" Meg inquired. "There was a murder last night on the subway. A man was killed for a bottle o' whisky."

Ian snorted through his nose, then aimlessly shooed away a fly which had come in through the front door, which was now shut. None of the MacDhuis made any comment about leaving it open a crack for the elves.

It was something "civilization" had already stripped them of.

"Ah guess Ah'll remember to drink mine an' discard the bottle befer ridin' the subway."

"Amazing the habits yuh kin change from readin' the news," came the sour rejoinder.

Ignoring the conversation, Storm looked up from the classifieds.

"Did yuh see this? Help wanted: dog groomer. Startin' salary 'commensurate' with experience. What does 'commensurate' mean?"

Ian stared at her in mild surprise.

"Yuh want me to clip dog hair fer a livin'?"

"Ah was thinkin' aboot applying fer it meself. Ah want to make some money."

In one fluid motion, he reached out, wrapped his long fingers around the paper and tugged it out of Storm's hands. She hissed in annoyance.

"Yuh're not to git a job; yuh're to go to school."

"Ah've been to school. Ah've learned as much as Ah need to know. Besides, what kin Ah learn what's really important? Kin Ah learn aboot sheep diseases? No. Kin Ah learn aboot –"

"Yer mother a'ways dreamed o' havin' her children college educated. It's my dream, too," he emphasized. "Would yuh rather yer father said his daughters was scientists than dog groomers?"

"Ah'd rather he said his daughters was sheepers."

Ian hesitated, sighed, then made another, more decisive attempt to shoo away the fly. The insect was unimpressed, but he did succeed in scaring away the pigeon.

"We've had enuf sheepin' to last us a lifetime. There's no money to be made raisin' sheep fer wool or meat. If there hadda been, we'd be back on the farm. Now unnerstan' that!"

With growing agitation, he pushed back from the table and began pacing around it in ever-widening circles.

"Do yuh fer one moment think Ah wanted to leave all Ah know? Do yuh imagine it was easy fer me to cume to a foreign country to make a livin'? Did yuh not see a part o' me die when Ah left yer mother's grave, the only sacred spot left me on this earth?"

It was the first real glimpse the children have seen of the enormous tension Ian was under. They cowered a moment from the intensity of his emotions, then slipped out of their chairs to stand before him. He understood their meaning, but it was a long moment before he trusted himself to touch them.

As his arms spread and they fell into his embrace, it was not without the hurtful realization that their relationship with Ian has subtly altered. The equality which existed on a small farm in Northern Scotland had disintegrated. The help he needed now was far more than they could provide. It was a sobering, aching awareness none of the three had anticipated.

After the hug had ended, Meg, the peacemaker, turned her back on him and crossed slowly to the stove.

"Ah think we could all use a fresh pot o' tea."

It is a tried-and-true remedy, a small attempt to grab back the normalcy. For the moment, it worked. But the moment was fading.

It was past midnight when Ian MacDhui roused himself from the lonely bed in which he had been lying, pretending without success, to quiet his mind for sleep. Growling in unaccustomed ill-temper, he drew on his trousers and tiptoed into the living room. The night air was still and heavy.

Padding to the window, he paused before it, wild eyes attempting to penetrate the smog and city lights to reach the heavens beyond. The moon, now well into old gibbous, was barely visible.

Five minutes passed, then ten and Ian did not move. It was only when a car alarm blared its protest into the uncaring artificial dusk that he was roused from his trance. Rubbing eyes, red-rimmed from concern and lack of sleep, he raised a clenched fist at the invisible perpetrator of his solitude.

"How kin a wolf howl into the night when the sky is a'ways grey an' he canna see the moon?"

A cry of despair wracked his thin frame. With impotent rage, he dropped to his knees, resting his chin on the paint-peeling sill.

"Meggie... Meggie MacDhui, Ah've done what yuh said. Ah've brought yer bairns to a new country, given them a new start. 'Git away frum the old ways,' yuh said. The land's tired; it's no longer a place where a man's thoughts kin roam free. 'A new beginnin' is what we need,' yuh said. 'Give Meg an' Storm a chance to be part o' sumethin' bright an' *innovative,* not mired in the muck. Let them be exposed to more than rompin' in the sheep dip wid boys who've no more future than do their fathers.'"

Shivering, not from cold but from fear, Ian held his hands out, palms up, toward the open window, addressing the wandering spirit of she, he could only hope, which had followed them to the new world.

"Ah coulda done it wid yuh, Megan MacDhui. Ah could do innythin' with yuh by me side. Yuh were my strength... my love. But on me own – who said Ah could do this terrible thing on me own?"

For a moment the curtain rustled as though in answer, but before he could hope of more, it died away, leaving him hollow and embittered.

The dawn was little different than the night. Low hanging clouds obscured the sun, making the day dingy and dirty. The car alarm which had begun just past midnight was still blaring its unheeded warning to the early morning commuters.

The classifieds, heavily marked in pencil, sat in desultory isolation on the kitchen table. Clan MacDhui had gathered in the bathroom, containing a toilet, cracked-basin sink and shower stall providing little by way of cheer.

Ian stood peering into the perpetually fogged mirror, shaving with a straight razor while his daughters critiqued his effort.

"There," he bragged in exaggerated accomplishment. "Have yuh ever seen such a fine job as this?"

The razor scraped away a stray whisker on his cheek, then deftly moved to the deep cleft in his chin. Meg and Storm winced a split second before he cut himself.

"Yuh kin a'ways tell when it's a State Occasion."

"Aye," Storm agreed in well-rehearsed conversation. "Ian MacDhui a'ways cuts hisself."

"On yer weddin' day, was yer face drippin wid blood?"

Ian ripped off a piece of toilet paper and stuck it to the cut.

"Not a bit o' it," he grinned.

"Why was that, then?" Storm pursued, already familiar with the tale.

"Me soon-to-be-bride shaved me that mornin'."

"Christ on the Cross, she sure was a wise woman. But how did she know yuh was not to be trusted wid a dangerous weapon?"

"Because me hands were shakin' like a calf wid the ague," he laughed. "What aboot me sideburns? Ah see the fellows here are wearin' then awful long. Shall Ah let mine grow, then?"

"Ah think yuh should shave yer head while yer at it," Meg offered, "an' yuh'll pass fer a convict jest released frum a work farm in Australia."

"Ah take that as a no."

While he rinsed his face, Storm inched closer, finally pressing her chin against his body.

"Ian?"

"Aye?"

"We'll no fergit, will we?"

"Fergit what, darlin'?"

"Where we cume frum?"

He reached down and tousled her hair in loving reassurance.

"No, Storm. We'll no fergit."

"Yuh promised to tell me... aboot her. Will yuh tell me... sumetime? Befer it's too late?"

"It'll never be too late, Ah promise yuh that. Ah'll tell yuh what," he declared, tossing the once white towel across the lip of the sink. "As soon as Ah git a job an' we have sume spendin' money in our pockets, yuh an' me an' Meg'll sit down and have ourselves a long chat. How would that be, then?"

Her shoulders sagged in quiet resignation.

"It's a'ways sume other time."

"Time," he smiled thinly, "is what we have plenty of. There. How do Ah look?"

"Like a spotted leopard."

Reaching up, Meg tore off the bits of paper decorating his face. With each removal, Ian rolled his eyes and made low "ouch" sounds.

"Better, now."

"As handsome a lad as ever courted lasses on the moors."

"Not that handsome, surely," he protested. The sentence was lightly articulated but behind the words lurked a sullen denial. He had asked for an obligatory approval, uncoupled from the illusion of times dead. The reminder now was unwelcome and startling.

"Handsome," Meg amended without understanding the look he gave her.

"Ah'm off, then to git me a respectable job. Be good an' dinna git into inny trouble."

"We never git into trouble."

"Well, Ah mean it, an' Ah want yuh to mean it, too. Stay poot."

*"Poot,"* Storm repeated, exaggerating his dialect, then dragging herself away from him. "What shall we do while yuh're gone?"

"Yuh might try prayin'," he suggested. Which was as much as to say, "Nuthin'."

It would be a long day.

It was late afternoon by the time Ian sagged wearily into a bus seat and buried his head in the sweat-obliterated newspaper. Where he had gone to apply for a job and been rejected, bold pencil marks crossed out the addresses. Where he had gone and been told to "Come back next year," he had tentatively made checks, until being advised by another applicant that the advice actually meant, "Go to hell."

It did not matter where he got off the bus so consequently Ian was not paying attention when his asphalt-weary feet touched yet another unfriendly sidewalk. Looking around himself with bleary eyes, he frowned at the street signs, then shook his head, trying to remember why they sounded familiar.

When realization came, his umbrella-mouth turned upside down.

"Ah know that address," he spoke aloud.

Opening the classifieds now clutched in his hand, Ian skimmed the fine print, finally finding what he was looking for near the bottom of the page.

"Dog groomer! It's providential! Ah wasna plannin' to cume here, yet here Ah am. It must be a sign."

Pausing to straighten his hair and reposition his wilted cap, Ian glanced at a clock in an adjoining jewelry shop window. It read 4:00.

"Not too bad," he observed, failing to notice the clock's hands were not moving and the jewelry shop was, in fact, a pawn shop.

Entering the door of the dog grooming establishment, he paused inside to acquaint himself with the setup. To his right was a counter and to his left, the waiting room. Several people, dogs on leashes, impatiently sat to be called. Ian did not recognize one single breed, which he naively attributed to the fact they must all be of mixed blood.

"Do you have an appointment?" a woman sighed at him.

Turning back to the counter, he removed his cap and approached.

"Ah've cume fer the job," he stated.

"What?"

"Ah've cume fer the job. The one advertised in the newspaper."

"What?"

Rather than repeat himself a third time, Ian held out the paper. She stared at it in dumb ignorance before finally taking his meaning.

"Oh. Sit over there," she directed.

He looked where she pointed. There was certainly an "over there," but the only possibility of "sit" was on the floor. The hair on the back of his neck rose in indignation.

"Ah am not a dog," he said. After his previous one-sided conversation, he did not expect to be understood. It was his first correct assumption of the day.

He crossed the room and stood by the wall next to a display of rubber dog toys. Out of curiosity, he examined one. Encased in a bubble pack, the "toy" was a red and yellow colored ball. The manufacturer advertised the item as "Amusement for the Sophisticated Companion."

The cost was $12.99.

Ian replaced it with a low whistle.

"Ah dinna know what they mean by 'sophisticated companion,' but it's mighty expensive amusement."

While he waited an hour and a half, the dog grooming shop sold nine of the toys and would have sold two more, but for the fact the purchaser could not find any in green and yellow.

Color, Ian noted, was highly important. It was a fact he was hard pressed to explain, inasmuch as dogs were color blind.

It was then he decided the "sophisticated companion" must mean "spouse."

"You can go in now," another clerk, this one a man, announced. Ian tried a grin but found the effort almost more than he could manage.

Moving with numb feet, he followed the man into a back waiting room.

"Mr. Joe will be with you in a minute," the man muttered, then winked at him. "Hope you get the job."

"Thank yuh," Ian replied politely, face turning red. He attributed his sudden flush to the heat, for the room was warm and he was desperately tired.

After a wait of another twenty minutes, Mr. Joe, a man nearly as round as he was tall, entered. He eyed Ian with the experience of a man already planning what hair to trim and how much to charge, not in that order.

"Where have you worked before? Did you bring references? I expect you have your own grooming tools?"

The words were spoken so fast Ian did not catch any of them.

"Ah've cume to apply fer the groomin' job," he spoke, hoping that was the appropriate response.

"The ad says, 'with experience.' I don't do on-the-job training. This is a classy joint. You have worked before?"

"Ah've never clipped dogs, but Ah'm a sheep man an' Ah've sheered more sheep than inny man in New York."

He hoped a small brag would not be out of place.

Mr. Joe took a step back, fearful least he catch whatever ailment the tall, flush-faced man suffered from.

"Mister, people bring their pedigreed pooches here to be made elegant – not to be 'sheered.' Christ, if they knew I had a sheep sheerer on staff, I'd be outta business in a week. Get out."

Forgetting to thank the man for his time, a practice Ian had steadfastly maintained until this moment, he trudged dejectedly out of the back room. The male clerk winked at him again as he brushed by.

"Sorry you didn't get the job. Mr. Joe's tough. What are doing tonight?"

Despite the friendly inquiry, Ian pretended he did not hear. What he would be doing tonight was trying to explain to his expectant daughters why he had failed to obtain a job, much less a respectable one.

Which would have had nothing whatsoever to do with the reply the clerk hoped to hear.

# CHAPTER 12

The door to the apartment was locked when Ian tried the knob. Frustrated, he twisted harder. The rusty handle turned an eighth of an inch but did no more than that. With a frown, he considered putting his shoulder to it, then changed his mind. With a patient forbearance he did not feel, he knocked.

Storm's voice came from behind the door.

"Who's there? An' make it quick!"

"Ian MacDhui."

Had she demanded proof, he would have been hard pressed to produce any.

Fortunately, his voice was recognized. The door was unlocked quickly.

"Why is the door locked?" he inquired, now more puzzled than annoyed.

"A neighbor was mugged this mornin', jest outside the flat." On his quizzical look, more from his expression than the information, Storm continued. "She screamed bloody murder, too. Yuh shoulda see'd the blood. Ah thought she was done, fer sure."

"Yuh dinna go down to help, did yuh?" he asked in a frightened voice.

"Ah was debatin' it right enuf, but befer Meg an' me could make up our minds, she got up from the pavement an' started chasin' the man what hit her."

"Did she catch him?"

"She was outta sight in a lick," Meg informed him, coming in from the bedroom. "We asked around later an' the 'general consensus' was, she dinna."

"Who did yuh ask?" he probed in shock.

"The neighbors. They were all gathered in the hall on the second landin'. They were makin' such a row, we thought there was anuther murder takin' place."

"So yuh went to see?"

"No. We went to help."

He was tempted to ask them who they were intending to aid – the murderer or the victim, but did not. He was afraid of the answer.

"There were nine or ten people standin; aboot, discussin' the news. Apparently, this type o' occurrence is quite common. We was advised not to worry aboot it."

"Aye. One old woman what lives here has seen one hundred and seventy-two muggings!"

The children were clearly impressed. Ian tossed his cap wearily across the room, landing it with efficiency on the couch. Seeing their news was not received with the spirit in which it was imparted, Meg pointed to the bathroom.

"Git washed up. Dinner's 'most ready."

Ian stared down at his soiled, empty hands, then shook his head slowly.

"Ah dinna get a job."

"Does that mean yuh're not hungry?"

"It means Ah dinna earn me keep."

Meg pretended not to notice his dejection.

"Megan MacDhui was known to say a man who tries his hardest earns his keep by the purity o' his heart."

"A man canna eat purity."

The statement was sacrilegious. The cloud of doom it portended hung over the tiny family a long moment before Storm dispelled it.

"Good Lord! Yer soundin' more an' more like me every day!"

It was not until Ian snorted that she knew she had won.

"The life an' times o' Clan MacDhui," he remarked, moving away. "Ah'll wash me hands."

As victories go, she had earned herself a trophy.

It was not until the supper was consumed that an air of despair settled over the small group. Sensing they could do no more to ease his pain, Meg and Storm excused themselves early, pleading a "bone weariness frum jet lag." Understanding their tact, Ian let them go, waving at them as they paused at the bedroom.

"Ian, shall we leave the door open?" Meg inquired. He could not tell from the tone of her voice whether she wished him to reply in the affirmative or the negative.

"Aye," he finally agreed, giving in to his soft heart rather than his raging emotions. "Leave it open a crack, so's Ah kin look in on yuh befer Ah go to sleep."

When he caught the sparkle of her grey eyes, he inwardly heaved a sigh of relief. It would not have done well for him to have guessed wrong.

Ian did not stir until his finely-tuned ears detected the rhythm of steady breathing. Then, with a sigh of rejection, he rose, his gangly frame hanging loosely from his bones. Had he been at home – had he been on the moors – he would have gone out, letting the familiar night scents rejuvenate him.

Failing in that, he would have walked two miles to Megis Crag, drawing himself toward the top by hand and footholds more ancient than memory. Once safely at the apex, he would turn northwest, then flatten himself into the stone. A man could not stand upright on Megis Crag for the winds were tricky and sudden. More than one man defying the elements had found himself at the foot with a splintered leg, or a broken back.

Someone unfamiliar with the moors might question why Ian MacDhui would climb such a perilous crag, much less face the northwest. There were no cities in that direction, no byways which might catch his passing interest. Only a native – a man who had lived in the area, or a man who had sad cause – would know what lay in that direction.

Only an alpha male who had lost his alpha female would find solace staring toward a kirk yard, where the only things stirring of a cold, lonely night were the spirits of those long departed.

Meggie MacDhui's spirit had never come to her husband while he lay in solitary vigil atop Megis Crag. She had never whispered, through manipulation of wind, nor communicated by a touch of ghostly fingers, but he knew she was about. He knew because he loved her and his love was greater than the bourne of death.

Ian MacDhui was not in Scotland and his jaded instincts warned him he would not find the spirit of his lost wife in Manhattan. He therefore paced the apartment, hands behind his back, head bowed, stray elfin locks draped across his brow like seaweed clinging to a derelict wreck.

This was not the way it was supposed to be. The dream, spoken from the lips of a flesh and blood woman, had been an entity alive; the dream, shared by two beating hearts had been a tangible, attainable reality. More than a figment of sleep, Megan's imaginings had risen, like Athena, springing from the head of Zeus, into reality.

Together, Ian and Meggie had built their castle, ringing the walls with laughter, peopling the rooms with little beings like themselves, yet entirely new and unique individuals. Not "heirs," as the moor folk had styled male children, but daughters to cherish and raise in a brave new land.

"An' how will we support all these bairns yuh're speakin' of?" Ian challenged, to which she had a ready answer.

"Yuh've gifts yuh've never dreamed of, Ian me darling."

"What 'gifts'" he demanded, pulling out the lining of his trousers pockets to show her his lack of worldly goods.

"Ah dinna mean gold an' that yuh know," she spun back, pushing him away with the flat of her palm. "Yuh're a special man, Ian MacDhui, though yuh dinna know it. Never mind what yuh know and what yuh dinna know, fer Ah know it, an' that's all that matters."

"Special?" he demanded, hands on hips, though carefully and at a distance, for if she chose, a well-directed blow from her strong right arm would send him tumbling.

"That's what Ah said, an' Ah dare yuh to tell me otherwise."

"Explain it to me," he begged, darting a feigned thrust, then sinking to his knees beside her. "Tell me what yuh see in me, fer Ah canna see it, meself."

"Ah see all the goodness in God's creation, stamped in yer face. Ah see wisdom where others see quiet. Ah see courage where others see naught but physical strength. Ah see faith where doubters see only patience.

"Ah see in yuh great deeds an' not the dirt beneath yer fingernails. Ah see the kindness an' the love that others overlook. Ah see the deep thoughts, what them moormen consider the wind whistlin' through yer ears.

"An'," she teased, "Ah see the handsomeness in yer face an' feature that yuh mistake fer commonness. There's nuthin' common aboot you, Mister MacDhui. Yuh're a man apart; a shepherd meant to watch over more than sheep."

"Now yuh've confused me more than Ah was befer," he protested, burying his face in the folds of her skirt. "Ah unnerstan' what yuh're sayin' a'right – an' had Ah the gift o' words, Ah mighta said the same wondrous things aboot yuh. But me? Yuh say them aboot *me*? That Ah canna see."

"Ah wish Ah could give yuh me eyes, then, Ian, because as sure as there's a God in heaven, Ah know of what Ah speak."

"Ah will never see it, no matter whose eyes Ah have. Yuh're crazy in love, Meggie an' that love is poisonin' yer thoughts. Ah'm but a penny-poor sheeper, too tall to fit in store-bought trousers an' too dumb to have an education."

"Ah'll teach yuh all Ah know, but it's not the book-learnin' education yuh're lackin' to make yuh a gentleman, Ian. There's them what has all the University learnin' in the world an' they've no heart to temper their knowledge. Widout soul, an educated man is no more than a walkin' encyclopedia. He can parrot the words but he dinna hold their meanin'. Yuh have the empathy to make a great human bein'."

"Awk, how kin Ah have this 'empathy' when Ah do not know its meanin'?"

"Ah'll tell yuh no more this night. If yuh're playin' games wid me, Ah'll play one back. Yuh go an' look up that word an' commit its meanin' to heart. An' then one day when awareness strikes yuh, yuh'll finally unnerstan'."

"Tell me now," he demanded, pressing his lips to her warm hand.

"Ah'll tell yuh nothin' more."

Looking up, he had caught her faerie eyes and grinned into them the light of his bright love.

"Ah'll tell yuh, then," he began, pressing his hand to hers. "Ah'll tell yuh that Ah'm naught but a man, an' being a man, Ah've other thoughts this night."

For which no further words were needed. They had kissed and hugged, then ran outside and made love in the tall, wild grasses until, passion sated, they had slept, two bodies as one, until the early morning dew woke them, and the warmth of a new day inspired the process yet again.

Rousing himself from memories, Ian sobbed, shook the kinks from his knotted shoulders then shuffled awkwardly to the door of their daughters' bedroom. Forcing himself to enter, he crossed to the bed to kiss the foreheads of those born to kindred spirits.

Before his act was completed, Storm's pale eyes fluttered open and her tiny, sculptured hand reached out to his.

"Ian, Ah was dreamin'," she whispered.

"Then go back to sleep, darlin' an dream again."

"Ah dinna want to dream." Pulling herself up by holding onto his arm, she stared sleepily into his matching orbs. "Tell me aboot Meggie MacDhui. Yuh promised an' Ah feel her close tonight."

Her words, coming upon his own thoughts, startled the father, scared the husband.

"Not tonight," he demurred, shaking his head."

"Please?"

"Ah'm too tired, wee one. Me ears is plugged. Ah canna hear me memories."

Bitterly disappointed, Storm pulled back, pupils contracting in anger.

"Then what have we cume here for, if we canna hear that what we need to hear?"

"We will hear it," he promised, but the lie was apparent and she withdrew further, hiding her hands beneath the covers. "Once Ah git a respectable job, me ears will open," he tried, as much for his own sake as hers. "Once we settle down, me heart will speak to me an' me lips will speak to yuh."

"Ah'm tired," Storm lied with a truthfulness equal to his own. "It's jest as well, for Ah couldna hear what it was yuh we're goin' to say."

"Aye," he agreed, averting his face. Then, "Good night. Sweet dreams."

"Ah dinna want what yuh canna have. Good night to yuh, Ian MacDhui."

Reacting to her blow, he sucked in air through nearly compressed lips, then drew away.

"Sleep, then," he ordered, to which she made no reply, her former answer standing, like a scarecrow, in a field of weeds.

The following three days were a reprise of the first. When he had exhausted all opportunities presented in the classifieds, Ian resorted, like the homeless Jane Eyre, to knocking on doors. And like that destitute lover, received for his trouble the merciless scorn of the world.

It was the tenth "Help Wanted" sign he applied at. This one was hand-written and placed in the window of a dirty, unpretentious fast food "joint." Pushing the door open with an enthusiasm equal to that of a condemned man waving away the priest, Ian started around the small area serving as both dining and interview room.

There were four men in line before a corpulent black man, who was seated at a table, a pile of forms, curling at the edges, pushed out in front of him. One eye was half closed, either from injury or disease. The man's nose had once been the most prominent feature on his face, but now stood as a bloodless reminder of better times.

When Ian's turn came, the man barely looked up.

"What experience have you got?" he demanded, the words spoken by rote.

To which Ian, in his newly acquired experience, responded, "Ah kin flip burgers!"

The man's reaction was so swift, a bubble of nearly translucent spittle flew from his mouth and settled on the table.

"What does a White Bread know about flippin' burgers?"

"Ah know how to eat 'em," came the reply. "An' Ah canna imagine as to how a man who knows how to eat canna learn how to flip!"

It was the desperation speaking, and Ian MacDhui did not recognize the sound of his own voice.

"Got a work permit?"

If it had been the first or the tenth time he was asked that question, Ian would have had one answer ready. But it was the hundredth time and his sigh served better than any assurances of "proper papers" and a "great willingness" to perform what was demanded of him.

Producing the well-creased form from his small pocketbook, he shoved it at the interviewer. The man glanced at it with perfunctory indifference, then finally raised his massive head.

"Can you read?"

"Ah kin read."

"But what kind of writing, Tea Cakes?" he joked. There was no humor in his voice.

"Ah kin read the Queen's English," the man, desperate for the job, responded. He had a sense he was being made fun of but did not see the punch line coming.

"The queen's English? There's a laugh, you damn queer. Keep your hands to yourself while you're here. Understand?"

"Ah-am-not-a-queer."

"All you English are fags. You wanna deny it?" But what he was really asking was if Ian wanted the job. He nodded dully.

"Ah want to flip burgers."

"Well, I'm not hiring a short-order cook. I'm looking for a jack-of-all-trades. Can you do that?"

Ian blushed, staring at the manager with suspicion.

"Tell me plain what yuh're askin'."

"Tell me plain what I'm asking," the man repeated. The cruelty was not lost on the other employees, who were as eager as he to hear the answer.

"Ah dinna unnerstan' the expression," Ian tried, modulating his voice to hide his fear.

The black man hesitated, then shrugged, blinking his one good eye in a grotesque wink.

"A mop man; a floor sweeper. You do what I tell you to do. Got it?"

"Aye. That Ah kin do."

"O.K. Just so we understand each other. You can start now. There's an empty locker in the back with a smock hanging on a hook. Put it on. You steal it, you're dog meat an' someone ends up 'flipping' you. Friday is pay day. Got it?"

"Got it! An' thank yuh, sir."

The manager drew back faster than if Ian had spit on him. Baring his crooked, yellow teeth, he waved the new employee away. "Sir," was not a word often heard in his world, and he did not trust a man using it. Not even one who spoke "the Queen's English."

The "Burger Joint" officially closed at 11 P.M., but Ian was not allowed to leave until he had mopped the floors and wiped the counters clean. Since this could not be done until the last customer departed, it was nearing midnight before he was "off the clock."

After rinsing the mop and the rags in an anti-germicidal solution made before the turn of the century, Ian wearily crossed to the sink, wishing to rid himself of the bacteria from the "mop cleaning slop."

Standing by the lockers were two waiters and the cashier. They had not introduced themselves formally and he presumed they wished to do so now. Affixing a crooked smile on his sagging face, Ian nodded toward them in a friendly manner.

"Going home, Tea Cakes?" one asked. It did not sound polite, but there was a lot in this new world which seemed one way and turned out to be the other. Ian gave him that benefit of the doubt.

"Me name's Ian," he tried, holding out his newly scrubbed hand. No one offered to shake it. "What's yuhrs?" he tried, feeling the hair on the back of his neck begin to rise.

"E-in?" the other inquired, scrunching up his eyes in mock astonishment.

"E-in? What's an E-in?"

"It's a common enuf name where Ah cume frum; in Scotland," he tried.

"Maybe he's E-in Fleming," the cashier suggested. This was followed by coarse, dirty laughter.

Ian did not recognize the writer's name and assumed the fellow had simply mistaken him for someone else.

"Ian MacDhui."

"McDooie?" He nodded agreeably. "If your name's McDooie, and you're a Scottish 'bloke', then why isn't your name Mac?"

"Because," the second waiter jumped in, "if they called all Scots by their names, there's be a terrible confusion." With a sneer, he cleared his throat and made a poor imitation of Ian's dialect. "'Hey, Mac!' 'Whadda you want, Mac?' 'Just thought you'd like to know your wife just ran off with Mac!'"

This was knee-slapping funny. The three employees, none of whom were born in the United States, nearly collapsed to the floor in effected mirth.

"Thanks for telling me, Mac."

"It's all right, Mac. There was this guy named Mac who run off with my wife, once."

"And why was that, Mac?"

"I paid him ten dollars and a sheep to take her, that's why, Mac."

"And did he come back and complain, Mac?"

"He sure did, Mac. He wanted another sheep to even the bargain, Mac!"

"I had a wife once, too. And you know what happened to her, Mac?"

"No, Mac. What happened to her?"

"She was hit by a Mac truck!"

Rather than reveal his true emotions, Ian stuffed his clenched fists inside his pockets and hurried off. He was nearly to the door before the manager hailed him.

"Broom-pusher," he yelled, to be heard over the din. "Report to work at ten tomorrow. You gotta get a PPD test." The stricken look on Ian's face prompted him to reply, where otherwise he would not. "It's to satisfy the health officials. To see you don't have TB."

"What is TB?"

"Fleas," the cashier explained, joining the manager.

"Ah dinna have fleas!"

"He's kidding you, Limey. Tuberculosis. It's a communicable disease. Congestion of the lungs. You know: consumption."

Ian nodded slowly, drawing in air through distended nostrils.

"Ah will cume in at ten, as yuh ask. But in return, Ah ask that yuh not call me names."

"Yuh ain't a Limey?"

"In point o' fact, a 'limey' is slang fer an Englishman. Ah am not English."

"Yeah," the cashier informed his friend. "He's a Scottish; you know. Like shortbread."

Yeah. Well, don't worry about it, Limey. Over here, when someone gives you a nickname, that means they like you."

The manager was a good enough actor to pull off the lie and was rewarded for the effort by a relieved grin.

"Good. Ah apologize, then. Ah dinna know. All yuh have to do is tell me. Ah learn fast."

"I'll just bet you will," the cook named Smash agreed, pushing away the cashier, who had gotten too close to his personal space.

They did not continue their conversation until the new "mopper" had left.

"What'd you hire him for, Drake? He's a queer duck."

"Because he doesn't have the right papers and he'll work for what I pay him without knowing I'm cheating him."

"Why are you bothering to get him tested, then?"

"Because I always comply with the law, that's why."

"You?" Drake shrugged, then stood up and moved away. "He won't stay long, you know."

"Long enough to give this place a good cleaning – which it needs. You bastards sure don't do a good job. You've been in this country too long – picked up slovenly ways." He went to the cash register and began counting receipts. "If I'm not here when he gets in, give him Greene's driver's license and social security card. He'll need identification at the clinic. But get them back from him."

"O.K. From Tea Cakes to Greene Sleeves in one easy switcheroo."

"You better watch it," the manager warned without looking up. "Call him what you will, but he's closer to Beef Cake than Tea Cake and if you get him riled, I wouldn't be surprised if he ends up putting you through the meat grinder."

Without bothering to reply, the cashier sauntered to the window, where he could still make out Ian's form, loping down the street. Pausing to stare at his own reflection a moment, Smash shook his head.

"You're wrong, Drake," he muttered to himself. "'Tea Cakes' is far closer to what that bastard has coming to him. Mark my words."

There was truth and jealousy in the premonition.

Ian MacDhui would have understood neither.

# CHAPTER 13

This time the door was not locked. Nor was it even closed.

Ian squared his shoulders, steadied his hand, then gave it a gentle push. Two sets of deep sunken gray eyes peered at him through the darkness of the apartment interior. In another lifetime he might have considered the fact he had recklessly blundered into a den inhabited by two Sabretooth tiger cubs.

He was late and they were worried. He did not need to remember the quote from one of Megan MacDhui's favorite authors: it came back to him without conscious thought.

"I was sick... sick onto death...."

Shamefaced, he paused before slipping through the door, then held out his arms. In a flash they were upon him, hurtling their own thin bodies against his with the force of dinosaurs.

"Ian MacDhui!" Meg cried, kissing his cold hand with her warm child's lips.

"We thought the damned city had consumed yuh!" her sister echoed.

"It's late an' Ah'm sorry Ah scared yuh," he tried, but the need for words was past. Had there been anything to forgive, the bairns had done so the moment they heard his familiar shuffle on the time-worn stairs.

"Ah got a job!" he cried, thus ensuring himself two dozen more kisses before they dragged him inside, closing the door firmly behind him to seal out fear.

"A job!"

"Aye, a job! An' look at what Ah brung home to celebrate!"

Managing to extract a hand from their grasp, he withdrew a paper grocery sack from his jacket pocket.

"What's in it?" Storm demanded, too excited to unwrap the contents.

"A pound o' mutton an' some dried barley. It's mutton stew we're to make this night, in celebration o' me great success."

Taking the package from him, Meg scrambled away toward the kitchen, eyes glistening with delight.

"Ah canna think o' no better way to celebrate! Mutton stew it is."

While she began the preparations for their much loved meal, Storm dragged him toward the couch, where a small radio sat perched on the arm.

"Look at what we've added to the decor," she bragged.

"What is it?" he gasped. While the identification of a radio was not beyond his grasp, seeing one in his apartment was.

"Dinna be daft," his child smiled, tears of pride illuminating her own face. "It's a radio set we've got."

"But – how?" Then, suspiciously, "Yuh dinna steal it?"

"Steal it?" Storm repeated, as if the concept were offensive to her ears. "We dinna steal it. We *obtained* it."

"Obtained it? What does that mean? Obtained it?"

"We went on a search-an'-seize mission."

Ian rolled his eyes.

"Yuh stole it!"

"No," Meg called from the kitchen. "Search-an'-seize means we liberated it frum the junk pile."

"Aye," Storm agreed. "An' yuh canna believe what people throw out. This is a perfectly fine radio an' it was in the rubbish heap."

"Throw out?" he demanded, head throw back in stark wonder.

"Aye. An' more besides. Go look into yer bedroom."

Nervous that he would discover a treasure trove of "obtained items" which would land him in prison, Ian inched his way toward the bedroom. It required more than a bit of courage and manipulation for him to crane his neck around the frame.

Inside, he saw a new dresser, a vase filled with fresh-cut flowers, a small throw rug at the foot of the bed and four mismatched throw pillows at the top. His gasp of astonishment was both genuine and horrified.

"Oh me God...."

"Yuh need no' worry, Ian MacDhui," Meg reassured him, joining her father and sister at the door. "We cume by 'em fair an' square."

"But... where?"

"It's all in the knowing where to look."

"Ah know, yuh said that. But tell me right quick so's Ah can start breathin' ag'in."

"Remember Ah tolt yuh aboot Drunk Al? The man on the street corner who lives in a flop house an' whose real name is Albert MacPhearson?"

"Aye," he dubiously acknowledged, mind in a whirl.

"We went out fer a walk," Storm began, but Meg elucidated.

"We went out to look fer yuh when yuh dinna return an' we run into Drunk Al. He said not to worry, he had seen yuh an' he thought yuh knew how to take care o' yuhrse'f. He said that rather than goin' in search o' yuh, we ought to go wid him."

"So we did!"

"Aye. He's a fine man, Ian MacDhui. He's fell on hard times but he knows where everythin' in this city is to be found. So we went wid him an' he showed us where folks drops off their belongin's they no longer want. He commonly goes through the piles his se'f, pickin' out items to sell."

"He helped us bring all this back. An' tomorrow we're to go wid him sumwhere else."

"Aye. To a new place. He thought we might get –"

"Wait!" Ian begged, holding up his hands for silence. "Yer goin' too fast. Where is this place?"

"Not far."

"We took the subway."

"Yuh took the subway?"

"Aye. Tis like the trolley, only it isn't."

"Isn't what?"

"Above ground."

"Well, that makes it a lot more clear," he confessed, utterly bewildered.

"It takes a bloke all around town an' yuh kin ride fer free iffn yuh know the tricks."

"Tricks?"

"We'll teach you," Storm promised.

"No matter," Meg glossed over. "We went through all the 'junk' an' he helped us carry it back."

"An' we're goin' ag'in tomorrow!"

"Aye, Yuh said. But slow down. Me head is hurtin'."

"Yuh're hungry," Meg diagnosed. "It's back to the kitchen fer me. Storm, yuh find a radio station to play."

"They go on all night," Storm informed him, leading Ian by the hand to the bed. "Jest set yerself down an' Ah'll have music fer yuh in a minute. Lay down iffn yuh want, an' rest yer head on yer new pillows." She observed him with pride as he did as ordered. "Tis fine, is it not?"

"Aye, tis fine," he admitted, overwhelmed and suddenly bone weary.

After several tries, Storm found a station playing soft classical music. They listened a moment in silence, then she spontaneously reached out, kissed his hand and skipped away.

"Yuh've done a good thing," he mumbled, more asleep than awake, then conducted St. Martin's in the Field with snores, until being gently roused to wakefulness an hour later.

"Time to eat, Ian," Storm advised. "Git up an' wash yer hands. The table is set."

Doing as he was told, Ian found himself in for another shock as he retraced his steps into the dining room. The flowers from his dresser had been brought in and placed on the table beside a bent but functional, four-prong candelabra burning three cheerful candles. His gasp of astonishment was reward enough for his scavenger children.

"Yuh like it, then?"

"Like it? It's fine... it's grand."

"Then sit down and place yer napkin unner yer chin for we're aboot to consume the grandest meal ever served in this here U-nited States o' America."

Sitting at the nominal head of the table, he wearily bowed his head, clasping hands together in earnest prayer.

"Oh, dear God, it's been a day o' firsts," he reverently acknowledged. "An' Ah'm thankin' Yuh fer this bounty. Amen."

"Amen," came the duel echo, in precisely the same tone of voice.

"Now, eat up an' tell us aboot this job o' yuhrs."

"Ah'm flippin' burgers," he started, pausing to chew and swallow between words. "Which means Ah'm moppin' floors. But Ah kin tell yuh widout shame that's it's an honorable job an' jest the beginnin'."

"Moppin' floors?"

"Aye, but Ah got on real well with the Boss. Ah wouldna be surprised if befer long, Ah was promoted. An' it means real money in our pocketbook. Think o' it. Once we save me 'salary,' we kin buy ourselves some nice things."

He was interrupted by the sound of a car alarm shattering the night air. All paused in hope it would cease the annoying din. After two minutes, Storm abandoned the idea and shouted at him.

"Kin we buy some quiet?"

"We kin move to the country. Ah know they have quiet there," Ian assured her.

"An' trees? Do they have trees there? An' birds?"

"Aye. Lots o' trees an' thousands o' birds."

"Can we bring Drunk Al wid us?"

"Aye. Iffn he wants to cume. That would be lovely."

"He can help with the gardenin'," Meg decided. "A man needs respectable work to keep his self-respect. Ah suspect he's been widout that a long time."

"Aye," Ian agreed, wiping his lips on the red and white checkered napkin. "Right as rain. A man needs to know he's contributin'. This fella, he sounds like a fine gentleman. But Ah dinna want yuh callin' him Drunk Al. That's disrespectful."

"He tolt us his name."

"Mebbe. But Ah wouldn't wonder if he became a whole lot better man wid a new name. A man lives up – or down – to a name. There are those what calls him Drunk Al that's bein' mean, an' he lives down to that name. Mr. MacPhearson sounds a whole lot better to me; an' Ah imagine it would to him, too. Or mebbe Kind Al," he added, noting their faces. "What would yuh say to callin' him Kind Al?"

"Ah like it," Meg declared, ending the suspense. "An' Ah think he will like it, too. Yuh're right, Ian MacDhui. A man's name ought to stand fer sumethin'. An' he's been kind to us. Meggie MacDhui would agree. 'Tis a fine thing yuh're doin',' she'd say."

Glowing with pride, their father finished his mutton stew, burped in tacit approval of his daughter's cooking, then patted his stomach.

"When Ah git paid, we're goin' on a shoppin' spree. What do yuh say to that?"

"We had better save our money."

"Awk," he expansively brushed them off. "O' course we'll save our money. But in the meantime, we'll go out into this grand city an' have a 'shoppin' spree.' We'll buy yuh some books, Meg, me darlin', an yuh some clothes, Storm MacDhui, fer Ah kin see yuh're growin' like a weed."

Pushing back from the table, he rose unsteadily to his feet, feeling the need for sleep pass through his over-excited brain.

"Now it's off to bed fer Ah have to be up early, me hearties."

They followed him to their bedroom, each child climbing into the bed, more full of questions than sleep.

"When yer settled, kin we cume an' see yuh work, Ian?"

"Ah dinna see why not."

"But yuh're only moppin' floors," Storm protested, anxiety and accusation filling her child's voice. "Is that a great an' wonderful job?" Ian did not answer. "Is it a respectable job?"

"Ah've a'ready told yuh it was," he tersely replied.

"How much money are yuh makin'?"

"Ah dinna ask the man, honey."

"What if it's not enuf?"

"Enuf fer what?" He was tired and his patience was at an ebb. She also had a knack of expressing his own fears – fears he did not want to hear, either from his own brain or from that of another.

"Enuf to buy a house; enuf to go on a shoppin' spree?"

"It will be enuf an' then some."

With waning faith, Ian attempted to extricate himself from his daughters. Before he could escape, however, Meg, the wise one, arrested his movement with a well-directed question.

"A shoppin' spree like the one we went to in Edinburgh, Ian? Wid Megan MacDhui? Do yuh remember?" He paused, caught between memories and flight. "We stopped in every shop we passed an' ate our fill o' sweets."

"Aye," he whispered. "Ah remember."

"Tell me aboot it!" Storm pleaded, trading her doubts for memories. "Yuh promised, Ian MacDhui! Yuh said when we were safely in the New World, yuh'd tell me.!"

"Ah did," he demurred softly. "But is this the time?"

"There'll never be a better," Meg declared, propping herself up on one elbow. "An' the best part was, Storm, yuh were there, too."

"Me?"

"Yuh were only a wee lass, Gail MacDhui," Ian recalled for her. "Ah carried yuh in me backpack, wid yer head facin' out over me shoulder, so's yuh could see what was cumin'. There were other fathers there, carryin' their bairns in backpacks, but they was all facin' away frum the action. An' Ah said, "iffn Ah was a babe in a backpack, which way would Ah rather be lookin'?' An yer mother had a right smart answer. She said, "Yuh'd rather be facin' the cumin' attractions,' an' so we turned yuh around!"

His grin was infectious. Storm grabbed hold of his arm, pulling herself up in bed with a desperation not lost on his watery grey eyes.

"Ah wish Ah remembered that. Make me remember. Please?"

He laughed and slid easily onto the side of the bed.

"Yuh were so wee, Ah had to feed yuh whipped cream from the tip of me finger."

"An' the puppet show," Meg pleaded, her own need for sustenance acute. "Tell her aboot the puppet show."

"Oh, yuh remember that, do you?" he inquired, arching an eyebrow in mock surprise.

"Ah do. Tell us aboot Meggie an' what she did." When he hesitated, allowing her the opportunity to continue, Meg fairly burst with shared joy.

"It was right in the middle o' the town square," she hurried to tell, words running from her mouth like dripping ice cream. "There was a big box set up in the street an' the players was inside, so's all yuh could see was the puppets. Ah thought they was real live bein's," she admitted, flushing slightly and earning for herself a tousle on the head from a loving hand.

"The players was inside?" Storm gasped, hardly daring to imagine.

"That's as true a thing as yuh will ever hear," he agreed. "There was a cloth draped all around it an' the puppets was set up through holes in the top. They was actin' out a play aboot sumethin', Ah fergit."

"It was aboot how they had flies all over their house an' they was discussin' how to get rid o' them," Meg promptly supplied. "The boy puppet wanted to go around swattin' 'em all, an' the girl puppet said that would take ferever. She wanted to open the door an' jest let 'em all fly out."

As she paused for breath, Storm prodded Ian.

"What happened?"

"Yuh'll never believe it," he sighed.

"Ah will! Tell me."

"Yer mother – Meggie MacDhui – went right up to the puppet show an' started talkin' to 'em."

"To the puppets?" she gasped in horror.

"Aye, she did. Rrrright there, in front o' all the people watchin'."

"What did she say?"

"She said, 'yer daft, the lot o' yuh, an' it's no wonder yuh have flies. Yuh canna swat 'em all an' iffn yuh open the door, there's more will fly in than will ever fly out. What yuh hav'ta do is poot out a dab o' heather honey on a piece o' paper. When they cume to eat, they'll get stuck. When that happens, all yuh have to do is poot the paper outside."

He laughed at the visual images dancing before his eyes.

"Were the puppets mad she spoke to them?"

"Nary a bit, wee one. As a matter o' fact, right befer our eyes, the girl puppet disappeared, then cume back up wid a piece o' paper wid honey on it. She poot it right out an' what do yuh think happened?"

"A fly landed on it?"

"That's right! Yuh've hit on it. A real-life fly flew up an' started eatin' the heather honey."

"An' everyone in the audience started clappin'," Meg continued. "Oh, it was a grand day. The puppets made Megan take a bow."

"Go on," Storm protested, but not in a way to make them retract their story.

"Aye, they did. An' Meg an' me an even yuh, too, wee one, was a clappin' right along wid them. Yer mother, she smiled and took a bow."

"She did," Meg confirmed. "An' it was a royal time."

"That it was. There wasna a thing yer mother couldna do. She was a magic one, that lassie. A wild one. If there was a thing to be done, she did it. An' yuh two are like her," he sniffed, wiping away a tear from his cheek. "There's a lot o' Meggie MacDhui in her daughters. Yer brave and *stalwart,* an' neither one o' yuh would be afeared to talk to puppets in front o' a group or an audience."

"Yuh coulda done it, too Ian."

"Awk, not me. Ah do not do well in front o' people. They frighten me. Ah'm a sheep man, darlin'. Ah kin talk to the wee beasties an' the clouds an' the crags, but Ah canna talk to people. Ah'm a poor, shy moor man, while yer mother was a people person."

"Could too," Storm sleepily corrected him. "When yuh git paid, will yuh take us to a puppet show?"

"Ah will. There's lots o' outdoor shows like that in Manhattan. We'll go out an' find one an' we'll see who o' us has the courage to talk to the puppets."

"Mebbe we could buy some puppets o' our very own. An' poot on a show, yuh an' Meg an' me. An' make a lot o' money."

"Mebbe we can," he agreed.

"Let's go out now."

"Ah have to git some sleep, me lambs. Ah'm off to work in the mornin', remember? Now, Ah'll kiss yuh good night."

"G'night, Ian MacDhui," Meg blessed him.

"'Night," Storm repeated, half-closed eyes full of story and dream.

Ian rose from the bed, took a step away, then turned back, head lowered, long, muscled arms hanging at his sides.

"This rememberin'... yuh've made me feel better, wee bairns. Better than Ah have in a long time. Tonight Ah feel yer mother right close to me, whisperin' in me ears. Sayin' all will be well," he reverently added. "A man needs his faith renewed now an' ag'in. Ah'm thankin' yuh fer it."

The daughters were asleep before he reached the door. Pausing a moment to look back, Ian ran a trembling hand through his hair, then took in a deep breath. Contrary to his usual habit of leaving the door ajar, he shut it tightly, as though to keep intact the memories, prohibiting them from following him out and thus diluting them in the empty spaces of the gloomy, foreign apartment.

For a long time he stood, back to the wall of the shuttered door, then with half stumbling, unseeing steps, made his way to his own bedroom. This door, also, he shut so as not to mix his feelings.

There was just enough reflected neon and filtered moonlight from the open window to starkly outline the cold, empty bed. With a moan of longing, Ian wrapped his useless arms around himself, cried in a low, hollow keening, then sunk onto the lumpy, sagging mattress.

"Meggie... Meggie MacDhui. Ah miss yuh. Ah miss yuh so bad Ah ache. Where are yuh when Ah need yuh? Where is me sweet, lovin' lass when her boy is hurtin' deep inside wid a need only yuh can unnerstan'?"

Clutching his own body only accentuated his longing. Sobbing with frustration, he grabbed one of the "new" throw pillows, clutching it to his breast with sudden, urgent fervor.

"Meggie, what is a man to do widout his wife? Ah was alone befer yuh met me, befer yuh loved me, an' Ah dinna know how a man an' a woman was like together. But Ah know now, an' Ah miss yer hand in mine. Ah miss the touch o' yer flesh as we lay together, unner the faerie moon."

Legs shaking with desire, Ian kissed the pillow, talked to it out of misery, rolled onto the bed, side by side with his sad substitute.

"Meggie, Ah miss yer lips on mine, yuh're hot breath in me mouth. The children, Meggie... the thought o' makin' children wid yuh; of me body inside yer body an' us wid not a care in the world but fer our lovin' an' our bein' one together."

Planting his lips on the imagined woman shape, Ian kissed it, then groaned in agony, for not even in the dreams of a lost and lonely moor man could he feel her respond.

"Megan... Megan Clarke MacDhui, Ah've never loved another. Yuh were the first an' yuh will be the last. Ah've smothered me feelin's fer so long, Ah've forgotten how. Yuh taught me an' yuh loved me an' now Ah'm alone an' achin' inside wid what Ah thought was dead.

"As dead as yuh.... Ah beg yuh, Meggie, cume to me now an' lie beside me an' love me as yuh used. Ah'm pitiful scared an' Ah dinna know what to do widout yuh. Yuh made a boy into a man, then left me wid naught but hollowness."

Crying into the night, Ian struggled with his trousers, slipping them down until his bare, swollen flesh rested against the mattress. Arching his back, he grappled with the covers and blanket, desperately balling them into an elongated human shape, needing to feel her under him, craving release from the torments of swirling emotions, too long suppressed.

"Meggie.... Meggie, cume to me this night, Ah beg yuh. It canna be too much to ask of a lovin' God. A God who made man.... A God who unnderstood the torments o' the body. Yuh tolt me that, Megan," he accusingly added, tearing away at his shirt until his skin was naked to the sting of night air. "A God who takes pity on his poor, miserable creatures. Yuh told me... so where are yuh, loving God? Give me back me Megan!"

As though in answer, the harsh, impersonal neon light outside the window snapped off with a crackle of death, shrouding the bedroom in solemn gloom. The grappling shadows sprang from man to wall, transforming solid being to formless ghost, as words of prayer were answered by amorphous denial.

"Ah love yuh, Megan MacDhui.... Ah love yuh, Meggie."

But the love was unrequited, and the lover's longing died an inglorious death amid the rumpled sheets and the loveless, faceless throw pillow resurrected from a trash bin.

# CHAPTER 14

Ian was up with the sun, shaved, showered, hair brushed and teeth cleaned by seven o'clock. Not to be outdone, daughters arose with him, eyes bright with expectation.

"Here's yuhr tea, Ian," Meg announced, standing by the door, cup in hand.

"An' here's yuhr toast," Storm provided, suddenly abashed by his looming presence. Noting her discomfiture, he graciously accepted the offering, then stooped to kiss her brow.

"Ah thank you, Miss Storm. Ah kin feel me stomach rubbin' ag'in me backbone. And Ah thank yuh, Miss Meg, fer the hot tea. Ah canna imagine startin' out a new job widout a cup o' tea to fortify me body."

"Aye," Meg agreed, also somewhat awed by her father's aura of Big City otherworldliness. "Right yuh are. It's our way o' blessin' yuhr day... and yuhr success."

Ian ate standing while his children watched with hungry eyes.

"Will yuh no be havin' innythin' to eat wid me?" he finally asked, growing uncomfortable under their weighty expectations.

"We'll eat when yuh're gone."

"Oh. Why is that?"

The answer was longer in coming.

"Because we've a mighty long day widout yuh," Meg conceded. "Eatin' an' cleanin' up will help pass the time."

He shrugged helplessly, then smiled. It was as well to believe, so others could more readily follow.

"It won't a'ways be like this," he promised. "When we git some money in our pocketbooks, we'll have time to spend together. Like we used to."

"Not like we used to," Storm demurred, then was silenced by a warning look from her sister.

"No," Meg smoothed. "But better, mebbe."

"Aye. Better," Ian agreed. "We've big plans. Once we git our permanent status, an' things is set up right an' proper, we'll have lots o' time together. Jest wait an' see. Ah had better be off, now."

He was almost out the door before a small voice hailed him.

"What time shall we have supper ready?"

"Ah dinna know fer certain. Ah suppose Ah'll be gettin' a permanent work schedule today so's Ah'll have a better idea tonight. After that, we kin make plans." He raised a hand in farewell. "Expect me when yuh see me."

He departed, fleeing for the stairs with a pace out of keeping with his optimism. Ian did not look back until he was out the building and down the street. Only then, with the absolute awareness of Meg and Storm's eyes upon him, did he find the courage to turn back.

His father's eyes found them in an instant, hanging out the upper story window, waving madly. With a grin and a mad wave of his own hand, he set out, as he had heard on countless American Westerns, "to face the music."

The bus stop was crowded. Pausing briefly to prepare his correct change, Ian hesitated, then stuffed the small farmer's pocketbook back into his trousers. For the first time in his life, he was ashamed to be odd. His ways were not the ways of native New Yorkers.

Rather than suffer the stares of incomprehension and ridicule, he opted to forgo the bus altogether. Setting off in an easy lope, he consoled himself with the fact he was saving money.

That was easier on his pride than admitting he was actually saving face.

The manager, whose name he learned, was Drake, was not at work when Ian arrived. The cashier explained to him, in a roundabout manner, about PPDs and sent him on his way. No explanation was given about the new name he was to assume and Ian did not question the matter. While there was a distinct flavor of dishonesty about the arrangement, he did not feel it his place to protest.

And thus, Ian MacDhui, honorable man, made one more concession to the mysteries of the New World. In New York, it was called "survival."

In Scotland, it would certainly have been labeled something less noble.

Back by 10 A.M., he was "put on the clock," and set to work. The burger joint, as he soon discovered, was more "joint," than "burger," more hangout than eatery. Familiar with drugs only through what he read in the newspapers and the conversations shared with Megan, whose grasp of the world and worldly affairs far exceeded his, Ian politely refused the few overtures he received to "have a smoke," and kept to the back when not actually required to perform his labors in the front.

With the naivety of a child, he mopped the floors, tidied the shelves, then dropped to hands and knees to scrub "where the sun don't shine," hoping that by hard work and careful consciousness to his tasks, he would ensure himself a place of welcome.

"Hey! Tea Cakes," the cashier called, drawing Ian's attention. "You missed a spot."

As Ian's eyes instinctively dropped to where the man pointed, the cashier deliberately spilled a cup of soda on the floor.

"Careless of you," another man observed, casually leaning against the wall. "You better not mess up," he warned, "or Drake'll fire you."

They waited until the spill was cleaned before dropping a bag of greasy fries, then crunching them beneath their feet.

"Hurry up!" he urged as Ian hesitated. "I see Mr. Drake coming."

Jerking spasmodically, Ian quickly stooped to pick up the mess. When he finished, the cashier grinned wickedly.

"Guess I was wrong. He's not coming, after all. He won't be in before noon. But it's nice to know you can obey orders."

Ian nodded briefly, the sad smile on his face fading into obscurity.

"Ah dinna mind yuh testin' me, friend. Ah unnerstan' Ah'm the new man here, an' Ah'll do as yuh ask. But Ah'd like to git along wid yuh."

"Yuh would, would you?"

"Aye."

"And how do you think you can do that?"

"By doin' me work an' keepin' to meself. Ah'm askin' yuh to be fair wid me. No more."

"He's askin' for you to be fair with him, Smash. And he put it so politely. You're a very polite fellow, aren't you, Air Holes?"

"Mah name is Ian. Ah'd be obliged if yuh called me that."

"Right you are, Mac. When you get done cleaning up the mess, Mr. Drake wanted you to get up on that stool over there and do something with the ceiling."

"The ceiling?"

"Yeah. He says it's full of cobwebs, and if the State inspectors ever see that, all hell will break loose. So hop to it."

Ian hesitated, then painstakingly replaced the smile on his face.

"Ah'm here to work."

"You're damn right you are, Limey. And don't forget it."

It was not until Ian was precariously perched atop the stool, stretched out at arm's length to swipe away the cobwebs with the end of a whisk broom that he discovered the true reason he had been asked to perform such a task.

"Nice body," the cashier leered. "A little on the lean side, but I could make do."

Confused and flushed with anger, the mop man dropped the broom from his hand, then hopped down with grace to retrieve it.

"Ah thank yuh fer the compliment, if that's what it was, an' Ah'm thankin' yuh to mind yer own business. Ah dinna unnerstan' what yuh want an' Ah'll be washin' the grease frum the exhaust filters, now."

Without waiting for the man to protest, Ian walked around him, taking care not to come within striking distance of the cashier's hands. There was something far dirtier about the man than his comprehension gave admittance to, but it made the chore of cleaning the filters far more desirable than batting cobwebs.

"He just put you down, Smash," the waiter, a youth of sixteen passing for eighteen, laughed. The crudeness of his humor would have curdled milk. "Maybe they don't do *that* overseas.

"Whatta you say, Mac? Do they do that where you come from?"

For the first time in his life, Ian felt a cold, unknowing fear creep down his spine. Feigning deafness, he ran hot water into the wash sink. Smash crept up behind him.

"You didn't answer the man, Mac."

Turning so suddenly he startled the cashier, Ian rose to his full height, glowering down at his small, weak tormentor.

"When Ah dinna answer yuh, it's best not to repeat the question."

Standing over six feet, two inches tall, with hard-earned muscles rippling down his lanky arms, Ian presented a formidable picture. Smash retreated a step then hitched his shoulder at a queer angle.

"Just don't come looking to me when you need a favor," he growled. "Understand?"

"Perfectly."

Before the conversation continued, it was broken up by the unexpected appearance of Mr. Drake. Frowning at Smash, he waved him away with a careless flick of the hand.

"You can take lunch at one, Mac. Employees are entitled to ten percent off whatever food they buy here. If you want, Smash'll run a tab for you. I take it out of your pay. That way, you don't have to go hungry... and you don't have to steal. O.K.?"

"O.K.," Ian stiffly agreed. Then, more respectfully, "Thank yuh." Drake had begun to walk away when Ian added, "Ah dinna steal."

The denial went unacknowledged.

While the manager was present, Smash and the waiter left Ian alone. When Drake was busy or stepped out, however, they were on him in a flash, pointing out imaginary spots he had missed, complaining about crumbs on the tables, criticizing the way he walked, talked – or remained silent.

It was close to one o'clock before Ian received his first reprieve.

"Take thirty," Drake ordered. Then, seeing the puzzled expression, rolled his eyes and pantomimed eating motions. Ian nodded agreeably, waited patiently in line to order "a burger an' fries, an' a small soft drink, orange." Receiving them without the perfunctory word of "thanks," Ian clutched his purchases to his chest and slipped out the back.

The alley which the hamburger joint let out onto was narrow, trash-littered and rank. Ian immediately switched from breathing through his nose, to an open-mouthed version of taking in air.

"Ah've smelled sheep dip all me life," he explained to himself, "an' Ah've cume acrost more than one dead animal what's been turned to mush frum the heat, but Ah've never smelt innythin' quite like this. Welcome," he grinned in self-deprecating humor, "to the Big City."

Picking his way carefully over and through the broken glass, crushed soda cans, balled up newspapers and animal dung, he finally spied a small, circular, sun-drenched area, serving as a crossroads for intersecting alleys. Drawn to it like a moth to a flame, Ian quickened his pace, hardly daring to breathe at all until he was bathed in sun.

Closing his eyes and throwing his head back, he soaked up the life-giving rays until his face was red from exposure. Only then did he shake loose from the hold nature had on him and settled into a natural squatting position to inspect his lunch.

Suspiciously sniffing the beef, he sighed and put it down, not trusting it to an empty stomach. The soda soon followed, for it held no taste remotely similar to an orange. While munching without enthusiasm on a French fry, he heard a noise behind him. As befit a creature of the wild, Ian turned with a slowness so agonizing, he did not so much as raise a head among the flock of pigeons gathered behind him.

A pot o' gold at the end of the rainbow could hardly have elicited a wider grin from his tired, depressed, prematurely-aged face.

"Rrrrock doves!" he pronounced, the sound closer to "cried" than "exclaimed." "Who'd have thought to find God's creatures in a place like this? Do yuh know," he inquired, leaning closer to the strikingly beautiful grey and white and black avians, "yuh have cousins in Scotland?"

More intent on the burger he had temporarily discarded than his words, the birds eyed him with hesitant suspicion. When Ian cooed, they crept up an inch, heads questioningly cocked to one side.

"Aye," he acknowledged with a crooked grin, "it'll be ham-burger yuh'll be wantin'. Ah canna say Ah recommend it."

Breaking off a bit of bun, Ian tossed it into the flock. Amid a sudden stretching of wings and the group activity of hopping an inch into the air, several birds immediately pecked at the offering. The crust was gone in a matter of three swallows.

"Now Ah unnerstan' the secret," he whistled through his teeth. "Yuh hafta gulp it down befer yuh kin taste it. Well, yuh're welcome to it, then, as Ah've no the knack."

Ian tore the hamburger into bits, dolling the treasures out, then scattering the food so no one pigeon got more than its fair share. When the meal was consumed, the fries followed.

Never satisfied but more than grateful for what they had received, the birds pranced around their lonely benefactor, whirling, cooing and fanning their tails in a show of splendor, for which the gift-giver was immeasurably grateful.

"It's nice to know Ah've made sume friends in my sojourn to the New World." And then, more quietly, as the awareness of time slipping away came into his consciousness, "Ah envy yuh yuh're flock. It's a good thing to belong. Ah belonged once, meself, but Ah dinna inny more. Ah'm a pigeon widout me mate. An' that's a sad thing.

"Ah wish," he added, standing up with enough animation to scatter his friends, "Ah were a pigeon."

He was not back inside the eatery a minute before receiving a stern rebuke from Drake.

"You're late. And don't feed them flying rats. I don't want to be accused of harboring vermin. If they keep on hanging around back there, I'm gonna put out poison." His back was turned as he finished speaking, but that did not prevent him from feeling the thrust of a thought, sharp as a blade, between his ribs. He spun quickly, arching an eyebrow when he saw Ian a solid ten feet away from him.

"No one," he spat, "likes pigeons."

"An' why is that?" came the question, as innocently articulated as a hangman asking the condemned if he had a last statement to make.

Drake's answer was not long in coming but spoken without the bite he intended.

"They're dirty, they shit on your head and there's too goddamn many of them."

"Yuh might be interested in knowin'," Ian casually began, "that rock doves are one of the few species of bird which are *anatomically incapable of defecating* in flight."

"What the hell does that mean?"

"They canna '*shit* on yer head.'"

More startled by Ian's educated statement than the fact he presented, Drake wrinkled his nose then made an obscene gesture of warning.

"Don't feed the fucking pigeons."

"Yer right," Ian slowly agreed in the manner of a wolf lowering ears to head. "Ah wouldna want to poison 'em."

When the manager slipped through the open door, Ian bared his teeth. It was a victory, but one which would cost.

And money, he was learning, was the soul of life.

At quitting time, no one spoke to Ian, a fact he greatly appreciated. Neatly replacing his mop, handle down to dry, and his rinsed pail in the small janitorial cupboard, he hurried out the front door, shoulders hunched, hands stuffed into trouser pockets. When a mated pair of pigeons flew overhead, he did not look up. Innocence, he was learning, had been banished from his life.

The revelation was not totally unexpected, though he seriously doubted that fact had been part of Meggie MacDhui's dream.

Fearing to spend money on bus fare, he loped city block after city block, learning to ignore the stares of the curious or the annoyed. New York was a fast-paced city, though no one seemed to appreciate that fact except when their own needs were involved.

With the ache in his heart taking root, rather than diminishing the further away he got from work, Ian finally paused to take stock of his dwindled resources. If he could not go home with a smile on his face, he would make an attempt at subterfuge by bringing presents. Meg and Storm would necessarily overlook his misery if he entered with an armload of groceries.

But the pocketbook held no more than five dollars and he bitterly remembered he had taken out the rest, hiding it in a safe spot, until direly needed. Five dollars would not purchase enough food to make a pigeon grin, much less a child. With a groan of despair, he turned one way then the other, seeking an intervention, no matter how temporary, for his dilemma.

The answer came via his own reflection, cast against the window of a shop. Startled, at first to see himself, hair disheveled, wolf-grey eyes wide with fright, he was repulsed, taking a step back in an effort to escape his own image. This offered him a new perspective, revealing that he stood in front of a pawn shop. As his face flushed with shame, his right hand went to his left.

"Forgive me, Megan MacD –"

But the dead wife had nothing to forgive, for the wedding ring, Ian MacDhui's constant companion for 16 years, was missing from his finger. Screeching with horror, Ian threw himself against the side of the building, tearing at his hand to retrieve that which was irrevocably gone.

"Me weddin' ring!" he sobbed. "Oh, Christ on the cross, Ah've lost me wedding ring!"

The discovery was shattering. Raising his head, he made a strangled attempt to howl. Failing in that, he growled, gnashed his teeth then beat the brick structure with his fists.

"Give it back to me! Give me weddin' ring back to me, you filthy bastards. Ah dinna know who took it, but Ah better git it back or Ah'll destroy in a day that which God took six days makin'!"

The threat was impotent. No one listened. Those of flesh and blood, seeing a man in furious affliction, shied away, not wanting to get involved. Those of higher powers, believing Man's lot on earth was to suffer, peered down without apparent interest, thus, by silence, giving tacit approval to the death of one man's heart.

In medical terminology, such a condition would be diagnosed as a myocardial infarction. In religious terms, a minister would speak of "mysterious ways," in explaining how one human being could exist without so vital an organ.

# CHAPTER 15

Ian pushed back from the table, wiped his lips with the cloth napkin, then sadly shook his head. The fare had been less than satisfying and the movement was more for his children than for himself. Left to his own devices, Ian MacDhui and his *nom de plumes* Tea Cakes, White Bread, Limey and Mac could have slid under the table and never eaten again.

Megan Clarke would not recognize the boy she had first met 17 years ago. In those eyes, she had never seen defeat. A shyness and awkwardness of person, certainly, but not an acknowledgement of loss. Her tall, lanky moor boy had fire in his eyes. When he spoke, there was no one who could doubt the conviction of his words, or the fire in his belly.

This man, the shrunken figure with hunched shoulders and knitted fingers bore little resemblance to her alpha male. He was frightened, quiet, haunted. The world had ceased to be a place of wonder, transforming both itself and the man into shadows portending doom.

Had Megan Clarke MacDhui stood beside her husband at the table, she would have known how to shake him up. She would have grabbed him by the hands and led him off into the mist and the mystery of their native land. First climbing a crag, his hands in her footholds, then down, across the wandering hills, she would have led him a merry chase, until, out of breath and at the peak of excitement, she would have laid with him, building passion into love and love into rejuvenation.

"There is nothin' a man canna do if he has faith in his heart," she would whisper into his red-rimmed, nearly pointed ears, as befit an elf-boy. And he would sing back, "There is nothin' a man canna do wid his wife by his side."

Megan MacDhui had not meant to die. That had not been part of her divine plan. She had expected to stand by Ian MacDhui as long as the March wind rippled over the rocks and the lowlands of their home, eroding their bodies with age, perhaps, but never touching the quick of their souls.

She had anticipated an age of life and been given half a measure. Slipping away, she had attempted to give him a substitute, or rather two. These duplicates were not to take her place, but rather to fill his heart with a different kind of love. It was a great, a terrible burden to bestow upon two such small heads, but Meggie had faith. Meg and Storm were her offspring as much as Ian's; and being such, they would keep lit the flame winter gales might otherwise extinguish.

But a child was not an adult, neither in wisdom nor in body, and Ian was alone. The bare walls of the apartment and foreign accents of their neighbors gave testimony to that. The unmade, lonely bed bore witness to the rest.

"Tomorrow," Meg began, hesitantly at first, then gaining steam as she pursued, "is Pay Day."

"Let's hear it for Pay Day!" Storm agreed. "Let that poot sume wind in yer sails, Ian MacDhui."

"Aye," he agreed, drawing back the heavy lids from his eyes with willful effort. "Pay Day. We hav'na had one o' them in a while."

Nursing the narrow, licking flame of expectation, Meg jumped to her feet and headed for the kitchen.

"Another pot o' tea to celebrate."

"When we have lots o' money, Ian, do yuh think we kin buy a house wid a big backyard? Ah'm thinkin' on it, an' it's like to drive me crazy fer the wantin'."

"That's the plan, me darlin'. Yuh dinna think we're to live in the likes o' this place fer ever, do yuh?" Her face fell too quickly to cover the obvious answer to his question. "Onest we've had a few Pay Days an' Ah move on to a bigger an' better job, then Ah'll git me papers straight an' there's no sayin' what the limit is. Ah'm a man wid a lot o' talents. All it takes is an employer to recognize me genius. He poots in a request wid the Immigration people, an' we're home free."

"How soon, Ian?"

"Ah canna say wid inny certainty, lassie, but wid that pot o' tea steepin' on the counter an' yer bright eyes lookin' into mine, yuh make me believe."

"Really?" Storm asked, her own innocent question bringing quick tears to his grey eyes. "Will it be that way?"

"Is that not why we cume to this land? To make a new start? Meggie, me love, was right when she said we've taken the sustenance outta the land an' need a new place to grow. She said Ah'm a 'man wid talents.'" He laughed cheerfully, but the joyous sound was flat on the ears of those who knew him best. They did not comprehend all, but a wee bit was enough.

"Ah think," Meg declared, pouring milk into their blue willow china, "that on our furst Pay Day, we ought not to worry aboot savin'. Ah think we deserve to splurge."

"An' what shall we buy?" he inquired, for in the telling it would make the expectation all the sweeter.

"We shall meet our obligations on the rent, o' course," she began, then paused as he interrupted her with a wave of his hand.

"Naturally. It's a promise made, an' we MacDhuis niver go back on our word."

"Ah'll drink to that!" Storm avowed, holding her newly refilled tea cup in her hand. With a nod of his head and a wink of his eye, Ian met her cup, clinking as firm a blow as he dared. Repeating the procedure with Meg's cup, the three drank their toast and found faith once again.

Blessed are the innocent who do not see the future, for it is only they who can retrain their childlike gullibility.

The morrow, as all morrows, came with the rising of the sun. Ian was awake, shaved and dressed before the two well-familiar pair of bright eyes were out of bed and following his progress.

"Back to bed wid yuh, me hearties, fer today is Pay Day an' Ah'm off frum work tomorrow. Clan MacDhui will be havin' a big time."

"Aye," came the dual answer, spoken by sleepy but excited voices. "Tomorrow we'll be havin' a big time."

Waving good-bye from their accustomed place at the window, Ian returned their salutations then skipped off to work with a light heart. With Pay Day around the corner, all things were possible.

The day was a long one, with no mention of any salary being distributed. Ian worked at his mops, pails and whisk brooms until 5:00 P.M. then looked up sharply as Drake dismissed him.

"Off you go, Shortbread. See you Sunday, bright and early."

Swallowing the bile which rose unaccountably into his mouth, Ian gave the man a weak smile, half fright, half modesty.

"Excuse me, Mr. Drake –"

The manager was busy working on his clipboard, barely lifting his eyes to see what his employee wanted.

"What is it?"

"He's quitting," Smash chuckled under his breath. "He got a job directing the New York City Transit. He'll be making twenty thousand a year, easy. Moving up to Yonkers."

Ian flinched at the unexpected, familiar location, then shrugged it off, for fear of losing the greater purpose.

"Tis Friday, is it not, sir?"

"That's right. And tomorrow is Saturday, just like Christmas comes after Thanksgiving."

"Is it not Pay Day, sir?"

"Oh. Yeah. I paid the others earlier. Where were you?"

"Ah was in the back all day," Ian replied, a trace of fear tainting the timbre of his voice. "Ah niver even took lunch."

"Yeah, well, that was your choice, not my decision. Don't expect me to pay you for that half hour."

"No. No, Ah won't, sir."

Drake walked slowly to the cash register, opened the drawer and retrieved a white envelope. The name Jim Greene was printed on the outside. As he accepted the check, Ian started at it with a puzzled air.

"Mah name is Ian MacDhui, not Jim Greene. Ah want me own pay."

"That is your pay."

"Why... does it have the name of sume other man on it?"

"You don't have work papers, Pampers. You want me to get in trouble with the authorities for hiring a wetback?" Ian slowly shook his head, brows knitting in the middle. "Remember when I sent you to the clinic? What name did you use?"

"Greene –"

"Right-O. And that's the name you get paid in. Jim Greene is an American citizen; with a Social Security card and a driver's license. Him, I can pay. Understand?"

"Aye. But yuh niver said –"

"You don't want it, I'll take it," Smash volunteered, holding out his hand.

Reacting as though the man's hand were a venomous snake, Ian shrank back, clutching the precious treasure to his chest.

"Ah want it. It jest seems... dishonest, is all."

"It *is* dishonest, you ignorant Brit. I thought you understood that. You're the one in this country on a tourist visa, not me, baby. You're supposed to be taking in the sights, spending money so good ol' American citizens like me can make a living bilking you. Now get out.

"And don't spend it all in one place," Smash added with what any other man would have discerned as a wicked dismissal.

"Ah won't," Ian promised, waving a good-bye. "An' dinna worry; tomorrow, me an' me bairns are off to spend our money like good tourists!"

"I won't worry," Drake promised, finally looking down. "See you Sunday."

As the mop man hurried out, he was spared the sarcastic question, directed to no one in particular.

*What the hell is a 'bairn'?*

Not until he was out of sight did Ian duck into a narrow, dirty alley and rip open the envelope. Hands trembling with expectation, he scrutinized the check, searching with mad hope for the dollar amount. When he did not see that which he expected, a low moan of confusion escaped his lips.

"What... what is this? There's been sume mistake."

The second part of the check had an explanation of deductions. Reading these words with more care, his lips moved in nearly inaudible horror.

"Federal tax, state tax, city tax, Social Security; food: eight dollars an' fifteen cents."

The sum total of his pay check was $24.43.

Stunned, shattered, nearly broken in half by the low, inconsequential number, Ian stumbled backward, finally breaking his freefall by striking the side of the building.

"How can this be? A week of me life for dollars twenty-four an' forty-three pence?"

His head was shaking but the reality of the check was beyond denial.

"For this, Ah came to the New World? For dollars twenty-four Ah took me children frum their homeland?"

Staring around, then up at the blue-grey, smog-laden sky, he shook an angry fist at unseen eyes.

"Megan MacDhui, yuh have betrayed me!"

The scream echoed off the walls, coming back to him time and time again, fading but never dissipated, until his own lament drove him crazy. Shrieking with bitterness, Ian shredded the list of deductions, then dropped the pieces, along with the envelope to the earth, stamping them into the ground until they blended in with all the other rubbish. Then, with loosely controlled fury, he pushed away, merging into the flow of human traffic, which neither saw nor cared to know his misery.

There was no thought now of taking the bus. First running, then trotting in a tireless gait, Ian traveled miles down congested city streets, turning his head away from any who would make eye contact, not trusting himself to meet the gaze of another person, lest their own, far more successful Pay Day, be registered in their eyes. Only after crossing and crisscrossing innumerable intersections until he was totally lost, did he stop to ponder his fate.

With less than twenty-five dollars in his pocket, there could be no shopping "spree," no books for Meg, no thought of a house with trees for Storm. After the rent was paid, they would not even have enough money for so humble a treat as porridge.

The ringing of his own blasphemy against his sainted dead wife still ringing in his ears, Ian started around, bleak eyes seeing but not registering his surroundings. Retracing his steps was impossible; asking for directions now unthinkable, for he did not trust his voice. Nor could it fairly be said he had a whit of faith in his fellow man. Betrayed yet again, every man, woman and child had become his enemy.

"How kin Ah go home wid this?" he demanded, wrinkling the check in his strong fingers. "What am Ah to say to them?"

No answer was forthcoming, nor had he, in his newly acquired wisdom, expected one.

Ian MacDhui was learning.

Ian MacDhui was learning the hard way.

No one, he recalled, had ever said life would be easy. He had never asked for ease. It was fairness he craved. That, he now understood, went hand in hand with "cheat."

The flashing neon sign "Checks Cashed" finally caught his eye. Resigning himself to the stark reality that no matter how long he clutched the check it would not grow, he yanked open the door and entered. A small, withered man with wire-rimmed spectacles stood behind a bullet-proof glass partition.

"Ah want to cash this," Ian demanded, showing the paper under the narrow slit. Not, "Ah would like to cash me Pay Day check," nor, "Would yuh kindly give me money for what Ah have worked so hard fer," but "Ah want to cash this." No claim to "me," no reference to "Pay Day." The check was a "this," and he was unworthy of any reference whatsoever.

The man behind the protective glass looked at the check with a bland expression.

"I have to see some identification."

"What do yuh mean?" Ian dully inquired.

"Something with your name and signature on it."

"What fer?"

"So I'll have proof you didn't steal it."

"Steal it?" Ian gasped. "It isna' worth the effort o' stealin'."

"I can't cash it without the proper I.D."

"Canna cash it?"

"No. Not without the proper I.D."

The sheep-man turned floor-mopper reached into his thin, empty farmer's purse and extracted a paper.

"Hold it up. Against the glass." Ian did as directed. The man sighed without surprise. "The name on that paper is Eye-an McD –" He made no further attempt to pronounce the foreign-sounding name. "Not James Greene."

"But..." Ian faltered, having forgotten that salient fact. "But it's mine." Then stronger, "Ah worked fer it."

"Maybe you did and maybe you didn't. But I don't know that. I can't cash a check if you don't have papers which say you are James Greene."

"The sign outside... it says 'checks cashed.' Ah want this mother-fucker cashed," he demanded, resorting to the language of the lost and the bitter. When the man did not react, Ian swallowed again, this time a mouthful of despair. "Please? Ah swear to yuh it is mine. Yuh kin call Mr. Drake. He paid me."

"I do not know a Mr. Drake. Get him to cash it."

Leg shaking uncontrollably, Ian tried again, hands wringing together in imitation of blood being extracted from a stone.

"Please. Please.... Ah need me money. Ah dinna know where else to go."

The man raised an eyebrow in well-rehearsed resignation.

"If I agree to cash this check – a check drawn on another man's name – then I must keep a portion of it as a fee; in case it later turns out to be stolen."

Ian's sigh was closer to the spleen than the heart.

"Take yer fee."

It was a foregone conclusion.

The clerk counted out several bills from his drawer, added a few small coins and slipped them under the window. Ian accepted the money without counting it, tipped his working man's cap from habit, then crawled away, head bowed.

Lessons, he was learning, were expensive.

And as hard to earn as Pay Days.

"He's cumin'." Storm warned, ducking back from the window as fast as her awkward position would allow. "An' his head is bowed."

Those were the code words. As though struck by lightning, Meg ran for the couch, leaped into midair the moment before her body would have crashed into it and ripped the hand-made banner declaring, in black magic-marker, "Happy Pay Day!!!!" from the wall.

Equally as sprite, Storm dragged a kitchen chair to the opposite side, where the banner was attached to the door frame, leapt up onto it and tore down her end. The frail paper ripped from the rough treatment. Neither child noticed. Nor would they have cared if they had.

Pay Day was obviously not going to be a new holiday on the MacDhui calendar.

Standing a moment in indecision, Storm finally shoved the banner underneath the couch, taking care to kick the frayed edges out of sight. Then, in quick rehearsal, she put a hand to her face and yawned.

Before there came a scratching at the outside knob, both sisters were draped over the arms of the couch, heads titled backward, eyes half closed, so that when Ian finally entered, neither did more than raise an eyebrow.

"Ah'm home," he tentatively announced, waiting for the rain of excitement to cascade over his sad parade. When none was forthcoming, he cleared his throat and tried again. "Ah'm home."

Rousing herself with apparent difficulty, Meg scratched, yawned, then ran her hands through her hair in unconscious imitation of her father.

"Supper is ready. Ah expect yuh'll be hungry. Ah hope yuh're not too tired to eat. Storm an' me cooked up sume bean soup. It ought to be ready aboot now."

"Bean soup?"

"Aye," Storm said, stretching out her toes, then spreading them wide, the way a cat does when awakened from a contented sleep. "Yuh caught us nappin'. We done a lot o' cleanin' today an' Ah guess we jest tuckered out."

"Ah'm tired meself."

"Then let's eat," Meg suggested. "An' then git us sume sleep. What do yuh say?"

"Sounds... like a good idea to me."

Their obvious lack of concern, the willful avoidance of anything related to money or Pay Day set Ian's mind to work, but his own heart was too heavy to pursue the matter. Watching his daughters prepare the meal a moment, he sighed loudly, then shuffled off into the bathroom to wash. When he returned, his well-scrubbed hands and cheeks bore close resemblance to his eyes.

The meal was consumed in silence. Once finished, Ian rose wearily to his feet and began collecting the plates.

"No need," Meg informed him. "Jest poot them in the sink an' we'll wash up tomorrow. Ah expect yuh could use a good lay down."

"Daughter..." The word did not sound right coming off his tongue, so he tried again. "Daughter." When the rest of the unexecuted thought died, Meg took up the dropped thread and slipped it gracefully through her silver needle.

"Father."

"Meg, me love.... Ah promised yuh we'd start yuh're library tomorrow. An' yuh, Storm, Ah said –"

"There's no hurry," Meg interrupted before he left the continuance of the conversation to Storm. "Innyway, Ah have not yet made up me mind what Ah want to read, so there's no sense buying a book Ah may not like. If Ah take it to mind to read a book, Ah'll have Kind Al take me to the public library. Ah suppose they have such creatures here, in the States."

"But Ah promised.... An' Ah intend to keep me promise," he suspiciously added, dreading the worst. "Ah said Ah would take yuh out on Pay Day –"

"No," she meaningfully corrected. "Yuh said yuh would take me the day *after* Pay Day. That's tomorrow. Let's let tomorrow go fer now, shall we?"

"An' what aboot yuh, Storm MacDhui? Are yuh goin' to let yer house an' yer trees go until 'tomorrow,' too?"

"Ah'm tired, Ian. Ah want to git sume shut-eye. Ah recommend yuh do the same. Ah suppose the damned house an' trees kin wait awhile."

Had she been older, Storm would have realized she said a tad too much, but being only nine going on ten-years old, her awareness went only so far. Meg came in fast behind her.

"Ah think rather than go on a shoppin' spree on Saturday, as we planned, we'd jest as soon go fer a walk. A long walk. Through the park. To stretch our legs. Wolf pups dinna like bein' cramped, yuh know."

"Aye," he sadly nodded. "Neither do alpha males."

"Tis agreed then, an' good night to yuh."

Rather than a final parting, both children paused long enough to make eye contact with their father. It was a moment of reaffirmation, of love shared, sorrow understood. When they finally broke away, he bent and kissed each on the forehead, diverting his hand briefly to make a half-hearted attempt at tickling Meg under the ribs. When she did not respond, he whispered something inaudible and shooed them off.

There was no laughter, no joy and little mischief left to his wolf cubs.

In the wild, grief was always the dominant emotion.

# CHAPTER 16

Facing an empty bed was more than he could bear, so Ian lay down on the couch, face turned to the backrest. Sleep was long in coming, and when it did, his dreams were peopled with herds of sheep, all of which had faces resembling Drake and Smash and the clerk at the check cashing store.

When he awoke a little past midnight, he tossed too suddenly, lost his balance and crashed to the hard, unpadded floor. Lying there a long beat until reassured his nocturnal rambles had not awakened his children, Ian reached a hand down to prop his weary body into a sitting position.

As he did, his fingers wrapped around something shoved under the couch. Drawing it out, he read, by the light of the reflected neon, the bold, proud handwriting on the sign: Happy Pay Day!!!! Stifling a sob, he crumpled the paper into a ball, then thought better of it and brought it to his lips. Kissing the sign with fervid emotion, he straightened that which was wrinkled, then lovingly replaced it underneath the couch.

He knew them too well. In the morning, or whenever the first opportunity arose, Meg and Storm would retrieve their banner and destroy it. If it were gone, they would fully comprehend their plans – and their emotions – had been revealed. That, he must never let happen.

Biting his lower lip to keep from disintegrating, Ian hugged his knees, bringing his deeply chiseled chin to rest upon them. When he found no solace in that familiar position, he unknotted himself and began pacing.

Tonight and for many nights since, pacing had brought no resolve, not a modicum of comfort to this displaced wolf. Stopping in the middle of the floor, he shook himself like a wet dog, then drew back his lips in defiant agony, the beast caught in the cruel steel trap, ready to bite off its leg for one last taste of freedom.

"A wolf does not like to be caged."

The words were spoken to no more than the walls, but as any lonely soul can testify, the unlived, unloved walls were a better companion than most human beings.

On impulse, Ian grabbed his cap, worked it around in his hands a dozen times, then tiptoed noiselessly to the door of his daughters' bedroom. Cocking an ear toward the inside, he held his breath and listened. When reassured they were, indeed, asleep, he flipped the cap on his head and headed out.

If there was a plan of action, it was not to be found cooped up inside a cage.

Taking the downward stairs three at a time, he emerged into the stale, humid night, drew breath through distended nostrils, then began his prowl. There were few people on the New York streets this late at night. Those who were, pulled back from the tall, gaunt, hollow figure loping down the sidewalk. All too familiar with hell, none wished to face the Devil on his own terms.

Three blocks, four blocks, two hundred and fifty thousand blocks, it made no difference. There was no one to watch, no one to time, no one to wait. For the first time in many months, Ian MacDhui was alone; as solitary as a beast on the moon.

Brooding in mind, thoughts dark, face misted in shadow, Ian traveled, pausing only now and then to stare at his reflection in an opaque shop window. What he saw there he no longer recognized. It was as well, for if he had, his sanity would have lost its tentative balance.

New World, Old World, future, past, present, all became a blur, until the overwhelming idea of money drove him to linger at a pawn shop. Gone were hopes of hocking precious items: now, the one prevailing obsession was to steal. If money could not be made by respectable work, then it might be obtained by theft.

With tongue lolling, ears pressed close to head, tail held at a thirty degree angle, the man-beast kneaded his fingers, cracked his knuckles and contemplated robbery. It made no difference that the pawnshop boasted "surveillance cameras." Had the sign proclaimed, "Thieves Shot on Sight," he would have broken the window and entered, just for the unlooked-for opportunity of being put out of his misery.

A moment, two moments, as he quelled his racing heart. The morality of the deed had made its call to his once stout conscience and failed. Megan MacDhui was moldering in the ground, three thousand miles away. No dead eyes to see and judge. Only the call, the desire, the lust for gold.

"Ah will.... Ah will," he swore, and meant it. But as the second moment slipped into three, then four, he knew he would not. Not because he feared being caught, for he feared nothing. He stayed his hand because there was not now enough riches in the entire world to sate his desire.

With a deep-throated growl of discontent, Ian shoved his itchy palms into the pockets of his trousers and walked again. His strides were no longer open and tireless, but were characterized by the listlessness of hopeless abandon.

The sign above the seedy establishment read "Mac's Bar and Grill." With a humorless chuckle at the now so familiar nickname, Ian placed his hand on the door and entered, just as some distant street clock chimed one.

"Do not ask for whom the bell tolls," he recited, without recalling where or from whom he had heard the quotation. "It tolls for thee."

The bar was half full, which also meant it was half empty. Shying away from deadened eyes, Ian sauntered to the bar at the far end, taking a seat toward the center of the unoccupied counter. It was a trick he had learned, once upon a time, when he had been just Ian MacDhui, dull-witted sheep man.

Taking a seat at either end was an open declaration he wished to be alone. Human nature surviving on perversity, it prompted men to sit beside him. Sitting dead center frightened people, because they did not readily understand the motive. In their lack of comprehension, they opted to sit as far away from the loner as possible, fearing a contagion of strangeness.

"What'll it be?" asked the bartender, who may or may not have been "Mac," and did not matter either way to anyone in the world.

"Whisky."

"Fifty cents."

Without thinking, Ian reached for his farmer's purse, remembering too late that it was frowned upon for a man to have a "Barbie doll" accessory in his pocket. As there was no help for it, however, he steeled himself, withdrew the soft, worn leather from his pocket, picked out the coins and set them on the bar.

The bartender accepted payment by replacing the silver with a small, scratched glass, half filled with ice. Ian deliberately removed the cubes, setting them side by side on the counter, then downed the drink.

"Another."

The bartender obliged, this time serving the drink without ice. For his trouble, he received an order for a third "an' one fer yerself." The drink was delivered and the change slipped into the bartender's slacks.

With two drinks in his blood to clear his head, Ian sipped the third more slowly, staring into the roundness of the glass at the image of a man. Not liking what he saw, he pushed the glass away, hesitated, then ordered beer. There would be no chance of seeing anyone's tortured face in the foamy head of a watered-down brew.

More from economics than desire, Ian poured the remaining whisky into the beer, then blew away the top inch of foam, pausing to stare the bubbles into oblivion before taking a drink. The beer was sour and impotent, which suited his mood. He nursed it, like a man dying of thirst on the vastness of the ocean.

When three peach-fuzz boys came in and placed themselves noisily at the bar, Ian reluctantly arose and stumbled toward one of the many unoccupied tables, inadvertently tripping over an unseen haversack on the floor. Righting himself with difficulty, he brought a hand to his head and tipped his cap.

"Excuse me," he apologized, articulating the words to emphasize his soberness, which they did not.

The man at the table, old by youthful standards at five-and-thirty, shrugged off the interruption.

"It's O.K." His voice was soft and pleasant, catching Ian off guard, for he had anticipated a quarrel rather than a forgiveness. "It's my fault. I shouldn't have had my overnight bag out in the aisle."

"Ah dinna see it."

"Didn't think you had. No harm done."

"Ah'm glad," Ian snorted, "fer Ah couldna afford to pay fer inny damages."

"Been there," the man replied with a well-mannered shyness. When he saw the tall man did not understand his expression, he waved his hand slowly and retried his own explanation of sympathy. "I know what it's like to be down on your luck; to need a friend. To need some... bloody money."

Perking up at the familiar swear word, Ian grinned lopsidedly at him.

"Been there," he repeated.

"Sit down, if you please. I've just ordered a sandwich and I hate to eat alone."

As he finished speaking, the bartender, doubling as the waiter, delivered a massive hero sandwich to the table. Eying it with hungry eyes, the man-beast licked his lips and accepted the invitation.

Letting the moment simmer, the man adjusted the position of the plate, ran the tip of his finger lightly around the rim of it, then subtly, without ostentation, bowed his head. Lips moving in unspoken grace, the man concluded his short prayer with a barely audible "Amen," then looked up.

"My name is Charles, by the way. Charles Denning. I'm a print editor. I was born in Jersey, actually, but I've been in Manhattan nearly all my life. A city can be a lonely place, sometimes. Funny, isn't it? With all these people, a man can feel as though he's lost in outer space."

"That's right," Ian agreed, hardly daring to stare at the man for fear he would disappear, proving to be no more than a figment of his imagination. "That's how Ah feel; pretty damn lost. Ah kin find me way amongst the swamps an' the moors an' the highlands like a wolf, usin' only me senses; but here, Ah canna find me way wid a map."

Smiling sadly, Charles placed a hand on Ian's, a comforting touch, no more. What a friend would do, sensing distress. Ian did not object, for he came from a man's world, where one shepherd's touch was a working relationship, a camaraderie. A shake of the hand, a nudge on the arm, a slap on the back: these were the working tools that bonded men as working stiffs, serving as an acknowledgement of moral frailty.

"Shall we eat?" Charles politely inquired.

It was an offer of breaking bread, of sharing food. Ian understood the ritual.

"Ah hav'na had innythin so fine since Ah left home."

"You are new here? I should have guessed. New York can be a hard place for a stranger to feel welcome."

"It's not the welcume, so much as..." He faltered for the words. "As the foreignness o' it all. Ah hadna expected so much... aloofness. Do yuh know what Ah mean?"

Ian leaned over the table until he was almost nose-to-nose with his new friend, earnest eyes seeking an affirmative that was immediately forthcoming.

"Oh, yes, I know exactly what you mean. And I'm sorry for you."

"Ah dinna want yer pity," Ian responded, surprised and hurt. He attempted to draw back, but this time Charles restrained him with gentle pressure from a hand on his shoulder.

"Not pity, certainly. You mistake; my fault. I should have said, 'I feel that way myself; alone and out of place.' That's all. You see, I work so much, I don't have time for friends. The people at work... well, you see, we work at our own desks, isolated from one another. We don't get to talk, to know one another. They're just as much strangers to me as anyone I pass on the street. I'm lonely," he confessed, then blushed slightly and turned his head away.

Now, it was Ian's turn to react. Sensing he had done or said something hurtful, his own face grew red from the neck up. He swallowed quickly so his words would be clear and articulate.

"It's a hell o' a place where a man canna git along wid those he works wid. Ah'm not used to it, meself. Ah mean, when Ah'm alone on the moors, that's one thing: Ah'm wid naught but the beasties an' the land. When Ah was wid people, we spoke the same language. Here, no one speaks like that. They're all talkin non-stop, but they're not sayin' innythin... kind."

"I never thought to meet anyone like you," Charles confessed suddenly, then, in imitation of Ian, cleared his throat. "To confess, when I saw you sitting at the bar, I thought you would have lots of friends."

Intrigued, Ian inquired, "Why is that?"

"Let us eat a bit and I will explain."

Charles cut the sandwich in half, placing his portion on a napkin so Ian could have the plate. Both men took small bites, then resumed their conversation.

"You're so good looking... so handsome. Bloody handsome," he added with an unequal smile. "In fact, you're the most beautiful man I've ever seen. I hope," he pursued, raising his eyes to meet Ian's, "that I haven't offended you by being honest. That's just my way. When I see the truth, I speak it. It doesn't always make me very popular."

"Ah kin imagine," Ian agreed, holding Charles' gaze. "Ah have a daughter jest like that. She was born wid a chip on her shoulder an' a tongue as sharp as the winter wind. That's why we call her Storm."

"We?"

"Aye. Me wife an' me."

"And you are –?"

"Ian MacDhui. Ah beg yuh're pardon fer not introducin' meself earlier."

"You, Ian MacDhui," he repeated, rolling the sound of the name over on his tongue like fine wine, "your wife and daughter came to New York together?"

"No.... Jest me two daughters, Meg an' Storm."

"And your wife? Your wife stayed behind?"

"Aye – no. Ah mean –" Tears came to his eyes and he finally looked down. "Me wife is passed on. Ah came alone wid me children to the New World because Meggie MacDhui a'ways had a dream o' the New Land. She thought we was better than what we was livin'. She had the gift, that one... but now, Ah'm not so sure," he added in a lower, shamed voice.

"No, sir," Charles protested. "I'm sure she was right. Just because you're having a hard time adjusting doesn't mean she was wrong. She would not want you to give up on her dream so easily, would she?"

"No." Ian looked up, eyes glistening. "When yuh poot it like that, no she wouldn't. But Ah've looked an' Ah've looked fer respectable work an' all Ah found was a floor moppin' job. Ah'm not particular," he hurried on, least he give Charles the wrong impression. "Ah dinna mind the work. It's the – it's the people Ah – canna git along wid. They're no' good people," he finished strongly. "An then..."

"And then?"

"Ah jest had me first Pay Day."

"Oh," Charles sighed. "Say no more. They cheated you."

"Ah dinna know," Ian confessed, wringing his long, smooth, classically sculptured hands. "But it was not what Ah was lead to believe. It was – a *pittance*. Do yuh unnerstan'? Nuthin' at all."

Sniffing away emotion, Ian squared his shoulders and looked around at the other patrons, none of whom were paying the least attention to them.

"And you need money," Charles prompted.

"Aye. Ah need money. Ah need a respectable job. Iffn Ah dinna git one, Ah'll be deported. Ah shouldna be workin' innyway," he added, allowing a trace of bitterness to poison his speech. "But iffn Ah git a job an' me employer makes a petition, then me and the wee ones kin stay. That's the Plan."

"I see. It is all perfectly clear to me, now. And very sad. Your plight is a desperate one."

"That it is."

"I think, perhaps, I know how to help you."

"Help me?" The astonishment was vivid.

"Earn a great deal of money."

"What kind o' money?"

"Fifty dollars a night."

"Yuh want me to steal," Ian gasped, repulsed by the idea. While he had contemplated such a desperate act earlier in the night, to have it suggested from the lips of a stranger made the idea seem monstrous.

Reacting spontaneously, Charles held up both hands as a sign of resignation.

"No. You mistake. Nothing like that, I swear. On my word as a gentleman."

"A gentleman?" Ian dubiously repeated, wanting to believe yet not quite certain his faith could be reinstated.

"Absolutely. What I am thinking of is completely honest. It involves no theft of any kind. It is neither illegal nor – immoral."

"A job?"

"Most certainly."

"What kind o' a job pays that kind o' money?"

"I cannot explain it to you here," Charles whispered behind a hand to his mouth to shield his lips from being read by idle eyes. "Come with me to my apartment; it will be far simpler there. There we may speak confidentially."

"Iffn it's not illegal, why canna we speak o' it here?"

"The answer to that is obvious. I do not wish to get in trouble. Nor would I presume you wish for get me into trouble."

"Trouble?"

"You said it yourself. You have no proper work papers; you need a position – job – so specialized that your employer will petition the authorities to get you a work visa. I can possibly offer you such a position, but I cannot do so openly. For to hire an illegal alien is to place oneself outside the law. I may be willing to do that for you – but I would not want anyone here to stand as witness against me."

He leaned closer, eyes staring earnestly into the other's.

"How would it look, if I or anyone else, went to Immigration, demonstrating your value to me, when anyone from this sleazy bar could come forward and say we met here, over a beer? Think of it and you will see that I am correct."

"Oh, Christ, Ah dinna know...." Ian cried, running his fingers through his dark hair. "Ah unnerstan' what yuh're sayin', but Ah'm afeared."

"Afraid of what? What have I said to cause discomfort?"

"This job yuh speak of – canna yuh tell me jest a wee bit aboot it? Shall Ah be moppin' floors?"

The question was piteously, almost pleadingly put.

"No," Charles smiled, flashing a mouthful of white teeth behind his thin, red lips. "Not mopping floors. What I have in mind is far easier – and more pleasant – than menial, janitorial labor."

"Certainly 'self-respecting,'" a woman commented, interrupting the flow of the moment.

Looking up sharply, Charles and Ian both stared at the speaker, who had come upon them unseen. She was a short woman, middle-aged and heavily made-up, with teased, cheaply-dyed red hair. Reaching out a hand, she ran one of her long, plastic fingernails around Charles' shirt collar.

"Leave us, Delilah," he grunted in obvious displeasure. "We're having a private conversation." Then, to Ian, "You see what I mean?"

"I'm afraid he does *not* see what you mean," Delilah pursued. "But then, that's not the idea, is it?"

"Go away, damn it." When she made no move to obey, Charles looked over toward the bartender, who may or may not have been "Mac." "Get her off my back."

"Oh, dearie," Delilah purred, "I wouldn't think of getting on your back. There wouldn't be any point – for either one of us – would there be?"

"Delilah," the bartender growled, without the least authority to back up his summons. "Leave them alone. They're big boys."

"One of them is, at any rate," she retorted, turning her large brown eyes on Ian. "A very big boy." Eying his broad shoulders and muscled forearms, she considered, then shrugged. "Big enough to take care of yourself, Big Boy?"

"Ah dinna know what yuh mean."

"No," she laughed, removing her hand from around Charles, then leaning over toward Ian, so her ample breasts nearly touched him. "I don't suppose you do." Noting his wide-eyed state, she pressed closer, forcing him back against the chair. "Like what you see, darling?"

"Ah'm a married man," he panted, gasping for air. "Ah dinna mean no disrespect, but –"

"Disrespect?" Charles hooted, finally daring to relax. Then, with a sneer, "You're not his type. He's a gentleman."

"Yes," Delilah agreed. "But what *you* mean by gentleman and what *he* means by the word are horses of a different color."

"Come on," the bartender urged. "Each to his own. Let him be."

She spun on her heels, making low chortling noises under her breath as she moved toward the bar.

"Let's get out of here," Charles urged. "As you see, we cannot talk privately."

"Tell me plainly what it is yuh have in mind."

"If you don't want to come –"

"No, no, please dinna git me wrong," Ian apologized quickly, fearing his chance was slipping away. "It's jest that… Ah'm afeared sume how."

"I wouldn't think anything would frighten you," Charles replied, playing on Ian's vanity. "Delilah is right about one thing – you're a big boy. You can take care of yourself. You're strong – you are strong?" he demanded suddenly, making it appear it was a condition of employment. "Not sick in any way?"

"Aye, Ah'm strong," came the too rapid reply. "Ah've been a sheeper all me life befer Ah came here, an' a man's gotta be strong to work at a livelihood like that. In fact," he added, feeling the effects of the whisky and beer for the first time, "Ah won a trophy at the Edinburgh Fair fer puttin' down any number o' city boys. Ah have a silver cup, engraved wid me name, to prove it."

"Oh, I believe you," Charles reassured him. "So, what do you have to fear? You've six inches on me and *I* never won a silver cup at any fair. I live alone; there will be no one at my apartment; just you and me. If you don't like my proposition, simply say so and leave. I don't see how I could stop you."

"An' what yer proposin' – yuh say it's not dishonest?"

"Not a bit. You have my word. I told you. I have a good job; a very good job. I earn in the six-figure bracket."

"How soon... how soon would Ah git paid?" came the question, spoken so low it was almost a whimper.

"Why, tonight, of course. Forgive me, I should have told you up front. You see, I want to be honest with you. I will pay you each and every night. And there aren't any of those troublesome taxes to worry about."

"No taxes?"

"Of course not. Not for the work you'll be doing."

"How is that, then?"

"There are certain ways a man may make money the government simply does not tax. You'll be an independent contractor. They don't regulate that type of commerce."

"Ah've never heard o' that type o' work."

"It's very common in the States. And certainly preferable to seeing half your salary go out the door before you ever see your money."

"An' how will yuh pay me? Ah canna git a check – in me own name," he dubiously amended.

"You don't have the correct papers," Charles agreed. "Believe me, there are a lot of people in the city just like you. I will pay you in cash, if that is agreeable. I might have you sign a paper, stating you received wages. Unlike you, *I* have to pay taxes. And, of course, you need some proof that you have a high income paying position. To satisfy the Immigration inspectors. So you may apply for a work visa. Everything," he added, "proper and above-board."

"Aye. That's sounds a'right."

"It is all right. I promise you. And I wouldn't promise you if I wasn't sure. Would I?"

"No. I believe yuh would not."

"Then you'll come with me?"

Ian hesitated, clearly torn.

"Yuh canna... jest show me the money?"

"Of course I can," Charles smiled, removing his wallet. "Here. See for yourself."

His billfold was well padded with currency. He riffled the paper, removed the corner of a twenty dollar bill to tantalize his audience of one, then drew it back, with what appeared to be reluctance. "But you understand, I cannot pay you before you have worked for it. I always say, treat a man fairly and he will do the same by you."

"That's right," Ian nodded. "Ah've said so meself. Ah would no' cheat you, Mr. Denning."

"I never thought you would."

Pushing back in his chair, Charles stood, then held his hand out to Ian. Thinking he wished to shake, Ian gave him his. Once attached, Charles' grip tightened like a vice. With the tall sheep man in tow, he moved toward the door.

"Good night, dearie," the woman at the bar called as they left. "Sleep tight."

There was an edge to her words, the meaning of which was not clear to one of the men.

To the other, it was a shared joke.

# CHAPTER 17

It was a short trip uptown. They took a cab. It was the first time Ian had ever been in a taxi in the United States, and he wrapped his fingers around the door handle in excitement.

"Wait until Ah tell me children," he gushed in unexpected, childlike joy. "Imagine – me ridin' in a cab! To go such a short distance, too," he added, as the thought struck him. "Yuh did say it was only a block or two?"

"That's right," Charles agreed, failing to share, much less comprehend the other's enthusiasm. For him, the mode of transportation was an everyday occurrence, worthy of no more than a raised eyebrow if the driver spoke English. He had other, far different pleasures on his mind and those thoughts required nearly all his attention.

After all, preparations for such an event were worthy of Olympic proportions.

"Ah needn't wonder that Ah've passed your flat many a time," Ian prattled on, unaware his words held no meaning to either of the cab's occupants. "Ah think Ah've left me footprints on jest aboot every sidewalk in Manhattan."

"I wouldn't doubt it," Charles muttered, merely to keep the conversation going.

"Ah knocked on many a door, too. But now that's over an' done wid, to be sure. Imagine: Ian MacDhui makin' fifty dollars sterling. Fifty dollars a night!"

"Imagine."

"Ah wasna' so sure at furst; Ah had me doubts," he confided, now pressing his nose to the glass so as to have better vantage of the passing landscape. "Yuh mustna' take that badly, fer Ah'm only bein' honest wid yuh. When a man speaks o' such sums, naturally another man's a bit suspicious."

The passing buildings nearly made him dizzy with delight.

"But yuh have a kind air aboot yuh, an' a good face. Ah wouldn't wonder iffn yuh had a wee bit o' Scot in yuh. What would yuh be sayin' to that, now?"

"I'm often accused of being Greek."

Reacting in wonder, Ian drew back from the transparency to stare at his new friend.

"Grrrreek," he questioned. "Now, Ah dinna see that. But I canna say Ah'm all that familiar wid the Greek. But 'Denning,' doesna strike me as being Greek. Perhaps yer father changed it – Americanized it, when he cume from the Old Country?"

"Perhaps."

"It's a cryin' shame such things is done, but Ah must confess Ah see the reason fer it. A'though they say this is a 'meltin' pot,' meaning a grrreat many nationalities mergin' together," he added to display his knowledge, lest Charles think him an uneducated peasant and rescind his offer of a respectable job. "Ah've recently discovered that it's no' differences Americans want, but similarities. They're afeared o' what they dinna unnerstan'."

"And you?" Charles demanded suddenly, startling Ian with the vehemence of the words. "Are you afraid of what you don't understand?"

"Ah hope Ah'm more o' a man than that. Ah a'ways said, them what fears the unknown are not men, but children."

"You would be wise to keep that thought."

"Thank you," Ian replied bowing his head slightly at what he perceived to be a compliment. "Ah will. An' will yuh look at that!" he cried, spying one of many "Check Cashed Here" signs along their route. "Thank God Ah shall niver hav'ta worry aboot that ag'in. Tis a poor way to make a living, do yuh not think?" When Charles did not answer, Ian continued, presuming his listener had not enough facts to draw a conclusion.

"Cashing checks fer men who dinna have the proper identification. Yuh know what Ah think?" he added, speaking faster, nearly tripping over his tongue in his eagerness to express his pent-up ideas. "Ah think they cash stolen checks. A pickpocket steals a purse an' runs off wid it. There may be a pay check or a check book inside, an' the thief wants to get that money."

His hands went instinctively to finger his poor farmer's pocketbook.

"Naturally, he canna pass himself off as 'Mary Smith,' fer obvious reasons, nor even 'Thomas Murphy,' because his face does not match the picture on the man's stolen papers. So he goes into one o' them shops, makes some lame excuse aboot not havin' his 'I.D.' wid him an' the man cashes it, takin' a hefty chunk out because he knows they're both doin' sumthin' illegal. Is that what yuh be thinkin', Mr. Denning?"

"I think you've hit the nail on the head."

"There must be a lot o' thievery goin' on in this city to make it profitable fer all them checks cashing shops to stay in business."

"Here we are," Charles interrupted, pointing out an apartment building on the right to the cabby. The man immediately pulled over a quarter inch, bringing the vehicle to a stop by the door.

Opening the left-side door and getting out without bothering to check traffic, Charles handed the driver a bill he had been holding in his hand, then motioned Ian up the stairs.

"Come on," he urged, taking the steps two at a time. "It's already late and I have a meeting I can't miss this morning."

"Would yuh rather Ah came back another night?"

"I said come on," came the order. "We'll see whether or not you come back."

The statement was meant to serve as a warning and to that effect did good service. Ian clung like a shadow to his benefactor, first towering over, then darting to one side and the other as they twisted and turned their way through the door and down a corridor.

Because of the late hour, the elevator, resting at the first floor, opened instantly. Charles hastened inside, pressed the round number twelve button, then leaned against the side as the car moved upward. In the dim overhead light, the bright, circular number shone like a beacon, drawing Ian's eyes to it as though it represented the floor on which salvation might be obtained.

"Tis a grand place yuh live," Ian admired. "There's a lift where Ah'm residin' but it doesna' work. Ah think it's more fer show than innythin'. Me daughters was sayin' the building was once a showplace in the '30's but if that's true, it's fallen on hard times. Meg said movie stars used to stay there but Storm told me it wasna movie stars but mobsters –"

The elevator door opened before he could finish the sentence and Charles ushered him out.

"Down here. Around the corner and two down on the right. Remember the directions in case I invite you back. I don't want to write them down."

"Ah have a good memory fer followin' a path," Ian overlapped but Charles was no longer listening.

"Number 1235. The door is usually open when I'm at home, but never enter without knocking."

"Ah wouldna think o' doin' inny such a thing."

Inserting his key into the lock, Charles turned the knob, opened the door, then stood back to allow Ian to enter first. When he was fully emerged into the darkness of the apartment, the tenant followed, taking care to shut and chain the door behind them.

The only light in the room came from a shimmering, illuminated lamp, the size and shape of a volleyball. As it rotated on an unseen axis, the red, yellow, blue and green colors rotated in ever-changing patterns, casting weird shadows along the ceiling and wall. The magnificence of it took Ian's breath away.

"Oh, my, how beautiful! Ah've niver seed innythin' like that. Ah wouldn't wonder if it were a magic lamp. Where in the world did yuh obtain it?"

"From a deranged genie. Follow me."

Tossing his jacket carelessly on the couch, Charles led Ian through the living room. Three doors led off a hallway. All were open.

"In here," the host indicated, pointing to the master bedroom. A thin, unhealthy sheen of perspiration had formed on his upper lip. As he turned back to see if Ian understood, the beads of sweat caught the light from the magic lamp, making him appear to have suddenly grown a multi-colored mustache.

"What's in there?" the Scot suddenly demanded, his own forehead now damp with cold warning.

"What do you think is in there?"

"Ah know a bedroom when Ah see one..."

"Congratulations."

"Ah dinna understan'. What business do we have in there? Ah think Ah would rather talk out here." The silence was deafening. Ian swallowed, then turned to stare at the lamp. "It's..." He was going to say "pretty," then changed his mind. "There's more room out here." Confusion tainted his soft voice.

"But it's more comfortable in the bedroom." The words held an ominous threat, not previously apparent to the untrained ear.

"Please..." The word was cried on an instinctual level, betraying barely suppressed terror.

"Please do – or please don't?" Charles retorted, relishing the syllables as living instruments of torture.

"Ah think Ah want to leave."

"An' Ah think it's too late for that," Charles parodied him. "Get in there and take off your clothes. I told you – I have a meeting in the morning and time... presses."

He laughed at his own joke as Ian moved back to the living room. Charles followed on his heels.

"What fer? Ah'll no be doing inny such thing."

"What fur?" the shorter man mocked. "What fur? What do you mean, what fur? You're not a boy." Then, with a dirty inflection, "Tell me you don't know how to turn up your ass to please a man."

"Turn up me arse?" Ian gasped, mouth dry, lips numb.

"That's right."

"Is that what yuh want? Is that why yuh brung me up here? To 'turn up me arse' fer yuh?"

"Bright boy."

"Ah will no' do it. That's dishonorable."

"There's no dishonor about it," came the answer, sneered over large, white teeth. "Taking money for sex is the oldest profession in the world."

"Never!" Ian screamed, voice strident with horror. "Ah dinna unnerstan' what yuh had in mind. Yuh said," he added accusingly, "what yuh were askin' me to do was respectable! This is not respectable! Ah want to leave."

Without bothering to reply, Charles stepped closer to his captive fly, then suddenly reached out a hand, placing it on Ian's groin. Frozen in horror, the taller man's eyes opened wide, betraying his shock. Stimulated by the look, Charles shoved Ian back, relishing the power at his command. Like a cat dropped from a great height, Ian never lost his balance. As he came to a stop several feet from the couch, Ian's own ire reached the flash point.

"Dinna lay a hand on me!" he warned, muscles in his jaw trembling with rage. When Charles only smiled, he raised a fist, shaking it in dire threat. "Yuh're crazy!"

Mistaking, or perhaps overplaying his hand, Charles attempted to repeat his past performance by placing a groping hand on Ian. Senses alert and fully functional, jaw tucked in, muscles tensed, Ian accepted the forward movement of the smaller man as a challenge.

Easily avoiding the touch, he grabbed Charles by the collar, shook him until his teeth rattled, then landed a blow to his stomach. As his "host" doubled over, pain racking his fine features, Ian snorted in triumph, than hit him again.

Discovering the physical activity a satisfying release after so long a time of reining in his emotions, Ian beat the man, pummeling him first with his right fist, then slapping him across the cheeks with his left.

Not satisfied with these blows, Ian drew breath in through distended nostrils, heaved his head back, teeth bared and howled to the ceiling.

"Ah am a wolf, an' Ah will not be treated like a dog. Yuh lied to me, an' so yuh will pay the price."

Before Charles could back away, Ian struck him again, this time an upper cut which sent him crashing into the wall. The vibration of the heavy weight caused the colorful round globe to crash to the floor, breaking into several large pieces. The room, once bathed in alternating colors, faded into black.

No genie escaped the magic lamp.

The destruction of so precious a possession brought Ian to his senses. With a sickening cry, half victory, half defeat, he held out his hands, wiped them in the air in a vain attempt to clean them, then danced away as Charles drew himself into a ball.

"Son of a bitch bastard," he cursed, wiping blood away from a bleeding mouth. "Get out. There's the door. Go."

"Yuh're damned right Ah will go," Ian threatened, taking a further step away from the vanquished, though not defeated, enemy on the floor. He was almost to the front door before Charles spoke again.

"One chance, Ian baby. And you better be listening, or you'll live to regret it." An instinct, as old as time, forced Ian to stop, back to his tormentor, and listen to his words. "I want your tight ass and I will have it, one way or another. If you don't – cooperate – if you walk out of here, then you had better be prepared to face the consequences."

"What... consequences?" came the low, uneasy question.

"I call Immigration in the morning and tell them that there's a certain Scot named Ian MacDhui, who isn't really a tourist – he's just a just penniless beggar. I'll explain to them that you've worked illegally under a false name."

"Go to hell."

"And that you left two underage kids alone in an apartment without adult supervision. In this country, that's called child endangerment, my friend. Rest assured, the authorities take a very dim view of aliens who come to the United States and abuse their children."

"They are not abused," Ian protested, confused, hurt and suddenly very, very frightened.

Charles ignored him, speaking over his protest.

"First, they take them away from you. Second, they throw you in jail while they make arrangements to deport you. Oh, they'll deport the kids, too. God knows where they'll end up; in some orphanage somewhere. That what you want?"

"No," Ian sobbed. "That's no' the dream...."

"It's up to you, sweetie. Say which way it'll be, right now."

"Ah swear, Ah canna do what yuh ask. It would kill me. Yuh're askin' me to give up me manhood."

"Not at all. What I'm offering you is a chance to *save* your manhood."

"Speak plainly," Ian demanded, but the words and their implications were already branded in his soul.

"You came to the new world for a new life, a fresh start."

"Ah came here fer a respectable job," Ian protested but the attempt was weak and unbecoming a man who already sensed his loss.

Charles nodded pleasantly.

"And you did not find one. What you found were low, degrading, poorly-paid positions. Hardly what you, or anyone else – your dead wife, for instance – would consider 'respectable.' You'll never find a better one because you have no skills."

"Ah'm a sheeper –"

"Which did not, apparently, keep a roof over your head in Scotland. Why should it in New York, where sheep are considered an endangered species?"

Holding one hand to his stomach where he still felt the effects of the blow Ian had delivered, Charles got slowly to his feet.

"How long do you have on your tourist visa? Six months? A year? By that time, you'll be begging in the streets for handouts . Or, worse yet, while the sheep man's away, his daughters will be prostituting themselves to the wolves, of which there are many in the Empire State."

"Stop!" Ian shrieked, placing his hands over his ears in supreme agony. "Ah dinna want to hear that."

"Perhaps not, but it would be foolish, naive of you, not to face facts. You're in this country on a tourist visa," Charles continued with a voice so cold it would have chilled the martini of any 5th Avenue purveyor. "No one of your class gets a work permit; the good ol' U.S. of A. doesn't want your type; we have enough failures of our own. If you have skills we need; if your coming to this country won't take jobs away from Americans; if you have money to start a business, hire American workers, fine and dandy."

He wiped the blood from his lip, all thought of personal pain forgotten.

"But a broken, penniless man with an obsolete skill? No. Add to the mix two underage daughters, and that makes three on the welfare rolls. Uncle Sam doesn't want that; the taxpayers, of which I am one, don't want that. So when your visa is up, it's back to where you came, Sheeper. And then what?"

"It won't be that way!"

"What do you do back in Scotland? Crawl around on the lousy hills or moors or whatever you call them, beat on your chest and declare yourself a failure? Or do you lose yourself in some hole in the wall in Glasgow and then sell your ass for twenty shillings a bang, or work the blow-job circuit for ten?"

Crossing to another lamp, Charles turned it on, adding illumination to his words.

"Get real, BaBa Black Sheep. Face the music; do a jig to the sound of bagpipes, wipe the snots from your nose and make up your mind."

"Ah... Ah canna do what yuh ask," Ian cried, sinking to his knees.

"No?" Charles whispered, brushing a leg against Ian's shoulder, then stroking his head as though he were an animal and not a man. "I think you can. I think you will."

"In the name o' God," came the broken-hearted plea. But the words were smothered into the carpet as his face dropped into the rich, luxuriant nap.

"Keep thinking, Ian," the master prodded, arousing himself by the sound of his own voice and the dire predictions he preached. "Of those bright little faces, waiting with expectation for their hero – their daddy – to bring home the money. If you don't, I've already told you what happens to them. They become whores in your place. And if you do bring home fifty dollars a night, you tell them a little white lie. Say to them you have a respectable job. That all their troubles are over."

Fingering his belt, Charles leered over the prostrate man.

"They don't need to know any more than that. In six months, a year, you have a bank account, a car, a home... and Immigration suddenly loves you. They can't give you a permanent visa fast enough. You're a hero, again, and no one's the wiser about how you obtain it."

"Yuh're killin' me. Yuh're killin' me," but the words had no relevance to his meaning.

"Good. I thought you'd see it my way. And besides, you're a pretty boy; a *very* pretty boy. Wasting all those looks would be a sin. And sinners go to hell."

"Hell? Yuh're pootin' me in hell."

"Vituperations only stimulate me," Charles laughed in sincere good humor. "Now, why don't you behave yourself and relax? Have a good time; enjoy yourself."

"Yuh're crazy."

"Oh, I've been called a lot of things," Charles agreed, maintaining the smile on his face. "But you know what they say: sticks and stones may break my bones, but words can never hurt me. As a child, I never found that rhyme to hold much truth, but as a man, I've widened my opinion. Knowing what you do, Mr. MacDhui, the choice is yours: either do as I say and earn your money... or your bastard children get taken away from you, or starve to death."

"Not – not bastard children," Ian protested, stunned by the equation put to him.

"No? Well, as you say. But answer me this: how much is your pride worth?"

"Me pride ?" came the startled, dismayed question.

"*Aye.* Your pride," he mocked. "And if you don't like that word, try another. How much is your *arse* worth? I offered you a chance and you hurt me. Now, you pay for that little extravagance before we get on with what you came here for."

"What – what do yuh mean?"

"I want you to beg my forgiveness."

"Beg yuh?" The words were strangled with horror.

"You heard me. You're already on your knees, so that's a good start. Put your hands together in supplication and beg my forgiveness. Or, I make a certain phone call and it's all over. You'll never see those kids of yours again."

"Oh, Christ on the cross. What in God's name have Ah ever done to deserve this?"

"You were born poor and you were created pretty," came the simply-stated answer.

With a groan of hideous resignation, Ian crossed his fingers then readjusted his weight on his knees. Once in that unfamiliar position, he swayed like a mighty oak in a winter gale before emitting a high-pitched noise, bearing no earthly semblance to articulate language.

"Beg," Charles demanded. "So I can understand you."

"Ah beg yuh," came the sentence, now carefully enunciated.

"Look up."

Ian raised his eyes, shining with emotion. When Charles found them, he held the stare, as a lover would hold the body of a cherished one.

"Pray."

"Ah'm prayin'."

A cold, calculating smile was his reward.

"Very good. Now, go to the bedroom and strip."

With a death rattle of defeat, Ian crawled down the hall, entered the bedroom and stopped a yard from the bed. Rising awkwardly to his feet, he began unbuttoning his shirt. With deadened fingers, the task proved nearly impossible. Yet, as an unsolicited miracle, the fastenings came undone and he stood, bare-chested, in the middle of the floor.

"Remove it, then proceed."

"Megan MacDhui," Ian prayed, this time to a different soul and with a different earnestness, "close yuh're eyes."

Discovering his right arm would not bend, Ian was forced to perform the work with his left. As the garment slipped off his shoulders, then dropped silently to the floor, he began on the button fly of his trousers. One, two, three, four buttons, each coming undone with a nearly indiscernible pop.

Wiggling his body without thinking, Ian pushed the pants down, leaving him in shoes, socks and thigh-length drawers. Charles took in the spectacle with undisguised delight.

"Where'd you get those?" he chuckled, pointing to the undergarment. "Out of the 1900 Sears Roebuck Catalogue?"

"They protect me when Ah'm out on the moors," came the whispered response. Having arrived in the Big City, Ian was learning shame. Like his farmer's pocketbook before it, he would now and forever, hold the wearing of so common a thing as long underwear to be an article of disgrace.

"Nothing will protect you tonight."

"Please –"

"Pull them down. I want to see you. Naked."

The pause between his sentences was meant to humiliate.

The tactic succeeded.

Working the clinging, sweat-adhered cotton underclothing down, first to his knees, then all the way to the floor, Ian did not raise his eyes, using the task as an excuse. Only when he stepped out of the clothing did he look up.

And died one thousand deaths.

"Pretty boy. Pretty boy," Charles sighed in hedonistic fantasy.

Two steps brought him into physical contact with the moor man. Running his hand down Ian's sinewy arms, he then placed a hand, palm down on the man's chest. Breathing heavily, his fingers played with one nipple, not satisfied until it was hard and aroused. Grabbed the long, dark locks, Charles drew Ian's head to his. Lips meeting in an open mouth kiss, he held the virtual prisoner to him until both men were nearly blue from lack of oxygen.

"Step back, darling. To the bed."

The words were soft, sweet, tender, belying the implicit warning of non-compliance. Ian backed a step, two steps, until his naked legs touched the blanket.

"Get on the bed." He complied and Denning smiled. "Now, for your first lesson. You must learn to please your customers. Undress me. Gently," he warned. Ian's hands groped out in compliance, but the effort was only partially satisfactory. "With your eyes open. Look delighted; astonished. Make small gasping noises of pleasure. Admire me. I want to be admired," Charles added with meaning.

"Oh, God.... oh, God. The body o' a man.... the body o' a man. Oh, Jesus Christ, what am Ah doin'?"

"You're earning a living for the wee ones in your den," Charles purred, throwing back his own head and closing his eyes. "Be nice, Ian."

"Oh, Christ, fine, fine, fine," the words came, tumbling out on one another, like acrobats on a high wire. And then again, "Fine, fine, fine."

As the clothing was removed, Charles began a slow gyration, using Ian's rhythm to choreograph his dance. Not unwary of the untamed animal on his bed, the hunter's caution was transmitted to Ian, who tacitly acknowledged it by drawing back his hands, then gently, ever so tenderly, running his fingers down Charles' belly.

"Fine, fine, fine...."

Sighing in hedonistic delight, Charles whispered, "You've come this far. A little farther, little lamb, and then I play ram to your ewe."

"No! No!"

"For your daughters, dear Ian. Remember them and all things are possible."

The statement, so very like what Ian had said at the King's Arms pub so many eons ago, came back to him in a flash. Not of inspiration but of despair.

*When a man has love, all things is possible.*

Had it been within his power, he would have stricken the expression from the universe. For he now knew it to be an untruth.

The first thing that struck Ian was the distant sound of a man sobbing. Puzzled at first, then frightened at the persistent, broken-hearted keening, he attempted to place his hands over his ears to block out the sound. He was distracted in this worthy endeavor when hearing another, far closer noise, this time in the form of words.

"Ian. Ian MacDhui."

Surprised to hear his own name being spoken in such a sing-song cadence, and in so close a proximity to the sobbing, he whined and twisted in bed. Crying in sudden pain, his hand flew to his back, coming away with a mixture of blood and sweat. Worse, the effort strained other muscles, which, until that moment, he had not realized were throbbing in dull, persistent agony. Groaning aloud put an end to the sobbing, bringing with it the harsh reality that it had been his cries which woke him. Likewise, the sadistic, grinning face of Charles Denning leering at him from across the pillow explained who had cooed his name. He instinctively pulled away in revulsion.

Laughing at the reaction, the overlord viciously kicked him off the bed with his bare foot.

"Get up," he growled, his voice now low and husky. "Get out of here. I have to sleep."

Heeding the words more from an innate comprehension than any physical capability to decipher them, Ian quivered, making retrograde movements across the carpet, no longer a man but a spineless creature caught in the bogs of the Underworld.

"Get your clothes and go," came the second warning.

A long, agonized pause ensued the beast on the floor spoke in a language he no longer understood.

"Me money? Me fifty dollars?"

"You can get it tonight."

"Tonight?" came the uncomprehending question.

"Next time. Some other time."

"Now.... please. Ah want me money, now." When Charles did not respond, Ian crawled on hands and knees toward the head of the bed. "Ah know yuh have it. Ah saw it.... yuh showed it me. Please. Canna Ah not have it now?"

"I said next time and I mean next time. You don't think this is the end, do you?" the man demanded, finally rolling over on his side to face the distorted features of the vanquished creature on the floor. "I own you. Lock, stock and barrel. When I beckon, you come."

"Ah... dinna unnerstan'."

"You will. Now get the fuck out of here!"

It was an order and Ian was no longer a free man, but a thing, an object to obey rather than to think.

With his nose dripping a long, thin stream of semen-colored mucus, he gathered his clothing and crawled away, having lost not only his pride and his virginity but a word from his vocabulary.

Respectable.

# CHAPTER 18

The cab ride from Mac's Bar and Grill to Charles Denning's apartment had seemed a short trip; the walk back an eternity.

By the time Ian reached familiar territory, it was nearing four o'clock in the morning. Stumbling over his shadow, he tripped, fell against a shuttered door, bounced and landed, palms out to break his fall, against a window.

It was not his own clumsiness, but the unexpectedness of staring into his reflection which caused Ian to pull back with revulsion. Crying with shame at his disheveled appearance, he toppled backward. This time, there was nothing to hold him and he hit the hard, cold sidewalk, tail-bone first.

For the first time in his life, Ian was acutely sensitive of his body. Emitting a high wail of misery, he rolled onto his side, turning his face away from the tell-tale glass. When this posture presented his countenance to the world, he flipped over, pressing nose to wall. Had he the power, Ian MacDhui would have merged into, then through the wall and onto oblivion without regret.

A couple, walking hand-in-hand, passed him. Neither paid him the slightest attention. "Down-and-outers" were beneath contempt.

Their proximity, however casual, caused Ian to suffer a sudden fit of chills and trembling. Drawing his arms around himself, he sniffed, moaned, then began banging his head into the wall. Without money, devoid of hope, such a desperate was the only way he knew to bring on stupor.

"Treat you pretty rough, did he?" a dispassionate voice inquired. From the sound, the speaker stood a million miles away. Without responding directly, Ian curled closer into himself and continued his downward spiral toward self-destruction. "That's no way to do yourself in," the voice continued.

This time, Ian paused in his repetitive action to raise a bloodshot eye toward this new source of torment.

"Leave me alone," he ordered, then snorted as the audacity of his command struck him. Bitter the idea of the lowliest of the low giving orders to anyone.

"I'd be glad to," the disembodied voice continued, maintaining a position out of his line of vision and therefore presenting only the feet and legs of a human being. "But you'll give the district a bad name. It won't do to have the cops pick you up around here. If you're intent on suicide, drag yourself down to the East River."

"If yuh'll point me in the right direction, Ah shall be eternally grateful," he hiccupped from having swallowed too much air with his sobs.

"That's not saying much, if your eternity ends in half an hour." The tone held no concern. The blunt statement of fact apparently required none.

"Aye, yuh're right," Ian agreed, wiping his nose on his wrinkled shirt sleeve. "But no' much is all Ah have to give."

"Then it's not enough. Get up and move your ass out of here."

"Me ass," he repeated with utter self-loathing. "Ah've a'ready 'got that up' once tonight. What more do yuh want wid me?"

"I told you. You stay here, you'll get picked up and carted away. Then the cops keep a sharp eye peeled for more of your kind and we're all in trouble."

"Ah dinna care aboot meself. Let them take me."

"You'd better care, baby. Once they put the mark on you, you're prime meat."

"Go to hell."

"Big enough for two, is it?"

"Leave me alone." Then, more softly, "Please."

"Only Park Avenue whores can afford self-pity, MacDhui. The rest of us have to pick ourselves up – literally. By our bootstraps as the old soldiers like to say. And some who fought other wars without boots."

The statement struck him as peculiar, but it was a word in the first part of the statement that caught his ear.

"How do yuh know me name?" And then, as the more potent statement sunk in, "How did yuh know Ah am a –?"

"Whore? Simple. Your pants are on backwards."

Eyes wide with shame, Ian dragged his eyes away from the talking legs to check his trousers. Surprisingly, they were on correctly. Frowning with an innocent lack of comprehension, he finally lifted his colorless, nearly translucent eyes up past the speaker's lower body.

"Yuh!" he gasped in complete astonishment. "The lady frum the bar."

"From the bar," Delilah agreed, shaking her head with a surprise equal to his own. "Now, get up," she continued, wondering at the same time why she bothered. "Stinking dogs attract flies."

"Ah am not a stinkin' dog. Ah'm a wolf." And then remembering, "an' a whore."

"You're a pretty boy and you paid the price. Now stand up on your goddamn feet and be a man."

Raising wet eyes to her dry blue orbs, he raised a hand, not for her to hold, but by way of punctuating his question.

"How? How kin Ah get back what Ah lost?"

The answer was written in the harsh neon of an overhead advertisement.

"You can't."

"Then... how kin Ah be a man?"

"The same way I can be a woman."

Awareness washed over the sufferer like a chamber pot emptied from a third story window.

"Not yuh.... Not yuh, too?"

She laughed derisively, as though seeing the joke.

"What do you think?"

"Ah think yuh're beautiful."

Anger rose, in the form of two red spots, rivaling the faded rouge on Delilah's cheeks.

"Take a closer look, honey. Pay my price and I'll show you the scars." And then, more suggestively, "Inside and out."

"No," he protested, gagging on the horror of her statement. "What kind of New World is this that Ah've cume to?"

It was just too funny. Bursting out into a gale of laughter, Delilah placed hands on hips.

"An upside-down world. That's why your pants are on backwards."

Blinking in hopeless wonder, Ian shook his head.

"But they're not." When she continued to laugh, he finally managed a grin. "Ah checked."

"And if you'd check further, you'd discover you're still a man. Now, get up. You'll find the world looks a little better when you're on your feet... Wolf Eyes."

"It sure as hell doesna look very good when yuh're on yer arse!"

"I'm glad to see you're getting some sense of humor back. Now, give me your hand."

Without waiting for him to make the first move, she grasped her fingers around his and hoisted him, with some effort, to his feet. The sight of his thin, muscular frame towering above her prompted an appreciative whistle.

"They grow them big where you come from. And where is that?"

"Scotland."

"What state is that in?"

"In the U.K. United Kingdom."

"Never heard of it."

"Scotland, England, Wales –"

"Oh," she interrupted, waving away the rest of the geography lesson. "What in God's name are you doing in New York?"

"Lookin' fer respectable work."

"You sure as hell missed that boat!" Then, looking upward, past the tousled hair on his brow, "Where are you staying?"

"In a flat – an apartment. Wid me two daughters."

"Wonderful. Two daughters. Two… grown daughters?"

"Twelve an' nine goin' on ten."

"You'll never win at craps with those numbers." Then, brusquely, "Come on."

"Where?"

"You'll need a place to wash up. A shower and a shave and maybe something on those cuts. You can't go home looking like raw hamburger. And you'll need time to concoct a story for those little prying eyes."

"Lie to me children?"

"You're catching on. I have a place above the bar. You can work on your face up there."

"Why would yuh do this fer me?"

"Let's just say, misery loves company."

With a nod of her head, Delilah walked off. Ian hesitated, then, like a pull-toy on a string, trotted after her.

The shower water was hot, but not hot enough. Adjusting the tap toward the left, Ian withstood the searing temperature change with a stoicism born of moors and misery.

He did not have to be told that all the hot water and soap in the world would not wash away his sins, yet he made a gallant effort, scrubbing away at chafe marks around his neck with vicious energy. When close to bleeding, he paused to throw back his head and, open-mouthed, let the liquid heat pound into the opening between spread jaws.

Gargling the water, he spat it out and repeated the process until his lips were red and the soft palate close to blistering. Still unsatisfied, Ian bite off a corner of soap like a naughty child and chewed it, stopping only when bubbles emerged through distended nostrils.

Hands, neck, face, mouth endured their cleansing without a sound. It was only when his reluctant arms reached his lower portions to wash away their transgressions that the moor man cried. Tears, hotter than city tap water, streamed down his cheeks, burning the tender flesh, scalding the soul beneath.

"Oh, God, Meggie MacDhui, how kin yuh ever forgive me? How kin yuh love me ag'in, knowing what Ah done?"

Her answer came in the form of several sharp blows to the bathroom door.

"Hurry up! And don't use all the hot water. I need to shower myself, and it don't come back fast."

Shaking with nervous energy at the reply he had not been expecting, Ian jerked the water off, leaving himself half covered with scum. Grabbing a towel, he made a rapid attempt at drying himself, then hurried to the door, opening it no more than a quarter inch.

Delilah, holding a portable steam iron to his shirt, glanced over her shoulder, making a "hurry up" gesture.

"Dry yourself off and get out here. I've only got so much mercy in "me" heart. I'm tired and I need to get some sleep."

The answer was immediately forthcoming, although, like the pounding on the door, it was hardly the one she expected.

"Ah canna."

"You 'canna' what?"

"Ah canna cume out."

"Why not?"

"Because yuh've got me clothes."

Her astonishment melted into uncontrollable laughter.

"Jesus Christ! You've just lost your' virginity' sleeping with a man for money, you're in the apartment of a prostitute and you won't come out because you're not dressed. That's rich! Ian MacDhui, if words were money, you'd be a millionaire!"

Making a valiant attempt to cover himself with the scanty white towel, Ian tiptoed out, face flushed from shame. Noting his color, Delilah sighed and took a closer look at her guest.

"There's 'hot,' and there's 'hot,' boy, and you've got them both. Turn around."

"What fer?"

"So I can look at you." When he hesitated, she made a whirling motion with her hand. Embarrassed, he complied, revealing the taut, muscular frame of a man used to hard work. "Good God, what you have, you ought to bottle," she replied with a low whistle.

"Ah'm naught but a –"

"Honey, do they have mirrors where you come from? Ever catch a glimpse of yourself in a pond? Ever see your reflection in a pane of glass?"

"Ah tried not to look."

"I don't mean just now. I mean ever. Don't you know?"

"Know what?"

"Where is this Scotland of yours? Next to Transylvania? You're a hunk and a half. You've not only got a movie star face, you've got a body to die for. I should have taken a closer look at you in the bar."

"Why?"

She opened her mouth to reply, then changed her mind in uncharacteristic reticence.

"Never mind. What's done is done. What is it they say: if it happens, it was meant to happen? Something about free will."

"Well, it had better be, because that's aboot all Ah kin afford," he tried with a shy smile.

"Maybe," she agreed. "Here. I've done what I can for the shirt. The rest of the wrinkles you'll have to stretch out over those damn muscles."

Ian dressed as Delilah watched, never taking her eyes off him. She did not speak again until he was forced to look down while buttoning his fly.

"What do you know about the business? About the men and women who sell their services for money?"

"Nuthin'," He admitted, working the buttons. "Except that which Ah learned this night."

"And it came as a revelation to you?" When he nodded, she continued. "It's one of the dirtiest jobs in the world. Not as bad as some... there are worse. But it's a hell of a way to make a living. If you're not cut out for it, it eats you insides out."

"What could be worse?" he queried, finally looking up to meet her eyes.

"Selling dope. Needin' it yourself so bad you'd sell it to a kid. Hooking others on it so you can supply your own habit."

"Aye," he agreed.

"Selling murder's another that's worse. Murder for hire. I've slept with a few of those; known some of them pretty intimately. They have dead eyes, Ian MacDhui. They have 'em and they cause 'em."

"Yuh've – slept with them, knowing what they do?"

She shrugged, then examined the end of a fingernail, finally biting off a hangnail as she spoke.

"Why not? They have money. It all spends the same. But we were talking about you."

"Me?"

She nodded.

"Working as a whore – a male whore – involves eating a lot of shit – and learning how to swallow it with a smile on your lips. It's giving and taking, with emphasis on the hard core, physical aspects of 'love.' What did Charlie do to you?"

"He... fucked me," Ian muttered, looking over her shoulder into the distance. "He made me... suck him."

"And he came near to strangling you – that much is obvious. What else? Did he tie you up?"

"Me hands.... while he was whippin' me wid a belt," he choked, drilling a hole in the distant wall.

"And you didn't fuck him?"

"No!" came the startled reply, as Ian's eyes were ripped away from his exploration for oil. "Why would yuh say a thing like that?"

"Because there are those who want what you have to offer. Most, in fact, expect you to accommodate them both ways."

"How – could Ah do that?"

She rolled her eyes.

"You have two daughters; I wouldn't think I'd have to draw you a diagram."

"But to be aroused wid a man... how could Ah? Ah dinna have that inclination."

"No? Maybe you don't think you do, but the act is the same. Where's your wife?"

"Me wife? Me darlin'? She's dead and buried," he whispered, blood rushing to his face.

"How long ago?"

"Three years."

"Three years. So... what have you done with your feelings?"

"Me feelin's?"

"Don't play innocent with me."

"Ah dinna have feelings," but the lie was apparent. Protruding his lower lip at his poor dissembling, Ian shook his head. "What Ah have, Ah've learned to poot away."

"Ever get aroused in the shower? Find yourself hot and bothered lying abed at night? Hold yourself for comfort, maybe, and spill a little seed into a balled-up pillow?"

"Ah dinna want to talk about it," he protested, holding his hands over his ears. She gave him a moment, then roughly drew his arms away.

"Maybe not, but your sexual feelings don't die with your spouse, no matter how you loved her. Your body keeps on functioning, day after day, night after night. Maybe you didn't consummate any new relationships, but you burned and you hungered, like any other man."

"Why are yuh sayin' this?"

"Just making a point. That you make 'love' in all sorts of different ways, just to stay alive; because you have to."

"Iffn me body's betrayed me –"

Delilah cut him off with a curt brush of her hand.

"Betrayed you, hell. You went through half the routine tonight; for all of that, the other way's easier."

"No.... Never!"

"Suit yourself," she sighed, putting a hand to her head. "I'm tired and you're giving me a headache. Get out of here."

Startled, yet sensing his chance to escape before further damage was done, Ian slid toward the door. When he looked back, she was not following him with her eyes. If she had been, he would have bolted, like a rabbit. But he was not a rabbit. His genus was canine, of the wolf variety. Not hunting, at the moment, but cautious.

Curious.

"You have more to say. Ah'm listenin'."

"Get out of here. I've said too much."

He shut the door, but behind him, effectively locking himself inside. With a madly pounding heart, Ian swallowed and repeated his statement.

"Yuh had more to say. Ah'm listenin'."

"I'm not promising anything."

"A'right."

"And I'm not saying life will be easy. Quite the contrary."

"A'right."

"The money's out there, Ian MacDhui. You've got what they're looking for."

"What... have Ah got?"

"A handsome face, a great body, a tight ass. And grey eyes. Wolf eyes," she added. "Cunning, wary, challenging... and something else. A sadness."

"Ah ought to bottle it," he tried, remembering her words. She reacted, first with a smile, then with a face as old and as grim as her occupation.

"Get out. Go home. Don't do any thinking; get some sleep. Tell the kids you got in a fight. Whipped the bastards good. They'll believe you."

"The pity of it is, they will."

"Then believe it yourself. You'll sleep better."

"Ah might at that," he admitted, finally slipping away into the cruel, harsh dawn of a New Day.

# CHAPTER 19

Meg was at the kitchen sink making rather louder than usual noises as she cleaned up after breakfast. Storm had gone downstairs to buy a newspaper. It was Saturday, the long-expected "day off," and they had decided to go to the cinema, in celebration. No mention was made of purchasing books or buying a home "wid trees."

"Ah'll jest be a minute," Ian promised, slipping into the small water closet and shutting the door. This was the moment he had been waiting for. With the children occupied at chores, he could guarantee himself five, perhaps ten minutes of undisturbed privacy.

What Ian MacDhui had to do was not easy and he had been dreading the chore since his arrival home that morning. Barely able to sit a chair, he had roamed the Spartan rooms with undisguised anxiety, jumping at the least sound, then spinning, cat-like, on the daughters, then making unnecessarily loud conversation to cover his tracks.

As befit their roles in life, neither had said a word; the questioning, all-knowing stares he so feared, had not appeared. There had been no reference to his nocturnal wandering. This, to his tormented mind, stood as one of the great miracles of the Age.

He had talked too much, he knew that, but he could not stop his tongue and they did not seem to mind.

"Ah couldna sleep," he had begun, wondering if they would believe the falsehood he was about to weave. "Ah found meself outside a bar an' Ah went in. Had a few too many," he confessed to their silent, wide-eyed stares. "Ah know Ah shouldna, but knowin' today was me day off, Ah thought, 'what the hell'? Fell in wid sum fellas an' they paid fer the drinks," he added, least they accuse him of squandering the family fortune.

He could not have guessed it was the last thing on their minds.

"Talked the night away," he bragged, feeling stronger in his lies, amazed at how easy it was to dissemble once the first step had been taken. "Jolly chaps, those. They wanted to know where Scotland was. Imagine that? Educated in this great country an' they dinna know."

Warming to his part, Ian had performed a little jig in the middle of the floor, laughing away any doubts they might be harboring.

"Ah tried to explain Scotland was part o' the U.K. an' what do yuh think they said?"

"What's the U.K.?" Storm supplied on cue.

Slapping his hands together in exaggerated delight, Ian nodded gleefully.

"Right as rain. 'What is the U.K.?' they demanded. Ah had to tell them, an' they were amazed!"

"I just bet they were," Meg agreed. Then, without prompting, added, "Did they know we have a Queen over there, or do they think she's an elected official, like the president?"

It was a test, a sounding board, a bit of bait twisted on the end of a hook. He snapped it up like a hungry bass.

"A queen? Furst o' all, they thought we had a king, an' second o' all, they asked aboot the guards at Buckingham Palace. Apparently they heard them fellas never talked if spoken to an' they wanted to know if it were true."

"What did yuh tell them?"

"Ah said o' course it were true. An' they asked if they had an itch, could they scratch it? An' Ah said no."

"And then what?" Storm asked, picking stray threads from the tablecloth.

"They wanted to know how a bloke cume to have a job like that, an' Ah told them they was soldiers in a cavalry outfit –"

"An' they started whoopin' up like cowboys an' Indians," Meg dutifully supplied.

Ian slapped his knee.

"Yuh might as well a' been there, yuh know the story."

Both Meg and Storm laughed in sad agreement, but their tempered emotion had nothing to do with Western films and actors made up to look like warriors. At that point, Meg decided to clean the kitchen and Storm to buy a newspaper. As Ian hopped, skipped and jumped to his dresser drawers "fer a quick change o' clothes," the two wise, old children assembled at the outside door.

"He's been in a fight," Storm whispered, the harshness of the statement belying the act she had just perpetrated for her father.

"No, he hasna," Meg demurred. It was not a denial as much as a show of support.

"He's gone an' gotten hisself beat up an' he doesna want us to know aboot it. Ah bet he spent the night in jail."

"Ah bet no such thing, an' keep yer voice down. He's done sumethin' bad, a'right, but Ah canna poot me finger on the deed."

"He's spent his last pence, that's what. A group o' fellas buyin' drinks. He must think we're daft. They saw him cumin' an' hit him up to buy a round or three. Ah suppose when he ran out o' money, they clapped the cuffs on him an' dragged him away."

"Aye, Ah suppose," Meg agreed, although she believed no such thing. Then, "Off wid yuh to buy that newspaper or he'll be askin' what's takin' yuh so long."

"Ah dinna want to go to the cinema."

"Well, it's that or listen to him lie fer another three hours befer he falls asleep on the couch. Have yer pick."

"Ah'm goin'," Storm groused and slipped away, her plodding footsteps audible two flights down.

Finally alone, and unnaturally comforted by the ease in which he had explained away his midnight sojourn, Ian steadied himself by taking in a lungful of air. It was, he reminded himself with unaccustomed dourness, "time to pay the piper."

Unfastening the buttons of his trousers, Ian gingerly tugged them down, thinking to let them rest at the midway point between his knees. When the touch of the material, suspended between groin and thighs caused him to dry retch in sick remembrance, he quickly threw them off, hands trembling.

Tossing the pants away, Ian wiped clammy fingers on damp shirt, then craned his neck, trying for a glimpse of his posterior. He did not know, yet had to know, what marks the brute had left. It was neither welts from the belt, nor imprints from the flat of Charles' hand, Ian feared, but rather, some other, more metaphysical stigma of his crime, branded into his flesh for all eternity.

When he could see no outward sign of guilt, he twisted further, hampered in part by his own stiff muscles, but more so by his tell-tale heart, pounding so rapidly he could not get oxygen to his brain.

Just before passing out, he whimpered and averted his eyes, pausing in this unholy quest to clear his head before continuing.

"Oh, me God, what have Ah done?" he inquired of the mirror. But like the walls, the looking glass held no verbal answers. Instead, it revealed the reflection of a man in torment; a man, whose face, so ruddy and innocent only a day gone by, was now lined and grey, to match his eyes.

"Ah am not afraid," he continued, jutting the clefted jaw in Celtic defiance. "Ah have nuthin' to fear, but fear itself."

It was a handy quote, one he had often heard Megan MacDhui use when speaking to her infant children.

"Naught to fear but fear itself, me darlin's," she had taught them. "Yer souls are pure an' yer hearts are good. The world is a hard place, but yuhr father an' Ah are beside yuh, holdin' yer hands as yuh reach out to take these furst steps. An' when the time cumes when yuh're on yer own, poot yer trust in God an' in knowing yuh're niver alone. Do what's right an' yuh canna do what's wrong."

He wished he had not thought of the rest of her words. Their meaning, once a source of inspiration, had become a black spot on his heart.

"Oh, Christ, Meggie, Ah canna see a mark... but *Ah* know it's there an' yuh know it, too. What in God's name am Ah gonna do?" And then, more agonizingly, "Ah kin *feel* it!"

Looking again at his buttocks, Ian saw only the smooth, taut, unmarked flesh. With his eyes thus occupied, he did not see the more tangible – and obvious – problem.

Standing by the door, open no more than a quarter inch, stood Storm MacDhui. She did not understand what he was looking for, nor why he cried, but inside her soul, she registered the hurt.

It was a pain she would not easily forget. Nor, when transferred to Meg, the diversion-maker, would she forget the burden, now for three to share.

The film they choose to watch at the cinema was a comedy. All three MacDhuis laughed at the appropriate places, clapped with the rest of the audience and threw popcorn at the screen whenever the scoundrel appeared. Announcing the day a "ruddy success," they went to bed early, each declaring they were "tired to the bone."

At midnight exactly, Ian rose from his bed, drew on his clothes and scribbled a note to his daughters. His bold, wide, looping penmanship declared, "Gone out. Got a good night job. See yuh in the morning. Love, Ian."

Paper in hand, he tiptoed to their bedroom door. Listening intently to be assured they were asleep, he hesitated, then, feeling the cold perspiration of guilt dripping from his armpits, lost his nerve and retreated.

Crumpling the paper, he paused by the grocery bag, doing service as a waste can, to throw it away. Once deposited therein, he felt no better. Imagining tiny fingers searching the dust bin for evidence of his deception, he reached inside and retrieved it. Discovering a second discarded paper, he took that, too.

By the light of the on-again, off-again neon from the window, he recognized the "Happy Pay Day" sign Meg and Storm had discarded. With a broken-hearted sob of hopelessness, he stuffed both into his trousers pocket and, like a rat deserting a sinking ship, scurried away.

It took him three turns around the block to work up his nerve, and then another wasted twenty minutes trying to retrace his steps of the night before. When he finally presented himself at Delilah's apartment door, it took the physical reassurance of his left hand on his right to bring it to the wood and knock.

"Who's there?" called the gruff, familiar voice.

"Ian MacDhui."

"Door's open."

This time he did not hesitate. Turning the knob, he found it unlocked, as promised. Considering that the first time he had not been lied to or tricked since arriving in the New World, Ian put on a happy face and entered.

Delilah was sitting on the couch, facing the door as he came in. Her features betrayed no emotion, neither happy nor sad. Taking her noncommittal attitude as a lukewarm welcome, he hesitated.

"What are you doing, working for the flies? Come in and shut the door. Management doesn't appreciate open advertising," she added, underscoring by implication what her words did not.

"Thank yuh."

With the door closed behind him, Ian faced the woman with his hands folded together, resting below his navel. Her expression did not alter.

"You paint a charming picture," she finally remarked, breaking the silence. When he did not reply, she rolled her eyes. "How'd you sleep?"

"Rough."

"What did you tell the kids?"

"Ah dinna tell them innythin'. Ah took them to the movin' picture show."

"The *movies*," she corrected.

"Aye. The movies. Ah fergit that's what yuh call the cinema. But Ah have to admit, it dinna sound inny better than 'moving pictures.'"

Delilah started to smile, then caught herself.

"What did you come back here for?"

"Yuh said... yuh might help. Ah'm a drownin' man. Ah need help."

"You need help, all right. But I'm not sure you need the kind I can give."

"Yuh've not had second thoughts?" he cried in desperation.

"I never second guess myself," came the flat reply. "There's no percentage in it. But you don't know what you're asking."

Squaring his shoulders, Ian repeated, nearly in order, what he had rehearsed to himself all day and half the night.

"When Ah was in Scotland, Meggie MacDhui an' Ah used to read the newspapers. They were full o' success stories aboot how a man might make a new start in America. Meggie knew people. She talked to 'em an' repeated what they said. Ah have it all here," he pleaded, placing his right hand over his heart. "If yuh canna git an immigration visa, an' Ah doubt you kin," he continued, words tumbling from his lips slower than the speed of his brain, "then go on a tourist visa. All yuh have to do is tell them yuh're cumin' back an' yuh won't have inny trouble. Not lyin', exactly," he hastened to add, "but not quite the truth."

He cleared his throat and swallowed hard before continuing with the precious words.

"Say yuh want to show yer family the U.S. of A. an' make them believe it. They'll let yuh out."

Ian paused, slowly unfolded his fingers, then scratched his head in simple puzzlement.

"Sorta sounds like bein' in Scotland is like bein' in jail. 'They'll let yuh out.' That's how she poot it. 'There's thousands befer yuh an' yuh hav'na the skills nor the money to git a work permit. So jest say yuh want a holiday an' then when yuh git to the States, find yuhrse'f a respectable job. Iffn yuh work so hard an' so diligent, yuh make yerself 'indispensable' then the fella what hired yuh kin apply to the Authorities fer a work visa. It happens all the time, she said. Ah wonder, now, if she weren't mistaken."

"You're coming of age," Delilah agreed.

"But no matter. We believed, an' here Ah am."

"What you've come to me for is hardly respectable."

He agreed by nodding his head, and did not belabor the point. That argument had died an ignoble death twenty-four hours ago.

"Ah have no home to return to, so there's no thought o' returnin'. Mr. Denning reminded me o' that, an' he made a good point."

She imagined Mr. Denning had offered a great deal of sage advice.

"He knows how to get under a man's skin."

Ian shivered at the undisguised reference.

"Ah know Ah canna earn money moppin' floors, nor flippin' burgers. Ah been to every place on the map beggin' fer a job an' what Ah'm qualified fer is not repeatable in front o' a lady."

She laughed and patted the sofa cushion beside her. He accepted the offer, demurely placing himself a foot away from her body.

"Ah've failed as a sheep farmer an' innyway, sheep is an 'endangered species' in Manhattan. So Ah have to think aboot me daughters."

"And what 'aboot' you?"

"Ah'll think aboot me later. When Ah have money in me pocket."

"That's what they all say, baby. All the innocents. 'I'm only doing it for the money.' Like the kids who take the Greyhound to Broadway, hoping for a Big Break. When it comes in the form of a porno movie and they're starving, they say 'I'm only doing it until something better comes along.'"

Compressing her lips a moment, Delilah might have been recounting a personal experience.

"Or the gambler who goes to Vegas, promising himself he knows his limit. First it's his pocket money, then all the cash he can draw on his credit card, then the savings bonds and finally his house. Everyone thinks they know their limit."

If Ian understood her illustrations, he gave no indication.

"Mr. Charles Denning said he would pay me fifty dollars fer one night's work. Was that a lie?"

"You're worth that. And more," she replied, arching one appreciative eyebrow.

"Why?"

"Because you're good looking, because you have a wild air about you, and because you haven't forgotten how to cry."

"Iffn Ah got what it takes, then Ah'm willin' to enter this dirty life o' yuhrs."

"Don't say I didn't warn you."

Reaching for her purse, Delilah stood, waited until Ian was on his feet then indicated the door. As they stepped out, she hesitated, then pursed her lips.

"This is none of my business, you know. You're nothing to me. You had better understand that from the start. Sink or swim, you do it on your own. Understand?"

"Aye."

"Then come with me."

"Where we goin'?"

"Downstairs. To the 'office.' I work out of Mac's and occasionally I throw a small favor his way. Do you know what I mean by a favor?"

"No."

"You will. Because you'll be giving them yourself. Come on."

With the door shut and locked behind them, the prostitute and the prostitute-in-training descended the stairs.

# CHAPTER 20

The bar and grill was more crowded than the night before. Most of the patrons were alone, sitting by themselves at tables. Four men sat at the bar, one with a woman he had obviously just picked up. The bartender was serving them doubles as Delilah brought Ian up for his special inspection.

"His name is Wolf Eyes and he's working out of here, as of tonight, Ed. He's O.K."

The man was older and more scarred than Delilah, but bore a vague resemblance to her. Ian thought instantly the prostitute trade made relatives of the oddest couples.

"As of *last* night," Ed finally remarked, wiping the counter with a faded blue and white checked rag.

"Last night was the Queen's Ball, and he's already paid for that. He starts tonight."

There was less challenge than fact in her voice. Ed hesitated, then shifted his eyes from Ian to Delilah.

"He ain't sleeping upstairs with you, is he? 'Cause if he is –"

"He's got his own place."

"Yeah. Well... I've heard that before."

"Not from me you haven't. Come on, Wolf Eyes." She paused pointedly until Ed moved away before continuing. "Keep an eye on me. Not an obvious one, but a discrete one. Get it? First couple of nights, I'll steer you in the right direction. I know most of the boys who come in here. They're all rough. This isn't one of the better places, but it's the only one I have an 'in' with. Watch me."

Leaving Ian at the bar, Delilah sauntered over to a man sitting by himself at one of the near tables. Making a low comment Ian did not hear, she was immediately invited to sit. Without being summoned, Ed brought drinks to the table. The man paid without being prompted. They sipped their drinks while Delilah made small talk. The man laughed.

Another drink later, they both stood and began dancing, cheek to cheek. Knowing that what she was doing was for his benefit, Ian experienced a flush as they glided close to where he stood. When the hem of her skirt brushed across his trouser leg, a cord drew taut around the base of his heart.

"Easy, Wolf Eyes," Ed whispered, placing a restraining hand on the new man. "Calm down."

"Ah dinna like it. That bastard has a dirty face."

"If that's his only flaw, it's a shining recommendation," Ed laughed. "You are a queer duck."

Not unaware of the emotions she had stirred in Ian, Delilah loudly declared she was "off to the powder room for a quick one," then purposely strode over to the bar.

"Dance with me," she ordered Ian. "Hands around my neck. Press real close, baby. I want to feel a man beside me."

As he eagerly obliged, she drew his head down and continued his education in remedial prostitution.

"Did you watch me? Casual is the name of the game. Let them make all the moves, unless you've got a slow one."

"How kin Ah tell?"

"You'll get to know. When you're here – and probably anywhere else, the bartender will hurry over with drinks. That's one way he benefits from our trade. Make the john pay for them."

"The 'john'?"

"You don't know what a 'john' is?"

"Ah know it's slang fer bathroom."

Delilah laughed in his ear as though the statement were the funniest thing she had ever heard. Her abandoned "john" at the table clenched his fists.

"O.K. You win that round; by default. It's also street talk for a customer. A pick-up. There are a lot of other words, more degrading, but most don't mind 'john,' so it works."

"Where did it originate frum?"

He felt her fingers stiffen around his arm and knew he had asked a stupid question.

"When you go up to a john, sit down. Usually he'll invite you, but if he doesn't, invite yourself. Easier for you than for me," she added as an afterthought.

"Why is that?" he inquired, desperate enough to take a chance asking another stupid question.

"Because you're prettier than I am. 'Pretty' opens a lot of doors that stay closed to 'ugly'."

"Ah think –"

She cut him off without emotion.

"Let me rephrase. 'Fresh' opens a lot of doors 'street-worn' keeps closed. That make it easier to understand?"

"Aye," tersely replied. She ignored the bitterness.

"Let the boy talk to you; talk back. Make small talk; listen to what he says. Appear interested. But for God's sake, don't get involved. You'll hear a lot of filth and some real pathos. One story means no more to you than the next. Remember that, or you'll really get your ass in trouble."

"Ah dinna want to do that!" he avowed with sincerity. Had Delilah believed him, she would have felt more comfortable.

"Let the boy know you're interested. Set-a-price," she stressed. "Start out with fifty dollars."

"What do Ah hafta do fer that great sum?"

The answer was simple and blunt.

"Anything."

"An'... if Ah do 'innythin' an' he dinna pay?"

Her expression hardened.

"If he tries to cheat you, take it out of his hide."

"Yuh mean, beat him up?"

"Beat the shit out of him. I think you're pretty well versed in where shit comes from."

"Aye. But what if he calls the 'local authorities'."

"Then you offer *them* what he didn't want to pay for. And hope to God they take it. For free," she added, fearing the worst.

"Me pretty face an' me tight arse?"

"And your tears."

"Christ on the cross," he swore. "That's a hell o' a thing to want frum innyone."

Grabbing him suddenly by his hair, Delilah drew his face down to hers. After an impassioned kiss, she whispered savagely into his ear.

"Everybody cries, baby. Sometimes, it's just nice to see someone else do it. Understand? You're supplying a service – let's say, several of them. You're not just a warm hole, you're an ear to talk to – a paid listener. So listen. Choke up some emotion. Just don't let it get to you. And play up your looks – flatter your customer. Words spoken by a handsome man mean more than an encyclopedia of love poems."

Dancing by the bar, Ian lifted his head to stare over her shoulder into the mirror. His face stared back at him. It seemed no different than on other occasions.

"There's been only one person ever called me handsome befer," he softly observed. "An' Ah married her."

"Then, honey, the world has done you a disservice." She offered him a derisive smile. "And don't worry – you won't have to marry any of your customers. Now, get to work."

Before she could disentangle her arms from around him, the man who had bought her a drink, approached, face pale with anger.

"What's going on here?" he demanded. "I got a vested interest in you."

Grabbing Ian by the shoulder, the "john" held a fist to the taller man's face. Ian responded without thinking, giving the potential customer a blow to the nose which sent him staggering into a table. Man, table, drinks and another man, this one a young blond sitting at the table, all went flying.

As the two bar patrons picked themselves up, the blond gave his inadvertent assailant a shove.

"Get outta here. Fast."

The older, shorter man knew good advice when he heard it. Muttering a curse at Delilah, he ran off, furiously disappointed.

The blond picked up the table, motioned the bartender for two drinks, then casually approached Ian. He did not look at Delilah, nor did she bother with him. They had no business together.

"Sorry you were annoyed like that," he opened with an apologetic smile. "How about dancing with me?"

"Sure, Ian agreed, then added awkwardly, "The lady's a friend o' mine. We work here."

Delilah spun away so fast the expression on her face was lost to both.

"I admire the way you handle yourself. New, are you?" the blond asked as he slipped his arms around Ian's neck. "My name is Sandy, by the way. What's yours?"

"Wolf Eyes."

Sandy drew back, studied the grey, canine-like eyes of his new friend, then nodded approvingly.

"Yeah. Sure are."

They danced through the rest of the canned music, then Sandy nibbled on Ian's ear. When Ian did not protest, he pressed his lips against Ian's. The kiss was not long, but passionate enough to excite interest in the paying customer.

With his stomach turning, Ian coughed into his hand to hide his discomfiture.

"Can I buy you a drink or are you horny enough without getting loaded?"

Sandy sounded hopeful and kind, yet behind the question stood a lifetime of experience.

"Fifty dollars," Ian replied, finally dropping his hand from his face.

He expected a loud exclamation of shock, protest, indignant insult. Instead, he received for his effort, a toothy smile.

"O.K."

Sandy reached into his pocket and Ian's heart rate accelerated, believing the "john" was going to pay him before leaving. Great was his disappointment, however, when all Sandy did was toss a bill onto the table for the two untouched drinks Ed had brought to the table while they danced.

"Come on. You'll like my pad."

Sandy turned toward the door, Ian catching Delilah's movement out of the corner of his eye. Obeying her gesture, he swatted Sandy on the rump. The "john" turned, grinned, then winked.

"Hey! Wolf Eyes! Look here!" Delilah called as Ian and Sandy moved off together. "Don't forget to use a condom!"

Turning expectantly, Ian caught the small, circular gold packet she tossed him. His blank look elicited laughter from the bar patrons observing the melodrama.

"What's a con-dum?" the neophyte inquired with curiosity. The customers broke up into raucous laughter.

Rolling her eyes, Delilah directed her attention to Sandy.

"That ups his price by twenty bucks!"

Sandy chuckled, patted his own groin and waved acceptance. In a reversal of roles, Sandy slipped his arm around Ian's and escorted him out, to the tempo of clapping hands and fading laughter.

Sandy No-Last-Name-Given lived in an old, well-maintained brownstone. When he unlocked the door and entered, motioning Ian to follow, he smiled graciously, sweeping his hand out as though entertaining royalty.

"Not much, but mine own."

"It's very nice," Ian truthfully admired. "Ah hope one day to have a place like this. It's more spacious than Ah would have guessed," he continued, walking through the living room in undisguised wonder.

"Yes," Sandy agreed, removing his light jacket and tossing it casually on the couch. "We like it."

"Oh," Ian remarked in surprise. "Yuh live here wid yer wife?"

"My wife? Not likely. Bill and I share it. He's away for the weekend."

"Oh." The sound of disappointment was not lost on the host.

"Do you want a drink?"

"No." And then, "Thank yuh."

Sandy proceeded to remove all his clothes, finally standing before Ian stark naked. He was a well-muscled man, fit and tanned, with light hair running from collarbone to groin. Ian stared at him a long beat before swallowing his fear and forcing himself to speak.

"Yuh've a nice body," he commented, remembering Charles' desire to be complimented.

"I appreciate you saying so. I try to keep in shape." Prancing around the room like a stallion on parade, Sandy came to a stop by the end table on the opposite side of the couch. Taking a small leather bag, closed with a thong, he opened it slowly, peered inside then held it out. "Want a snort?"

"A snort? O' booze?"

Sandy blew air through his nostrils.

"Snow."

"Drugs, yuh mean?" Sandy nodded. "No. Ah dinna take drugs. An' yuh shouldna, either."

"Drugs are a way of life, Wolf Eyes."

"They're a way o' death."

"Well... who wants to grow old? Social Security'll be broke before I ever get old enough to draw it and besides, coke expands the mind. It helps me see the world for what it really is."

Without bothering to pursue the matter, Sandy laid out his white line, administered the powder to himself, then breathed deeply. His face immediately changed color and his eyes drew into slits.

"Let's have some fun, shall we?"

Making a curt, authoritative motion with his hand, Sandy led Ian into the back bedroom. Like the room in Charles' flat, this one, too, had a four-poster bed. The difference was, wrist cuffs hung suspended from the two front uprights. Along the back wall were lined an array of whips, chains, and costumes.

"No!" Ian protested, freezing in his tracks. "Ah dinna want inny part o' this. I came here to –"

"Screw and be screwed? Open up, baby. There's a hell of a lot more to the world than sex. And a hell of a lot better sex to be experienced than by getting on a bed and going through the motions. This," he suggestively added, "is what you might call character playing."

"Ah dinna want to play a character."

"Oh, but you are, already. 'Wolf Eyes' is a character. A facade; a face you put on when you sell yourself. All well and good, but he's not the character *I* want to play with. I want something entirely different."

"Stand back," Ian warned, raising his hands in a defensive-offensive position. Sandy stared at him a moment, utterly unthreatened. He had read his pigeon correctly.

"You came here to earn fifty dollars."

"Fifty an' twenty is seventy," came the rapid, yet uncertain reply.

"You came here to earn seventy bucks. So, earn it, or leave. The door's open. I don't want any trouble. I'm not going to force you."

Ian pointed a shaking hand toward the devices hung on the wall.

"That looks pretty forceful to me."

"No. No. Oh, sure," Sandy laughed, believing his head remarkably clear and insightful from the drugs raging unchecked through his brain. "But that's part of the role playing. It's called willful submission."

Pausing to rub his already erect penis, Sandy shook his shoulders in impatient expectation.

"You ought to appreciate my scenario. I play Richard Topcliff, Elizabeth I's rack man. You can play a Jesuit priest. They were much hated in those days. Here," Sandy continued, rewriting the script as he spoke, growing more and more aroused as he imagined the scene. "It's perfect.
"You're a Scot. So, you play someone who's trying to free Queen Mary from her unjust imprisonment. Father... McDoohan. That sounds Scottish." On Ian's blank look, he grew increasingly verbose. "Surely you're familiar with English history."

"Ah know aboot Queen Elizabeth an' Queen Mary –"

"Good. So, here's the scene. You conspired with the Spanish Catholics to free Queen Mary and lost. Unfortunately, you didn't have the foresight to fall on your sword. Elizabeth's men captured you and brought you to the Tower, to... elicit a confession. Oh course, you know any confession for treason means a very unsavory, prolonged death. In your case, it also means torture. We'll begin with some minor whipping before you're placed on the rack. Later, of course, you'll be disemboweled, drawn and quartered –"

"Yuh canna do that!"

"No, of course not," Sandy laughed reassuringly. "I'm just explaining what might have been, four hundred and some odd years ago. We're not going that far, believe me."

"Ah dinna think Ah do. Ah think –"

"Be careful what you say," Sandy menacingly warned. When Ian clamped his jaws shut, he continued. "We're just playing. Remember that. You'll get hurt – and you'll get screwed – and do some screwing, too," he predicted, raising an eyebrow. "And I guarantee it'll be the best intercourse you've ever had."

"If Ah had a penny to me name, Ah'd take that bet."

"Well, here's one you'll 'no' be betting against. Have you ever had a master?"

"No."

"You'll have one tonight."

Taking one of the short, ten foot long whips from the wall, Sandy ran his hands lovingly over the weapon, caressing it as though the leather were a living, breathing entity. Without warning, he took a step back and cracked it. A sound as loud as a gunshot split the night air, the tip of the weapon snapping a half inch from Ian's ear, tickling his face with the force of the displaced air.

Jumping back, Ian held out his hands, thinking to catch the sting of death when it came again. But Sandy was not looking for that type of confrontation.

"There," he indicated. "In the box beside the bed. Open it."

Ian did as ordered, drawing back the heavy, cedar chest lid to reveal piles of neatly folded costumes.

"Look toward the bottom. You'll find a habit. Take it out."

Ian found the article of clothing and removed it. The habit was more like a loose-fitting robe, tied at the middle with a cloth belt. It was black and might have been sold in a small, back street shop under the label, "One Size Fits All."

"Strip," Sandy ordered. "Then put on the habit."

Ian followed the instructions, laying his clothes neatly on the back of a chair. As he stood, naked, ready to slip his arms through the sleeves, Sandy whistled in appreciation.

"Yes. You look like a Jesuit. They're the sensual ones. I think Richard Topcliff will want to know all about your sexual activities on Queen Mary's behalf."

"Roman Catholic priests are no' supposed to have sex," Ian protested, his head already swimming from dreaded anticipation.

"Of course not. That's why Master Topcliff will enjoy hearing of your exploits," he grinned. "Now, get dressed and we'll begin. I'm eager for the fray."

This time, when "Richard Topcliff" cracked his whip, he did not miss. Before the victim could recover, he found himself chained to the "rack," hands raised high over his head, legs stretched out and bound by other cuffs Ian had not seen.

Sandy sneered, then agilely leaped atop the bed.

"Welcome to hell, 'Father Wolf Eyes'!"

Ian closed his eyes and prayed for sanity.

By seven o'clock the next morning, the light could no longer be kept from the room, despite the black curtains covering the window. Sated yet still exhilarated, the master torturer, minus his rack man's costume, stretched, then kicked the man at his feet. Ian groaned but made no further response.

The Defender of the Faith; the conspirator who had tried and failed to install the Catholic Queen to her rightful throne; the whipped, battered, beaten man who lay on the floor sobbed from the punishment he had endured. His bare arms were around his head, his legs splayed, one knee bent the wrong way. His breathing was strained, laborious.

He was kicked a second time with like result. When he still refused to move, his head was grabbed and shook, until his teeth rattled. Without further words, the master waved six 20 dollar bills in front of the executed's face, then dropped them, one by one, onto his bare chest.

For one of the men, the cost of his entertainment was cheap. He would have paid four times that amount for a front row ticket on the Great White Way.

And not found the acting nearly as convincing.


When the knock came, Delilah did not bother to acknowledge it. Sitting with her back to the door, she groaned slightly, then made an ineffectual waving motion with her hand. The knock was repeated. Striking an awareness deep within her consciousness, her head jerked and she made an attempt to speak. Her voice was husky, deep.

"Who is it?" she demanded, but her demand would not have shooed away a fly.

"Ian MacDhui," came the too-rapid response.

"Go away."

"Ah want to see yuh."

"I doubt it," she sighed. Then, with resignation, "What am I? A den mother?"

She arose from the chair, walking with old-lady steps to the door, opening it no more than a crack. One eyeball peeked out at her unwelcome visitor.

"What do you want?"

"A friendly face."

Grinning with demoniacal pleasure, Delilah opened the door to admit him.

Slipping through the narrow space allotted, Ian closed and would have barricaded the door had there been the material handy to perform such a task. It was only when he was assured of their relative safety that he looked at his hostess.

She was battered from head to toe. Both eyes were blackened, her face red from constant slapping. Her hair was in total disarray, while one strap of her dress draped uselessly over her exposed left breast.

"What in bloody hell happened?" he gasped, shaking with such violence a saucer on the kitchen table rattled.

"I earned my money," she casually replied. "Our 'friend' from the bar came back. He extracted his due for buying me a drink."

"No! No!" Ian screamed, quieting only when she put a finger to her lips, indicating silence.

"And so did you, I see."

First stunned to silence, then prodded to activity to control his shaking, Ian reached into his pocket, retrieving a wad of bills.

"Ah made me one hundred an' twenty *bucks.*"

Delilah stared at him a moment, then turned away as the right side of her mouth began to twitch in uncontrollable, unanticipated, unremembered, emotion.

"Shit on the cross," she swore with hatred. "What have I gotten you into?"

She made a move, then her knees gave out, plunging her forward. Only by the sharpest-honed instincts did the former sheepman catch her before she struck the floor. Looking wildly around the unfamiliar apartment, he spotted the bedroom. Lifting the poor, beaten creature into his arms, the wolf carried the ewe into her cave.

It had been a night, and would be a day, of opposites.

# CHAPTER 21

It was the unaccustomed sound which woke her. Raising her head, instantly alert, Delilah reached for the wicked-looking kitchen knife under her pillow. Silently withdrawing it, she slipped out of bed, paused only a moment to clear her head from the effects of too much beating and too little rest, then tiptoed, weapon in hand, to the closed door of her bedroom.

Lips pursed together in determination, she flung it open, assuming a fighter's stance, ready to take on any and all comers. Great was her surprise, then, to discover, not thieves stealing her 12-inch portable TV and her radio, but two girls. Coaching them in their work, apron wrapped around his waist, was Ian MacDhui.

Slowly, almost reluctantly lowering the knife, Delilah instinctively ran a hand through her hair to smooth it, then straightened, feeling foolish. She compensated for her entrance with false bravado.

"I've heard of Snow White cleaning the home of the Seven Dwarfs, but you're too tall," she said, indicating Ian, "with a serious deficiency in the boob area to be Snow White... and if you're dwarfs," she continued, looking sharply at the children, "why are you helping *him* clean?"

"Because he asked us to," Meg replied.

Taken aback by the polite tone as much as the statement, Delilah could not help asking, "Do you always do what he asks?"

"Yes."

"No." This, from Storm.

The children spoke simultaneously, their answers overlapping one another's. Ian swelled with pride, then spread his arms, encompassing his family.

"Tis Clan MacDhui yuh're feastin' yuhr eyes on. This is daughter Margaret an' this is daughter Gail."

The correction was not long in coming.

"I'm Meg an' this is Storm."

"Storm?"

"It's a play on words," the so-named child explained. "Me given name being 'Gail,' as Ian wrrrrongly introduced. It's been said," she pursued, eying her father, "that Ah have a temper worse than innyone, so 'Gail' – as in 'g-a-l-e,' meanin' a terrible wind, translated into 'Storm.' Ah prefer it," she meaningfully added.

Delilah marked her, nodding sympathetically.

"'Ian?'" she questioned, wisely changing the subject. "You mean, your father?"

"They were born to take care o' me," the proud papa explained, a smile radiating over his face. "Jest as Ah was meant to raise them. Callin' me by me furst name just cume natural. More equal-like."

"I see. Well, pleased to meet you, Meg and Storm MacDhui. I'm Delilah."

Which raised two eyebrows, one for each child.

"Is that yuh're real name?" Storm pointedly inquired.

"Yuh kin see they dinna add much to me, socially."

Rather than be offended, however, Delilah laughed.

"No, Delilah is not my 'real' name. It's my stage name."

"Are yuh an actress?"

"I sure as hell am, honey. One that plays a great many parts." Putting a hand to her face, she offered a rueful smiled. "One which changes every night. You might say, I play rep. That's short for repertory," she winked at Storm.

"Where do yuh work?"

This time it was Meg who asked. Making the quick determination the children played off one another, assuming parts dictated by circumstance, Delilah met them head-on, immeasurably appreciating and matching their role-acting.

"At a club. That's where I met your father."

"At a club?" came a unison of astonished question.

"He's the house bouncer. When customers get rough, he wrassles them out the door. It has its awkward moments, as you've undoubtedly noticed, but the pay is good, and it's not generally considered a hazardous occupation."

Stamping her foot in annoyance, Storm turned accusingly to her father.

"Yuh dinna tell us yuh were a bouncer!"

Caught between a rock and a hard place, Ian weakly offered her a tepid grin. Faced with the choice to go along with the plausible lie Delilah established for him, or explain the truth before it went even further, he swallowed and lied.

"Aye...Well, that's becuz Ah thought yuh might object. It bein' a bit on the dangerous side. But as me friend jest explained, it's no' –"

"– generally considered to be a hazardous occupation," Meg finished.

"It's better than moppin' floors!"

The desperate, almost pleading look on Ian's face did not coincide with his words. Both children suspected something terrible amiss, but instinct warned them it was neither the time nor the place to challenge him.

"Besides," he continued, falsely sensing they were weakening. "Ain't Ah the best wrassler in Scotland? Dinna Ah have the trophy to prove it?"

"Aye, yuh do," Meg, the peacemaker, agreed. Then, to Delilah, "Did yuh know he had a trophy?"

"No. Actually," she added in a lower voice, "I know very little 'aboot' him at all." To Ian, she continued, "So, you have a trophy?"

"Aye. Frum the Edinburgh Fair."

"I don't know where Edinburgh is, but if it's as tough as Manhattan, your wrassling skills will serve you well."

"They already have!" Storm declared. Two sets of guilty eyes shifted to her.

"What yuh mean?"

"Yuh're job at the club. How did you get the position? Did yuh have to throw out the old bouncer?"

Confronted with the necessity to create a background to the Lie, Ian flushed and nearly flubbed his lines.

"What do yuh know aboot bouncers, in the furst place?"

"Awk," she dismissed with a wave of her tiny hand. "Ah know all aboot 'em. From the picture shows. Every saloon has one."

"We were speaking of a club," Delilah tried as Ian nervously shifted his gaze toward her. Reading his silent call for help, she was more than willing to step in an extemporize. "The man who had to job before him made so much money, with tips and all, that he retired to the country. Bought a pretty little house with lots of trees."

"Really?!"

"Sure. And your father will have the same opportunities. It's a *much* better job than mopping floors," she finished, flush with her own success.

"Ah'll say," Meg agreed, rubbing her hands together in pleasure. "A respectable job."

"Finally," Storm seconded. "Yuh shoulda tolt us. We was worried."

"Ah know...."

What he knew was that he had lied to his daughters, giving them a false sense of pride. The hurt went deeper than any assaults already sustained. Seeing his eyes water, Delilah made shooing motions with her hands.

"All right, you three. Enough cleaning for one day. You make me nervous. I have to take a shower and wash this – grease paint off my face. What I can of it," she admitted. "Sometimes, not even cold cream removes that damn make-up. Why don't you all go out and buy something special, for a party? Here, Ian," she hailed, making a move for her purse.

"Niver mind," he responded. "Ah have money. Ah git paid every night Ah work," he added for his daughter's benefit, which came out sounding better, as it was a truthful statement. "This celebration is on the MacDhuis."

The ring of veracity in his words perked Meg and Storm up appreciatively. With thoughts of parties and respectable jobs filling their heads, they scrambled for the door, eager to begin a second chance at a new life.

Returning soon after, grocery bags filled to the brim, Clan MacDhui set about preparing food for a feast. Delilah, fresh from her dressing table, had the professional's skill in altering her appearance, leaving few traces of her beating visible.

The lady of the house presumed she was ready for anything, but seeing a brand new, red and white tablecloth, complete with four cotton napkins already placed over her dining room table gave her a start. Clutching her heart in theatrical dramatics, she approached in astonishment.

"What's all this?"

"Yuh canna have a party widout accouterments," Ian suavely informed her.

"It's a tradition," Meg explained. "Meal time is supposed to be a civilized affair. That's what Megan MacDhui a'ways said. We dinna know iffn yuh had a tablecloth –"

"An' napkins," Storm added.

"So we purchased them."

"Well, I suppose you can never have too many," Delilah meekly agreed. "And I was lacking... napkins."

"Sit down," Ian invited, making a low bow. "We're aboot ready."

If the erstwhile matron thought she was surprised before, nothing could have prepared her to see Ian, standing behind her chair, drawing it back as she approached. Closing and then rolling her eyes, she accepted his invitation, going so far as allowing him to push in her chair, before motioning him to follow suit.

He did so, while Storm poured lemonade into mismatched jelly glasses. Moving from one side to the other, she inadvertently jostled the stem of the table. Being unsteady, the drink spilled.

"I'm sorry. This table was never intended for company. My Colonial Oak Dining Room Set is... out to the cleaners," Delilah apologized.

"Have no fear! Ian MacDhui is here!"

Ian bent down, assessed the problem, then slipped off his seat, disappearing from sight. Meg and Storm made faces at one another, then winked at Delilah.

"We call him Mr. Fix-It," Storm explained, intending and succeeding in bringing a smile to the elder's face.

"That's becuz he canna fix innythin'."

"Untrue!" came the disembodied voice.

The table jumped, titled one way and then another before finally settling into a faintly lopsided position. A rustling of the tablecloth announced his coming reappearance.

Maneuvering out from beneath the table on hands and knees, Ian grinned at Delilah, then suddenly blushed to the roots of his hair. His eyes faded to a washed-out grey, as a row of perspiration appeared out of nowhere across his brow.

In all his life, Ian had never felt cause to be ashamed of crawling around on all fours. The events of the past two days had altered this perception drastically, and as awareness struck, his body trembled from shame.

Instantly aware of his predicament, Delilah placed her own unsteady hands around the rim of the table and rattled it, thus creating a diversion. Popping up, he resumed his seat.

"Ah dinna think yuh fixed it," Storm commented, more intent on the table than on her father.

"So, Ian. You're no handyman?" Delilah came in quickly, offering an excuse for his red face.

Faltering for a ready reply, Meg innocently filled in the silence.

"No. But iffn yuh ever need a hole poot in yer wall, he's yuh're man."

Ian's groan was Delilah's cue to pursue the topic.

"A hole in the wall?"

Meg served the rest of the food then settled down to tell the "tall tale." It was a story they often recounted and she rattled on rapidly, Storm easily interrupting her sister in their eagerness to explain MacDhui lore.

"Aye. One year when wool prices was a wee bit high, we had a windfall. We treated ourselves to a 'modern convenience.'"

"We bought an electric stove."

"O' course, Ian knew all aboot electric stoves. He had used one once in Glasgow."

"What he meant was, he had *seen* one used."

"An' o'course, he dinna need to read the instructions."

"So we plugged the bugger in an' decided to make us a pot o' tea to try it out."

"Now: what do yuh boil water in?"

"A kettle," Delilah guessed.

"Right as rain. We filled the kettle wid water an' placed it in the oven."

"We thought we'd have a nice, hot cuppa in seconds."

"Split seconds. Lightnin' fast."

"We went into the livin' room fer some reason –"

"Ian MacDhui said it were Meggie MacDhui lookin' out fer us –"

"Because when the kettle blew, the door went one way and the rest o' the oven went the other, makin' a hell o' a hole in the wall."

"Iffn we'd o' been in the kitchen, we'd all o' been blown to Kingdom Come!"

"Amen!" Ian agreed.

"Well, what could we do? We buried the poor dead oven alongside the pots an' pans."

"Out back; in the MacDhui graveyard."

"You – buried it – along with the pots and pans?"

"Ain't that what yuh do wid dead things? Bury 'em?"

"Ah'm afeared," Ian interrupted, "Me children are a bit too knowledgeable aboot buryin'."

"I'm sorry."

And, to her immense surprise, she was sorry.

The rest of the meal was consumed, amid idle chatter, to the great pleasure of all. When each partygoer declared her or himself satisfied, Delilah pushed up from the table. Seeing her rise, Ian sprang up, deftly removing the chair from her way. Shooting him a "we'll have to discuss this later" look, she pointed toward the kitchen.

"You make some coffee, Wolf Eyes, while I hear the story about why the pots and pans gave up the ghost."

"Wolf Eyes!" Meg exclaimed in wonder. "Why – that's what we call him!"

Quickly realizing she has said something better left unmentioned, Delilah quickly repaired the damage.

"Yes. He told me that. So when he needed a stage name at the club, I suggested he use that."

A moment passed while Meg and Storm digested this bit of news, then both gave a spontaneous thumbs-up.

"Ah like it!"

"So do Ah. As long as he remembers he's no' a Lone Wolf."

"Ah won't," he promised.

"But he really is a wolf, yuh know," Meg continued, as they walked into the living room. "We MacDhuis all are."

"We howl at the moon," Storm added.

While Ian wrassled with the coffee, Delilah settled herself down in her chair. The girls sat opposite, on the couch.

"You do?"

"Aye."

"Why is that?"

"Becuz we're wild. Becuz the moon reminds us what freedom o' the soul is all aboot."

From the kitchen came the clattering of a cup as it broke. Delilah quickly dismissed the accident.

"Tell me about the pots and pans."

The story commenced with no one to see the tears in Ian's eyes over the long-ago memory.

"We were in Edinburgh on holiday, watching this programme on the telly through a shop window."

"It was all aboot how people on this far away planet lived wid terrible wind storms."

"They dinna have inny water, so they hung their pots an' pans outside on a line, an' the wind whipped them clean."

Speaking in an overly loud voice to blot out Meg's use of a now hated word, Ian called, "We thought that sounded like a good idea."

"Aye," Storm agreed. "We figured we lived in a pretty windy place ourselves."

"An' bein' as how we dinna like washing dishes –"

"Ian strung a rope along the side o' the house, an' we hung out the pots an' pans fer the wind to clean."

"We'd a poot out the plates, too, only we couldna figure out a way to do it."

"Which turned out fer the best," their father commented, making an appearance with a tray set with coffee cups.

"The next day we hung out sume more an' the day after that. We waited until –"

"We were out o' pots an' pans –"

"Then went out one bright summer mornin' to cut down a pot fer porridge."

"They were not exactly wind-blown clean," Delilah surmised.

"They were not," Ian agreed, dispensing the hot beverage.

"They were crawlin' wid maggots –"

"Amongst other small beasties –"

"So instead o' makin' breakfast, we buried 'em."

"Handles up," Ian helpfully supplied. "To serve as headstones."

Delilah looked from one to another, unsure whether to laugh or cry.

"Well? What did you do then?"

"Cooked over a spit until we could afford a hot plate an' new pots an' pans!" Ian concluded.

"Scotland must be a very interesting country," was all Delilah could think of to say.

"It tis," Meg agreed.

"We'll show it to yuh one day. When we save up enuf money, we're goin' back to the moors," Storm insisted.

"Oh?"

"They have one dream, an' Ah have another," Ian sadly admitted.

"We're sheepers daughters, an' our place is wid the beasties. Where a pack o' wolves kin howl to their hearts content."

"Where a wolf kin see the moon," Storm added.

"That's why it's so important Ian got hisself a self-respectin' job. Meggie MacDhui said in New York, immigrants would git a fair shake."

"How insightful of her."

"She wanted us to stay in the New World, but Ah dinna think she knew yuh couldna see the moon."

"Ah dinna remember her very well," Storm confessed. "But Ah think she'd unnerstan' our feelin's."

"Yes,' Delilah agreed, turning her blue eyes on Ian. "I think she would understand everything."

"Ah dinna know," Wolf Eyes replied, dropping his head to stare at the naked ring finger of his left hand. "Ah dinna know... aboot innythin'. Aboot what she'd think... or no' think. But Ah know what Ah think."

"There's thinking, Ian MacDhui and then there's doing. I didn't know her, but I see her in you – and in them," Delilah said, indicating the children. "And I think Meg is right."

"Well, God bless the innocent," he replied. "As He seems to do a pretty poor job with the rest o' us."

"Drink your coffee before it gets cold."

He obeyed her command, feeling cold enough inside to need the warmth.

# CHAPTER 22

It became a time of confusion; of strobe lights and blurred hours, black lights and blaring music. Faces merged together as easily as one body fit into another. The act of making love became a dreary routine, a mechanical in and out, where kissing was meant only to stimulate, and whatever raw emotions existed had nothing whatsoever to do with love.

The only break in the routine was a literal one. Repairs to the body being easier to heal than those of the soul, pain became accepted as a way of life. As time went on, Ian got better at identifying which "johns" were likely to employ violence, those who played games of humiliation, the men and youths who did drugs, and thus avoided them.

Without ever making friends, "Wolf Eyes" became a familiar face among those haunting the fringes of "boys who do with boys." Some became regular customers, occasionally paying him as much as three hundred dollars a night for a special event or a group orgy.

More often, they paid him "bonuses" in advice, providing him phone numbers of likely clients, offering him hand-me-down suits, shirts and shoes fit for a king of Scotland. They pointed out those men with the easy smiles, taught him how to spot a user, avoid a fight. And all the while, they educated him in the ways and means of how to please a man. They were not easy lessons to learn, but they were the essential tricks of the trade, and he learned them well.

One thing these men did not have to teach Ian MacDhui was how to keep his mouth shut. After his experience with Charles Denning, Ian never again mentioned where he lived or with whom. He would be asked those questions, often by those who would never think to use such information for blackmail, but never did he answer.

"Ah'm the lone wolf, the solitary wolf," was all he would say. And after a while, they believed him and stopped asking.

When the alarm buzzer rang, the two men lying side-by-side jumped, startled by the sudden noise. Only Ian, lounging on a nearby chair, did not move. Gone forever were the days when he quivered at the slightest noise, flinched and cringed at any unexpected intrusion on his world.

He was not the same man and his fears had changed.

"Jesus!" the short man on the bed swore. "That damn alarm scared the hell out of me."

"Me, too," his partner complained, rubbing sleep from his eyes. "I'm sorry. I forgot I set it. I suppose I should have taken it off."

"No," sighed the other. "I have to take a shower and be out of here by nine. I've got to meet a client at ten. He's keen on that Oldani property and if I can give him the right price, which I think I can, we'll both go away happy men."

"You – Wolf Eyes," his partner observed with something akin to awe. "Why didn't you jump when the alarm went off? You must have nerves of steel."

"Ah saw what the clock was set to an' was jest waitin' fer it," he lied. Lying came easily these days.

"Even so. Doesn't anything scare you?"

"Ah'm a wolf, remember? A wolf is a predator; a hunter. It's in his nature to expect the unexpected an' to remain calm, no matter what."

"Yeah. Well, if you're hunting rabbits or cattle or whatever they eat, that makes sense. But you're a man."

"Am Ah?" he rhetorically questioned. "Ah had no' noticed."

"Well, we did," laughed the first, reaching over toward the bedside stand. Pulling open a drawer, he removed a wad of bills, pre-counted, then handed them to Ian. "Thanks for a great night."

"I feel as though I could fly," his partner remarked, stretching stiff muscles. "See you tonight, Wolf Eyes?"

"No' tonight." Then, on their looks, which held a silent accusation of jealousy, "Ah'm no' workin' tonight. It's me night off."

"What does a wolf do on his night off?"

"Yeah. Are you leading a double life? Like Clark Kent, or something?"

Ian did not know to whom they referred, but it would have made little difference to him if he had. He would neither have understood nor appreciated their reference to Superman.

"Ah'm goin' to sleep," he grinned. "That's what a wolf does on his night off."

"Well, I hope you have a featherbed or something."

Ian might have replied that he had taken to sleeping on the couch, for the idea of lying in a bed – any bed – had become repulsive to him, but did not.

Just as their reference to Superman went over Ian's head, so too would his explanation of why anything even remotely resembling a bed held a repugnance to him.

Drawing on his shorts and trousers with the acquired ease of a man used to being stared at, Ian slipped the money into his pocket. As he withdrew his fingers, he did not notice a small packet fall to the floor. It was only after he was gone that one of the men stooped to retrieve it.

Playing the item around in his hand, he sighed, then tossed it to his partner.

"Souvenir," he joked.

The second man caught it, held it up to the light, then grinned.

"We'll save it for next time."

Slipping out of bed, he headed for the shower, dropping the unopened condom on the stand as he passed.

When Ian awoke at four, Meg and Storm were seated at the table, reading the newspaper. After a brief trip to the bathroom, and a quick examination of a healing black eye in the mirror, he reappeared, smelling of cologne and whistling an old tune.

"What shall we do tonight? Go to the movies?" he guessed, unconsciously inserting into his speech the words of the New World. Standing on tiptoe he attempted to read over Meg's shoulder. Anticipating his action, she closed the paper before he could see her area of interest. The point became moot, however, as Storm voiced her desire.

"Ah'd rather go night clubbin'."

"Night clubbin'?" he demanded in shock. "Where'd yuh hear that expression?"

"Ah've been askin' around. Aboot the kind o' places what hires bouncers. A night club seemed to be the most likely. Do they have topless dancers where yuh work?"

"No! An' yuh ought not to be askin' around."

"Why not? Afeared what we might learn?" This time, it was Meg who spoke, making it harder to answer.

"Ah'm no' afeared o' anything."

"Then when are yuh goin' to take us there?"

"Take yuh where?"

"To the place yuh work. Yuh said we could see it."

"Aye... but Ah meant sumetime later in yuh're lives. Yuh're too young to git in. There's an age requirement. Eighteen. An' neither o' yuh kin pass fer that, no matter how worldly yuh might think o' yerselves."

"Take us in the back way. You work there. No one will say anythin'."

"Oh, no? Yuh think not? Then yuh better think ag'in, because they're very particular aboot that. They could lose their license, an' Ah could lose me job. What do yuh say," he continued, rubbing his chin, "that we read aloud frum a book?"

Meg and Storm exchange glances, smiling thinly to one another.

"Like we used to," Meg quietly replied.

"Aye.... Like we used to. Ah'd like to do sumethin' familiar."

There was a small but impressive library in a newly purchased bookcase. Meg got up from the table, passing the newspaper to Storm as she did. In a moment she was back with the reading material.

"Where shall we sit? On the couch?"

"No!" Ian answered, too rapidly. Quickly, he made an attempt to soften his denial. "It's lumpy."

"Then why don't yuh sleep in yer bed?"

"Ah tolt yuh," he grumbled, looking off. "Ah miss yuhr mother. Ah dinna like sleepin' alone in a big bed."

But he had told them no such thing. His admission now raised unseen eyebrows.

"Ah've changed me mind," Meg suddenly blurted. "Ah'm hungry. What say we go out to eat an' then cume home and read the book?"

"All right by me," Ian agreed, suddenly claustrophobic. "Ah could eat a bear."

It was late when they returned. A full moon shone over an unusually clear night sky and they enjoyed reminiscing about their days on the moors until it was close to eleven.

"Ah hope it's not too late to read," Meg observed, seeing Storm stifle a yawn behind her hand.

"No, Ah dinna think so," her parent reassured her. "Yuh two git ready fer bed, an' Ah'll read a chapter or two fer yer listenin' pleasure."

They scrambled to obey, reminding him with acute pain, of how young and impressionable they really were. A supper, a walk around the park and an hour of reading meant more to them than all the money in the world.

If only he could explain that nothing came without its price; that even such simple pleasures had to be paid for. Without a job, there would be no food, no apartment to come back to, no book to read.

Without a job, there would be no life, yet the job itself was death.

There was a word to describe his plight and Ian MacDhui fought with his jangled nerves to remember it. It came to him with a jolt of a past lifetime.

Conundrum.

With the curtain parted to admit the bright white rays of the full moon, Meg and Storm settled themselves in bed, shoulder-to-shoulder. Ian could not bring himself to look at them.

"Once upon a time," he began. They interrupted him with childlike enthusiasm.

"That's no' how that book begins."

"It isna? Oh, Ah must have read it wrong. Ah'll start ag'in. 'It was the best o' times, it was the worst o' times –'"

"Not that, either!"

"By God, yuh're correct. Ah must need readin' specs. Now, let me see if me old eyes kin make out the real words...."

He read to them until they were asleep, chins drooping down onto their chests, eyes tightly closed, breathing deep and regular. Usually, it was a delight to read, but tonight, the words had blurred before his eyes and it took more concentration that he possessed to turn the pages, one after the other.

There was a restlessness rising within him, a wildness too strong to be ignored. Dropping the book to the floor, he left the room and ran to the living room window, thrusting his head and shoulders out in a desperate attempt to draw power from the moon. From his confined angle, however, the silent satellite was not clearly visible, driving him nearly mad.

Without thinking, without the ability to reason his actions, Ian raced for the door, flung it open and bounded down the stairs, feet barely touching the steps in his haste. Once on street level, he discovered the moon obscured by the tall buildings. Cursing with fury, he bolted into a run, finally settling into his long-strided wolf gait. Wherever the moon was, wherever he could see it best, he would find, if that journey took him half way around the globe.

He traveled in this manner for fifteen minutes, then broke his pace, darting into a back alley. There, amid the trash-strewn walkway, moon beams poured, like salt from a shaker. Gasping in total need, he held up his hands, seeking to feel the light, to touch the rays. Then, raising hands to face, he washed the twinkling into his eyes, bathing in its purity.

Thus cleansed, his arms dropped to his sides in well-rehearsed pantomime and he drew back his head until it was extended as far as his neck would allow. Baring his teeth, canine-fashion, Ian attempted to howl, to bare his soul, to reestablish himself as a wolf, an ancient moor creature, a free man.

No sound issued forth. He swallowed, tried again. Nothing. Gritting his teeth this time, Ian clenched his fists and willed the howl to issue forth. Silence.

Wolf Eyes had been struck mute.

With an agonized sob of despair, he ran from the alley and into the street, plunging headlong into the traffic, regardless of oncoming cars. If he could not howl in an alley, he would have to seek some other place; some refuge where the trees were green and the rustle of their leaves would stimulate his soul.

By the time Ian MacDhui reached the park, the moon was beginning to fade. Trembling with impotent rage, he placed himself as squarely as possible underneath the pale beams and threw back his head. No sound. He tried a scream of rage. He might have been rendered dumb for all the noise he made.

Once more, this time with a concerted effort and a prayer, directed upward, past the wolf moon, to the stars. Somewhere, in the heavens, lay heaven. Somewhere, the spirit of the Alpha Female had to be looking down at her Alpha Male. Surely such a spirit had the power to unfreeze the vocal cords of so desperate a petitioner.

Ian's prayer was wordless, more jumbled than coherent. Just as his voice failed him, so too did his words. She would have to understand.

God would translate.

Taking in a deep breath through flared nostrils, Ian set himself, head back, arms at his sides and howled. He howled and howled and howled but it was not the call of the wild he sang, but the utter wretchedness of one who could not utter a note.

His howl was as silent as the grave.

Ian MacDhui had sold his soul. He had become "Wolf Eyes" to the world and lost his identity. Megan MacDhui no longer recognized him. He did not know himself.

The realization was shattering. Crumpling to a heap on the dry ground, he buried his head in his arms. As the wind rose, it kicked a balled-up piece of hamburger wrapper into his lap.

In the great city of New York, he had become just one more receptacle for garbage.

# CHAPTER 23

Mac's Bar and Grill was more lively than usual. Ian had not planned on going there this evening, but his sudden unexpected, devastating inability to howl had altered his plans. Now, he wanted nothing better than to get hooked up with a rough "john" – or a dozen of them. He was not interested in making money tonight: he had sold his soul for money.

Tonight, he was seeking pain.

Wearing a pair of jeans, loafers without socks and a white, short-sleeved shirt, open three buttons down – the same attire he had worn while walking with his children – Ian swaggered through the door. Added to his formidable physique and handsome face, were new additions to Ian MacDhui. Where once his grey eyes had held innocence and naiveté, now they darted around the room with a professional's detachment.

Where once he had slumped his shoulders and jumped at each unexpected noise, now he was one with the radio music playing in the background, naturally swinging his hips to the tempo.

Where once he had dreaded work, feared the men who cast sidelong glances at him, now he sought eye contact with them, establishing, by silent communication, his willingness to do anything for a good Pay Day.

This night, however, none of the men looked up as he entered. Annoyed by not having his own desires immediately gratified, he headed for the bar, slapping his hand, palm down, for attention.

Ed looked over at him in mild surprise.

"Evening, Wolf Eyes. Didn't expect to see you in here tonight."

"Why not?" Ian casually inquired, leaning over the bar in blatant self-advertisement.

"Thought you were going to take a night off."

"Awk, yuh know me," he bragged, raising his voice. "Ah love me job."

"Yeah. Well, what'll it be?"

"What does the House recommend?" he asked, stretching the full length of his body.

The bartender hesitated, then reached behind the counter and brought down a bottle. Without bothering to ask if his choice were acceptable, he poured a double into a glass, swished it around then handed it to his customer. The ice was conspicuously absent.

Ian took a sip, then nodded approvingly.

"What is it?"

"Something to drown your broken heart in. Fast."

"But Ah dinna have a broken heart," came the softer, more puzzled protestation.

"Well, something's eating you. One of your kids sick?" he guessed, for the sake of making conversation.

"Ah dinna have kids," Ian lied. This night he lied badly.

Finishing his drink, he made a point of paying for it, then ordered another. Ed complied, then sidled away.

Ian sipped his second drink, then remembered why he had come and finished it in four swallows. As the bartender predicted, the alcohol went rapidly to his brain, taking the edge off his "broken heart."

With batteries recharged, Ian turned, back to the bar, to survey the customers. When no one looked over at him, his face flushed in anger. It was one thing to be ignored when he was frightened and scared; another thing entirely, when he was on the prowl.

"What's a matter wid yuh bastards?" he demanded to a group of men sitting at a table in the corner. "Ain't there a man amongst yuh what'll give Wolf Eyes fifty bucks fer a blow job?"

"Leave us alone, you fucking gay prick," one of them spat, clearly annoyed by the intrusion. Rather than repulse or insult him, the words raised his ire.

"Gay? Gay is it, then? Gay means happy, an' Ah've niver been more miserable in me whole fuckin' life!"

The men looked away, clearly uninterested. It was not a night to be ignored, however. Striding up to them, Ian grabbed the speaker by his jacket and pulled him to his feet. Startled, the man attempted to escape, but was held fast.

"Ah came to this fuckin' country wid only one goal in mind – to find me a respectable job. An' what happened? Ah sold me soul to the Devil an' Ah'm no longer a wolf. Widout me identity, Ah'm nuthin'! Do yuh unnerstan'? Nuthin'!"

Tossing the terrified man back into the table, Ian turned around, addressing all the startled patrons.

"Ah'm not askin', Ah'm tellin'. Where's the man – or men – big enuf to take me on?"

The other three men from the upturned table exchange glances, then accepted the challenge for their friend. Without a word, they jumped on Ian from behind, knocking him, face down, to the floor.

Recovering from his initial surprise, the champion of Edinburgh threw one off, struggled to his feet and landed a punch to a third before receiving a kick from behind. With air gushing from his lungs, he fell forward into one of the men from another table. Sensing an easy victory with five or six men against one, the fighters crowded around, each hoping to land a killing blow and thus inherit the bragging rights.

Ian did not go quietly. Roaring after the manner of a wounded beast, he flailed with his arms, scratched, clawed, kicked and finally spat.

The confrontation was over almost before it began. When Ian was on his face, pressed to the floor by two bodies sitting atop him, another placed killing blows into the small of his back. Ed finally broke up the contest.

"All right!" he shouted, shooing away the pugilists as though they were flies and not men. "Break it up. You've had your fun."

"He started it," one accused.

"Yeah. The sonofabitchbastard fag. What did he think we were, anyway?"

"Get out. All of you," Ed ordered. When they hesitated, uncertain whether there was still a chance to land more blows, he used a threat more potent than physical force. "Or I'll call the cops and give them your names. There's two hundred dollars damage to this place, easy. Who wants to pay for it?"

The verbal insecticide was effective. Gathering together, the group dissipated, hurrying away before the threat could be carried out. Following them were several other disappointed patrons. They had hoped for some more definite conclusion to the argument, but with the police undoubtedly coming, they did not want to be interviewed, either for complicity or as witnesses in a law suit.

"Get up," Ed ordered the prone Wolf Eyes. "And get out of here. I am gonna call New York's finest because I'm gonna have to file an insurance claim. But don't think that'll get you out of paying damages. You I know. When you come to work tomorrow, you'd better have some cash in your jeans."

"Go to hell," Ian groused, but did as he was told. Delilah had warned him against antagonizing Ed and he knew the longer he tarried, the higher the tab for damages was likely to get.

Staggering outside, ears ringing from shooting pains along his rib cage, blood dripping from an open cut over his left eye, he tripped over his own feet, nearly losing his balance. He would have plunged to the ground, had not a man streaked out from the shadows and caught him.

Surprised, Ian began to pull away from the restraining arms, assuming the stranger wanted to finish the job he had started inside.

"It's all right," the man pleaded in a surprisingly gentle voice. "I'm not here to hurt you."

"Why not?" Ian demanded, furiously blinking his eyes to bring them into focus. "Ah'm free game tonight."

"I wasn't one of those who hit you. I'm sorry for what happened."

"Sorry?" Ian drunkenly hiccupped. "Why be sorry? Ah went in lookin' fer it an' Ah got what Ah deserved. Only," he miserably added, "Ah had hoped one o' them bastards mighta done me in. Put me outta me misery."

"You mustn't say that."

"It's a free country, isna it?" Ian bitterly demanded. "Land o' the brave an' home o' the free. It's a song, correct? A patriotic song? Ah remember learnin' it. Ah believed it, too. Christ on the cross, Ah was born dumb."

"No. Not dumb. We all learn from our mistakes."

"What are yuh?" the drunken man demanded, drawing back his head in exaggerated surprise. "Sume sorta preacher?"

"No. I'm not any sort of preacher. But I heard your proposition to those men at the table."

"What prop-o-sition was that, then?"

"About a blow job. Fifty dollars, I believe, was the price you named. Are you still interested?"

Ian laughed, holding his ribs from the pain.

"Well, Ah dinna know that Ah'm worth that now. Ah'm a wee bit the worse fer wear."

"Come home with me." When Ian hesitated, clearly torn, he added, "Please?"

"Please? Please?" the wolfman snorted. "Dinna yuh know that's not a word to use wid a whore? Yuh fergit all the social graces when yuh're buying sumeone's services. That's part o' the game."

"I'm not playing a game. I don't like game playing."

"Oh, right," Ian scoffed, blowing blood-tinged air through his bleeding nose. "Ah know all aboot yuh boys. None o' yuh play games until yuh git me home, an' then it's whips an' chains an' 'devices o' insertion'."

"We're not all like that."

"That's what Ah've heard," Ian replied, suggestively raising an eyebrow.

"I mean it. I won't try and convince you here. Please. Come home with me."

"Why? Yuh think Ah'm too drunk an' too beat up to demand me Pay Day?"

"No. It's because I'm lonely and I don't want to go home to an empty house."

Something in the tone of the man's voice conjured up a mouthful of saliva. Turning to spit it out, Ian shook his wounded head.

"Whatever yer trouble is, Ah dinna want inny part o' it."

"My best friend just died. I miss him so much my insides are all eaten away. You don't have to do anything... physical. I don't need a blow job. Just your company. For which I will pay you," he added.

"No one pays jest fer company."

"All right," the man conceded quickly. "Fifty dollars for a blow job. In advance."

Reaching into his pocket, he withdrew a leather wallet. Taking out fifty dollars, he handed the money to Ian.

"Ah think Ah'd rather go home wid one o' them rough-houses," he protested, finding his fingers accepting the paper. "Ah'm more fer fightin' than lovin' tonight."

"Please?"

Ian groaned, then nodded acceptance.

"A'right. But no more talkin'. Me head hurts. An' no more 'pleases.' That is the kinda word which Ah dinna want to hear. Niver ag'in."

"I won't say it. Can you walk, or shall we take a cab?"

"Ah kin walk."

The stranger slipped an arm through Ian's and guided him down the sidewalk.

"This is very kind of you," he continued, uncertain whether Ian understood him or not. "I just don't want to be alone tonight."

In twenty minutes they reached a small neighborhood. For most of the walk, Ian kept his eyes clamped shut, for fear of seeing any moon beams. He did not want to be reminded of what and of whom he no longer was.

Pausing only long enough to unlock the door, the man guided Ian through, turned on a light switch, then shut the door.

"You can open your eyes now," he said. His words were kind. Ian choked, coughed, then spit blood into his hand. "I'm afraid you're really hurt. Would you rather I took you to an emergency room?"

"Ah'm no hurt," the beast demurred. "Banged up but no hurt. Ah'll survive."

"Thank God for that."

"Ah'll no be thankin' God fer innythin'. If God is in His heaven, He's no friend o' mine."

"Here, sit down. Can I get you anything to drink? Some coffee, maybe?"

"Whisky."

"No. I don't have any in the house."

"Yuh do, but yuh're no' goin' to offer me inny."

The man grinned, then pointed to the couch.

"Sit down, pl –. Sit down."

Ian started to comply, then shook his head.

"Where's the bedroom? Ah came here to do a job."

"The bedroom's through there. The second one on the left, please." He cringed at the unanticipated use of the forbidden word, then sighed in relief as Ian seemed not to notice.

Following the directions, Ian walked into the hall, pausing briefly at the first door on the left.

"This is a bedroom," he unkindly observed. "What's wrong wid this bedroom?"

"It's the one I shared with my friend."

"Aye. The one who died. What did he die of?"

"He... had a venereal disease."

If he meant to shock Ian, his attempt failed.

"Aye. Ah might o' known. Are yuh infested wid it, too?"

"I don't know. Probably."

"Yuh shoulda been more careful," Ian hissed. "Did they not tell yuh to wear a condom? Or was it frum a blood transfusion?" he added. His intent was to hurt, but the shock effect failed.

"No. It wasn't from a blood transfusion. It was from another friend. A long time ago. He had been suffering for years."

"Well, then, Ah'm glad he's dead. Sufferin' is bad for the soul," he added. "An' bad fer yuh, too." Speaking louder, Ian shuffled past the forbidden room to the next, unbuttoning his shirt as he walked. Entering the room, it was he who turned on the light. "Ah recommend a good screw. That'll take yuhr mind off yuhr troubles."

The man, who had not identified himself, said nothing. When Ian had stripped to bare flesh, he indicated the bed.

"Lie down, if you will."

The request was not immediately complied with. Noting the hesitation, Ian suggestively patted the mattress.

"Cume on, little darlin'. Cume sit beside me. Ah dinna want to catch a cold." The man did not move. "Rrrright here. Snuggle up tight an' let me take yuh on a wondrous journey." Nothing. "Dinna tell me yuh're a shy one. If yuh canna make 'love' in the light, turn it off. It dinna make no difference to me."

"You've been badly used. I'm sorry. Deeply sorry."

"Save yuhr pity fer yuhrse'f. Ah'll no be wantin' it."

"We all need pity at one time or another."

"If it's pity yuh're wantin', yuh've cume to the wrong man. Ah'm no' sellin' pity. Ah'm sellin' me body. Now – tell me what yuh want. Yuh're fifty dollars to the good. Ask, an' Ah'll produce."

"Anything?"

The single word sent a chill through Ian's naked body. Wiping the sudden cold sweat from his brow, he smiled thinly.

"Now, that's better. Aye. Innythin'. Yuh'll get a bargain this night. Innythin', an' all fer fifty dollars. My usual is one hundred an' fifty. An' Ah'm worth it, too."

"I believe you."

"Then ask. Break out yer devices. Poot on yer costume. Wave yer arms over yuhr head an' beg fer the screw o' yer life."

"Get in the bed. Under the blankets and the sheet."

Ian did as requested. The man hesitated, then turned out the light. In the silence which followed, Ian sensed he was removing his clothes. When he finally sat on the bed, the action was tentative.

A glib comment on his tongue, Ian bit the words off and said nothing. By the ticking of the small alarm clock on the bedside table, he counted five minutes before the man slowly swung his legs over the edge; until his full weight rested on the mattress.

Another minute passed, then a second. The cold sweat reappeared on Ian's lip and his heart pounded at twice the rate of the second hand. With his brain fogged, he could not fathom what new and horrible tortures the man had in store for him.

"Order me," Ian said suddenly, startling himself with the hollowness of his voice.

"Hold me."

Without hesitation, Ian wrapped his arms around the man's bare chest. He expected this to be the beginning of the nightmare. The only thing he did not anticipate was nothing. Which is precisely what happened.

With a dread so palpable Ian could feel the arteries in his temples throb, he decided he must make some move, create some impasse from the terrible anticipation mounting in his brain. With a fatalistic resolve a soldier might experience lifting his head out a bunker into the sure and certain fire of enemy marksmen, Ian nibbled on the man's ear.

He got no response. Puckering his lips, he kissed the man's cheek. It was cold to the touch.

"Christ," Wolf Eyes whispered. "Yuh're like touchin' a corpse."

"I am a corpse," came the hollow voice.

"What do yuh mean?"

"I told you. My friend just died."

"Yuh're friend.... Not *yuh.*" But Ian was not as convinced as he wanted to be.

"We lived together for fourteen years. We were – we considered ourselves married. Do you know what it's like to lose someone you love – someone you've shared your heart and soul with for fourteen years?" The man choked over the words. A small rivulet of spittle ran down the right side of his mouth. He made no attempt to wipe it away.

Like tears, it would return.

"Aye. Ah do," Ian blurted, breaking, for the first time, the cardinal rule he had established for himself after his first, brutal experience with Charles Denning.

"I thought so. I thought... I saw that kind of hurt behind your eyes."

"Listen," Ian demanded, drawing back, eyes wide with fear. "Ah dinna unnerstan' what yuh want. Furst yuh say yuh want a blow job an' then yuh say you dinna. Tell me, for Christ's sake, what yuh're settin' me up fer."

"My name is Jim."

"Ah dinna want to know yuhr name."

"My friend's name was Bill. Two pretty common, everyday names. Jim and Bill. James and William. Who would think?"

"Think what?"

"So much love could be conjured up by the mere mention of those two names."

"Ah dinna want to think."

Jim ignored him. Or if he did not, then it was his demand for the "services rendered" clause for which he had hired Ian.

"I call him my friend. Friend. It sounds so... casual. Our relationship was anything but casual. I loved him, with every fibre of my being. We were married. But when you're gay, you can't say you're married. That's a dignity the 'straight' world denies us."

He sniffed and this time, wiped his nose.

"Some religions – not the major ones – allow us some sort of marriage ceremony, but no one is really comfortable with it. For church members, it's a concession, a bone they toss out. It makes them feel Christian. Charity. If they really understood charity, they would concede the fact that love is the one universal constant in the universe. Not a qualified love – not a 'love' between a man and a woman, for that's not what they mean; they don't mean *love*. They mean sex. Sex for the sake of procreation."

Beneath the sheet and the blanket a small tremor began.

"Using their definition, childless marriages are sham unions; affection between husband and wife is not good enough."

"Ah dinna want to hear this. Here. Let me fondle yuh. Yuh'll fergit –"

"Don't touch me there!" Jim screamed, pulling back from Ian's touch as though he had acid on his fingers. "I told you. I'm grieving. My heart is broken. I'm just... afraid of the dark. Afraid to be alone tonight."

Ian withdrew his hand but he could not shake the sensation of coldness.

"The last sight I had of Bill was lying in a cold, sterile hospital bed, the tip of his tongue protruding between his teeth. His eyes were half closed, the pupils rolled up into his skull, the skin of his face a –" He laughed bitterly. "A deadly pallor. His fists were clenched."

Inside the tremor two fists clenched.

"Don't ever let anybody tell you death is peaceful. That's a damned lie! Death is never peaceful. It's an ugly, horrid rite of passage. The last, ineffectual gasps for breath, the quivering of the heart muscle.... The wild stare... the light burning out."

"Shut up, will yuh?" Ian screamed, trying to get off the bed and away from a horror even worse than the ones he knew so well. "It's no' like that!"

"But it is. I saw it. I wish to God I hadn't, but I did. I sat at his bedside, all night long, holding his hand. Once in a while, he'd squeeze my fingers." Jim began to weep, the salt tracks staining his broken heart. "No. That's not true. I'm glad I stayed. I promised him, you see. Promised I'd stay with him. Pray for him. See he died with dignity."

Ian put his hands over his ears but the words penetrated the flimsy barriers without difficulty.

"Do you know what the worst part was? The very worst part? Not watching Bill die. I knew he had to die; he needed release. It was watching the nurses come and go. They didn't come often – once an hour or so, just to look in. It wasn't his passing which made them uncomfortable – it was my holding his hand. One man, holding the hand of another."

Ian's hand went numb.

"It's queer, you see. Against nature. Not even in death are we accorded any pity. If I had been a woman; if I were Bill's wife, they would have touched me on the shoulder, brought me coffee, whispered words of solace. Not very much to give, really. Just enough to let me know they cared. One human being to another. Because I was a man and not a woman, no one said anything. Not one word. Not one... blessed word."

"Ah'm sorry," Ian stammered, shaking under the burden of Mankind he unwittingly carried.

"Thank you. Thank you for that. I appreciate it."

They cried together, the fresh grief and the old grief finding common ground. When Jim lifted his head, finally, to stare at Ian, he did not need to repeat his former request.

The wolf man hugged the gay man, neither of them "human" in the eyes of the "fish and fowl" world.

# CHAPTER 24

"Let me pay you," Jim said as Ian swung his cramped legs off the side of the bed. It was morning.

"Yuh a'ready paid me. Besides, Ah did no' give yuh a blow job."

"I didn't want one."

"Ah did no' screw you."

"I did not want you to."

"Yuh did no' fuck me."

Jim shook his head sadly.

"I was married and now I'm widowed. I have no interest in sex. Besides," he added, sniffing back his memories, "It's too dangerous. I would infect you. You have to be careful."

"Use a condom."

"Who can be sure?"

"Then Ah dinna want inny more o' yuhr money. Ah dinna earn it."

"Your time has value." Jim's voice was tired, drained of emotion.

"Ah git paid fer action, no' time."

"Your compassion, then. That's worth more to me than –" Ian shook his head. "Then let me make you another offer."

"What other offer?" came the suddenly suspicious interrogative.

"Move in with me. Live with me. Stay with me. Watch over me; just as I watched over Bill. Maybe you can... care for me. I'm going to need help. I'll pay you." Ian retreated a step. "Maybe in time you can come to love me. I'll make it worth your while."

"Love yuh?" Ian whispered.

"The thought so repulses you? You could not love a man?"

There was sadness for a moment before the terrible hollowness returned to Ian's voice.

"Ah canna love. Not yuh – not innyone. That's the point. Can yuh no' see it? Ah've loved once an'... lost. Like yuh," Ian added. "Ah dinna have no more heart. It's turned to stone. Dinna ask what Ah canna give."

"You can't say that."

"Ah kin an' Ah will. Ah dinna want to love here," he explained, holding hand to heart. "Ah only love here," he continued, pointing to his naked body. Then, accusingly, "No one's iver asked me fer that kind o' love befer."

"You could love me – as a friend?"

"Ah canna love! How much clearer kin Ah make it, man?"

"I beg you. I'm afraid to be alone. Afraid of the nightmares. Afraid of this house."

Jim reached out a hand, trying to touch Ian's arm. Jumping back, the tall, stone-hearted man shook his head, wild-eyed.

"No! No more touchin'. Not that way. Beat me, if it will make yuh feel better. Thrash me. Stuff a dildo down me throat. Tie me up an' rape me. Dress me up an' –"

"Shut up! I don't play games! I'm not like that!" Then, more softly, "I thought you understood."

"No, Ah dinna unnerstan'! Ah dinna unnerstan' innythin'! Ah'm a married man. Ah canna be stayin' wid yuh. Ah canna care fer yuh; Ah canna love yuh! Look!" he shrieked, holding up his left hand. "Canna yuh no see what Ah mean?"

He meant to display his wedding ring, but there was no ring on his finger. Both men stared at the naked place where a ring should be, neither commenting. It was only when Ian shook his hand, then grasped it with his right did Jim make any attempt to speak.

"You've taken it off – when you bathed, perhaps –"

"No! Ah lost it! Ah fergot! Ah had it... an' Ah lost it. Oh, Jesus, Ah have no memory...." Ian staggered backward, still hiding his disfigured hand. "Meggie. Meggie. Ah lost yuhr ring an' look what's becume o' me. Ah swore to yuh Ah'd git a respectable job an' here Ah am, dishonored, disgraced, made naked by me own hand!"

Thrusting out the offending digit, he slammed it into the wall.

"If a part offend thee, cut it off," he remembered from somewhere in the depths of his religious training. "Cut it off," he repeated. "That's what Ah'll do. Cut it off."

Spinning wildly, Ian searched for some weapon, some means to detach his ring finger from his body. Sensing the despair yet feeling the insanity far more acutely, Jim forced himself from the bed, tottered on unsteady legs, then pointed toward the door.

"Leave here!" he commanded. Ian started at him in stark incomprehension. "Leave here. I asked you for help, and I would help you, but I can't. For God's sake, go. And I beg you, don't hurt yourself. Not over a missing ring. Life is too precious."

"Precious?" Ian spat, eyes narrowing in righteous indignation. "Precious? How kin yuh say that when yuhr best friend is dead?"

"Because I know he would want me to live. To find happiness with what time I have left."

"Yuh're daft," Ian shuddered, shaking his head. "There is no happiness. No' fer me. Niver. No' ag'in. Ah kin no' even howl. Ah tried an' Ah failed. Ah'm nuthin'. Do yuh know what that's like?"

"Yes. I think I do."

"But Ah dinna want to find happiness an' yuh do. So we're no' the same. Yuh must go one way an' Ah another. Ah kin only work now fer me – fer two someone's elses. No' fer meself."

"Then I feel sorrier for you than I do for myself."

Ian made a move, then jerked in spasmodic realization that he was naked. Grabbing his clothes, he shoved stiff legs through trouser legs, numb arms into narrow sleeves.

"Good-bye, then," he growled, pausing at the door, back to Jim. Slowly turning, he raised his right hand in simple farewell, started to wave, then thought better of it and slipped away.

Once outside, he broke, not into a lope, but a run. He ran until his mind gave out and then remembered no more.

When Ian awoke, it was to a piercing beam of light shining into one eye. His first thought was that he had been unconscious all day and was now coming to as the moon rose once more. Struggling to maintain control, he licked his lips, swallowed and made a weak attempt to howl. Whatever noise he made was lost to someone speaking over him.

"Just a minute. He seems to be coming out of it."

"Don't hold him down!" came a second, vaguely familiar voice. "Let him alone. Leave his arms free."

"He may hurt himself."

"No. He won't."

The piercing beam vanished with the click of a pen light. It had not been the moon, then, for moon beams were not turned on and off at will.

The voices moved away, forcing Ian to strain to hear what they were saying.

"There doesn't seem to be any concussion, but if he complains of a sharp, persistent headache, he should go to the hospital. Keep him off his feet until you're sure he's cognizant. And don't let him drink. Booze."

"I won't. Thank you."

The speakers moved away. Money was exchanged, the sound grating to Ian's acutely attuned ears. More waiting, then he felt the smooth, cool touch of a hand in his. Remembering the shame associated with his hand, Ian groaned, making a weak attempt to raise his head.

"Where am Ah?" he asked.

"Neither heaven or hell."

"Delilah?"

"None other."

Finally opening his eyes, Ian smiled weakly into her troubled eyes.

"How did Ah git here?"

"I found you outside the bar. Ed and I dragged you upstairs."

"Oh," Ian muttered, remembering. "He's mad at me."

"He'll get over it. You're quite an attraction these days, baby. You bring in the customers. How do you feel?"

"Like me old mother used to say, 'like death warmed over.'" She patted his hand reassuringly, then, noting his reaction, draw back. "Ah'm sorry," he apologized quickly. "Ah'm feeling low."

"So I gathered."

"Ah lost me weddin' ring."

Delilah stared at his hand, considered, started to make a comment, then changed her mind.

"You don't look too good."

"Who was that man? A doctor?" She did not reply. "Yuh paid him," he accused. "Yuh've got to let me make it right wid yuh."

"He's not a doctor and I didn't pay him."

"Then who was he?"

"My brother."

"Aye. An' Ah'm the Duke o' Edinburgh."

"You're learning," she smiled approvingly. "He's not a doctor. We call on him sometimes when we need medical care and don't want to go out for it."

"Who's 'we'?"

"The girls and I."

"So, Ah'm one o' the girls." It was the first time he grinned.

"And a damn tall one," she agreed. "But we've been through that. Not enough on top to get by, sonny boy. And you'd have to do something about this," she teased, running her hand familiarly against his chin.

"What time is it?"

"Half past ten."

"At night?"

"Day."

"Oh, me God! Meg an' Storm'll be wonderin' where Ah am! They'll be worried."

"Take it easy. They've already been here."

"Where, here?"

"Here, here. To my place. When you didn't come home, they set out in search of you. And found you."

"Like this?" he cried.

"No. I just told them you were sleeping off a hard night of 'bouncing,' which isn't far from the truth. I told them you'd sleep here and they went back home."

He sighed, then laid an arm over his face in sad resignation.

"What would Ah do widout yuh?"

She shook her head thoughtfully, as her finger wound around a stray lock of his long, dark hair.

"I don't know. Have a 'respectable job' by now? Be able to howl at the moon?"

The arm flew away and he leaned up, eyes wide with wonder.

"How – how can yuh know? How is it yuh unnerstan' Ah canna howl at the moon?"

"I make it my business to know everything," she evasively replied. He shook his head.

"No. That's no' it. It's becuz yuh're a wolf, too."

With lips pursed, Delilah withdrew her hand, feeling the closeness of his body, the intensity of his confession, the stirrings of emotions she would rather not pursue.

"Who me? No way. I'm not a wolf. And if I were, I'd be the original lone wolf."

Ian unhappily dropped his chin.

"There is no such thing as a lone wolf."

"Like hell there isn't."

The room was growing close. Finding it hard to breath, Delilah pulled away, first to the corner of the bed, then standing, she turned her back to him.

"Get some sleep. Your 'pups' won't be around to collect you before lunch."

"A'right," he agreed, leaning back and closing his eyes. When she left, he let out a sigh of relief. Like her, he was glad to be alone, but for different reasons.

Life was moving too fast, in too many directions. He needed time to think; time to sort through his emotions.

Time to come to grips with the New World. It was not easy for a man more wolf than human being.

Meg and Storm took the slow route back to the Sea Breeze Apartments. They might have hailed a cab, for with Ian's new job as club bouncer, money concerns had been erased. But there was in them that inborn reserve when it came to spending money.

"We Scots are tight as a drrrrum when it cumes to parting wid a pence," Ian had once announced. He had meant it more as an observation than a tenet, but his daughters had adopted the saying as a way of life. Fortunately, it worked well with their financial situation, so they never had cause to repent.

"Let's go through the park," Storm suddenly suggested. "Ah have to see a tree or Ah'll go mad."

Diverting their route, the two children crisscrossed streets like the natives they were becoming, arriving at their destination half an hour after leaving Delilah's apartment.

"It's no' much," Storm complained, scooping up a handful of dirt and running it through her fingers.

"The soil or the park?"

"Both."

"Take heart. Wid Ian's new job, we're closer to a house o' our own every day."

"Ah know. But Ah wonder what kind o' a house it will be."

"What yuh mean? How many trees?"

"A happy house or a sad house." Meg stared off in the distance at a group of youths coming their way and did not answer. "He's changed, yuh know," Storm continued, lost in the workings of her own mind. "Sumethin's happened to him. What do yuh suppose caused him to end up at Delilah's last night? A bad fight?"

"Aye. A bad fight," Meg agreed without conviction, never taking her eyes off the approaching gang.

"It musta been four or five o' them ag'in one. Ah wonder they dinna take him to hospital." No answer. "Yuh suppose he'll be a'right?"

"Ah suppose. Delilah said so."

Annoyed at her sister's seeming disinterest, Storm tugged on her sleeve.

"An' what aboot them two, innyway?"

"What aboot them?"

"Ah think he likes her. Do yuh like her?"

"Aye. She has sense. She likes him, too."

"What do yuh suppose she does fer a livin'? Bein' a dancer or sumthin'? Ah looked in all the papers an' Ah dinna see nowhere advertised where they have repertory plays like she described. Not the kind o' places where they employ bouncers."

"Ah know."

"What, then?"

"Ah know that boy," Meg indicated with a nod of her head. Alerted to the danger by the tone in her sister's voice, Storm sharply looked up.

"He lives in the Sea Breeze. Ah see him go out at all hours o' the night an' day," Storm agreed. "He's a bad one. Kind Al says he deals drugs."

"Let's go."

"Ah'll no' be runnin' –"

"It's them queer foreigners," the boy in question shouted, pointing at the MacDhuis. "Them who talks queer."

"Watch who yuh're callin' queer," Storm warned, eyes flashing.

"I'm calling you queer. Just like your old man."

"Ian MacDhui is no' queer!" It was Meg this time, fists tightened in anger.

"He is, too, queer. He's a fag. He goes out all night an' comes back in the morning all done in. I followed him, once –"

"He's a bouncer," Storm continued. "An' iffn yuh know what's good fer yuh, yuh'll keep yer dirty mouth shut!"

"Dirty mouth is it?" the boy laughed. "What's that in your hand? It looks like dirt to me. I've got something better for you to have."

His licentious gyration of hips, while holding out a small bag of white powder, brought the red flush of fury to both offspring of Ian and Megan MacDhui.

"We know all aboot yuh. Yuh're a dope pusher an' Kind Al says yuh'll be dead befer yuh're twenty."

"Oh, 'Kind Al,' is it? That's a laugh. He'll be dead tonight," the youth bragged. "I'll sell him something bad and he'll be rolling around in that dirty alley of his, screaming that the bugs are eating him alive!"

"He dinna use drugs! An' iffn yuh touch a hair o' his head, Ah'll kill yuh!"

"You'll kill me, little girl?" Tossing the packet to a friend, he beckoned her forward with his hand. "Come on. Maybe you'd like a taste of what your old man is dishing out."

Not as frightened as she was realistic, Meg placed a restraining hand on Storm.

"It's seven ag'inst two."

"Ah dinna care if it's seventeen ag'inst two. Yuh heard what he said. Are we supposed to take them dirty words from that piece o' crap?"

Her sentiment struck Meg where it hurt. Shaking her head, she moved slightly away from Storm, assuming a boxer's stance.

"Let's see if a city boy kin take on the heirs o' the wrasslin' champ o' Edinburgh," she challenged. "Ian MacDhui beat a man ten times yuh're size an' has the trophy to prove it. Cume on, then."

Laughing at the seeming absurdity of the challenge, the boy winked at his friends, then made a dash at Meg. Having moved into an open space, however, she easily darted away from his lunge, licking him as his grasping hands missed her.

"Bitch!" he cursed, spinning back, eyes wild with artificial courage.

He attacked again, this time landing a blow to Meg's chin and then two quick jabs to her ribs. She staggered but did not fall. Recovering faster than he expected, Meg kicked him again, this time in the groin. As he bent over from the unexpected force of the strike, two of his companions jumped Storm.

The three street youths had height, weight and age advantages, but their fighting skills were dampened by their inability to think clearly. They were flying high and none of them considered two girls any kind of threat.

Pushing Storm to the ground, the boy on top spread his body over her and began making humping actions, laughing for his friends to see how easy a time he was having. He had not anticipated the enemy's wiles, however, and before he realized his mistake, Storm sunk her teeth into the lobe of his ear. Biting down with all her strength, she came close to ripping the flesh off before he managed to pull away.

"Dirty whore," he screamed, pummeling her face with his fists. "Dirty bitch!"

Striking her again, he gritted his teeth and tore away at her shirt, ripping the cloth at the shoulder. Meg roared in righteous indignation, leaping on his back in an attempt to pull him off. Before she could hurt him, however, his friends wrapped their arms around her and yanked her away.

"We'll give you a taste of New York you haven't seen before, *tourist,*" one laughed in her ear.

Meg struggled, but could not free herself. Cursing through gritted teeth, she kicked, then tried to gouge the eyes of her captors, to no avail. Another blow, this time to the side of her head, stunned her into momentary submission.

"Come on, little girl," the first was whispering to Storm. "Give me what I want."

Wrapping his hands beneath her trousers, he managed to slip them half way to her knees before Storm reached into her pocket and withdrew a small bag. As the boy pressed down closer on her, she struggled for position, held her breath, then summoned her strength. As his face pressed down over hers, she brought her left hand up, smashing the bag against his cheek. Its contents exploded over his face.

Screaming with surprise, the attacker drew back, allowing Storm time to roll away.

"Shit! Shit! Shit!" he shouted, spitting the vile slime from his contaminated mouth.

This was the opportunity they needed. Exchanging quick glances, Meg and Storm took off, running for all their might. Before the others could divert their attention back to their victims, the two were far enough away to make pursuit impractical.

Meg and Storm did not stop running until they had covered twenty blocks. Only when they ascertained they were not being followed, did they duck into an alley to recoup their dignity.

"Are yuh a'right?" Meg puffed, blowing air through distended cheeks.

"Aye. That bastard made me feel sick to me stomach. But Ah got him. Not exactly in the way Ian MacDhui would o' beat him, but in me own way." Holding up her hands, also covered with foul smelling muck, she smiled proudly. "Sheep dip. Ah tolt Ian Ah brought sume an' he dinna believe me."

"He'll be glad to believe yuh, now!"

"Aye. But we canna tell him. If he thinks we've been in a fight, there'll be a hell o' a ruckus."

Meg nodded in sad agreement, ruefully rubbing her bruised face.

"True. Cume on. Let's git outta here. We had better be cleaned up befer we have to go an' fetch him."

Realizing the truth of her words, Storm yanked triumphantly at her ripped shirt, ran her fingers through her messed hair, then straightened her shoulders.

"Bloody bastards. Ah'll git them, yet. An' iffn he ever touches me like that ag'in, Ah'll cut his prick off wid a knife."

"Not widout my help," Meg vowed, eyes narrowed. "Let's go. Ah know jest where to git some knives."

"Wait a minute." Looking around the alley, Storm easily found that which she sought. Pausing briefly to refill her bag with dog feces, she grinned toothily. "Not as effective as sheep dip, but it'll do the job, Ah wager."

Returning her grin, the two small fighting MacDhuis hurried off.

She was watching television and did not hear him come out of the bedroom. When his shadow crossed over the screen, she gave a start and looked up sharply, expecting to see –

But what Delilah saw was not what she expected. Ian MacDhui, sleepily rubbing his eyes, grinned as he caught her startled expression. As usual, he misunderstood her look.

"Sumethin' happen in one o' yuhr stories yuh wasna expecting?" he asked, indicating the soap opera.

"Sumethin' happened, a'right," she agreed, staring in stark appreciation at the man before her. Clad only in a long shirt, the tails of which draped low but not modestly over his anatomy, he was a sight to behold. It was not the first time Delilah had seen his body, for she had taken every opportunity to assess his physique, but it was the first time she had seen him *nearly* naked.

The difference between unclothed and alluringly undressed was dramatic.

"Honey, if clothes make the man, I never want to see you in anything else," she confessed, feeling both foolish and aroused.

"Ah jest wanted to ask iffn Ah could take a shower."

"How are you feeling?"

Which was not as innocent as it sounded.

"Much better."

Turning off the television, Delilah stood, hesitated, feeling suddenly shy, then shook off one mood in exchange for another.

"You know, Wolf Eyes, you make me feel –"

"Won't yuh call me Ian?" he interrupted.

She stopped, considered his request in light of her present situation, then demurred.

"No. It's better that I don't. Not now. Not when I feel the way I do. You know, Wolf Eyes, you're doing something to me."

It was she who made the advance. Standing on tiptoe to throw her arms around him, her lips found his and they kissed. Without either fully understanding what was happening, the embrace turned passionate and desperate.

Before she could break it off long enough to get him into her bedroom, he pulled away, the color completely drained from his face.

"No," he choked, trembling violently.

"Why not? You're the first man I think I've ever really wanted."

"Ah canna –"

"What do you mean, 'yuh canna'? You damn sure can."

With a face torn by anguish, Ian back-stepped, hands out to ward off an imaginary blow.

"Ah'm a married man. Married past 'till death do us part.' Megan MacDhui is a part o' me; a part o' me, now an' forever."

"She's dead, Wolf Eyes."

"She lives fer me –"

"She doesn't keep your bed warm at night."

The crassness of the statement gagged him and his eyes misted.

"Ah love her –"

"Love her all you want. I'm talking about physical attraction, for God's sakes."

"Please, Ah'm askin' yuh not to say inny more."

"You're a fuckin' prostitute, Wolf Eyes! You've screwed around more in the past year than you've ever done in your life!"

"Aye," he agreed, swallowing his shame. "Wid men. But no' wid women. There's a difference. Wid men – wid most o' the men Ah serve – it's jest pure sex. Games, mebbe, aye, an' beatin's. Not love. What's between a man an' his wife is sacred."

"So, what does that make me?" she demanded with scorn. "Everyman's wife?"

"Ah think what men do to yuh is a sin."

"I'm not asking to be your wife, damn it. All I want is to get under the covers with you and generate some heat."

"No. Ah dinna want it to be like that between us. Ah dinna want to be yuhr 'john.'"

"I'm not asking you to pay me! I'm telling you, I want you."

"But in my wantin' there's more besides. How kin Ah take yuh to bed, as Ah took Meggie and she took me, when Ah have nuthin' to offer yuh; when Ah have no' the right to love yuh, knowin' Ah have to let yuh go out, night after night to earn a livin'?"

"Jesus," she spat. "One whore is asking another whore to screw around and he gives me the Sermon on the Mount. Spurn me, will you?"

With her head in turmoil and her pride severely wounded, Delilah rushed him, fists out. Landing blow after blow to his chest, which he took without any attempt at self-defense, she finally gave up, pushing him away from her, instead.

"Get out of here, you fucking prick! I don't understand you and I don't want to mother your kids. I'm sick of lying for you!"

Delilah continued to push him until Ian was at the door. Pausing only long enough to open it, she shoved him with such a vicious effort, he lost his balance and went sprawling, face down, into the hallway.

"Cover your own 'arse' from now on!" she screamed, slamming the door, then locking it. In a moment, the sound of the TV, at full blast, filled his ears.

Stunned, not from the attack but from the display of raw emotions, Ian twisted his long legs under him, hiding his face in his hands. The movement drew the shirt, already tangled, well up his back.

Thus, naked and exposed, Wolf Eyes curled into a fetal position and wept.

It was a far cry from howling.

# CHAPTER 25

The official line went something like this:

"There were seven of them, the bitches."

"They told us to meet them in the park; they lured us there, promising what girls promise."

"When we got there, they called us over and then came at us with knives and clubs, the dirty dykes."

"They had some kind of shit smeared all over themselves. It was disgusting."

"We tangled pretty good, but then these other guys came out of the bushes. What could we do?"

"We'll get 'em when they come home."

What the gang had not counted on was that Meg and Storm anticipated their plans and went into the apartment by climbing up the rear fire escape.

After waiting three hours, the gang had dispersed, gone off in search of other, more viable game.

Not much for a pack of wolf cubs to howl over.

Ian was waiting for them at the door, hands on his hips. To hide their entrance, they had climbed in through an exit on the sixth floor, then taken the stairwell up one flight.

"Yuh're late," the father announced, lips pursed.

"Aye," Meg nonchalantly agreed.

"Ah thought yuh were goin' to meet me at Delilah's."

"We met Kind Al on the way over and went on an excursion. Lost track o' time."

"Ah kin tell a lie when Ah hear one."

"Ah lie, yuh lie, we all lie together."

"What does that mean?"

Meg and Storm slipped past him, into the apartment. He shut the door behind them.

"It's a rhyme."

"It doesna rhyme. Tell me plain what yuh've been up to."

"We will, if yuh will," Meg replied, kicking off her shoes.

Ian's face flushed with anger.

"Ah asked yuh a question."

But she was through speaking. Storm took up the slack.

"Yuh've changed."

He hesitated, his own guilty awareness getting the better of him.

"Aye. Ah have."

"An' not fer the better."

"I'm survivin'." And then, "Ah'm makin' money. Good money."

"Which is not to be confused wid respectable money."

With the veins in his neck tightening, Ian clenched, then unclenched his fists.

"Ah dinna want to fight wid yuh. Tell me plain what yuh've been up to."

"We will, iffn yuh will."

"Stop!" he cried, already stretched to the breaking point. "Ah dinna know what yuh mean. Ah've changed an' not fer the better. A'right. So Ah have. Ah'm sorry fer it, but there's no goin' back."

"Aye, there is," Storm pouted, her own body trembling with emotion.

"What yuh mean?"

"Back. Back to Scotland. Now that we've saved money, Ah want to go back. Home."

"Our home is here."

"No. It isna. Our home is on the moors. Where Megan MacDhui is buried," she spitefully added, pointing an angry finger at him.

"Where her spirit roams," Meg suddenly blurted. "We canna find her here. An' neither kin yuh."

"Dinna tell me what Ah can an' canna find."

"We dinna want to stay here."

"A'right," he softly conceded. "Ah'll look fer another flat. Ah shoulda done that when Ad started makin' good money. But give me sume time."

"We dinna have time. Ah want to git out tonight."

"We canna make arrangements that fast. An' yuh know it."

"Then we'll move in wid Delilah."

"Yuh canna do that, either."

"Why not?"

He hesitated, but his truthful nature got the better of the lie his tongue was concocting.

"Ah had a fight wid her."

"Jesus!" Meg swore, throwing her head back in misery. "We've all been in a fight today."

Slumping down onto the couch, Ian dejectedly held his head in his hands.

"If that be the case, then Clan MacDhui lost, all the way around."

It was a sad admission.

While Meg went to lock the apartment door, Storm slammed shut the outside window, scaring away a nesting pigeon.

The summer wind was hot, bringing no relief from the searing temperatures. While it was always cool in the homes of his customers, returning, day after day to an un-air-conditioned flat cast a depressing pall over the spirit.

Despite his promise he look for new lodgings, Ian had made no attempt to relocate his clan, and neither child mentioned their request again. Any reference to that fateful day, when Ian quarreled with Delilah, Meg and Storm fought the gang of boys, and accusations of lies hung suspended in the air like dead dreams, was assiduously avoided.

Ian never questioned why his daughters cast furtive glances over their shoulders when they walked with him; they never inquired why the family was never invited back to Delilah's. In either case, answers would have necessitated untruths.

As Meggie Clarke MacDhui would say, "Let silence be yuhr best reply."

The cache of money under the mattress had grown enough for the MacDhuis to live comfortably. They no longer needed to furnish their home with castoffs, yet the trips with Kind Al were a ritual not to be ignored. They ate porterhouse steak, bought top cream for their coffee, ate steel-cut oats "imported from Scotland" and drank orange pekoe tea brought in from Canada.

Storm sported a new pair of "tennis shoes," meant for walking, Meg used a set of colored pencils to sketch the wildlife, which did not include any beasts of the canine genus, and Ian learned the lyrics to all the "Top 40" hits so popular with the young, working crowd who patronized the club where he was employed.

No one spoke of trees, books or respectable jobs.

The New World had become depressingly similar to the Old World as far as great expectations were concerned.

"Ah'm off," Ian announced, emerging from the bathroom, freshly shaved and smelling of Old Spice. Storm wrinkled up her nose as he passed.

"What?" he inquired, seeing her look. "Did Ah use too much?"

"Inny a-tall is too much," she complained. "Ah jest canna git used to yuh smelling like a city bloke."

"What would yuh rather Ah smelled like – sheep dip?" When she did not answer, he was sorry he asked. "Be good while Ah'm gone. Stay outta trouble."

"Dinna go innywhere, niver open the door to strangers an' be kind to one another," Meg quoted by heart. In the beginning, their repetition of his admonitions had been a game they played. This time, her tone of voice indicated the ritual had worn thin.

"Aye," he agreed, not to her words but to the sentiments behind them. "Ah'm thinkin' it's aboot time yuh started school."

"We canna go to school," Meg felt obliged to point out. "Not when we're in the country on *expired* tourist visas."

"Dinna lecture me," he snapped, then apologized with a curt gesture of his hand. "Ah know. Ah think it's aboot time Ah asked me employer to put in fer a proper work permit."

"Ah dinna see how you qualify," Storm groused, picking a tuft of lint from the threadbare couch. "There must be lots o' Americans what kin bounce a drunk on his head."

"Thank yuh fer that rousin' endorsement o' me skills an' talents," he replied, slinging a summer-weight jacket over his arm. It was too hot to wear, but it was, he explained, "Part o' me costume."

He habitually lost a jacket a week. He lied and said the hat check girl mistakenly gave it away and that his employer "made good his losses." Storm had suggested he order jackets in bulk, to save money, and there the matter dropped.

It was early, not quite 6 P.M. but Ian was restless and the idea of lounging in the flat with nothing to amuse himself but the dark stares of his daughters prickled the hairs on the back of his head. The fact they did not complain when he announced his early departure suggested they felt the same way about his perpetual scowl.

The elevator in the Sea Breeze Apartments had been repaired, but Ian chose to take the stairs, not trusting life and limb to what Meg described as "a disaster waitin' to happen." He had therefore worked up a sheen of perspiration over his lip and small wet spots beneath his arms when he emerged into the street.

Three men were lounging on the steps of a neighboring apartment building, smoking away the hours in idle nothingness. When they saw him, one poked another. All discarded their cigarettes, and stood as he approached.

"Hey. You," one called.

Once upon a time, Ian would have responded with a friendly grin and a greeting, but he had become too well versed in the American Way to bother turning his head. This evening, however, the salutation was more than a perfunctory meaning.

"Brit," a second man called. He tossed a five dollar bill on the sidewalk in front of Ian's feet. "That's for you."

Ian would have preferred to avoid them, having some vague memory of recognition, but tarried out of uneasy anticipation of worse to come.

"Ah dinna want yuhr money," he replied, sidestepping the offering.

"Not enough?" the third inquired. "How much does a queer like you make? Ten dollars a night? Twenty?"

"Pretty easy money, right, Irish boy?"

The top of Ian's hands broke out into a cold sweat, causing him to shiver uncomfortably.

"Lay off," he warned.

"That's a peculiar expression," the first laughed without humor. "Lay off. I bet you do a lot of that in your profession."

"Yeah; laying on and off."

"Ah dinna know what yuh mean," Ian retorted, moving away with what he hoped was an indifferent attitude. He had seen enough men with hate in their eyes to fully comprehend where these three were headed and wanted no part of it.

They fell in behind him, shadowing his movements as he hurried out of eyeshot from the twelfth story window where two sets of grey eyes were undoubtedly watching.

"We don't want your kind around here."

"Ah'm no' Irish," Ian replied. As a diversion, it failed, as he knew it would.

They drew closer, one making a half-hearted effort to grab his jacket. Jerking it away from the outstretched fingers, the Scotsman quickened his pace. Not until he was two blocks away from the Sea Breeze did he stop and face his accusers.

"Iffi yuh know what's good fer yuh, yuh'd better back off," he warned.

"You heard what I said; I said we don't want faggots living on our block."

"Especially queens like you. We got enough of our own without importing them from other countries."

"Ah-am-not-a-queen."

"You're not, ugh? Well, 'Mister Mac-Dooie,' the fact of the matter is, we know what you do for a living and it makes us sick."

"Fucking pervert. Why don't you go home?"

"Why dinna yuh go back to pickin' the wings off flies?" Ian demanded, his ire rising. "That's all yuh're good for."

He should have kept his temper, bitten his lips, blown off their cruel accusations, but his nerves were jangled and his pride stung. Words, as any sensitive person knew, were far more destructive than "sticks and stones," childish rhymes notwithstanding. He had been reminded of that once and the memory, too easily brought to mind, stung.

"How about we bash your damn head in and then kick your nuts off? I bet that'd put a crimp in your 'love making.'"

One of the men began moving to Ian's left, the other to his right, effectively encircling him. He knew their type, their hatreds, their prejudices.

He knew that three against one were bad odds.

"Maybe you need a little lesson."

"Maybe he needs a *big* lesson," laughed the third. "Taught to him by *men.*"

"Men?" Ian snorted, wanting nothing better than to see these three "men" taught a lesson in manners. "Ah know yuhr kind."

"And what kind is that?"

"The kind o' men who canna earn the love o' a good woman, so they hafta buy one. An' at that, they're so damned impotent, they have to pay her extra to keep her mouth shut aboot their ineffectualness."

Ian MacDhui had learned a great deal since his arrival in the New World.

"You dare say that to us, fag? When all you ball is some other fag's ass hole?"

"You wouldn't know what to do with a woman if she stood naked in front of you."

"Would yuh?" Ian demanded, his face changing from red to purple.

They came at him together, arms outstretched, fingers grasping. One had a knife, the other two short, stout lengths of pipe. Ducking under one wild lunge, Ian lashed out a fist, striking against an extended jaw, then grimacing under the slash of the sharp blade. Seeing blood, the attackers became careless, intoxicated with the belief a "fag" could not defend himself.

Taking advantage of their beer sodden assault, Ian backtracked, then caught the man with the knife as he thrust the point forward in what could have been a killing blow. Twisting his arm behind his back, Ian easily dislocated his shoulder, then sent him sprawling into the arms of his companions.

Temporarily stunned by the prowess of their victim, the men hesitated long enough for Ian to make a hard decision. Facing the brutal fact that if he were reported to the police for roughing up three citizens, he could be deported without a trial, he turned his back and began running, leaving his jacket behind, in yet another instance of the hat check girl giving it to the wrong man.

They followed him a block, then lagged behind, finally letting him escape into the crowd of evening traffic. With the sound of their crude, derisive taunts filling his ears, Ian ran the rest of the way to Mac's Bar and Grill, futility attempting to wear off his sense of cowardice by exercise.

Arriving out of breathe and disheveled, he paused outside the door to regulate his rapidly beating heart. Before going in, he also took the time to glance at his appearance in the shop-front glass. It was not the action of a vain man, nor one who appreciated his own good looks, but merely the hard-learned habit of one who earned his living by selling his body.

A man who looked like a bum was paid like a bum. This was the new order, the dictate of life for someone who had given up all thought of a respectable job. Gone were the days when a man was judged by the strength of his arms, the knowledge in his head, the sentience of his soul. What mattered to a john was the cut of his hair, the stamina of his bedroom skills and the amount of pain he could endure.

Walking into Mac's with an assumed air of nonchalance, Ian began whistling a tune. His hips swayed gently to the beat as he sauntered to the bar and ordered a drink. He had learned the tricks of the trade well.

"What'll it be, Wolf Eyes?" Ed inquired.

"The usual," Ian replied, nodding toward his special bottle.

"Only the best for you," The bartender replied in a quiet, respectful voice which carried across the dance floor.

Reaching for the bottle, labeled Chivas Regal, he poured a double shot of warm tea into a glass, then slid it across the polished counter top. In another two years, that same bottle would actually contain aged Scotch; in five, when Ian was a confirmed alcoholic, it would hold "two dollar" whisky.

Leaning, back to the bar, Ian sipped his drink and took in the customers with a practiced eye. Because it was early, the pickings were slim. Rather than the typical customers, well-dressed women sat around several tables. A number of them were staring at him with causal appreciation. These looks he ignored, or more accurately, did not see. They held no meaning for him; it was the lustful stares of men he had trained himself to spot.

Money was the name of the game.

Paying him no more attention, Ed accepted a tray of food from the back, carrying it over to one of the tables. He did not see a wet spot on the floor and slipped, falling hard. The contents of the tray spilled over one of the women.

Seeing the disruption, Ian hurried over to give his friend a hand up, then reached into his pocket for his clean, black pocket linen. Handing it to the woman, he smiled apologetically.

"If yuh get to that fast, it may not stain."

Hesitant at first, the woman finally accepted the handkerchief, using it to blot out the splash of mixed drink.

"Thank you," she replied, finally handing it back. As he reached for it, her hand lingered over his, a smile of gratitude on her face. "How kind of you to offer it."

"It's me pleasure," Ian replied, taking back the cloth. Thinking no more about the incident, he returned to the bar, where he saw, for the first time in two months, a familiar friend waiting for him.

"Hello, Wolf Eyes," Delilah said. "How goes it?"

"It goes."

He began to add her name, then cut himself off and looked away. His omission was not lost on her.

"Why won't you say my name?"

"Because Ah dinna know what yuhr real name is."

"What difference does that make? I called you Wolf Eyes just now."

"It makes a difference to me," he mumbled, feeling awkward and embarrassed.

This time, she ignored his emotion, turning instead to indicate the woman to whom he had given his linen.

"You made an impression on her."

"Did        Ah?"        he        asked        with        indifference.

"Yes. In fact, I would say there are at least... three or four women in here tonight who can't peel their eyes off you."

"Ah'm no' interested."

"Woman have lust, too, you know."

"Aye," he agreed, finally looking back. "So Ah've been tolt."

It was meant to be a slap. Delilah's eyes hardened. It took a concentrated effort for her to modulate her voice.

"How are the kids?"

"A'right."

"Meg has her books an' Storm visits her trees in the park, I expect?"

"Aye."

"What do they do all day while you sleep?"

"Spend their time hatin' where they are. They hate the flat, they hate the city. They hate me."

"What are you doing about it?"

"Savin' me money."

"To go home?"

"This is me home," he spat, then regretted the outburst and looked down. "Ah'm sorry. Ah'm a wee bit strung out."

"Something happen?" she asked, her inquiring eyes noting the blood stain on his shirt.

"Aye. Sumethin' happened."

She turned to Ed, holding up two fingers. He brought them both a drink, this time from the real Chivas Regal bottle.

"My treat," she explained on his look.

"Yuh dinna need to be treatin' me. Ah have money."

"I know. But you're saving it. Remember?"

They drank together, then Delilah disappeared. He did not look after her, though he followed her in his mind. She returned a moment later, carrying a small basin of water and bandages.

"What's this fer?" he demanded, suddenly embarrassed and ill at ease.

"Take off your shirt."

"Here? In frunt of everybody?"

"Why not? What have you got to hide?"

With her words stinging more than the wound, Ian slowly unbuttoned his shirt, beginning at the bottom and working his way slowly to the top. While the procedure was not meant to attract attention, the manner in which he performed the simple task was an example of well-practiced enticement.

Naked from the waist up, his muscles firm, his skin pale under a light dusting of fine black chest hair, Ian MacDhui found himself an object of attention. Ashamed for the first time in many, many months, he directed his attention toward Delilah.

"Yuh dinna have to do this, yuh know. It's only a scratch."

"Might get infected."

"Who cares?"

"Lift your head up," she commanded. He did as ordered, his piercing grey eyes staring into the mirror behind the bar. Almost by accident he caught the reflection of the woman he had helped. She and her friends were staring at him with undisguised interest.

Lowering her voice, Delilah spoke as she bandaged his arm.

"I can think of a way for you to make better money."

"What's that, then? Robbin' a bank? That's got to be more respectable than what Ah'm doin'."

"Servicing women." Before he could object, she hurried on. "They pay better prices than men do – although they expect a better product. More than a pretty face wearing cheap cologne."

"Ah've a'ready had that once tonight," he complained. She considered, then shrugged.

"Men will sleep with any warm hole; women have to be more discriminating."

"Why is that?" he asked for the sake of hearing himself talk.

"Women have better taste. They generally want someone who's kind – and exciting. Not a prick who could double as a serial killer."

"What's that to me?"

"Maybe something. Maybe nothing." She lowered her lips, forcing him to drop his head to hear her words. If he had not, she would have finished her first aid and disappeared. The fact he did encouraged her to continue.

"How would you like to go into partnership with me?"

"Partnership? What do yuh mean?"

"I know how we can make money; real money."

His answer was slow in coming.

"Yuh an' me?"

"That's right."

"Nuthin' illegal?"

She snorted, then finally met his eyes, dancing with them as she displayed a shrewdness he had never before seen.

"Nothing more or less illegal than what you're already doing."

"Doin' what?"

"Using my experience and your body."

"Speak clearly."

Delilah shook her head.

"Not here. If you want to know more, come upstairs with me and I'll explain it. If not, it's nothing to me."

But it *was* something to her, and he clearly understood her implication, if not her meaning.

Ian had faced and run from one confrontation already this night; to flee again was against his nature.

The nature of a wolf man, if not a moor man.

"A'right. But on one condition."

"Which is?"

"Yuh let me pay fer the drinks."

Delilah finally smiled.

"A gentleman, in wolf's clothing."

"Or lack o' clothin'," he grinned back, pointing to his bare chest.

"It's a start," she agreed.

They left together, draining the bar of what little excitement it possessed.

# CHAPTER 26

When she shut the door behind him, Delilah waved Ian away from her, then turned to stare at him. Her gaze was so direct and so pointed, he colored under the scrutiny.

"Get used to it," she warned.

"Used to what?"

"Being stared at. By a woman. Move around." He shifted weight from one leg to the other. Her lips pursed in good-humored annoyance. "Walk. Walk around. Move."

He took two steps, then stopped, grunting in embarrassment.

"Ah feel like a ram at the Edinburgh Fair. Are yuh goin' to lift up me tail to have a look at what's under it?"

This time, he succeeded in making her laugh. That reaction was not exactly the one he had in mind, but the sound of her joy filled him with pleasure.

"Oh, yes, indeed, I am going to look at what's under it. That is, if a ram's male anatomy is where a man's is."

This time, he was he who laughed.

"Ah suppose it is. Iffn Ah got on all fours." Then, more seriously, "Will Ah have to do that sort o' play actin' wid women?"

She hesitated before answering, not because she did not have a reply, but to better express her thoughts.

"Some, I'm sure. But what I'm grooming you for, you won't mind as much. They won't be games of humiliation. Or contests of strength – or endurance. That comes later."

This time, he knew he was being set up and rose to the occasion.

"Fer what?"

"For bedtime."

They laughed together and it was a good sound; a harmonious blending of two over-wise souls sharing an oblique joke.

"Walk. Walk. Walk," she ordered again. He obliged, making the circuit of the living room.

"Hold your head up; shoulders back. How would you rate a ram who hunched its shoulders?"

"No' very highly," he admitted.

"Remember that. Every time you go out from now on, you're going to be judged. Think of the streets as an extension of the fairgrounds. You're a walking, talking advertisement of your wares, baby boy."

"Now yuh make me sound like a bitch in heat."

She started at the word, caught herself, then realized he was not using it in a derogatory sense, but in its actual meaning.

"Wow," she said, more to herself than to Ian. "You're going to raise a few eyebrows."

"Eyebrows is one thing; skirts is another," he agreed. This time, she picked up a throw pillow and threw it at him. Deftly catching it, he stopped and made a low bow. "Well: do Ah git the blue ribbon?"

"Honey, this contest isn't won in a day." Reaching down, she retrieved a small shopping bag from behind the couch. Removing an extremely skimpy pair of black silk briefs, she tossed them to him. "Put these on."

"What are they?"

"Drawers. Appreciate them; they cost a bundle."

"Not frum the quantity of material, surely."

"For the style. Long johns and thigh-length briefs are all right for men, and may be sexy under the right conditions, but when you're undressing in front of a woman, she wants to see you in something tight and revealing."

"Men niver complain," he groused, forgetting that once-upon-a-time he had worn long-legged drawers and been chastised for it. Turning the underwear one way and then the other, he made a vain attempt to determine front from rear.

"Wolf Eyes, men know what you have underneath your drawers. They know how you carry yourself, how you feel, what it looks like. To a woman, your penis is a foreign creature. It's an oddity they never quite get used to seeing."

"Yuh mean yuh want me to sleep wid virgins?" he whispered in horror.

"Virgins, hell. Women want –" She considered, then continued. "When a man goes into a strip tease club, what's he going there to look at? A woman's breasts," she quickly supplied before he gave her a lecture on his unfamiliarity with such establishments. "Her rear end – arse, to you. They want to see her flesh for two reasons: One, seeing a woman naked makes a man feel superior. Two, men don't have breasts. None to speak of, anyway. They don't have large, round buttocks. They don't have –"

"Ah know what they dinna have," he protested, holding up a hand to stop her from elaborating.

"All right. So they want to feel superior and they want to take a good, long look at what they don't have. You think a woman is any different? She wants to feel superior and she wants to see what she doesn't have. That's pretty straight forward."

"Ah have to admit... Ah niver thought o' it like that befer."

"Yes.... I suppose you haven't. Most men don't. They think about what they want to see, and don't pay any attention to what their partner wants. That's called 'selfish,' baby. And don't tell me your wife never looked at you with hungry, appreciative eyes." Ian tried to protest but she talked over him. "I know she did. If she was the wild lass you say she was."

"Ah niver said innythin' o' the sort!"

"Oh, brother, take a look in your eyes sometime when you're thinking about her. They glow with remembrance. You two had some high times out there in the tall grass and it wasn't one-sided. Now take off your drawers and put on those briefs."

Holding them up, Ian dangled the skimpy silk in front of his nose.

"Where's the fly?"

"There ain't no fly."

"Then how do –?" Her loud guffaw abruptly silenced his unspoken question. "A'right," he agreed. "Ah kin figure it out fer meself."

"Good boy. I knew you were the cerebral type."

Slowly unbuttoning his trousers, Ian let them drop to the floor, then stepped out of them. She noted with approval as he wiggled his hips, testimony to the lessons he had absorbed from his former lovers. Slipping off the jockey shorts that had become another part of his "costume," Ian presented himself naked before her. Waiting for her nod of approval, he struggled manfully into the briefs, then hoisted them up, stopping at what appeared to be an insurmountable obstacle.

"They dinna fit!" he gasped.

"Stuff yourself in."

More awkward manipulations followed, accompanied by assorted grunts and groans before Ian managed to comply with her order. The result was a very pretty picture of a prominent male anatomy, leaving little, but enough, to the imagination.

Following her downward gaze, he blushed.

"Ah look like a fool," he declared.

"You look sexy; and vulnerable. You're a knock out, Wolf Eyes!"

"Ah'm a grown man past thirty-five years o' age."

"Honey, women may want to look at naked twenty-year olds, but they don't want to be screwed by one. Good sex takes experience, not just in bed. And you, Ian MacDhui, have lived life."

His head shot up faster than the proverbial brag concerning a head of a different "color."

"Yuh called me by me real name!"

Realizing her mistake, Delilah's eyes hardened and her mouth drew into a tight line.

"Here," she indicated, tossing him the shopping bag. "Put on the rest of these clothes."

Staring curiously into the bag, his eyes opened with astonishment.

"You've a whole suit o' clothes in here. Where did they cume frum?"

"Oh, I had them lying around."

The lie was badly told, leaving him uncertain whether she meant for him to question her or not. He decided in the negative.

Removing a long-sleeved shirt first, he started at the clothing as though unfamiliar with so fine an article, then shrugged and fitted his arm through the sleeve. Delilah shook her head disapprovingly.

"Take your time. Do it slowly. Women like to watch a man dress – or undress. It's very sensual. Remember: you're not at the races. This is a ritual, a part of the foreplay. Women don't want to be rushed. They like to work up a mood slowly; anticipate what they're getting."

"Buying, yuh mean."

"Watch your mouth," she warned with dire seriousness. "Talk like that and you're out on your ear."

"Ah'm sorry."

"No crassness, Wolf Eyes. You're going to be a high-priced stud. A gentleman for hire. And I mean a gentleman. Soft spoken, mannered. Kind. Get it?"

"No. Ah have no' decided... Ah tolt yuh –"

"Get over it," she warned. "Your days with men are numbered. Sooner or later, you'll end up getting your head busted, or you'll get syphilis. Woman are safer and they pay better."

"How-do-yuh-know?"

This time, her laugh was bitter and self-deprecating.

"I'm a woman."

"Yuh surely dinna pay fer –?"

"Don't be an idiot. All right," she continued, on his look, "I get around. I talk. I listen. I know people. That's our new partnership."

"Explain it to me, please," he requested in a softer, more humble voice.

"I have the contacts. You have the bod."

"Yuh're gonna be me pimp?"

"Pimp; procurer; call it whatever you like. Start with, I'm going to be your teacher."

"But Ah know how to –"

"You think you do. But a wife is one thing; selling your services is another."

"Yuh mean to say, Ah need tricks?"

"You need technique. Style. And, yes, experience. I'm not saying you have to hang from the ceiling, suspended from a chandelier; I'm not going to turn you into a trained monkey. Just someone who's been around the bend. And lay off the booze. You're drinking too much lately. Women don't want a lover who's a sot; they get enough of that from their husbands."

"Delilah.... What yuh're sayin'... it makes me sick. Ah canna do this." Knitting, then disentangling his hands he turned wet eyes to her. "What was it yuh said aboot a partnership?" Caught at the crossroads, she failed to hold his gaze and whispered something he failed to grasp.

"Say ag'in, please."

He had almost forgotten how to say the word and mean it.

She tried a second time but failed. This time, he was ready for her.

"The deal is, Ah work an' yuh dinna."

Clutching her heart, Delilah shivered, half from shame, the rest from the hope of the innocent girl she had once been. Without being told, he had guessed her trump card.

"Yes."

Summoning the bravery of a wolf facing a two-legged beast with what it comprehended to be a weapon of deadly power, the ruff on the back of his neck rose. Not in anticipation of a one-sided fight that would inevitably go against it, but with the indomitable will of the alpha male defending its territory at any cost.

"Wid those terms, Ah'm agreeable."

Having no appropriate reply for she was not the alpha female, she indicated the bag with what she considered to be unemotional indifference.

"Put the rest on. I want to see how you look. And do it slowly. Men may want you to get your 'arse' out of their apartment on the quick, but women generally don't. They want to watch you dress. They would like to believe you're... hesitant to leave. As though the night meant something to you. That," she coldly concluded, "is part of the technique."

He finished buttoning the shirt to the collar, slipped the vest over it, taking care to button it, then took out the trousers and fitted them over his slim hips. She waited for him to complete the operation then stepped closer, unbuttoning the top three buttons of his shirt. Not quite satisfied, she undid the bottom button of the vest.

"Ah canna sleep wid a woman fer money."

Fully aware of his tenuous grasp on respectability, she opted for the sharp tongue which came as naturally to her as his pride came to him.

"Who the hell said anything about sleep? You're gonna provide stud service, laddie buck, not sleep with 'em."

He sniffed, then looked down at himself.

"Yuh know what Ah mean."

The acute suffering in his voice finally prompted her to retreat. Face clouded with emotion, she let down her guard.

"Yes, Ian, I know what you mean. And while I can't speak for the dear departed, I can speak for Meg and Storm MacDhui."

Face blanched to a deathly pallor, Ian reached out a hand she did not accept.

"Ah dinna want to hear no more!"

"Honey, how long do you think that club act of yours is going to fool them?" Accurately reading the expression on his face, she hurried the rest of her explanation. "Or maybe they've already guessed."

Hearing the truth came near to shattering him. Covering his face with his hands, Ian trembled in utter agony.

"Oh, sweet Jesus, what have Ah done?"

He was in her arms in a moment, clinging to her, head buried in her long, red hair. It was not a sexual embrace, but Delilah intuitively understood that, in his misery, it could be. But it was not the time.

"Baby, your daughters are young women with a great deal of harsh experience already in their heads. Can you possibly imagine they could hold *anything* against you?"

"Ah dinna know.... Ah dinna know." Still shivering, Ian pulled out of her embrace, desperate now for answers. "Is that what they think? What they *know* Ah do fer a livin'? Tell me true an' dinna lie."

"Your doubts are answer enough."

"But –"

"But, nothing. Have they said anything to you? Confronted you? *Blamed* you?"

"No, but –"

"Then let it go at that. When the time comes, you can talk to them. But I'll promise you one thing: they'll take it a lot better if they think you're doing something safe."

"Their mother.... They'll think Ah betrayed her."

"If you really think that – if you truly believe that – then I'm wrong. Change your clothes and get out of here. Living with your conscience is hard enough for me; I don't want two more consciences on my shoulders."

It was a gut-wrenching decision she was asking him to make. He stood, hands drooping at his sides, tears rolling down his cheeks.

One minute, two minutes. He did not leave.

"All right. Start walking. It's all right to lope like a wolf, but it isn't all right to walk like a lumberjack."

"I'll walk," he agreed, resuming the lesson.

"When you've got that down, you'll practice putting on a condom. You'd be amazed how enticing a man can be, applying a little, fire-engine red, polka dot latex sheath to his prick."

"But, Ah dinna like them things. Men dinna like them," he added defensively, correctly interpreting her expression.

"Well, women do. So get used to them."

"Ah canna imagine why they would."

"Oh, you 'canna,' can you? Then put your mind on this, *Mister* MacDhui. Number One: venereal disease."

"A'right, Ah know aboot that," he began. This time, she came in so fast on him he nearly lost his nose.

"Number Two: Pregnancy. You don't have to worry about that serving male clients, honey, but it's a whole 'nuther ball game with the ladies. Most of the women who call you will be married. They don't want a bouncing baby with dark brown hair when they're married to a blond. One phone call to a divorce lawyer and it's all over. She loses everything, even though her husband has two or three girls on the side. That's called a double standard. Ever heard of that?"

"Aye. Ah know what yuh're sayin'. "But Delilah had more to say.

"It used to be that the law presumed any child born to a married man and woman was the flesh and blood of the husband. No argument. Any baby his wife had, he was legally responsible for. Not anymore. So a woman has to be a lot more careful. To say nothing about her own preferences. There are few things worse than having an unwanted pregnancy."

"All right. That makes sense to meh."

"Number Three: And listen to this one real close, Wolf Eyes, because if Number Two doesn't mean a hill of beans to you, Number Three will." She spoke over his protestations. "How would you feel walking down the street one day and running smack into a grey-eyed, dark-haired kid, the spitting image of Ian MacDhui? Not possible, you say? Think again."

He groaned and turned his head away.

"You want to take the chance of fathering a child out of wedlock? A child you may never know exists? Or what about a child dumped on your doorstep? I wonder how Meg and Storm would take such an unexpected addition to your little clan?"

Hand to head, Ian reeled from the weight of her arguments.

"Bring on the condoms!" he cried. "The hell wid walkin' and talkin'! Lesson Number One is 'Fire-Engine Red.' Lesson Number Two is 'polka dots.' An' Lesson Number Three is –"

He stopped in mid-stride to catch her stare. Reading approval there, he broke contact, scanned the room and saw what he wanted. Literally leaping toward the object, he scooped it up in his hand and returned, holding the condom out as though it were a priceless gem which, in fact, was not far from the truth.

"A spare instead o' an heir!"

"I never thought of you as a wit!" she laughed. "I guess I'll have to change 'me' tune."

After which they both collapsed into one another's arms, tears of laughter running down their faces.

As Delilah would say, "Enough said."

Ian MacDhui did not work for a week, while Wolf Eyes went to school. Delilah proved an adept teacher, instructing him in the proper manner of a New York gentleman, which was, by his account, a far cry from a Scottish one.

After the walking and the talking and the condom lessons, there were classes on polite conversation, the do's and don'ts of social behavior, dressing – and undressing – and the inevitable but necessary creation of a "mystique" for the man providing late-night escort service.

"It's all right to be Scotch," Delilah remarked, listening carefully to his soft drawl.

"Scotch is a whisky," he commented dryly.

"No," she corrected. "Scotch is a fine old Scottish tradition. May I buy you a sample of my native brew?" she rephrased.

"Scotch is no' brewed. It's distilled."

"You-get-the-point."

"Aye."

"And never, ever, drink too much yourself. Remember?"

"Aye. She's escapin' frum her drunk husband an' doesna want a drunken lover," he dutifully repeated.

"Correct. Now: you may keep any presents she gives you but never ask for one. That sounds like begging."

"Ah dinna want to sound that like!"

"Learn to pace yourself; never push. Women like conversation; they want to build up to their romance slowly. If she's suddenly shy with you, go for a walk. Hold her hand. Whisper sweet things in her ear. Flatter but don't be obsequious. A beautiful woman already knows she's a looker and a plain woman is perfectly aware of her defects. You start gushing all over her and you'll make her feel a fool. Above all, be kind. To yourself, as well."

"What yuh mean?"

"No man's first time, every time. You'll strike out once in a while. Not too often, I hope," she added, "but there will be nights you just don't have it. Be honest. Make sure she believes it's not her fault. It probably won't be, but even if it is, you're the performer, Big Boy. If it doesn't work out, it's *always* your problem, not hers."

"The customer is a'ways right?"

"Never mind the advertising slogans. Apologize. Shed a few tears if you can. Be humble. Tell her you'll make it up to her some other night."

"Fer free?"

Delilah considered.

"That's your call. Play it by ear. But remember: the woman you stiff – the woman you *don't* stiff," she amended with a smile, "is the woman who tells all her friends about you. For good or for ill. I can put you on the right track, but it's your race, MacDhui."

"Ah'm followin' yuh."

"Once word gets around, women will call you because they're received good references. That's how you move up the ladder. I know some ladies, and they know other ladies. A hairdresser tells her customer, who tells her boss and, with any luck, you move from the first floor to the penthouse. That's the idea, anyway."

"It all sounds so complicated. Ah'm... afeared."

"It'll be rough, at first. Just like it was with men, but in a different way. You'll get used to it."

"But what aboot... love?"

"Love?" Delilah stared at him is stark disbelief. "If they want love, honey, they subscribe to the Romance Novel of the Month Club. You're only there to provide some physical pleasure; a relief. A thrill. Be dangerous; mysterious. Play a different character every night. But don't look to give or receive love."

"What aboot yuh?"

"I'm very good at playing parts."

"I meant love." She made no answer. "Do yuh subscribe to the Romance Novel o' the Month Club?"

"I can't read."

Which Ian MacDhui, d.b.a. "Wolf Eyes," knew for an untruth.

# CHAPTER 27

The maroon Cadillac pulled up to the curb and tarried just long enough for the tall, well-dressed man to stoop down, peer through the tinted glass and be waved inside by the driver. He accepted the invitation immediately. In a moment, the vehicle merged into the flow of traffic and was gone.

At the same time, a phone was ringing in Delilah's apartment. She answered it with an authoritative "Hello?" Listening a moment, she nodded, then crisply informed the caller she would "put them on hold."

The telephone was new and so were the furnishings. Replacing her old, uneven dining room table was a Colonial American dining set with six matching chairs, two of which bore the designation of "captain's chairs." That was because they had arms, the astonished salesman explained. The set had not come with two captain's chairs, but the purchasers had insisted, or they would "bloody well take their business elsewhere."

When the dining room set was delivered, there were two captain's chairs, cannibalized, no doubt, Delilah explained, from another set, which would be sold, "as is" to a family "buying over their heads, and not too proud to have the 'captain' sit in a chair devoid of arms."

It might be noted that when Meg and Storm MacDhui were invited to eat at Delilah's, they were the ones who sat in the captain's chairs, thinking it grand sport to throw their lanky legs over the arms after dinner "to expand our stomachs."

The driver of the Cadillac nor the occasional passenger was not Wolf Eye's date. He had grown accustomed to these new ways, the "sizing-up" period by a female friend or relative before his own arrival at the home of the paying customer. After several initial blunders, he had grown to appreciate the brief interludes before getting down to work.

But only after the purpose and technique had been explained to him.

Lesson One: if the driver was a woman, never ask her name. That caused immediate consternation and invariably a lie. Delilah explained that when caught in such an embarrassing position, women inevitably used their middle and maiden names.

Lesson Two: Make a generic compliment about the car but never phrase it so as to appear as though he had never ridden in anything better than a farm wagon. And absolutely never seek an explanation for any items hanging from the rearview mirror or found on the seats or floor, invariably forgotten in the quick clean-up of the dash and the upholstery.

Lesson Three: Never mention anything as crass as money unless the driver brings up the subject. Never refuse to take money offered, except in rare cases when it is less than the agreed upon fee-for-service.

Lesson Four: Confine small talk to matters of local interest; nothing controversial. No sports.

Lesson Five: Do not waste breath on compliments to the driver, if she is a woman. If she was also interested in obtaining that which he is providing for her friend, politely thank her and remark that "me evening is a'ready full, but Ah'd be honored if yuh would call me in a day or two."

Lesson Six: Never volunteer to drive the car. The driver's position was the seat of power. Driving gave a woman a sense of control and authority. If invited to do so, politely decline.

Lesson Seven: Never, ever speak of other women, not even if pointedly asked. Remind them that "reference by word of mouth" is better than "telling tales." Never acknowledge having known any women who are mentioned by name. If the matter is pressed, simply state that nicknames of endearment are always used in place of actual first names, or that, "Ah dinna remember, Ah'm sorry," implying that he understood the value of the expression, "silence is golden."

Lesson Eight inadvertently came from Storm MacDhui: "Dinna drown yuhrse'f in perfume. It makes the room close an' the head swim." While the youngest clan member did not precisely understand where or in what business her father was working, her perception of appearance was acute.

Ian's new job was a source of wonder to his daughters. When pressed, he informed then he had been promoted from bouncer to entertainer. As he never seemed to practice lines from a play in their presence, they decided "entertainer" meant "bein' the fluff what opens the door an' seats them what's cume to be entertained." Delilah's hearty endorsement of such an idea clued them they were not exactly correct, but there the matter rested.

Proving that discretion was indeed, the better form of gallantry.

Waving a small, respectful good-bye to his chauffeur, Ian fluidly slipped out of the leather seat and sprang, with hard-muscled legs, out onto the pavement. Remembering Lesson Nine to never, ever check a piece of paper for an address or apartment number, he strode to the entrance, whispered a code word to the doorman, passed him a small remuneration and was admitted into the world of "those what have it made."

Making his way through the lobby, Ian paused by a mirrored wall to check his appearance and adjust a stray lock. His intention was not to replace the strand back into his well-brushed head, but to set it free.

"Women like hair," Delilah had instructed. "If they want a Marine drill sergeant type, or a businessman with a crew cut and shaved sideburns, they don't have to look further than their own backyard. Just as a man likes hair he can run his fingers through, a woman wants to see some vulnerability. Short hair is a statement, just like a beard. It sets men apart ; it's an offense. Females want their lovers to be romantic and sentient. A man who abandons the dictates of fashion, wearing his hair past his collar, is exciting. It invites sensuality, rather than superiority. She gets enough of that from her husband."

Ian learned his lessons well. Gone was the primitive moor man, the Scottish sheep farmer, whose bow to respectability had been an appearance at church with a well-shorn face and clean, albeit broken fingernails. That creature was replaced by a modern, well-groomed, high-styled, handsome dandy.

What remained, however, was the innately good man inside the package. That was what set Ian "Wolf Eyes" MacDhui apart from the rest of the gigolos selling ambulatory stud service.

As he admired himself in the mirror, part of his true self shone forth. With a silly grin, he declared, "Who ever thought Ian MacDhui would be a well-dressed 'man *aboot* town'?"

Still smiling, he glided toward the elevator, pressing the "up" button with a jaunty air.

"Well, Thomas an' Louis an' Mae," he continued. "Ah expect yuh may inform Mister Angus Meager that Ah have 'made it.' Ah have money in me pocket, a set o' fancy clothes on me back, an' a bank account, kept directly under Meg an' Storm MacDhui's bed!"

He did not continue the dialogue by answering whether his four friends would be allowed to "cume fer a visit an' a loan." While the loan of money was now possible, the thought of them coming to the New World and seeing just exactly how the former sheeper had "struck gold" was utterly abhorrent.

As Delilah had warned, which, in retrospect seemed eons ago, making a living as a whore was a mean, rotten, dirty business, where a man – or a woman – sold what little soul he or she had left for a few dollars a night.

Ian was earning far more than "a few dollars a night," but she had been correct about the soul. While he found it easy to stare into a mirror to adjust his hair before going to the penthouse, he never performed such an act when he was not working. The sight of his face had become repugnant to him; and his soul, if indeed he still possessed one, belonged no more to himself, nor to a loving God, but to that despised creature who collected the unearthly remains of the evil and the unworthy.

Ian MacDhui had learned how to play games; he knew when to smile on command, when to boast of imaginary accomplishments, what fables to spin of his life away from the bed chamber. He was a former jock, a writer of mystery tales, an aeroplane pilot rescuing hikers lost over glaciers or within dense forests.

He was a male model, a stunt double for a famous actor whose name he would rather not mention; a mountain climber or a NASCAR driver in his spare time. He was James Bond undercover, seeking out the enemies of Her Majesty in daring and unbelievable ways.

Wolf Eyes had no children, was never married and had been in the United States for years, having immigrated at the tender age of eight or ten or twelve by stowing away in the baggage compartment of a tourist ship. Occasionally, his background started after being sent "abroad" by his noble mother who had borne him in Ireland while on "holiday," or confessing he was the "spare" to the heir and America had proven a better choice than the more traditional religious orders.

Ian MacDhui was everything, in fact, but a former displaced sheep man from the lonely moors of Scotland

Acting, he had learned, was as much a part of the service as the actual physical demands of sexual gratification. No one wanted tales of woe; those were as common as workers sitting behind cubicles in innumerable nameless offices. The commodity he was selling was escape, and he the fantasy prince, constructing castles in the air.

What Ian MacDhui had also learned, but which came as no surprise, was that no one cared to look behind the magic and the make-up. He was an actor from the cinema, a baritone from Broadway, stepping, however briefly, off the stage to provide a personal one-man play over chilled cocktails and beneath crisp sheets.

Modest wealth and word-of-mouth fame had brought neither happiness nor respectability to the moor man. His grey wolf eyes shone with reflected light, no longer sparkling with inner love of life. That, along with the Dream, had died. And like Megan Clarke MacDhui, had been buried in a poorly marked grave, without the simple dignity accorded pot and pans and ovens.

Another night, another client, another act. Lying stretched full-length on her white, long-napped rug, Ian displayed the treasure he had brought for her amusement, speaking in his decidedly Scottish dialect and rolling his R's to good effect.

"Ah saw them in a toy store window. They'rrrre called Lincoln Logs, afterrrr the Great Rrrrailsplitter who became yuhr sixteenth prrrresident. There was this grrrrand display o' cabins an' barns. Ah was so taken wid it, Ah thought to meself, why not build the same wid other material, so Ah bought these...."

Spilling a velvet bagful of shiny round, colorful objects onto the rug, Ian held one up for inspection.

"Condoms. Ah dinna know iffn yuh're familiar wid such, but –"

The woman at his side laughed delightedly, more childlike than sexual, staring with rapt attention as he began his "log cabin."

"I'll never think of Lincoln Logs the same way again."

"Aye," Ian agreed, piling the condoms, one on top of another until he had created a small house. "But then, ag'in, there's another way to think o' a Lincoln *Log.*"

Drawing the woman to him, he kissed her passionately, pressing his "Lincoln Log" close to her negligee-clad body. In a moment, they were rolling together, attached at the day-glow, piña colada-flavored Lincoln Log.

One month, two months, three months. Delilah's phone rang with callers. Dutifully talking down first names and phone numbers, she would check the appointment calendar of "Wolf Eyes," make the date and post it on the wall. As Ian had no phone, not wishing his daughters to intercept a call, he got in the habit of dropping by her apartment every evening for a drink and an update on the "work situation."

Occasionally she would have a new outfit for him to try on, a fresh supply of bikini underwear, or a collection of "toys" for the female audience requesting "something new along the lines of adult entertainment."

Her own wardrobe and appearance had improved dramatically, as well. No longer did she answer his polite rapping at the door covered in bruises or dressed in ripped chemises. Her hair was professional dyed and coiffured, her nails shaped and lacquered in colors setting off her complexion, while her clothes reflected a professional, rather than a working woman.

They kissed and occasionally drew arms around one another in platonic friendship, but they were not lovers. Those "goods" were saved for the paying customers.

When she heard his familiar footsteps on the steps, Delilah met Ian at the door, welcoming him with a smile and a loud, bawdy "Hello." Grinning in return, he slipped inside, then flopped on the couch in uncharacteristic resignation.

"I have one on for tonight; could make it two, if you get out early," she offered, ignoring his mood she could not quite place.

"No," he demurred, shaking his head, then running his hands through his long hair in a gesture she knew so well. "Yuh know Ah dinna like that. The ladies is payin' good money an' they deserve the whole night."

"What they deserve and what they get is up to you. You make the rules now, Wolf Eyes. Besides, it's a waste."

"Ah di'na serve more than one man, or a group o' men, a night, an' Ah'll no be cheatin' the ladies. Besides... if they think Ah'm off to another bed, it makes them nervous. Then Ah'm no' a date but meat on the hoof."

"Who called you that?" she demanded, thinking to have discovered the reason for his discontent.

"Ah jest heard it here or there. Ah do git around now, yuh know."

"I know," she hesitantly agreed. "But you're hardly meat on the hoof, honey. You don't call a man making six hundred dollars a night that." Then, eliciting no response, "What's the matter?"

"Me tourist visa is long expired."

"So?"

"Ah have no employer to petition me to stay in this country."

"Is that all? So what? You've already dropped out of sight. No one can find you. Immigration has better things to do than track down tourists who permanently extend their stay. The country is full of them."

"I'm here illegally."

"That makes you one in two billion."

"Aye. Ah'm unique," he tonelessly agreed.

Joining him on the couch, Delilah wrapped an arm around his shoulders, holding him tight.

"Is it the children? Did Storm accuse you of being a wetback, or something?"

"No. They dinna mention it."

Assuming that for a lie, she shrugged it off.

"Tell them you've applied for permanent residency. They'll never know the difference."

"Ah suppose not," he agreed. "Ah've lied so much, Ah'm pretty good at it by now. Even to them," he morosely added.

"Then tell them the truth, if you don't want to lie. I doubt their world will come crashing in around their heads."

"They need to go to school. How kin Ah enroll them when they dinna belong here inny more than Ah?"

"Hire a private tutor. You can afford one."

"Aye. Ah might do that," he agreed.

When the idea did not cheer him, she removed her arm, got up and fixed them both a drink.

"You running dry? Running out? Not drinking enough fluids?" she teased, clinking her glass to his. "You're working too much, maybe. No big deal. All males, even wolves, come up empty once in a while. Sleep here tonight. I can cancel your date."

Ian set his untouched glass on the end table and stood, shaking his leg in nervous agitation.

"It's no' that," he restlessly demurred. "Ah'm a'right."

"Not coming down with anything? A cold? The flu, maybe. It's going around."

"Ah feel a'right... here," he replied, placing a hand on his chest. Then, slowly bringing it up to his head, he continued, "It's *here* Ah dinna feel good. It's me head what's all messed up. Even given that Ah've poot away all thoughts o' self-respect, Ah feel bloody useless."

"Useless?" she reacted in consternation. "We're making more money than I ever dreamed possible." Then, suspiciously, "You think you're sharing too much with me? That I don't pull my weight? You don't have to give me so large a cut, you know. We can... negotiate." He made no reply. "You don't have to give me anything, if you don't want to. I understand.... You're a big boy, now; you can handle your own affairs. I can go back to work –"

Ian swung on her so fast she spilled some of the alcohol from the cut crystal glass in her hand. The expression on his face changed from placid to wild and violent.

"That's no' it! Savin' yuh frum that hellish life on the streets is the only respect Ah have left to me. It's what keeps me goin', night after night.... After night."

"Then, what is it, baby?" she whispered, lost and suddenly bone-chilled frightened.

"Ah tell yuh, Ah feel useless! I'm no' but fluff. When Ah was a sheepman, Ah thought Ah knew all there was to life. It was gettin' up in the mornin' and workin' till way past dark, tendin' me animals and lovin' me wife an' daughters. Day in an' day out, Ah niver questioned me life. Ah was happy...in me own way. We niver had a dime to spare, but Ah didna miss what we dinna have."

Picking up his abandoned glass, he stared into the amber fluid before continuing.

"Now, Ah'm no' so sure. Thoughts is crowdin' in me head so fast Ah canna make sense o' them. Ah've bought Meg a library full o' books, an' Ah'm lookin' at buyin' a house wid trees fer Storm, but Ah canna say Ah'm happy. Ah'm fuckin' miserable, an' Ah dinna know why. Ah try an' work it out, but that's as fer as me thinkin' takes me!"

Shoving his hands in his pockets, Ian began pacing, head hung low, eyes on the carpet. Delilah stared hesitantly at him, not knowing what to say. In her own life, money had always seemed the answer to everything. Money, no matter how obtained, was her escape from hunger, a respite from fear. It was beyond her ability to view wealth as a problem in itself.

The phone rang, startling them both. When he expressed no inclination, Delilah went to the telephone and picked it up.

"Hello?" Her tone was guarded, half resentful. "Yes. You can leave a message here for Wolf Eyes." She wrote down a name and number, her expression changing as she performed the task. "Just a minute."

Snapping the hold button on her new telephone, Delilah glanced over at Ian, torn between saying anything or simply hanging up the receiver.

"It's that bitch, Sally Richards. The 'escort killer.' Remember her? She was the one who threw you out before you got your jacket off. Shall I tell her you've –" She was going to say "retired," then changed her mind. "That you're all booked up?"

She could see from his look he was clearly not interested. Before she could reconnect the line, however, he crossed to her, roughly clasping a restraining hand on hers.

"What the bloody hell," he snarled. "In me present mood, maybe we'll kill each other an' poot us both out o' our private miseries!"

Delilah hesitated, torn between her original thought and his current desire. She finally shrugged and jabbed the hold button.

"Yes, he's available tonight. What time would you like him to arrive? Seven o'clock? Are you sending around a car?" She listened a moment before answering. "If he takes a cab, Miss Richards, the charge gets added onto the fee." This was apparently agreeable, for Delilah nodded curtly. "He'll see you then."

Dropping the phone onto the cradle, she turned to Ian with a pasted-on smile.

"You've got a date, Sweetie. I'll cancel the one I had already arranged." When he didn't comment she added in a lower tone, "God help both of you."

"God, Ah'm very much convinced," he retorted in a snarl, "Will be lookin' the other way. Sumethin', Ah might add, He's very good at."

The temperature in the room dropped. It was as good a celestial answer as any.

# CHAPTER 28

The "flat" was neither flat, nor did it bear any relationship to ordinary apartments. The tri-level home boasted a water fountain, a magnificent, mirrored bar and an entertainment system providing music to every corner, kitchen, halls and bathrooms included.

A Black Forest grandfather clock chimed nine as Wolf Eyes arose from the couch to stretch his legs. Sally Richards, a middle-aged woman, attractive and nervous, poured herself the last dregs from the bottle.

"Get another," she ordered, indicating the bar with a nod of her head. Ian hesitated, then did as he was commanded.

"What yuh want?" he sang out from behind the semi-circular structure.

"The same."

"Ah dinna see any. Where do yuh keep it?"

Sally looked over, started to rise, then abruptly changed her mind.

"If there's none on top, try below, under the taps. Check the cabinets. They're not locked."

Finding what she wanted, Ian returned with the freshly opened bottle. He poured her a drink, paused to light her cigarette, then positioned himself on the padded arm of the couch. When she made no obvious objection, he bent to kiss her neck. Two more kisses brought his face to her breasts. Placing his hands on them, he attempted to kiss the flesh through her blouse, but she withdrew rapidly from his touch, face taut.

"Don't touch me there. I'm paying you to do as you're told. No more. I didn't give you permission to kiss me – anywhere."

Shrugging in silent acquisition, Ian wandered aimlessly away when she offered no more by way of conversation, or desire. Pausing by the mantle of the marbled fireplace, he admired the array of photographs displayed above.

There were seven pictures, all of which included the lady of the house. From the people in the photographs, it was easy to follow the progression of her life. The earliest was a photo of her, holding an infant child. Two more were of Sally and the child as he grew. A forth depicted "Mrs. Richards, executive of the year," as she clutched a large trophy. The last was of Sally and a man standing beside the boy, now grown to adulthood, at his college graduation. The face of the elder man had been cut away, leaving only his headless body.

With nothing to lose, Ian disregarded one of the Cardinal Rules of his profession and picked up the last photograph, trying a smile of interest.

"What happened to this bloke?"

"Divorced."

"Bad apple?"

"Depends on your point of view. Put it back." She waited until the photo was returned to its position, then stood, wringing her hands in agitation. "Let's go upstairs."

Ian nodded agreeably, hurrying to catch up as she led the way.

The master bedroom was spacious and dark, illuminated by an open window. Sally made no effort to turn on the overhead, so Ian wandered to the side of the bed nearest the window, standing with his back to it.

"Would yuh like me to git undressed?"

"Yes. All right."

Not understanding her reluctance, he removed his suit coat, vest and shirt, unbuttoning each article with deliberate slowness. Bare chested, he flexed his muscles, made low groans under his breath, then perched on the edge of the bed and slipped off socks and shoes. Looking over his shoulder, he ascertained she was looking at him but in the gloom, could not read her expression.

He was tempted to stand and strip his trousers off, doing his well-rehearsed routine, but did not. Rather, he slowly passed the pants over his hips and let them drop to the floor with a soft swish. Then, clad only in his briefs, he stood and turned to face her.

"May Ah undress yuh?" he whispered. She did not reply. Five, ten seconds passed before he summoned his own waning courage and approached. It was not physical violence he feared but an emotional outburst from a woman clearly torn by the situation in which she found herself.

With instincts warning him to dress and leave, Ian instead reached out and placed both hands on her covered breasts. She responded immediately by slapping them, terrified and horribly aghast at his action.

"Go away!" she screamed. "Leave me alone. I never said you could manhandle me!"

Ordinarily, such a command was law, but not tonight. Sadly shaking his head, Ian removed his hands, holding them up, palms outward.

"It's a'right," he explained, the words sounding distant and strange because of the pounding in his eardrums. "Ah unnerstan'."

"You're a man," she spat, arrested by his nearness. "You don't understand a damned thing!"

"Aye, Ah'm nought but a man, but Ah *do* unnerstan'."

"Don't touch me," she warned. "I'll call the police. There's a phone over there," she indicated.

He did not look to where she pointed, but rather, inched a step closer, hands still held out in a non-threatening position.

"You think I'm frigid," she accused. And then, bitterly, "That's what they all think. That's the easy answer."

Again, he shook his head.

"Me wife, Meggie MacDhui. She had the tumor, too. She had a breast removed."

"What are you saying?" Sally gasped, lower lip trembling with emotion.

"Ah felt the prosthesis downstairs when Ah touched yuh. Yuh've had a mastectomy."

Even in the darkness of the room he could sense the color draining from her face.

"You – you know?"

"Aye. Ah know."

"You're... not repulsed?"

"Repulsed?" He choked, feeling his own countenance grow red from the onslaught of distant memories. "Ah regard yuh the more fer it."

"What do you mean?"

"Meggie an' Ah had no secrets frum one another. When she was told aboot the cancer, we discussed all her options. She was afeared, as you are afeared. Frightened that Ah'd think her less a woman."

"Yessss," Sally hissed through clenched teeth.

"We talked long into the night.... into many a night and many a day. We looked at the padded brassieres, the prosthesis. We talked aboot her physical sensitivity... the scars." Tears rolled down Ian's cheeks as he continued, voice flush with love. "Ah remember when she cume home frum the second operation, me wee's an' Ah all took off our shirts an' announced ourselves as 'The Four Flat-Chested MacDhuis'."

He did not realize, nor did he care he had revealed his true name.

"It... didn't matter to you?"

"Matter?" he demanded, spittle flying from his wet lips. "What mattered to me was that Ah had another day wid her. An' a day after that. Ah dinna marry her fer her breasts; Ah married her fer love. Do yuh think a doctor kin cut that away?"

Sally's jaw hardened at his passionate avowal.

"Yes. A doctor cut away my husband's love, the same time he cut away my breast. I believe," she added bitterly, "that was the only thing which did not make it to the hospital bill: one amputated love."

"No," Ian disagreed, shaking his head. "If that's the case, then he niver loved yuh to begin with."

"Stan always said he loved perfection. I was no longer perfect."

"Then Ah bloody well hope he enjoys fuckin' Christ, because He's the only perfect human bein' there is!"

Despite her horror, his words brought a smile to her lips.

"I never thought of it like that," she hesitantly admitted.

"Let me care aboot yuh," he invited, arms held wide. "Let me remember, an' God help us, let yuh fergit."

Slowly, ever so slowly, she fell into his arms. The first kiss was for rewriting memories and the second for healing.

In the dark of the night before dawn, the man and the woman lay intertwined, neither needing time, for blessed sleep had stolen over them.

Through the open window, where the curtain fluttered like the wings of a dreaming rock dove, a full moon shone.

An hour later, in the far distance of the great New World, came the sound of a wolf howling.

Leaving two other matters Wolf Eyes had to accomplish before his soul was sated. The first required a visit to an address he had sworn to forget and remembered with all the clarity of a new born babe's fist wail. Knocking on the door to the house, Ian waited a moment, then turned the knob and entered, sensing it would be unlocked.

Crossing through the living room, he passed the first bedroom on the left without glancing to see if it were occupied. He knew it would not be.

Entering the second, he stood in the doorframe, eyes glowing with emotion.

"Ah have cume to love yuh," he whispered. "No' to screw yuh, no' to fuck yuh; but to love yuh. To hold yuh an' comfort yuh an' keep away the nightmares. One night, friend Jim, yuh dinna have to be alone."

"You came back," came the hushed response from the lonely guest room bed.

"Ah niver truly left."

"Where are yuh goin'?"

"Out."

An exasperated sigh punctuated the pronouncement.

"He's due home inny minute."

"He is, or he isn't," Storm retorted with slightly more than casual indifference, whether from the fact "he" had replaced "Ian" in their lexicon, or her desperate need to escape had reached the boiling stage.

"He'll be tired when he gits home. He won't appreciate it iffn yuh're gone."

"He won't even notice." Turning to her sister, her own grey-green eyes flashed. Flashed, Ian MacDhui might have observed, had he been there, "wid the intensity o' smolderin' peat."

"That's an untruth," Meg cried, defending him with waning courage. "Fust thing he does when he cumes in is to call our names."

"No," came the curt denial. "The furst thing he does is try an' slip inside widout a peep so's he can lie to us aboot the time in case we're asleep."

"Well, after that," Meg sadly conceded. Observing Storm was only listening with half an ear, she repeated her earlier question. "Where are yuh goin'?"

Chin jutting, she replied in defiance although Meg's demand was hardly worthy of a harsh retort, "Ah have a date."

"A date?"

"Why should *he* be the only one what goes out on the town?"

The statement reeked of blasphemy and shook Meg to her already unsteady foundations.

"He-goes-ta-work."

"Aye. Ah've been givin' that a lot o' thought lately. Ah spoke wid it to Kind Al."

"What did he say?"

"A bloke what goes out stinkin' o' perfume an' fresh shaved ain't goin' to work. Least not the respectable kind."

"He nevir said that!"

The shock in Meg's voice caused Storm to amend the statement.

"A'right. He said it weren't no work he unnerstood."

"That's better." Hands akimbo, she pursued, "Who's yer date?"

After a long hesitation, she responded, "Kind Al."

"Oh. Yer goin' out fer breakfast?"

"In a manner o' speakin'."

"What other way is there?"

"We ain't gonna eat."

Wincing at her sister's deteriorating grammar, Meg edged the conversation closer to the brink.

"Who's goin' to eat, then?"

"The wolves."

"There ain't no wolves in New York City!"

"Yes, there are. Kind Al said so."

"Aye. In his drink –"

"No! In a place called the Bronx Zoo."

"I've heard o' that," she softly conceded.

"Rrrright. In the book."

The once cherished reference book purchased another lifetime ago by one Megan MacDhui, its dog-eared pages long forgotten amid newer, less painful remembrances in Meg MacDhui's bookcase.

"Yuh'r goin' to the Bronx Zoo? At night?"

"It'll be light soon enuf."

"It's a fearful long way away."

"Closer than Scotland an' that was meh furst choice."

"I'm goin' wid yuh."

She waited for an objection and when none was forthcoming, she hurried to the closet, now filled with an assortment of outerwear, selected a jacket and jammed her fists through the sleeves. She was almost to the door of the bedroom when she remembered something and turned back. Holding up a corner of the mattress, she extracted a Kerr jar, unscrewed the top and extracted a $20 bill. Thinking better of it, she exchanged it for two $10s then reaffixed the lid and returned the glass to its "secure hidin' place."

Offering one to Storm, she jammed the other in the pocket of her blue jeans before staring around the living room.

"Now, what?"

"Ah'm thinkin' we ought ta write him a note."

"Aye. A whole en-cyclo-ped-ia."

"Ah said a note!"

Rolling her eyes, Storm quick-stepped into their shared bedroom, drew down the blanket and placed both pillows side-by-side on the mattress. Casually covering them with the blanket, she deftly made several indentations to approximate human shapes, considered, then retrieved a pair of slippers. Balancing them on their heels, she placed the pair at the feet of the closest pillow and re-covered them.

As Meg joined her in appraising her handiwork, Storm concluded, "It might no' fool a man in his rrrright senses, but he has no' had them in a wolf's age, so here's to believin' he'll 'peep in,' take a look-see an' figure he's got away wid another lie."

The tragedy was, Meg knew she was correct in her assessment. At any rate, it saved her having to leave a note and they hurried out, taking care to lock the door and protect "the innocents inside."

They found Kind Al waiting for them two blocks away at the designated meetin' spot. Seeing them approach, he smiled and held out his arms. Both children rushed up and allowed themselves to be engulfed in his arms. Before he let go, Storm wrinkled her nose.

"What's that awful smell?"

Perhaps sensitive to the fact he had told too much to inquisitive ears, the old man grinned.

"Shaving lotion," he bragged. "I found a bottle in the waste can from that fancy hotel they just put up," he bragged. "More'n half full, too. I thought since we was going out on an excursion of grrreat significance, I ought to doll myself up. I shaved, too," he added, reluctantly releasing them.

Staring in wonder at the attempt he had made, they ignored the stray patches of whiskers remaining and offered him a thumbs-up.

"Yuh'r as handsome a fellow as ever walked the moors," Meg praised.

"Oh, the blood-lettin'," Storm seconded with a grin.

As the bus rolled up to the stop, Al pretended to check the watch he wasn't wearing.

"Right on time."

The first to climb the steps, Meg offered a handful of change to the driver.

"This is fer the three o' us. We'll be transferin' by-an-by."

Familiar with the MacDhui children who had become adept at "bus ridin'," he tipped his cap and waved them down the aisle.

"A far cry frum our furst ex-perience wid public transport," she continued, slithering into a seat and scooting to the window so Storm and Al could fit beside her.

Less forgiving, Storm scowled.

"Ah'm still on the look-out fer our haversack. If ever Ah see some bastard wid it, Ah'm gonna –"

"Call the cops?" Al tried.

"Nah," she boldly disagreed. "Poot a knife between his ribs. That's called New York justice. It won't even make a note in the newspaper."

He nodded. Perhaps too readily.

After several transfers, all of which Meg paid for, they arrived at their destination just as the early morning sun was making an appearance over the horizon. The front gate was locked.

"We've cum too early –"

Shaking his head, then putting a finger to his lips, Kind Al motioned they follow him. Taking a tour of the fence encircling the vast property, he finally came to a stop, glanced around to see no one was looking, then motioned them closer.

"There's a break in the fence here."

"Yuh made it?" Storm exclaimed in wondrous appreciation.

His face fell but only for a moment.

"It's been here forever. All the kids know about it. It's a way of getting in without money."

"Ah kin pay," Meg protested but he shook her off.

"The zoo's not open this early. If you want to see 'em feed the animals you gotta come before they let the payin' customers in."

"Why is that?"

He smiled, revealing a mouthful of teeth destroyed by alcohol.

"It's grizzly."

"Meanin' it's bears?"

"Meanin' it's bloody."

"Ah'm all fer it!" Strom gushed in excitement.

"The city folk don't like to see *carnivores* tearin' and rippin' apart their food. It makes 'em uncomfortable."

"What do they expect? Ta see 'em use a knife an' wipe their lips on a napkin?" she asked in disgust.

He debated and then nodded.

"Yes."

"Oh, Saint Andrew, protect us frum fools."

They slipped through the hole in the fence, he quickly led them through the grounds. Crisscrossing several trails, they eventually came out at the carnivores enclosures. Bypassing the bears and other meat-eaters, they arrived at the area housing the "American *lupus*." Dog-like in appearance, there could be no mistaking the wild demeanor of the beasts as they madly tore away at their early morning meal.

"Oh, meh God, Ah niver thought to see such beasties ag'in," Storm whispered in reverence.

Checking to make certain none of the keepers lingered in the area, Al permitted the two kin of the wild beasties to press their noses against the bars. Shoulders shaking in excitement, the sight transformed them back to a faraway place once called home.

"Look, Storm!" Meg pointed. "That's the alpha male."

Tearing her eyes away from the feasting, Storm confirmed the identification, then scanned the enclosure, finally indicating another.

"An' there's the alpha female. Yuh kin tell," she explained to Al, "by the way the other wolfs defer to her. She's got the big hunk o' meat. They'll sup on it when she's done."

"Why is that?"

Amazed that he did was not in possession of so common a fact, she was only too eager to explain.

"Becuz it's the right o' the dominant breedin' pair to have furst rights to whatever there is to eat. They're the ones what will bring wee ones into the world. It's a way o' preservin' the leaders – the ones who lead the pack. Survival o' the fittest, they call it. But, in actual fact, it's the way o' preservin' all of 'em. The strongest take care o' the weakest."

"Why is that?" he asked a second time.

"It takes a pack to bring down prey. A lone wolf might git a rabbit or a lamb, but to take on a ram or a big brute requires the might o' many. Sume what chase it away from the others, sume ta take the furst nips at its heels, another to attack the flank an' then the neck. It may no' be pretty," she added in disdain, "but it's the way o' the wild. A lamb feeds one but a stag feeds the pack."

"And you wouldn't be sad to see a lamb eaten?"

"Aye, o' course Ah would. As a sheeper, it's me duty to preserve all meh sheep. An' Ah no' generally like to see a fawn go down or a doe, but it's nature an' nature sumetimes seems cruel. But, in the scheme o' things, every creature has a right to survive."

"And that's respectable?"

"Aye. It tis."

"Sort of what your pa is doin'? Working to protect his lambs?" She started to reply, then bit her lip. Al stuffed his hands in his pockets. "Surviving," he shrugged, "is hard. And it's seldom pretty."

They spoke no more, spending the rest of the morning with their eyes glued to the wolves. At ten o'clock the first visitors appeared at the exhibit. Men alone, mothers with children, boys eager to see a fight break out. All looked, trying to absorb the scene they viewed on only one level then drifted away to view the elephants or the "pretty pink swans."

The three interlopers to the realm of detachment remained mute and it not until a small child reached into a red and white-printed paper bag and threw a peanut into the perimeter that Meg offered advice.

"They dinna eat peanuts," she tried, using her polite voice.

The child frowned.

"I eat peanuts."

"What do they eat?" the mother accompanying her child asked in curiosity.

Meg debated how best to answer, then grinned.

"Ham-burgers."

Rather than be offended, the lady smiled.

"Oh. I see. Thank you." Turning to her child, she translated. "The wolves eat hamburgers. They get them from the store."

"Aye," Storm mumbled. "But, they no' poot ketchup an' pickles on 'em. They're pizzon to a wolf."

"Really. How interesting."

The pair drifted away as Storm scuffed her foot in the dirt.

"They shit in the outhouse, too."

Meg poked her, but with a gleam in her eyes. No one knew everything, she was learning. And, there was always two ways to view life. Applicable to words as well as history. "Respectable" being a case in point. One, she realized, Megan MacDhui fully comprehended. It was only just that her cubs followed suit.

The real "Wolf Eyes" watched the dawn brighten the New World with shared awareness. Rather than return to the Sea Breeze Apartments, he had promises to keep. Not those expressed in words, but those of an itinerant traveler having chosen the road less traveled by.

Delilah was sleeping when Ian entered her bedroom. Rubbing the tiredness away, she stared at him in silent wonder, responding to the glow around his head with a quiet smile.

"Would yuh like to cume home wid me?" he asked.

He did not have to tell her the story about how Megan Clarke MacDhui had once requested he look up the word "empathy," or how she had whispered in his lover's ear that one day, when awareness came upon him, he would understand its meaning. It was all expressed in his wondrous grey eyes.

Delilah slowly nodded, her own heart alight with the wonder of the revelation.

It was half past one o'clock in the afternoon when Meg and Storm MacDhui returned from their sojourn. As planned, albeit for a different reason, their absence had not been missed. Each with a finger to her lips, they tiptoed into their father's bedroom. The alpha male and his new alpha female were entangled in one another's arms, his head upon her bare shoulder. Both were sleeping soundly.

Exchanging glances, Storm reached inside her shirt and retrieved the cord around which was suspended Ian's wedding ring. After reverently kissing it, she passed it to her sister. Meg repeated the ritual, then held it out in blessing.

"Wid this ring, Ah do thee wed," she proclaimed.

Creeping closer to the marriage bed, Meg suspended the cord from the top of the headboard, so that the gold band draped down between the newly married couple.

"Amen," Storm whispered, then backed away, Meg gently closing the door behind the slumbering pair.

A moment, no more, then over the din of mid-afternoon traffic and commuter aeroplanes carrying people to and from the great city o' New York, rang the sound of wolf pups howling.

The End

GSFE

ALSO BY: S.L.KOTAR AND J.E.GESSLER

A character based historical 1950's courtroom based murder mystery entitled "**The Hugh Kerr Mystery Series**"..

- Book I          **The Conundrum of the Decapitated Detective**
- Book II         **The Conundrum of the Absconded Attorney**
- Book III **The Conundrum of the Sins of the Fathers**
- Book IV **The Conundrum of The Two-Sided Lawyer**
- Book V          **The Conundrum of the Clueless Counselor**
- Book VI **The Conundrum of the Loveless Marriage**
- Book VII        **The Conundrum of the Executed Defendant**
- Book VIII       **The Conundrum of the Jettisoned Jury**
- Book IX **The Conundrum of the Perjured Pigeon**
- Book X          **The Conundrum of the Haunting Halloween**
  - **Party**
- Book XI **The Conundrum of the Tuneless Tunesmith**
- Book XII        **The Conundrum of the Meddling Motorcar**
- Book XIII       **The Conundrum of the Blundering Bear**
- Book XIV        **The Conundrum of Shooting Fish in a Barrel**
- Book XV         **The Conundrum of The Girl with the Emerald**
  - **Eyes**
    - **To Be Continued!**

Next a series is "New Beginnings" a 1950's medical drama.

- Book I          **The Believer**
- Book II         **The Heretic**
- Book III **Arrow Song**
- Book IV **Peas In A Pod**
-

  **To Be Continued!**

**"the ReproBate saga"** is a character-based series in the 1860 American Civil War

- Book I          **Beneath the Rose**
- Book II         **skull and cRossBones**
- Book III        **Redefining Bastions**
- Book IV         **thicker than Blood**
- Book V          **prioR Battles**
- Book VI             **Requited Blasphemy**
- Book VII            **The waR Between**
- Book VIII           **To Richmond or Bust**
- Book IX         **carrying Battlescars**
  - **To be Continued**


**"the Hellhole saga"** is a character-based series from the American West

- Book I          **First Draw**
- Book II         **Audition for a Legend**
- Book III        **Strange Bedfellows**
- 

**"The Kansas Pirate Series"** is another character-based series from the American West

- Book I          **Pirate Treasure**
- Book II         **Strawberry Fields**
- Book III        **The Drinking Gourd**
- 


Stand-alone novels include:

- **Catman** *He was every man; he was no man*
- 
- **ONE** Science Fiction space travel
- **Shepherd of the Kingdom** a modern-day horror classic

Non-Fiction
"**The Kepi Magazine**," A publication specialized in the Civil War and 19th century life.:

- **The Kepi Volume I and II**
- **The Kepi Volumes III and IV**

www.ingramcontent.com/pod-product-compliance
Lightning Source LLC
Chambersburg PA
CBHW030531130626
46554CB00009B/1399